ONCE

BROTHERS

Also by this Author

Mystery/Suspense:

Looking Over Your Shoulder
Lion Within
Pursued by the Past

Young Adult Fiction:

Breaking the Pattern:
Deviation
Diversion
By-Pass

Between the Cracks:
Ruby
June and Justin
Michelle (Coming Soon)

Stand Alone
Tattooed Teardrops
Don't Forget Steven
Those Who Believe
Cynthia has a Secret
Questing for a Dream
Once Brothers

ONCE BROTHERS

P.D. Workman

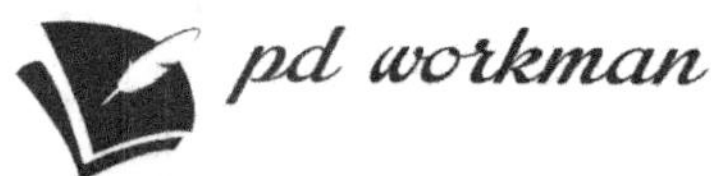 pd workman

Copyright © 2015 P.D. Workman

ISBN: 9781988390024

To all of the brothers in all kinds of families.

Acknowledgments

I wish to personally thank the following people for their contributions and knowledge and other help in creating this book:

Beta readers Luke Taylor and Cindy McGrath.

Tom Grusendorf, Jr. for editing.

Chapter One

THINGS WERE TOO QUIET lately and Sarin pondered what to do about it. He rolled several ideas around in his head, mulling them over for a few days, before selecting one to put into action. He called together a meeting of the Kittens. Sarin was, of course, President of the Kittens, the junior half of the Wildcats motorcycle gang. Sarin had been elected by the older Wildcats to look after the Kittens.

The boys assembled, with plenty of joking and jostling and speculation on what Sarin had called them together for. Sarin watched them, noting who was there and the dynamics of the room. He stood up, straightened his leather jacket, and folded his beefy arms across his chest. He cleared his throat. The conversations dropped off to a few isolated whispers. Sarin looked around, raising one eyebrow, and the whispers faded away.

"It seems to me," he announced, "that since Hanley and Carlos got busted, and Platt and Storm were promoted—" Platt had joined the senior Wildcats and Storm was killed in a bar fight. "—I'm thinking we could use some fresh blood."

There were of nods of approval. A few scowled but stayed silent.

"You got someone in mind?" Andrews asked.

Sarin nodded. "I do, actually... I don't know how it's going to go over with you boys, seeing as some of you might think he's yellow..."

"We don't want him!" Travis barked.

"Shut up, Travis. You'll get your say. Right now I'm talking, so shut your trap." He waited for further protest from Travis. Travis just shook his head and waited. "So, like I said, some of you might think he's yellow. He's been known to walk away from a fight."

He thought there were going to be fireworks then and there. No one wanted the guy. They couldn't figure out why Sarin would suggest him in the first place. It was like a slap in the face.

"Then how come you're interested in him?" Keith asked.

Sarin waited, letting the tension build. Making them wait for it. "It isn't because he's yellow that he doesn't fight. It's 'cause he's too good. One punch and the other guy wakes up wondering if he ever finished putting up his mitts."

There were cautious mutterings of approval.

"Who is he?"

"I'll get to that," Sarin teased. "Patience. You guys remember Escobar and his goons coming to school looking like they'd been hit by a train? They told some tall tale and the truth never leaked out. Well, I'm leaking it now. It was one against four and none of them were standing when my boy walked away from it. Bare hands."

"Come on, Sarin, give! Who is this guy?" Keith asked in exasperation.

Sarin gave them a dramatic pause before answering. "Think he sounds good?" There were impatient growls from the Kittens. "You got my word for it that he's good. Jacob Donell. Anyone know him?"

"He's old enough to be a Cat," someone protested.

"He's fifteen," Sarin corrected. A guy couldn't be promoted to the senior Wildcats until he was at least seventeen.

"That bruiser Coach Patterson was killing himself to get onto the football team last year? Is that who you mean? Dark hair? Scars?"

"He's the one."

Everyone started talking at once and Sarin held up his hand to silence them. "One at a time."

"There's no way he's fifteen," one of the Kittens blurted.

"No, he's right," Jackson argued. "Donell was in all my classes in elementary. He's fifteen."

"Couldn't be the same guy," Keith protested.

"He's pretty hard to mistake, isn't he? I'd know him anywhere. I'd know him fifty years from now," Jackson challenged, his face getting red.

Sarin intervened before they came to blows. "I checked around. I thought he was held back too. But he's fifteen, so drop it. That's not the point. I'd recruit him directly to the Cats if I wanted. But I'm not. I'm recruiting him to the Kittens. He needs training. Anyone got anything to say about him? Andrews?"

"I don't know that much," the boy said, "except he's big. He doesn't hang around anywhere—"

"He's a loner," someone interrupted.

"Shut up," Sarin snapped. He nodded for Andrews to go on.

Andrews shrugged. "Nothing else."

"Next?"

Hi-Top glanced around and raised his voice. "I remember him from grade seven. You guys remember…? When he knocked down Taylor?" Hi-Top looked around at the others for confirmation. A few grinned and nodded.

Sarin raised his eyebrows. "What? Tell me about it."

Hi-Top considered. "You remember Taylor? He wasn't around for long."

Sarin nodded.

"Sure. Fancy-pants English major. Thought he was gonna save the world. Or at least inspire a few hoods along the way."

Hi-Top agreed. "Always pretending he cared. Trying to get kids to confide in him. Donell was one of his special projects. But Donell wasn't cooperating. He wasn't asking for help. Taylor told him to stay to finish a homework assignment or something, but Donell ditched."

Sarin grinned, nodding. What juvie wouldn't?

"When we got to class the next day, Taylor flipped right out. He was pissed. And Donell was the target." Hi-Top shook his head, remembering.

"He went after Donell like he aimed to kill him," Marcus jumped in, his voice high and excited. "There was gonna be bloodshed! I never seen a teacher act like that. He must've been drinking all night to be so out of control."

Hi-Top scowled, giving Marcus a shove. "I'm telling it! Before Taylor could lay a finger on Donell, the kid wound up and laid him out cold with one fist!"

Impressed, Sarin chuckled and motioned for the next Kitten to offer his opinion.

"Don't know nothin' about his fists, but he must have something going for him. He's been dating Megan Stuart for two months."

"Two months? Nobody can hold onto *that* chick for two weeks."

Sarin didn't know the girl in question, but the expressions of the boys who knew her or her reputation told the story. She was obviously a prize. "Next?"

"He's got a limp," someone in the back offered. "Can he run?"

Sarin pursed his lips. He looked over the Kittens. "Anyone?"

"He can run. I've seen him," Keith contributed. "Besides, you think Coach would want him on the team if he couldn't?"

"Good point." Sarin's eyes stopped on Travis. "Trav?"

"Nope. He's yellow. I don't care how big he is."

The remaining comments were brief. Sarin looked around the room to make sure that all had been given the opportunity to voice their opinions. He looked at Lanny Talet, who rarely passed up the chance to make trouble. Everyone quieted to hear what Talet had to say.

"I don't think I've ever seen him without a black eye or some good bruises." Talet folded his arms across his chest and leaned back against the wall. "They say it's his old man. So if he can hit a guy that hard, hard enough to knock him cold the first shot, how come he puts up with that garbage?"

There was total silence.

"Anyone know his pop?" Sarin asked.

Negative.

"Well, someone will have to look into it. I'm taking it to the Cats."

Sitting down with a cold beer, Sarin sighed and stretched his legs out in front of him. Chopper finished handing beers around to the other senior Wildcats lounging around his basement suite. Holding onto the last bottle, he twisted off the cap and took a long drink. He wiped his mouth with the back of his hand.

"So what've you got?" he asked Sarin.

"A prospect for the Kittens. We've got to fill out the missing positions if we're going to keep the Wildcats running smoothly."

Chopper nodded and claimed his seat in the sagging recliner, putting his feet up on the coffee table.

"Did you pick him out or did the bloodthirsty Kits?" He tipped up his bottle again.

"I did. Most of the Kittens know who he is. The general feeling is that he'd be a plus. Fifteen, throws a good punch, not too hotheaded."

They waited for Sarin to go on. He glanced around the company. The Cats were a smaller group than the Kittens, but bigger, more experienced, more battle-worn. You couldn't find a room of tougher guys.

"Jacob Donell. Anyone know him?"

Most of them shook their heads. Sarin raised an eyebrow at Larry, who nodded. "Donell. Big kid. Walks with a limp."

"Yeah."

"He works for Billy's. Been there about a year now. Young to start, especially in construction. But he's got the skills."

Sarin put aside his beer bottle and lit up a cigarette.

"He's a good worker," Larry said. "Learns quick. Works hard. Careful."

"How does that limp affect him?" Sarin said. "The Kits said he can still run."

Larry grunted. "It doesn't slow him down. He's up and down ladders and structures all the time. Walk a beam with an armload without looking down."

"Anyone else know him?" Sarin asked.

"Hang on," Larry protested. "I'm not done."

Everyone waited for him to gather his thoughts and go on.

"This one day, I was a bit buzzed on the job. Not bad, but I know it ain't the smartest thing. Anyway. He comes up to me, this big, quiet kid. Wants to know if I checked the cable before hooking the last load for the crane. Thinks it looked stressed." Larry shook his head. "Lucky I didn't chuck him on the spot. Told him to take a hike. So he walked away. Then I hear this high, screaming sound. That's the sound those steel cables make when they're about to snap. I look up, the load is straight up above me, a bunch of framework. Next thing I know, the kid's slammed into me. Threw me good. I was still in the air when I hear the load whistling through the air and hitting the ground. I rolled a few times and when I open my eyes, he's standing over me, brushing himself off and checking things out. That load landed right on top of where I was. He saved my life."

Others murmured approval.

"He didn't turn me in, either," Larry added. "Didn't tell Billy that he thought I'd missed a problem with the cable. But he did tell me he didn't think I oughtta be drinking on the job."

Nods of approval from around the room at this sign of loyalty.

"He had a point there," Larry admitted. "Scared me off drinking." He took a swig from his bottle. "On the job," he added with a wry smile.

Some of the Cats chuckled. Then they were silent as they considered Jacob Donell's qualifications.

"Vote we recruit him?" Sarin asked.

Hands or bottles were raised around the room. Sarin looked around. It was unanimous. Jacob Donell would be a Wildcat Kitten.

Jacob shook his head. He couldn't understand why random bullies were always getting on his case. He didn't bother anyone. He let everyone else live their own lives without interference. Why did they always think it was their calling to interfere with his?

He continued on at a quicker pace, turned a corner, and crossed the street partway down the block. Jacob slipped into a narrow lane and waited. He knew the streets and alleys in the area.

The banger came along looking down the other side of the street to where Jacob should have been, afraid he'd lost his mark.

"Looking for me?" Jacob asked as he walked by.

The other boy jumped and whirled around with a switchblade in his hand. They both looked each other over, assessing the situation. The boy might have a blade, but Jacob was much bigger and stronger and had the drop on him. Jacob had a feeling the boy wouldn't have pulled a blade if he'd had time to think it through. He didn't want to threaten or stick Jacob right in the middle of a busy street. Jacob swallowed.

"What do you want?" He kept his voice low and unemotional.

The boy's grip tightened on the knife, his knuckles turning white. His lips were pressed together tightly and his eyes darted back and forth. "Nothing," he sneered, surer than he looked, putting a lot of force into the word.

"You've been tailing me for at least three blocks," Jacob pointed out. "You want something."

"I don't know what you're talking about."

Jacob couldn't understand what the boy was afraid of. Jacob wasn't known for beating people up. He had a reputation as a coward, avoiding fights whenever he could. He couldn't stand to see other people hurt. To be the cause of it. But the kid was scared. Jacob took that to mean there weren't any other Wildcats close by to help out. The boy swallowed, inching back from Jacob as if he was afraid Jacob was going to attack him.

"You're a Wildcat. Is this business?" Jacob suggested.

The kid cleared his throat, shifting back and forth like a little boy trying to ask a strict teacher for permission to go to the can. "Yeah," he admitted finally.

"What do you want?"

"Sarin wants to talk with you."

Jacob's eyebrows traveled up. Sarin Mace wanted him? "What about?"

The boy shrugged uncomfortably. Biting his lip, he finally withdrew the switchblade and put it away, looking down at the ground. "Couldn't say."

"Where?"

"Huh?"

"Where did he want to see me?"

"Oh… your place… I was…" he ran his fingers through his hair. "I was supposed to find out where you live…"

"Where's Sarin now?"

"I dunno." He got red in the face and turned away, probably knowing his blush gave away the lie. Jacob didn't say anything. He just stood there looking at the Wildcat. The boy did a little more of his gotta-pee dance.

"I don't know!" he insisted.

Jacob shook his head, considering. "I'll bet he's hanging out at Antonio's about now. Come on, let's go see."

The flush drained from the boy's face. He opened his mouth to argue, but apparently he sensed that there was no point. Maybe Sarin was at Antonio's and maybe he wasn't, but arguing over it wouldn't change things one way or the other. He nodded sullenly, and he and Jacob headed over to Antonio's in silence.

When they got to the cafe, Sarin was outside, sitting on his motorcycle in the parking lot, his helmet resting on his knee as he talked with a Wildcat with a tattoo on his throat. He was involved in the conversation and didn't see Jacob until he was within a few feet. His eyebrow twitched up.

"Hello, Donell."

Jacob took note of the fact Sarin knew him by sight. He hadn't just heard Jacob's name or something about him and decided he wanted to talk. He knew what he was doing. Jacob swallowed and stood his ground. He was quiet and shy, but he was straightforward. And showing any weakness in front of the gang leader wouldn't benefit him.

"You got one of your Wildcats following me," Jacob accused, motioning to the kid, who was now as pale as a ghost and looked like he was going to throw up.

Sarin glanced at him. "Maybe you and him were just going the same place, huh?"

"I know a tail when I see one."

"Yeah? Where'd you learn that?"

Jacob breathed out, trying to relax his tight muscles and keep his temper. "What do you want?"

Sarin's eyes flicked over him. "Where do you park your bike?"

"Few blocks away."

Jacob couldn't exactly keep his bike at home, where Duke might see it and start asking questions. It was *his* bike. He'd saved the money for it, and he didn't want to get it taken away, either because Duke took a fancy to it, or because he thought Jacob was going to get himself in trouble.

"I'll double you over and we can talk privately," Sarin said, with a glance at the other Wildcats.

Jacob nodded. Sarin put his helmet on and did up the strap. While he turned on the motor, Jacob slid on behind him. It was probably a good thing that they were only going a few blocks, as their combined weights put quite a bit of stress on the suspension. But they were at Jacob's bike a few minutes later and he transferred to his own ride.

"Just follow me," Sarin instructed over his shoulder.

He roared away. Jacob gave him a lead and then followed. Sarin led him on a speedy tour of the neighborhood and nearby highways, obviously testing how well Jacob could manage his cycle and the traffic. Then Sarin led him to a strip of trees by the river and they parked. Sarin took his helmet off. He offered Jacob a flask from the inside pocket of his jacket. Jacob shook his head. Sarin took a swig and stowed it back away.

"I need another member for the Wildcats," he said.

"No."

Even if Jacob had the inclination to join a gang, and he didn't, where was he going to find the time?

"I'm afraid it isn't quite that easy," Sarin countered.

Jacob waited without saying a word.

"The Wildcats have already voted you in."

"It isn't that easy," Jacob echoed.

"Oh?" Sarin smiled, anticipating the ensuing discussion. "You've got the bike and the skills. You're already halfway there."

Jacob shook his head. "I'm flattered. But I'm not interested. Lots of guys want in… pick one of them."

"You haven't been around the guys. How do you know you wouldn't like it?"

"I'm not into gangs."

"We can protect you. Take care of those guys trying to prove themselves by jumping you."

Jacob was startled. He looked quickly at Sarin's darkly tanned face.

"You think I haven't done my research?" Sarin grinned.

"I can look after myself."

"Can you? If four guys can't beat you, maybe five could. Or six. Thugs can still count. They can figure it out. Next time, maybe you won't be able to beat them."

Jacob ran his thumbnail through the grooves in his motorbike grip. He didn't understand why guys wanted to fight him. What point was there in beating up a random kid? Jacob didn't run in their circles. He wasn't involved in gang politics. He'd never crossed these guys or ratted them out or challenged them. He was just big and they wanted to look tough.

"There's other things we can do for you," Sarin said, watching Jacob. "We've got pull." His dark eyes bored into Jacob's and he changed track. "We're family. We look out for each other. You telling me you don't want someone watching your back?"

"*You're* the one behind my back," Jacob pointed out.

"So… you want me to be for you or against you?"

Jacob shook his head, frustrated. Sarin took two steps toward him. With a lazy gesture, Sarin pulled a deadly-looking pistol from under his jacket. He tapped the barrel against Jacob's sternum.

"Look, Donell." He lost the friendly, easygoing manner. "You can make this easy or hard. But the result is the same either way. You're in the gang." He drew a small circle on Jacob's chest with the tip of the barrel. "Now, maybe you're the target and maybe it's someone else. That cute girlfriend. Someone in your family." He shrugged widely. "I don't really care. You can be part of the gang, and get all the benefits that come with that or you can be on the receiving end. And if you think you can handle it because you've beat down a few random bullies, you'd better think again. 'Cause that's nothing compared to what's going to happen to you if you dis' the gang."

"I don't know why you want me," Jacob pointed out, trying to swallow the dark foreboding rising in his chest. "I'm not… your type. I'm not like the others…"

"We take all kinds. We can make you." Sarin smiled. "We can make you or break you, Donell. What's it gonna be?"

Jacob's initiation looked more like bear-baiting than a beat-down. Sarin watched the Kittens swarm him, only to get thrown off or knocked down within seconds. Jacob couldn't avoid getting hit, not with so many attackers, but he certainly held his own for much longer than anyone Sarin had ever seen before. Sarin probably should have enlisted the older Cats to take part to unbalance the scale a bit more.

He was only supposed to be allowing two minutes for the beat-down, but Sarin ignored the time, evaluating Jacob's skills in defending himself against the attackers. He wasn't able to defend himself effectively against so many and it wasn't long before his nose streamed blood and more blows connected with his body than he was able to land. But he kept his feet. Even after five minutes, he wasn't on the ground, at the mercy of the gang's feet.

That was where the worst injuries occurred. Feet and boots inflicted far more damage than bare fists.

The other Kittens started to slow down. They'd put all of their energy into the first minute or two of the attack. Jacob delivered a right cross to Jackson's temple that knocked him cold. The other boys tried to kick Jackson out of the way. That didn't work and two of them grabbed him by the arms and dragged him off to the side, so they wouldn't be tripping over him.

Sarin was impressed. Even tiring against so many opponents, Jacob was still able to do damage. He hadn't dropped anyone when he'd been fresh. Had he held back in the beginning and simply held the Kittens off? Watching him, Sarin wondered if Jacob had some kind of formal training. It wasn't any form of martial arts that Sarin recognized, but Jacob was definitely a disciplined fighter and Sarin had never seen some of Jacob's moves before.

There was a flash of steel and several of the Kittens stepped back away from the fray, looking at Sarin to call an end to the fight. Lanny Talet had pulled a knife. Who else? Talet's face was red with anger. He was naturally slim and his face was more battered than Jacob's. He'd put himself in the way of Jacob's huge fists too many times and he'd had enough.

Jacob managed to grab Talet's arm. He twisted it rendering the knife harmless, but not disarming him. The other Kittens held back, looking at Sarin to call the fight. Jacob took a few steps back from the others so that they were all in front of him when he turned his eyes to Sarin.

"You said no weapons."

"That's the rule," Sarin agreed. "Do whatever you like with him. I won't interfere."

Jacob's brows drew down at this response. He forced the knife out of Talet's hand and closed it, putting it in his own pocket before releasing Talet and pushing him away. Talet whirled back around, angry at being embarrassed in front of the gang by a green, untrained initiate. Jacob circled, his eyes alert, watching for a further attack, maybe more weapons. Talet dove in and in the blink of an eye, Jacob had him in a sleeper hold. His muscled arm closed around Talet's throat and held there for the few seconds it took Talet to black out.

"Call it," he ordered Sarin. "You said two minutes. Call them off."

Sarin nodded. "You're done."

Jacob transferred Talet's limp body to two of the Kittens standing closest to him, but they simply dropped Talet to the ground. Hi-Top gave Talet a kick in the ribs for good measure, cussing him out for dishonoring them by breaking the rules.

Keith handed Jacob a rag. Jacob wiped his face and then pinched his bleeding nose with it. "That was some brawl," Keith observed. "Where'd you learn to fight like that? I ain't seen half those moves before."

Jacob didn't answer Keith's question, eyeing Sarin.

"I let it go over," Sarin admitted. "I wanted to see what you could do. Two minutes wasn't long enough to evaluate your skills." He paused. "I've never seen an initiate keep his feet for that long."

Jacob's mouth and nose both bled and one black eye was already swollen too tightly shut to see out of. His slow movements betrayed his exhaustion.

"Come on, come have a drink and take a load off," Sarin invited, motioning to the condemned building that acted as their current base of operations. The rest of the gang headed inside. Jacob followed. Normally after a beat-down, the initiate was unconscious or too badly injured to participate in the festivities. It was novel for Jacob to still be on his feet and they pestered him with questions and comments. But he was reserved, not responding to the chatter.

Sarin saw to Jacob's comfort, giving him a drink and a chair to rest his bulk. The boy was going to be mighty stiff and sore by the next day.

"What kind of training have you had?" Sarin asked, watching Jacob take a swig of his drink and then hold the cold bottle against his bruised face. "You don't learn to fight like that street-brawling."

But Jacob was keeping his cards close to his chest. "Just picked it up," he said tersely.

"Picked it up where? From who?"

He shrugged and didn't answer.

Chapter Two

DEKE WATCHED JACOB TALK with Sarin—or refuse to talk to Sarin—and nursed his own cuts and bruises. Jacob packed a powerful punch and Deke had been clipped a few times during the beat-down. He couldn't recall ever seeing an initiation like that before.

Deke's own recruitment to the gang had been far different. He wasn't courted by the gang like Jacob. He had to work his way in. On his own on the streets, he did what he had to in order to survive. He'd badly needed a gang. A family. Stability and protection.

It was Larry who brought him up. Now a full-fledged Wildcat, Larry was one of the Kittens then, but senior enough to have his say in gang politics. Deke remembered standing there, slightly behind Larry, as he was presented for the first time to the gang as a potential recruit. His knees shook like he'd climbed a hundred flights of stairs and he felt queasy and faint. He covered it the best that he could with bravado, putting on a tough face and attitude. He folded his arms across his chest and looked challengingly at the established members.

"This here is Deke," Larry introduced him. "New in the neighborhood. Looking for some protection."

Deke steeled himself against the catcalls and mutters.

"What is he, twelve?" Someone laughed.

Deke swallowed and drew himself up, trying to look taller. Tougher. More experienced.

"He's fourteen," Larry said, looking at Deke's slight frame. "Don't worry, we'll put some muscle on him."

"I'm strong," Deke protested, swaggering. "I might not look it, but—"

"Keep your shirt on," Larry counseled. "Don't let them get to you."

Deke did his best to reign in his emotions. "I'm tough," he said in a quieter voice, unable to leave it without one last protest.

"Sure you are," sneered Vincent, a boy long since gone from the gang now. Deke couldn't remember what had ever happened to him.

"He got references?" another voice piped up.

Deke looked for the owner of the voice, but couldn't pick him out from the crowd of Kittens.

"He's got no references," Larry said. "All he's got is this."

With that, Larry reached behind Deke's back and shoved him toward the other boys, propelling him straight into the group. Deke had no warning this was going to happen. No way to know that when Larry brought him before the gang that he was going to be forced to defend himself or be killed.

They all started punching and kicking him, shouting and swearing and calling names. Someone grabbed him from behind and Deke couldn't escape the grasp no matter how hard he pulled and twisted. He was held there in front of the rest of the gang, with no way to defend himself, while they fought with each other for the opportunity to use him as a punching bag. He heard his nose break. Dark patches and bright lights filled his head so he couldn't even see in front of himself. Ribs cracked.

The boy behind him got tired of holding him up and dropped him to the floor. Kicks landed in his kidneys, his ribs, his head, and his groin. Blindly, Deke tried to grab their legs to pull them down, to sweep his legs out to trip them up.

He was still conscious when someone said, 'time's up,' and the punishment petered out. Deke lay there gasping and sobbing, soaked with sweat and blood and tears and his own urine, his whole body a mass of quivering jelly.

"Not bad," one voice said. "He's tougher than he looks. He was still fighting back at the end there. Wouldn't have thought he had it in him."

"Mama's boy," another sneered. "But he's got promise."

"Can you get up?" someone asked from nearby.

Deke tried to open his eyes, but even if his head hadn't been spinning, and the whole world flashing in and out of consciousness, his eyes were already swollen too much to open.

"I'm just… gonna stay here a while…" Deke croaked. He couldn't even imagine moving an arm or leg to get up.

There were chuckles and some jeers from the gang. They left him laying there on the floor, untended. Deke wasn't sure if he could make it through the night and the days to follow. Maybe they'd ruptured or broken something vital or he would just bleed out while they walked around him. He was just thankful that the beat-down was over before he even had a chance to worry about it.

Deke survived his initiation, though that first night and the following few days were a blur of pain and confusion. The Kittens were usually pretty good about not killing their initiates. Usually. Deke was sure he'd been pretty close to death. But his will to survive was strong and he was tougher than he looked. In a few days, he was able to get up, move around, and walk without assistance. It took much longer to heal all of the bruises and broken bones. Several of the gang seemed to take great pleasure in jostling him when they walked by, seeing how high they could make him jump.

The emotional scars ran pretty deep too. Deke still had nightmares now, years later, about having to go through it all again. Having to endure another horrific beating at the hands of the boys he needed so desperately to accept him.

But he was part of the gang. He succeeded in his goal. He had a home and a family. Maybe not what his real brothers would call a family, but it was a place he belonged. They watched each other's backs. That was more of a family than where he came from.

Now Jacob Donell was part of that family too. He was lucky to get off so easily. Lucky that he was bigger and stronger and better skilled than the usual recruit. Jacob appeared to be settling in and relaxing now, having finished off a couple beers. He was starting to realize that he wasn't in danger anymore. He belonged somewhere now. He didn't smile at Sarin or the other boys, but he seemed less tense. His neck and shoulders were hunched, making him appear a little shorter. Deke didn't know whether he normally sat like that, or whether it was the pain and fatigue of the fight and the soporific effect of the alcohol.

As Deke watched him from across the room, Jacob roused himself and looked at his watch. "I gotta go."

"Go?" Keith demanded. "You don't have to go anywhere. Where do you gotta be?"

Jacob looked at his watch again, a frown line forming between his eyebrows. "I gotta… take care of some things. I didn't know I was gonna be so long today."

Keith snickered. "You're lucky to be able to go anywhere tonight. Come on, your girlfriend can wait for another night. This is your party."

Jacob's face reddened.

"Be a man," Travis urged. "Tell her she's just gotta listen to what you tell her."

Jacob got still redder and scowled at the floor. "Ain't my girlfriend. It's something I gotta take care of."

He struggled to get up out of the chair that he had sunk into. It was obvious from his movements that he was stiffening up. But his face remained an expressionless mask, not showing any pain. It took a few moments to climb out of the seat. Jacob massaged his muscles and worked out the kinks.

"See'ya 'round," he said to the gang as he headed for the door.

"Donell," Sarin called after him.

Jacob turned around and looked at him.

"You're here tomorrow after you're off work. And no ducking out early."

Jacob looked him over for a moment, not saying anything, and then left.

Chapter Three

SAMMY HADN'T CHOSEN TO join a gang. He wasn't even a good prospect. He was too young, too small, and too shy. Unlike Jacob or Deke, he did have a mom. But that didn't keep him away from the local gangs. Living right in the projects, there was nowhere else for him to go. As soon as he walked out the door, he was in gangland. There was no avoiding it. He knew the bigger players, knew as much about the various gangs as any of the cops who patrolled the area. It never occurred to him to join any of the gangs, but it also never occurred to him that he had any choice. All of the older boys were in gangs. Most of the older girls too. Some of the boys his age or younger were already affiliated with a gang, through a father, cousin, or older brother.

Sammy's induction into the Sixth was nothing formal. He was still uninitiated, though he wore their colors. He had simply been walking to school one day, dragging a stick along the fence, and he stopped when he saw the big, black car pull over. He didn't want to get into the middle of something. He didn't want to get in the way of a drive-by or a drug deal or some other kind of transaction. So he just stopped and hung back against the fence, waiting for the boys to finish what they were doing and go on.

One of the Sixers, Marcos, swaggered up to the limo, tugging at his belt-loops to let his pants ride a little lower and adjusting the cocky tilt of his green cap. The dark window of the car went down, and the man inside, with lots of gold jewelry, greeted the banger. They bumped fists and they talked in loud, bragging voices like they had nothing to hide.

Sammy's heart sank lower and lower. He was going to be late for school now. As it was, he'd been running too late to make it in time to get a free breakfast. Marcos and the limo man continued to talk loudly like they had all day to finish. There was no way for Sammy to sneak by them. Any movement he made would attract attention, and attention was not good. Not good at all. He tried to remain invisible.

Eventually, Marcos stepped away from the car and he looked around, up and down the street, like he was searching for something. His eyes caught on Sammy and he tilted his head to the side slightly.

"You. Kid." His finger jabbed toward Sammy. "Come over here."

Sammy didn't move. He stood there, frozen, hoping that if he didn't respond, the man would give up on him and find someone else. He wished he could just close his eyes and fade from view. But that wasn't going to happen. Marcos continued to stare at him, raising an eyebrow.

"You hear me, kid? I said get over here."

Sammy bit his lip, trying to keep from crying. The Sixer waited, and Sammy eventually managed to get his feet to move. He shuffled a few steps closer. Then a few more, until he was finally close enough for Marcos to inspect him and make a decision.

"You live around here, right? Over on Fifth Street?"

Sammy nodded, gulping.

"You know the Sixes' crib, just down from your house, eh?"

He nodded again. How could he not know where the gang holed up? Marcos pushed a package into Sammy's hands.

"You take that over. You go straight there and don't stop to do nothing else on the way. Got it?"

Sammy looked down at the package in his hands in terror. He didn't want to be involved in any gang transaction. He tried to hand it back, but the man wouldn't take it.

"Go on. Deliver it for me. Straight there."

Sammy's hands shook. He looked up at the banger's face. Marcos looked back at him, scowling. "Do you understand?"

The jewelry-decked man still watching from inside the car chuckled. "You going to trust that little moron? He's obviously got no clue."

"He'll do it," Marcos asserted. "He just doesn't talk much."

He raised an eyebrow at Sammy. Sammy finally gave up and headed back the way that he had come. He looked back over his shoulder once or twice while he walked down the street. Marcos watched him until he was out of sight. After he got around the corner, Sammy stopped and tried to catch his breath. He swallowed, staring down at the innocuous package. He could just dump it, but Marcos knew where he lived and how to find him if the delivery went astray.

Sammy forced himself to go on. He went back past the house he lived in—families crammed into single rooms. Hallways that smelled like rats and skittering noises inside the wall.

Sammy walked past the building, further down the road to a bungalow. But no family lived there. Sammy stood at the end of the sidewalk, not turning into the yard. For as long as he could remember, he'd been told to stay away from the place. And now he had to deliver a package there. He was terrified to go in and he was terrified not to.

He stood there for a few minutes, unable to convince himself to go in. Eventually, a younger gang member strode out of the house. "Get out of here, kid! You can't hang around here."

Sammy shook his head in protest. "N-n-n-no. I g-g-g-got…"

"What are you babbling about? Come on, move on."

Sammy tried to get control of his words, but couldn't get anything coherent out.

"What are you, some kind of retard? Get out of here!"

Sammy held the package out like a shield to keep the other boy from physically removing him from the property. The boy looked at it. "What you got there? You delivering this? That for Sixth?"

Sammy offered it to him.

The boy shook his head, holding his hands up. "No, I can't take it. Bring it in."

Sammy stood there, unmoving. The boy grabbed him by the arm and pulled him up the sidewalk toward the house. Sammy went with him, a lump in his throat. The young Sixer pushed him through the door.

"Delivery," he sang out.

One of the older gang members appeared. Pinky. "Hey, Maury."

Pinky's gaze shifted toward Sammy. He looked Sammy over and pulled the package out of his grip. Sammy was relieved to finally have it out of his hands. He turned to go.

"No, no, no," Pinky said, grabbing his shoulder. "Where'd you get it? Who sent you?"

Sammy motioned in the direction he'd come. "F-f-from…"

The man felt the package and used his nail to peel up one corner, peering inside. His mouth curved up slightly.

"My man Marcos. That where you got it?"

Sammy nodded.

"You know who Marcos is?"

Sammy looked down at his own feet, nodding. Of course he knew who Marcos was. Everyone in a six-block radius knew who Marcos was.

"How about Zed? You know him?"

Sammy nodded again.

"He's hanging out over by the Big Box. You tell him a message for me—"

Maury nudged Pinky, shaking his head.

"What?" Pinky demanded.

"He, uh, doesn't talk."

They both looked at Sammy. Sammy bit his lip. His mouth was as dry as a bone. He wanted to protest, to explain that he could talk, he just couldn't get the words out sometimes. But for that, he'd have to speak.

"Oh, he's that one," Pinky looked down at Sammy with dawning understanding.

Sammy twisted his fingers together and tried to leave again. The man kept a grip on him.

"No, stay. Just wait here while I get a piece of paper."

Sammy waited. The older Sixer disappeared into another room. Maury kept an eye on Sammy, making sure he couldn't take off. Pinky came back a few minutes later with a folded-up piece of paper. He gave it to Sammy.

"Take that to Zed. Got it?"

Sammy sighed. Pinky patted him on the shoulder. Sammy left the house to make his second delivery for the gang. He'd been making deliveries ever since. Sometimes he got to school in between, but often he didn't. He was a part of the Sixth now.

Chapter Four

JACOB GLANCED AROUND BEFORE unlocking the door, making sure that everything was in order. He emptied the mailbox, but it was all flyers. He went into the house, walking to the bedroom in the back corner without turning on any lights.

"Hey," he said softly, before turning on the bedroom light. "Sorry I'm so late. I didn't know…"

He switched the light switch on and blinked a few times, getting used to the light. Nicholas, his older brother, 'big brother' Jacob jokingly called him, sat in his chair. He blinked sluggishly, obviously having been asleep.

"Sorry. I thought… it would just be an hour or two, and then I could get back here."

Nicky's eyes turned to him. Jacob saw his lids widen and his pupils dilate in spite of the light being turned on.

"I'm okay," he assured Nicholas. "Really. It probably looks bad, but it isn't. I'm okay."

Jacob explored his puffy eye and split and swollen lips with cautious fingers. He forced a smile and a light voice. "I've had plenty worse."

Nicholas knew that was true. Jacob sighed and went to work. His movements were stiff and clumsy, so he slowed down, not wanting to hurt Nicholas. He undid the straps that held Nicholas upright in the chair, and once he was free of the restraints, Jacob scooped Nicholas up in his arms and deposited him gently on the bed. He changed Nicholas, then propped him up and connected the g⁻ tube to feed him.

"I'm sorry," he apologized again. "I should have come home for supper before. I thought I'd only be a little while and then I could come home and we could eat and get you off to bed."

Nicholas's eyes went from the bagged formula that Jacob held above him to Jacob's face.

"I already ate," Jacob said. "Well, drank. Guess we both had liquid suppers today!"

Nicholas's eyes narrowed at the corners.

Jacob shrugged. "I'll have breakfast," he promised.

He waited, watching the formula drain. The house was silent. There were sirens outside, but inside it was safe and warm. Duke was still away. It took about twenty minutes for the bag to empty, and then Jacob disconnected the g⁻ tube and got Nicholas ready for sleep.

"That feel better?" He restrained himself from apologizing again. If he kept saying how sorry he was, Nicholas would just get more stressed out. As he turned Nicholas onto his side, the older boy started coughing. Jacob thumped his back lightly to loosen the congestion. Once Nicholas stopped, Jacob felt his cheek with the backs of his fingers.

"No fever. You feeling okay?"

He studied Nicky's eyes closely. Nicholas blinked a couple of times. Jacob ran his fingers through Nicky's short blond hair.

"Okay. Better to get back to sleep."

He pulled Nicholas's blankets up over him and tucked him in. Jacob cleared away the garbage and disposed of it. Then he returned to the room and turned the light off again. He felt for his blankets on the floor and settled himself for sleep.

"Night, Nicholas," he whispered.

He listened to Nicky's slow, even breathing and drifted off to sleep.

In the morning, Jacob gave Nicholas a quick sponge bath and his morning formula and dressed him for the day. He strapped

Nicholas into his chair and wheeled him into the kitchen. He angled the wheelchair so that it caught the morning light, but so that the sun was not in Nicky's eyes.

He looked in the fridge, sighing. His head pounded and his stomach felt sea-sick. Jacob turned and looked at Nicholas. Nicky's eyes narrowed slightly.

"I know," Jacob said. "I said I'd eat, but…" he trailed off.

Nicky's gaze held steady. Jacob started the coffeemaker going. There was a half loaf of bread in the fridge. He took out one stale slice and dropped it into the toaster.

"Okay, I'm eating."

They waited for the coffee to brew.

"I gotta be out tonight." Jacob's eyes wandered to the window and then to Nicholas. "Sarin says I gotta be there after work and I'll probably be pretty late. I'll come home between school and work so you can eat. I'll put you down for bed so you won't be up late like last night."

He studied Nicholas's face, a little worried. But he didn't see any disapproval or anxiety there. He sighed.

"Okay. That's what we'll do."

The coffee machine finished at almost the exact same time as the toaster popped. Jacob worried down as much as he could and put the dishes in the sink to look after later. He returned Nicholas to their room, and after saying goodbye, he headed off for school.

Chapter Five

DEKE AWOKE WITH A groan, rolling over and covering his eyes against the light in the room. Someone was talking close by in a loud voice. He wasn't sure who it was yet or what they were talking or arguing about. He tried to go back to sleep, squeezing his eyes tight and pulling a blanket over his head. But the arguing went on and he was too wide awake now to get back to sleep. His head felt like it would split in two.

Groaning again, Deke pulled the blanket off and forced himself to his feet.

"Rise and shine, sleeping beauty," Keith mocked, seeing him get up.

Deke squinted at him. "What are you so cheerful about?"

"It's a beautiful morning." Keith had a wide grin, obviously delighted to needle Deke. "Sun is shining, birds are chirping… Sarin is hung over…"

Deke looked around for the leader of the Kittens. Sarin was normally a hard drinker, without any noticeable next-morning consequences. So him having a hangover was news. Sarin wasn't in sight.

"Sarin is hung over? What'd he drink?"

"I think he was trying to keep up with Donell." Keith laughed. "But he doesn't quite have the same body mass."

"Donell didn't drink that much," Deke argued. "Two or three beers…"

Keith shook his head. "You must not have watched for long."

Deke looked around again to make sure that Sarin was not in earshot. "How sick is he?"

Keith snorted. "Puking his guts out."

Deke tried to suppress a smile. Keith laughed again, nodding. Deke stretched his shoulders and arched his back, wincing at the stiffness and pain that had set in after the fight the previous night.

"Oooh, that Donell packs a punch," he grunted.

"Yeah," Keith agreed. "I'm feeling it this morning too."

They looked each other over. Both had bruises and split lips. Deke rubbed his ribs. "That guy's gonna be a great asset in a rumble."

"He's good. As long as he doesn't run from a fight."

Deke nodded. He looked around. "Is there any booze left from last night? Or did Sarin and Donell drink it all?"

"See what you can find."

Deke sighed and went back to the common room where they had partied the night before. Others were still sleeping. On their usual mattresses like Deke had, for those for whom the building was home. Others passed out on the floor or in other positions. In the common room, a few were sprawled on the chairs and furniture. There were a few girls still in evidence, sleeping soundly, mouths hanging open, disheveled, not looking nearly as attractive as they had the night before.

Deke cast around for some bottles that weren't yet empty but most contained no more than a swallow left in the bottom. Eventually, he found two beer cans that hadn't been opened and popped the top of one. A couple of Percocets and he'd have a pleasant buzz and be feeling no pain. After swallowing them, Deke wandered over to the window and gazed out at the street. It was late morning, but there were a few kids on their way to school. Or he assumed they were on their way to school. They could just as easily be skipping school, with completely different plans in mind. Deke watched one boy lead his younger brother down the sidewalk, holding hands, both wearing backpacks.

There was an ache in Deke's chest that had nothing to do with bruised ribs. He pressed his hand to his breastbone. Deke had once had brothers too. He remembered them walking him to school. It seemed like a long time ago. Another life. But now he had his gang brothers. Plenty of guys to watch his back. Or to fight with. They were just like brothers. There was no difference.

Deke swallowed a couple more percs to ease the pain.

Chapter Six

Get up! Get up, you good-for-nothing! It's a school day!"
The jarring kicks to the ribs roused Sammy from his exhausted slumber on the floor. He pulled away, rolling over to get further from the source, and collided with kitchen cupboards behind him. He tried to protest that he was up, the words getting lost in an incomprehensible string of sounds. He sat up, warding off the blows with his arms.

Sammy blinked, trying to clear his eyes and focus on the attacker. It was, of course, his stepfather. The latest in a long line. Now that Sammy could see the blows coming and avoid them, Hector stopped kicking him.

"Why can't you get yourself up in the morning?"

Sammy tightened his blanket around himself. "T-t-t-tired."

"Everybody's tired. I can get myself up."

Sammy nodded.

"Get me some coffee," Hector ordered.

Sammy stumbled to his feet. Hector left to grab a quick shower before anyone else could get in ahead of him. With the blanket still around his shoulders, Sammy fumbled with the thin filter paper and measured the coffee grounds. He tripped over another figure curled up on the hard kitchen floor when he went to the sink to look for a cup.

"Not yet," Tiny murmured. "In a few minutes."

Sammy smiled and shook his head. He watched the coffee machine, letting his eyes close halfway again, dozing on his feet.

The shower shut off and Sammy forced himself to move. He jiggled the coffee machine anxiously, trying to hurry the brewing process. Hector would not be happy if he got back downstairs and the coffee was not ready before he went to work.

"Is that coffee I smell?" queried a deep voice. Sammy turned, knowing it was the father of the Bachers, the family that lived in the room next to Sammy's family. Hector complained that there were too many people living in their own room, but the Bachers had five children and they all slept in the room. Hector put up with the baby and the toddler sleeping in the same room as him and Sammy's mom, but he wouldn't allow Sammy to sleep there. It was too crowded, he said, and they needed privacy. The house was filled to the gills and the kitchen was the only place that Sammy and the other surplus children of the house could find to sleep.

"H-h-h-hec…" Sammy kept protectively between the coffee pot and Mr. Bacher.

"Hector's?" Bacher smiled broadly. "When's the last time Hector bought coffee? He's happy to drink it, but he never buys it. Everyone else contributes."

He pushed Sammy aside and shoved his coffee mug between the coffee maker and the pot to catch the stream. His hands were big, heavy with thick calluses.

"N-n-no," Sammy tried to push his way back in to protect the coffee until Hector got down. Bacher shoved him again, spilling coffee on the counter.

"Back off, kid. It's coffee. First come, first served. And I'm the first one here."

"N-n-n…"

Bacher ignored him. Sammy tried to grab the mug away and Bacher pushed him aside. This time, Sammy grabbed a big knife from the knife block on the counter and pointed it threateningly at Bacher.

"You little punk!" Bacher growled, putting his mug down on the counter. Sammy breathed a sigh of relief that Bacher had relinquished the coffee. Bacher slapped Sammy across the head and grabbed the knife from him. Sammy's ears rang with the force of the blow. Tears sprang to his eyes. Sammy stared up at Bacher. He'd never laid hands on Sammy before. He had all those kids and he was always friendly, seemed like a nice guy.

"You think you're a big gangster now?" Bacher demanded. "You think that hanging around with that gang makes you a bad guy? A big, bad dude?"

Sammy shook his head, trying to keep the tears from escaping. Bacher picked up his mug and took a sip.

"You're a little kid. Not a bad-ass. You stay away from that gang and be a good little kid."

Sammy sniffled and wiped his nose with the back of his hand. "C-c-can't!"

"You can. My kids stay away from gangs. You can too."

He gave Sammy a long look, then walked out of the kitchen.

Sammy looked at the coffee pot. Between the coffee that Bacher had taken in his extra large travel mug and the coffee that had spilled, there wasn't enough for a full mug left.

There was a movement below him and Sammy looked down to see Tiny sitting up with his blanket wrapped around him. Sammy wasn't sure when Tiny had woken up, how much of the confrontation he had seen.

"You can make more coffee," Tiny squeaked.

Sammy poured what was left in the coffee pot into the mug that he had scavenged from the sink. It only half-filled the mug. Sammy dumped out the grounds and the filter and set it up again. But of course, Hector was back before it had finished brewing.

"What's this?" He looked into the coffee cup. "I told you to get me my coffee. And this is what you do?"

Sammy opened his mouth to explain. "B-b-b…"

Hector flung the contents of the cup in Sammy's face. When Sammy closed his eyes and jerked back, Hector walloped him on the opposite side from where Bacher had slapped him. Sammy might have been surprised by Bacher's attack, but he wasn't surprised by Hector's. He'd been taken off-guard, not expecting the scalding liquid in his face, but he wasn't surprised. Sammy backed away swiftly and looked for his chance to get past Hector, out of the kitchen, to where he could escape the house.

"You worthless little piece of crap!" Hector kicked Sammy, trying to sweep his feet out from under him. "I let you stay in my home and this is the kind of thanks I get? You can't even make me a cup of coffee?"

Sammy tried to avoid the blows, which only made Hector angrier. Sammy turned to take a kick aimed at his crotch in the leg instead and Hector followed up with a punch that caught him square in the belly. Sammy got the wind knocked out of him and retched, spewing up a splash of yellow bile that landed on Hector's shoe. As Hector was distracted and bellowed about his soiled footwear, Sammy managed to slip by him and escaped the house. He stumbled down the front steps holding onto the railing, still heaving and trying to get his breath back.

Chapter Seven

JACOB HAD GOTTEN IN from a night out with the Wildcats in the wee hours of the morning and fell into his bed—onto the blankets on the floor—to try to get in a few winks before he had to be up for school. He had accumulated a considerable number of tardies in the past few weeks since joining the gang and he knew there'd be trouble if he were late yet again, but there wasn't much he could do about it. No discipline that the school could inflict could compare to the consequences of skipping out on the gang.

Even though he hadn't wanted anything to do with the Wildcats initially, he was enjoying the new camaraderie. He'd never been a part of something before, always a loner, and the time spent with his new brothers in the gang was a revelation. He hadn't actually expected to enjoy himself. But they shared his enthusiasm for motorbikes and the wild freedom of the road. They were quick to share a beer or smoke with a brother, or to help out with a place to crash or advice on girls. Once he got over his initial nervousness about being arrested or Duke finding out about his gang involvement, Jacob actually started to enjoy himself.

"Jake! Get your skinny butt out of bed, Jake!"

Jacob awoke with a start and pulled away from his father's kicking feet, rubbing his eyes swiftly in order to focus in on Duke to figure out what to do.

"Dad," he got to his feet quickly to avoid any further kicks. "You're back."

"Damn right, I'm back," Duke agreed. "So you'd better get back on the ball. Vacation's over."

He sounded drunk already, slurring his words slightly. Jacob glanced at the window to gauge the time, wondering if he'd already slept through the morning and should have been at school. But it was still dark, the sky just starting to lighten with early morning dawn. Duke had put in his shift, apparently gone out to drink afterward, and was just now getting home.

"Yeah," Jacob looked around, trying to figure out why Duke was kicking him awake, other than just pure bloodymindedness. "Glad to see you."

"Get some dinner on the table," Duke growled. "A man's gotta eat after a hard day's work."

Jacob nodded in agreement. "Sure, Dad."

With the evening shift, Jacob had thought to avoid Duke's angry suppertime abuse; it hadn't occurred to him that Duke would still be coming home after a long shift, hungry and looking for trouble while Jacob was still home.

There was a change in Nicholas's breathing. Jacob glanced over at him and saw by the dim light coming through the window that his eyes were open. Jacob shuffled his feet, looking to get around Duke without any further abuse.

Duke let him get past, but followed him toward the kitchen. "You should be up by now for school anyway."

"Yeah," Jacob agreed.

If he was going to get to school for his first class, he needed to allow time for feeding and caring for Nicholas. He would need to be up pretty soon.

"You been skipping school?" Duke demanded, closing in on Jacob.

Jacob opened the fridge, scanning to see what was available to make for Duke's dinner. He grabbed a bottle of beer and handed it to Duke, hoping to placate him and avoid a confrontation. Duke took it and shoved Jacob backward, into the counter.

"You know better! Skipping is going to get you into trouble. You need good marks if you want to amount to anything."

"I'm not skipping. I went to school the whole time you were gone."

He tried again to get started on cooking something for Duke for dinner, filling a pot with water and putting it on the stove to boil for pasta.

"Yeah? Then what was the pile of messages from the school that I came back to today?" Duke demanded.

Jacob's stomach dropped. "I—I was late a couple—a few times. But I went, I didn't skip…"

He was still clumsy from sleep and he didn't manage to avoid Duke's swing. Duke's fist caught him across the jaw, making Jacob's head snap back. He stumbled into the stove, bumping the hot pot and nearly upsetting it.

"You're lying to me!" Duke bellowed. "You think I don't know what's going on here? You think you can just skate through life because of my position? You're going to have to make something of yourself, just like I did—"

"I will, Dad." Jacob tried to come up with the right words. "I'll work hard like you. I'm sorry."

Jacob tried to move further away from the stove so he wouldn't end up getting burnt.

"I don't expect top marks from you," Duke grumbled, and he twisted off the top of the beer bottle. Jacob breathed out, still anxious, but relaxing a bit when it didn't appear that Duke was going to continue the abuse. "I expect you to be there and not getting in trouble over missing classes."

"Yessir."

He opened the fridge again and Duke moved back, out of the way. Jacob withdrew a package of ground beef and half a bottle of spaghetti sauce. He wasn't sure how long the hamburger meat had been in there, but it still looked okay.

"Boys will be boys," Duke muttered to himself. "Skipped school a time or two myself. And my dad whaled on me for it, too. If you're gonna skip, you can expect a beating for it."

Jacob poured pasta into the boiling water. "I won't skip." He glanced nervously over his shoulder at Duke. "Why don't you go sit down and turn something on? I'll bring dinner to you when it's ready. You've been working so hard…"

Duke took a sip of the beer and studied Jacob with slightly bloodshot eyes. In spite of Jacob's height, he still had to look up to his dad. He didn't know anyone who could top Duke. Not in real life.

"Nice to be home," Duke observed. "Missed yeh while I was gone."

Jacob swallowed. "Missed you too, Dad… why don't you go sit down…"

Duke took another drink of beer and turned around, walking out of the kitchen and into the living room. Jacob listened to the TV turn on and to his father settling into his favorite chair. Breathing out a long sigh of relief, he moved around the small kitchen, getting Duke's dinner prepared. It would make sense for him to eat too and maybe save some for supper before he had to go to work, so all he would have to do was to warm it up. But looking at the amount of food, he knew there wasn't enough. Duke would want all of it and more if he hadn't loaded up at the bar before coming home.

When Duke started to snore, Jacob went back to the bedroom to get Nicholas up. The room was getting light now as the sun was above the horizon. He looked to see if Nicky's eyes were open.

"I'm turning on the light," he warned, and waited a couple of seconds before doing so.

Nicholas was lying in the same position that Jacob had left him in the evening before.

"Morning," Jacob greeted softly. "You have a good sleep?"

Nicholas's eyes were wide. Jacob smiled reassuringly.

"I'm okay. He wasn't bad today. He's already asleep."

Nicholas's lids lowered slightly.

"It's okay," Jacob tucked a lock of Nicky's wavy hair behind his ear. "Let's get you some dinner too." He propped Nicholas up. As he prepared the g- tube, he raised his eyebrows at Nicholas. "I made dinner for Dad. Is this dinner or breakfast for you? Guess it doesn't much matter if it all tastes the same, huh?"

The outside corners of Nicholas's eyes angled up. Jacob chuckled to himself. He sat on the side of Nicky's bed, holding the formula bag up and watching it drain. He tried to think of what interesting news he could share with Nicholas.

"He's got the office Christmas party coming up. Said he wants me to come." Jacob rolled his eyes. "Always wants to show off how much I've grown. How I'm taller than all of the guys that he works with now. Thinks it's funny that his son is bigger than any of the grown cops."

Nicholas's eyes were steady.

"If I just knew he wouldn't get drunk at it this year…" Jacob sighed. "No chance of that, I guess."

Nicholas's eyes shifted slightly toward the door. Jacob listened for a moment. Duke was moving around, but settled again and started snoring.

"Some of the others," he said, continuing on with the commentary on the Christmas party, "some of 'em are okay. Like Thompson… you remember the first time that he came here?"

It was a long time ago now. Jacob thought he'd probably been in about grade one at the time. Not so long after their mom died. Her death had hit Duke hard. At first, Duke went out and got drunk a lot, but his pals at work talked to him and Social Services came a lot, and eventually he evened out again. He started bringing home some of the other guys from work, and that helped him get over the rough spots, the lonely times that consumed him.

Jacob remembered the first time that Thompson came. Both boys were in the bedroom. Nicholas was sitting in the dusty sunlight with his eyes shut. Jacob was amusing himself with a toy car on the floor. The door slammed and Jacob stood up. Then he heard Duke talking to someone else and didn't go out to greet his father. He heard Duke get a couple of beers out of the fridge and they sat down in the living room.

"Nice place," Thompson commented. Jacob had his suspicions that Thompson's place was much better. The house had been getting more and more run-down lately, despite the visits from Social Services. After a moment, Thompson asked, "Do you live alone?"

"There's a cleaning lady who comes in once a week." If she felt like it. And when she did, she didn't do much more than stir around the dust. "And my boys," there was only the slightest hint of an 's' at the end of the word. "Jacob, come out here," he shouted.

Jacob hesitated. He looked at Nicholas. Nicky's eyelids had opened and they stared into each other's eyes for a minute.

Jacob stood up. He touched Nicky's shoulder as he went by. "Be right back." Jacob went out to see the living room. He stopped in the doorway and looked in. The visitor was a tall, slim cop. Dark hair and clear blue eyes. Younger than Duke.

"This is Officer Thompson," Duke introduced. "Well, come on," he chided when Jacob didn't move. Jacob went the rest of the way into the room. He obediently went over to stand beside Duke.

"Hello there, Jacob, how's it going?" Thompson smiled.

Jacob mumbled a reply, looking away shyly.

"Speak up, boy, don't act like an idiot!" Duke remonstrated, cuffing Jacob's ear. Jacob cringed away.

"Duke!" Thompson's voice was shocked.

There was a moment of silence. "I'm sorry... I don't know what came over me."

"Have you talked to anyone about this?"

"This..." Duke's voice was awkward. "It's the first time, Jack. You don't think that I'd..."

Thompson looked Jacob over carefully, then turned his eyes back to Duke.

"I've seen the results of abuse, Duke. I won't stand by and let it happen to someone I know."

"Of course not," Duke was earnest. "I wouldn't either. But I swear to you, I've never hit the boy in my life." There was a pause. "Jake, why don't you go warm up some dinner for us, okay?"

Jacob nodded. "See-ya, mister." He retreated into the kitchen.

"He's got quite a limp," Thompson said conversationally after a few long minutes of silence.

"Yeah… he broke his hip when he was just a little tyke. I was out of town and his mother didn't get looked after soon enough."

"I understand it can be very hard to tell with children when they have broken bones."

"It was obvious enough. His mother… well, she had some issues."

Thompson made a sympathetic noise. "Is it painful for Jake?"

Duke grunted. "He gets by."

There was silence for a few minutes. Jacob slid the previous day's Mexican casserole into the stove to warm.

"He must miss his mother," Thompson offered.

"I suppose so. He doesn't talk much. She and I were… separated for a while and he didn't see her while she was gone… she wasn't back for long before she died, so I don't know how much he really remembers about her."

Jacob heard the slosh of liquid as one or both of them took a drink.

"I'm sorry, it must be hard on you to talk about her. I shouldn't have brought it up."

"It's all right Jack. It happened. A person can't ignore it."

"How old is Jake? He must be about the same age as my daughter."

"Grade one."

"Just the same! We'll have to get together sometime, your family and mine, for a picnic or something. Introduce the kids."

"That would be nice."

They never did get their kids together, but Duke and Thompson stayed friends. Thompson was the only one that Jacob could ever remember defending him from Duke's abuse. Jacob assumed that everyone else was too afraid of Duke. Thompson was the only one who stood up to Duke.

* * *

Jacob strapped on his helmet and headed over to the Kittens' headquarters. His thoughts jumped from one thing to another. He was being pulled in so many different directions. Trying to keep Duke happy, staying out of trouble at school, getting to his job, spending time with the Wildcats, Megan, and Nicholas. It seemed like every second of the day, there were at least two different places he ought to be.

Riding his bike, that was when he felt relaxed and free. Just riding away from it all. One day, he'd like to just keep going. Ride out of town. Out of the county. Far away, where nobody knew him. Where he had no responsibilities. But he couldn't leave Nicholas. No matter what else was going on, Nicholas depended on Jacob for everything.

Sighing, Jacob pulled his bike alongside the group of bikes already outside the HQ. Taking off his helmet and running his fingers through his hair, he went in.

Mostly, they were sitting around drinking. Jacob approached the group and perched on the edge of a packing crate. He had no interest in settling in. If they weren't going to go out riding or actually do something, there was no point in getting comfortable. Why stay?

There were greetings from several of the boys. Jacob caught Sarin's eyes on him, and turned his face away slightly, his ears getting hot. He wasn't sure why he bothered to turn his head. It wasn't like he could hide the ugly bruise. Everyone could see it. It covered half his face.

"You know, man, you're so black and blue all the time now, we oughtta call you Black," Hi-Top commented lazily.

There were snickers from the other boys. Sarin nodded, his eyes glittering.

"Not bad." Sarin's closed halfway as he looked Jacob over. "Black, huh…?"

Jacob shifted uncomfortably under Sarin's gaze. "Are we going out anywhere?" He stared down at his work boots.

"Sure, Black. Just keep your shirt on."

Jacob shuffled his boots, looking for a more comfortable position on the crate. He didn't see any reason to wait. The others were just sitting around bored. He tapped his toes impatiently. With all the different directions he was being pulled, sitting around doing nothing was almost painful. He wanted to go out and ride, have some fun. And if the Kittens were just going to sit around today...

Jacob stood up.

Sarin's eyes followed him. "Where do you think you're going?"

Jacob thrummed his fingers on the outer shell of his helmet, held at his side. "I'm gonna go out. Maybe I'll catch up with you guys later..."

Everyone was immediately looking at Sarin.

"Why don't we all go out?" Keith suggested. "What are we doing just sitting around here?"

Jacob paused, waiting. Others nodded and chimed in.

"Come on, Sarin," Talet encouraged. "It's time to move."

Sarin looked at them, his eyes narrowed slightly, calculating. "We're still expecting a few more guys."

"Hell, I'm not waiting for stragglers," Talet protested. "They can find us later or go somewhere else. Let's ride."

"You in charge of this gang?" Sarin challenged, his voice hardening.

"No," Talet's voice got higher. "Are you?"

Sarin swore and jumped to his feet. Shrieking with laughter, Lanny Talet dashed for the door. Everyone got up and chased after him and Sarin, eager to see the fight. By the time Jacob got to the door, Talet was on his cycle, roaring off down the street. Sarin's face was white with rage. He leveled a glare at Jacob. He wasn't about to forget who had started this. He threw his leg over his own motorcycle.

Everyone was pushing to get to their bikes. Since Jacob was the last one to pull in, his was on the end and easy to get out. He shouldered his way through the other boys to get to it, and strapped on his helmet. He pulled out just behind Sarin as he chased after Talet.

Darkness was just starting to fall, the city lighting up around them. Jacob breathed in deeply and savored the fresh air; exhaust fumes and all. He easily kept up with Sarin and the two of them were closing in on Talet. The other Kittens were behind them, trying valiantly to catch up.

Jacob didn't care whether Sarin caught Talet or not. It wouldn't hurt his feelings to see Talet get a taste of Sarin's fury. Talet was a troublemaker and Jacob had been on the receiving end of the trouble he stirred up more than once. All Jacob cared about was the feeling of freedom as he rode in the open air, the wind blowing over him.

As they rode through the city streets, Jacob started to get an uncomfortable feeling. He checked his mirror a few times, then rode up beside Sarin. He flipped up his visor and motioned for Sarin to throttle back. Sarin slowed down.

"What's up?"

"We got a tail," Jacob shouted back.

Sarin shot a glance over his shoulder. "Oh?"

"Third car back. Red Chevy."

Sarin checked again. "Just some guy rubbernecking."

It wasn't unusual for people to show interest in a dozen black-jacketed teens on motorbikes when they were out and about. Jacob shook his head, leaning to pull in closer to Sarin.

"He's a cop. Undercover."

Sarin shook his head.

"He's undercover," Jacob insisted. "His name is Levi."

Sarin looked back at him, brows drawing down. "You know him?"

"Take it to the freeway. He'll have to drop us or make himself obvious."

Sarin nodded and shifted up as Jacob did. The rest of the gang sensed the change of atmosphere and grew more riotous.

Chapter Eight

DEKE'S HEART THUMPED FAST with excitement as he followed Jacob and Sarin's lead. He didn't know exactly what was going on, but it was obvious from Sarin's movements that something was up. They took the freeway exit. Looking back, Sarin watched a red sedan take the exit as well and then pointed to it for the rest of the gang to see.

Deke and the rest of the Kittens slowed down to surround the red car. Deke tried to get a look at the occupant. It wasn't a rival gang member or anyone from around the neighborhood that he knew and Sarin wasn't one to just target random bystanders. That only left one possibility.

The cop was forced to slow down to avoid clipping any of the motorcycles. Sarin and Black had slowed as well. They all rode in close, crowding the cop and slowing him down more and more. The driver rolled down his window an inch or two and feigned ignorance.

"Hey, what's going on?" His face was ashen.

"You tell me, copper," Sarin responded.

"Huh? What? What do you want?"

The Kittens who hadn't yet figured out that the target was a cop tossed Sarin's words back and forth, making sure that everyone knew.

"We want you, pig."

"Pull over!" Travis yelled.

The Kittens were riding dangerously close to the car. Even though he had slowed down, the cop could do major damage if he made a mistake or overcorrected. Or if he decided that the only way out of there was to ram his way through the group. Jacob was riding just behind the cop's mirror, so close that his handlebar was almost touching the window. His face was hidden behind the black visor of his helmet. He didn't say anything, not participating in the yelling and catcalling going on between the rest of the Kittens, but the driver's eyes riveted on the tall, broad boy.

Eventually, the cop rolled his window up tight, made sure all the doors were locked, and stopped on the shoulder. The Kittens parked their cycles around the front, back, and driver's side of the car, and most of them dismounted. Inside the car, the cop was frantically calling for back-up.

"Tip it!" yelled Talet.

The boys lined up on both sides of the car, and started to push on the car. It took a few moments to get into a rhythm, rocking the car back and forth, back and forth. They pushed harder and got more momentum. Before long, the tires were lifting off the ground slightly with each rock. A little bit longer and they would be able to tip it right over, maybe even roll it. Deke was on the driver's side, and assumed that they would tip it onto the passenger side, toward the edge of the highway where no one had parked their bike. But mistakes could be made, and he watched the car carefully, ready to jump back if it decided to roll toward him. He'd seen what could happen if you didn't get back fast enough when the car tipped over the wrong direction. It wasn't pretty.

Deke realized that Jacob hadn't dismounted his bike. He stood watching them, without making any move to participate. He was the biggest guy there. They needed his help.

"Hey, Black!" Deke shouted, jerking his head for Jacob to join them.

Jacob put his hand up to his visor as if he was going to flip it up. Then he froze, not touching it. Instead, he revved his engine and pulled out onto the freeway. Sarin's head jerked around to see Jacob disappear around the next bend. His mouth dropped open in disbelief.

"What the——?"

The gang lost the rhythm to tip the car over and tried to recover. Deke focused on the push-rest rhythm, trying to get back into it. Before any of them saw or heard the approaching back-up, the cops were on them. Deke swore and made a run for his cycle, but the cops were jumping out of their cars to duck behind their doors, guns drawn and trained on the Kittens, yelling orders. Deke stopped where he was.

"They ain't gonna shoot," Travis yelled. "No one's showing any iron."

On his own advice, he tried to make it to his cycle to make an escape. A shot rang out from one of the cops surrounding them. Deke couldn't tell whether they had fired toward Travis or into the air. Travis jumped back, swearing. He looked at the cops in disbelief.

"I'm not armed! You can't shoot me!"

"Lay on the ground with your hands behind your head," a bullhorn-amplified voice ordered. "Any other response will be taken to be a threat and you *will* be shot."

Travis' bravado faded and he stood there, with his cycle a few steps away, stuck between the idea of getting on his bike and escaping and of doing what the bullhorn had instructed.

"*Everyone* get down on the ground!" the order was repeated.

Deke realized that they were all still standing around, watching Travis and trying to figure out what to do. No one was surrendering. He looked anxiously at Sarin for some sign. Sarin wasn't going for his cycle or trying to make a break for it, but he wasn't lying down on the pavement either.

None of the cops were moving in to arrest them. They stayed sheltered behind their car doors, guns trained on the Kittens. They weren't going to put themselves in harm's way. As much as Deke wanted to obey the instructions and avoid the possibility of getting shot, he couldn't be the first one to surrender. He wasn't going to look yellow in front of the gang.

"Everyone on the ground!" the order came again.

With a relaxed smile, Sarin raised his hands in the air. "Don't you guys think you're overreacting just a little?"

"Get on the ground, Mace."

Sarin smiled and looked around at the others. "You heard the man."

Deke exchanged glances with Keith and they both looked over at Travis. Travis' throat was flushed, the red creeping up toward his face.

Sarin leveled a stare at Travis. "Get down, Trav. You're making everyone nervous. You draw fire, maybe one of us gets hit."

"They can't shoot us when we're not a threat," Travis insisted, his voice higher than usual, like he might burst into tears. "No one's got any weapons out."

"You feel like getting shot today?"

"They can't *do* that."

"You got your lawyer here?" Sarin mocked. "You think they're gonna wait while you call him?"

Travis opened his mouth to argue again.

"Just do it," Sarin snapped.

With the eyes of all of the gang on him, and all of the cops with their guns trained on the gang, Travis slowly knelt down, then lowered himself to the asphalt and put his hands behind his head.

"And the rest of you," Sarin told everyone else.

Everyone moved at once. No one had wanted to be first to surrender to the cops, but Sarin had taken care of that.

Sarin looked around to make sure that everyone was moving. "You too, Deke."

Deke realized that he was standing there watching everyone else. Giving himself a shake, he bellied down and laced his hands behind his head. He had his head turned so that he could see Sarin lie down as well, with a long sigh.

Once they were all down, the cops moved in. Deke lay still while one of them put a knee on his back and frisked him. "Weapons or needles or anything sharp in your pockets?"

"I got a knife," Deke said. "No heat."

The cop found his knife and pulled it out, handing it to another officer standing nearby who was bagging evidence as quickly as he could.

"And drugs," the cop noted, pulling Deke's pockets inside-out and retrieving the contents. "What have we got here?"

Deke turned his head to look and the cop pressed it down to the pavement again. "Don't move."

"I was just looking. You asked what I had." He had a better view now, even though he couldn't raise his head. "Percs, X, and crack." He grinned. "But it ain't mine, I'm just holding it for a friend, you know."

"Like I haven't heard that one before." The cop patted down Deke's legs and body. "What's your name?"

"Richard Taurus. They call me Deke," he explained. The cop pulled his hands around to cuff him and then raised him to his knees, then his feet.

"Richard Taurus, you're under arrest." The cop rattled off the usual spiel while walking Deke to one of the squad cars. He pushed Deke into a seat and shut the door A minute later, another cop brought Sarin over and sat him beside Deke.

Sarin grinned at Deke and he turned his attention to the scene outside. "Something I don't get here," he mused.

Deke raised his brows. Everything seemed pretty straightforward to him. "What?"

"Donell. Black," Sarin amended, with a crooked grin. "How did he know the cop?"

"He just sussed out the car," Deke suggested. "Acting suspicious. Too many antennas…"

"Uh-uh. He knew the cop's name."

Deke frowned, thinking about that. "Knew the cop's name? I dunno… maybe he's been arrested by him before."

"How many pigs do you remember by name? No, something weird going on here. Then he takes off right before the force show up."

Deke considered. "It's not like we didn't know they were going to come."

"He's not yellow; why did he take off? So we get cooled for a night. That's no big deal."

Deke didn't say anything, thinking about it.

Chapter Nine

SAMMY HAD AN ERRAND to run for Zed, but he made a detour back to his house before taking care of it. His stomach had been growling for a couple of hours and he hadn't seen his mom that morning, only Hector. Hector would be at work now and it should be safe for Sammy to stop in.

He went up the stairs to his family's bedroom. The door was closed, but there were no locks so he went straight in.

His mom was walking the baby, pacing back and forth with him on her shoulder, patting his back. She turned quickly at the sound of the door opening, startled. Her face relaxed when she saw Sammy.

"Oh, it's you. Why aren't you at school?"

"L-lunch," Sammy hazarded, though he didn't have a watch or a phone to check the time and it probably wasn't noon.

She looked him over, her eyes sharp. "You're out messing around with that gang again. Why don't you stay away from them?"

Sammy went to the dresser and pulled on the top drawer. It was sticky. The track that the drawer was supposed to run on was broken, but Sammy wiggled the drawer patiently and got it open. Pawing through the food packages, he found a sleeve of crackers and the peanut butter. There was a hole chewed in the cracker bag.

"C-c-can't." He lived just a couple houses down from the gang. They knew where he lived. Did she want the gang to come in looking for him?

"Just tell them that you won't help them."

Sammy used a cracker to scoop out some peanut butter and looked at her in disbelief. "K-k-kill mm-m—"

She snorted. The baby fussed, and she patted him tiredly on the back. "They wouldn't kill you, They couldn't do anything to you. You just go to school and stay away from them."

Sammy shook his head and munched on the crackers. He stirred the contents of the drawer to see if there were any drink boxes, but didn't find any. He stuffed some more crackers in his mouth.

"The police were here, asking questions about you," she said. "You want to end up in Detention?"

Sammy wiped cracker crumbs from the corners of his mouth. He'd heard that the police had been asking about him in other quarters as well. On one hand, he should be proud that he was important enough to attract their attention. They knew he was with the gang and the work that he was doing for them. But he didn't feel proud, he felt scared. If they sent him to juvenile detention, even for a day, he'd get killed. A puny runt like him, who couldn't even speak properly; they'd eat him up.

The baby squirmed, drawing his knees up tightly, and started to cry. His mom slapped the baby sharply on the back a few times and gave him a stern shake. "You stop that!" she hollered in his face.

The baby was silent for a minute, startled. Then his face crumpled up and he started crying harder, face turning red. She shook him harder, but it didn't help.

"C-c-colic?" Sammy asked.

"Hungry, probably."

Sammy looked into the food drawer. There were no cans of formula. He picked up the food stamps envelope. It was too thin. Empty. He opened it to be sure. No more stamps. Sammy looked at his mother in disbelief.

"He sold them." Her voice held no emotion.

Hector.

Sammy looked through the drawer for anything that the baby might be able to eat. No milk, no juice, no pablum, applesauce, or bananas. Sammy picked up a plastic plate, and crumbled a few of the crackers into it, crushing them into as fine a powder as he could. There was a baby bottle filled with water on the dresser that the baby had obviously refused to take. Sammy unscrewed the nipple and poured some of the water over the crackers, stirring it into a thin gruel. He continued to stir and mash it, trying to get all of the lumps of cracker out and all dissolved. His mom watched this process with a frown.

Sammy sat down on the edge of the bed and she sat down beside him with the baby in her lap. The baby continued to sob and squirm.

"Psst. Hey," Sammy whispered, putting a bit of the makeshift pablum on the end of the spoon and trying to get the baby's attention. "Shhhh. Look."

With a bit of encouragement, Sammy got the baby to pay attention, and got a little of the mixture into his mouth. Most of it came back out. Sammy caught the rest on the spoon and reinserted it at the next chance.

"Shhh," he continued to soothe, as the baby hiccuped and whined. "Eat up."

It took a long time to get all of the cracker mush into the baby, but eventually he had cleaned the plate. The baby started to cuddle with his mom and get sleepy-looking. She shook her head.

"You're a smart boy. I don't know why you won't go to school."

Sammy sighed. He licked a bit of cracker pablum off of the back of his pinky finger. He touched the baby's pouting lip.

"I'll g-g-g-get f-f-orm—"

"How can you get formula? You don't have any money."

"I c-c-c-can!" Sammy insisted.

She shrugged, not bothering to argue it any further. Sammy looked around the room, a knot forming in his stomach as he realized why it was so quiet.

"B-b-b-bun...?"

She looked at him for a minute before answering, her face a mask. "Bunny's not here."

"W-where?"

His mother shook her head and wouldn't answer. Sammy swallowed and looked around, as if there might be some clue as to where Bunny might be. He had to know where she was, to know that she was safe. Bunny's not here. Did that mean that she was in one of the other rooms? Maybe another parent with a toddler was keeping an eye on her while his mom struggled with the fussy baby? Had Social Services come and taken her away, as they had with others in the past? Had Hector taken her with him? Sammy felt sick at that idea. If Hector had taken the little girl...

"Where?" he nudged his mother's arm.

Again, she just shook her head. Images flashed through Sammy's mind. Bunny sick, or hurt, or even killed. If Hector hurt her too badly, what would he do? Just dump her little body in a dumpster or in a shallow grave in the park.

They wouldn't tell Sammy anything. The little girl would just disappear forever.

Sammy left the house and went to find Zed. He was supposed to be at the gang's crib, so Sammy didn't have far to go. He didn't hesitate at the gate like he used to. It wasn't good for the cops to see him hanging around outside. Instead, he zipped quickly up the sidewalk and let himself in.

Maury was on guard at the door again. He gave Sammy a friendly nod.

"Sammy, baby!"

Sammy shifted, looking around.

"Who you need?" Maury asked.

"Z-z-zed."

Maury nodded. "Wait right here. I'll get him."

Maury disappeared into the back hallway. He came out a few minutes later with the big, heavily tattooed banger.

"What'cha got?" Zed asked.

Sammy pulled the envelope out of his deep pocket and handed it over. Zed ripped it open and pulled out a wad of cash and a scribbled note. He glanced over it and grunted.

"Good. Thanks."

Sammy knew that he was dismissed, but he stood there, trying to figure out what to say and how to form the words. But his brain and his mouth wouldn't cooperate and he just stood there looking like a moron.

"There's no return," Zed nodded at him to leave.

Sammy still didn't move. Unable to speak, he held out his hand, shaking slightly; palm up, rubbing his thumb across the pads of his fingers. Zed looked down at his hand, and then exchanged a disbelieving glance with Maury.

"What?" he looked back at Sammy. "You want me to tip you?"

Swallowing, Sammy nodded. Maury giggled. Zed glared at Sammy.

"I don't tip you. I don't pay you. This isn't your job. You do me a favor. To stay on the good side of the gang."

Sammy nodded again. But he still didn't leave.

Zed shifted his stance, his eyes growing curious. "What do you need money for?"

Sammy took a deep breath and tried. "B-b-b-baby…"

"Baby?" Zed repeated. He laughed. "You're a bit young to be worrying about having babies!"

Sammy could feel himself blushing. He shifted, looking down at his feet.

"You don't have a baby, do you?" Zed teased.

He shook his head, trying to swallow a lump in his throat. Zed's smile faded. "Who is it? Baby brother?"

Sammy nodded. "H-h-he's h-h-hun-hungry…"

Zed considered this, not teasing anymore. After a moment, he inserted his thumb and finger into the envelope in his hand and withdrew a couple of bills.

He handed them to Sammy. "We don't let babies starve around here."

Sammy shoved the bills down into his pocket. "Th-tha-thanks."

Zed slapped him on the back. "Now get outta here."

This time, Sammy turned and left.

Sammy headed toward the small grocery store a few blocks away. There weren't a lot of places to shop in the projects and the convenience stores that stocked formula sold them at a high premium. He would get a much better price at the grocery store, and even better at the superstore, but it wasn't within easy walking distance.

He was only a block from the grocery store, within sight, when they closed around him. Three boys in green gang colors. Young Sixers. Older than Sammy, but not by a lot. Definitely bigger, though. Sammy stopped walking, looking from one to the other anxiously. They didn't look like they had a job for him. They didn't stand like they were holding or concealing something that they wanted him to deliver. Sammy took a step backward.

"Oh no, you're not going anywhere." Hicks wore a big smile.

He reached out for Sammy's arm and Sammy pulled back to avoid getting caught. But the other two were ready and grabbed him to hold him still. Sammy twisted to free himself. His instinct was to hit and kick and elbow, to do whatever he could to get away from them. But they were Sixers. They were in the same gang as him. And if he fought them, he risked running into trouble with the gang. So he tried to free himself, but he didn't strike out. It would have been hopeless anyway.

"In here," Hicks muttered, motioning.

The two sidekicks dragged Sammy after him into an alley, so he was hidden from the view of the street.

Sammy tried to jerk away. An alleyway was not a good idea. Guys got killed in alleys. He didn't know what the Sixers were up to, but the fact that they didn't want anyone on the street to see was not a good sign.

"Settle down, there, Sammy," Hicks soothed. "We're not here to hurt you."

Sammy stopped resisting and looked at him. Did Hicks have a job for him? If so, why didn't he just tell Sammy straight out? Why did he have to hide, to drag Sammy into an alley?

"You got something that we want, that's all," Hicks said.

"Wh-wh-wha—?"

"You can't think of what it is that we might want?" Hicks laughed.

Sammy shook his head.

"Check his pockets," Hicks ordered.

When he realized they were after the money, Sammy fought back in earnest. He nearly escaped, but Hicks laid into him, punching him in the gut and in the face until Sammy couldn't fight back anymore. He sagged in their arms, gasping and sobbing. One of the boys forced his hand into Sammy's pocket and pulled out the cash that Zed had given him. He handed it over to Hicks.

"Yeah," Hicks smiled. "There you go. You forgot you had to pay your taxes, didn't you? Thank you very much for your contribution."

Tears ran down Sammy's face. His mouth was bloody and he couldn't catch his breath. "N-n-no," he tried to protest.

"You shut up!" Hicks put his face close to Sammy's, brows drawn down in a scowl. "You shut up and don't tell no one about this."

Then he withdrew and stood with his thumbs in the belt loops of his sagging jeans, his head at a cocky angle. He nodded to his cohorts and they let Sammy go. The three boys walked away, leaving Sammy in the alley.

For a while, Sammy just stood there, leaning against the wall of the building for support, the tears and blood dribbling down his face. At first, he was confused. How had they even known that he had money? He never had money. Mugging him was a ridiculous prospect, considering that all he usually had in his pockets was lint, and little enough of that. But there had been someone else in the room other than just him and Zed. Maury had been there, watching the whole thing. Maury, who was young, like Hicks and his goons.

Sammy pulled up his t- shirt and used it to wipe his face. He tried to breathe evenly, ironing out the sobs and the ragged intakes of breath. He swallowed. He still had to get the formula for the baby. Even if he didn't have any money. He sniffled loudly and started on wobbly, jelly-like legs, continuing on his way to the grocery store.

Before he went into the store, Sammy zipped his jacket up part way, hiding the blood stains on his shirt. Then, trying to look inconspicuous, he crept around the cashiers and went to the baby food aisle. He knew where it was. It wasn't like he hadn't bought supplies for the little ones before. There were a few other people around and Sammy tried to look casual, studying out the various kinds of food on the shelf. He grabbed a couple of the small jars of food and put them in his pockets. Bunny had really liked the peaches when she was a baby. He inched down toward the formula. He considered the boxes of pablum for a minute, but they were too bulky. He wouldn't be able to carry both pablum and formula out of the store without being spotted. With another glance around, Sammy drifted down to the formula. Powder was the most compact way to carry it. The pre-mixed cans would take up way too much room. He took a can of powder down and pretended to be checking the label for something important. After a quick glance around, Sammy slipped it inside his jacket, against his body, and started for the door.

As he approached the check-outs, there was a shout from behind.

"Hey, kid!"

He turned around and saw a security guard walking after him. Sammy forced an innocent 'who, me?' expression, and kept walking backward, getting closer to the doors.

"Hold on, I want to talk to you."

Sammy gauged the distance to the door. He stopped, as if he was willing to comply, to put the security guard at ease. He'd get a lot further if he could take the man off-guard. The man visibly relaxed and slowed his approach. Sammy let him get another step or two closer and then made a break for it, whirling around and heading for the doors at a sprint. The guard's shouted curse rang out behind him and then they were both running, Sammy was desperate to get away, to escape with the formula for the baby. Who was going to feed the baby if he didn't?

He was fast, adrenaline boosting his speed considerably, but the guard was tall, with a much longer stride. His steps ate up the distance between them. Sammy was out the doors and halfway down the block, but the guard didn't give up. He kept coming after Sammy.

Sammy was prepared for a flying tackle, a collision that would knock him off his feet. He would hit the pavement hard, with the man on top of him. Probably break his teeth in the process. Maybe some ribs too. He'd seen it happen. But the guard simply overtook him and grabbed him by the back of his jacket, throwing him into the sad little pocket of grass and weeds beside the sidewalk.

Then he grabbed Sammy tightly by the arm and held him in a steel grip. "Stupid little punk! Nobody shoplifts in my store!"

Sammy didn't protest. There was no point. He had been shoplifting and the man had caught him at it. Wasting his energy and the breath to stammer out an argument would be pointless.

They were both breathing heavily. Sammy was dragged along back to the store, people gawking at him the whole way, pointing and whispering to each other. By the time they got back to the doors of the store, there was already a police car waiting. Sammy swallowed, forcing back tears. Here it was. His first arrest. The Sixth would be proud of him. Graduating. Becoming a man. But what Sammy desperately wanted was to feed his brother. His rep wasn't important.

"Nice job," the policeman complimented, climbing out of his car at their approach.

The security guard cleared his throat. "Well. Couldn't just let him get away."

The policeman took hold of Sammy's other arm and the guard released him, leaning up against the squad car to catch his breath. The cop looked Sammy over. Sammy's eyes rested on the officer's name bar. Smith. That was easy enough.

"Put your hands on the car." Smith pushed Sammy toward it.

Sammy knew how it was done. He leaned forward to put his hands on the car, putting his feet far apart and well back. Smith proceeded to frisk him, pulling out the formula and jars of food and putting them on the top of the car. He looked for weapons or drugs, carefully checking all of the usual hiding places and turning Sammy's empty pockets inside-out.

"Turn around."

Sammy straightened up and turned around.

Smith's eyes traveled over him. "What's your name?"

"S-s-s-smm…" The words stuck in Sammy's throat.

"Slow down. Just relax. I need your name, that's all."

"S-s-samm."

"Sam?" Smith repeated.

Sammy nodded.

"You do this on a dare or something? You and your friends thought it would be funny?"

He shook his head.

"What are you going to do with baby food? Eat it?"

Sammy shook his head again. What did the cop *think* he would steal formula for?

"I bet he uses the formula to cut drugs," the guard suggested eagerly. "Coke or heroine or something."

Smith's eyes searched Sammy's face. Sammy felt like he was caught in the glare of headlights. Exposed. Like a cat about to get run over in the street. He looked away.

"Maybe," Smith agreed. "But what about the jars?"

The guard frowned, shrugging. "Maybe he just wanted a snack."

Smith didn't believe it. "Unzip your jacket."

Sammy obediently pulled down the zipper, separating the two sides of the jacket. Smith pushed back first one side, then the other, staring at Sammy's bloodstained shirt and noting the green bandana. Sammy sniffled, his nose still running or bleeding. Smith looked back at his face.

"Open your mouth."

"You think he's smuggling drugs in there?" The guard got closer for a look.

Smith didn't bother to answer. He silently pulled on a pair of blue gloves, then pushed back Sammy's swollen lip, pulled his cheek out, and pressed his fingertips against Sammy's teeth, forcing him to open his mouth further. He withdrew his hand and let Sammy close his mouth.

"Who beat you up, Sam?"

Sammy looked down, then back up again.

Smith's eyes were intense. "You're Sixth Street's new messenger."

Sammy just swallowed. His mouth was as dry as if it had been filled with cotton and he didn't know what to say, even if he could speak.

"It's gotta be to cut drugs," the guard repeated.

Smith glared at him. "I'm conducting an investigation here," he said firmly.

"Just trying to help," the guard groused.

"You're not. Maybe you should step back inside. I'll come take your statement when I'm done here."

Reluctantly, the guard went back into the store. Smith's searchlight eyes focused back on Sammy. "You get mugged?"

Sammy cleared his throat. He thought he should explain, but what would he say, even if the words flowed naturally? That his own gang had jumped him? So he just stared down at his shoes and nodded.

"Who is the baby formula for?"

"B-b-b-broth-ther."

"You were coming to buy it and they took your money?"

Sammy nodded confirmation.

Smith continued to stare at him. "How old are you, Sam?"

"I'm t-t-t-ten."

Smith expelled a loud breath. Eventually, he moved, opening the back door of the police car. "Get in."

Sammy obediently climbed in. This was it. This was his first arrest. Smith shut the door, and Sammy knew he was on his way to the police station to be booked. But Smith left him there and went back into the store. Sammy put his head back and closed his eyes to wait while Smith got the security guard's statement.

It was a while before Smith returned. Sammy's lip and cut-up mouth were throbbing. There was an ache in his ribs and belly, but as long as he didn't move, it was tolerable. His legs were stiffening up after running and then being forced to sit still in the back seat.

Smith made his way around to Sammy's door and opened it. Sammy waited to be told that he was under arrest and that he had rights.

"Come here."

Smith reached to close his hand around Sammy's shoulder and escort him out of the car. Sammy was confused and resisted. He didn't want to have to go back into the store, to face the security guard or the owner or whoever Smith wanted to put him in front of. But Smith kept a firm grip and merely led him around to the other side of the car. He opened the front passenger door and motioned for Sammy to sit. Sammy obeyed, but he still didn't understand what was going on. He looked up at Smith, waiting. The cop sighed and leaned against the top of the doorframe, looking down at Sammy. He put a shopping bag down in Sammy's lap. Looking into it, Sammy saw the formula and baby food. Evidence? Why was Smith giving it to him? He looked at the cop in confusion.

"That's for your brother." Smith's voice sounded strained.

Sammy closed his hands around the bag. He didn't dare hope that he had understood. He was still being arrested. He was still going to be in deep trouble when they put him in juvie and he wasn't big enough or confident enough to stand up for himself. He looked worriedly into Smith's eyes.

"You need to get away from the gang," Smith told him. "They're only going to get you hurt and in more trouble. Do you understand that?"

Sammy nodded briefly.

"You need to go to school. The only way to get out of this place is to get educated. That's the only chance you've got. If you continue to associate with the gang, work for them... you're going to end up in more trouble."

Sammy had no idea how he was supposed to stay away from anyone who lived in the neighborhood. They were practically next door. And refusing to work for them... what did the cop think, that the gang would just let him off the hook?

"I know it's hard," Smith sympathized. "You look up to these guys. They're tough and they get what they want. You want to be like that, to emulate them. But they aren't getting anywhere in life, Sam. It may look like they're getting everything they want, with their drugs and their guns and their money. But they're just going to die. And they can't take any of that stuff with them. They'll get killed in a drive-by, or a drug overdose, or gang warfare. It's going to happen to all of them, sooner or later."

Sammy didn't say anything or make any sign. Smith straightened up. He shut the passenger door and walked around to the driver's side. Sammy watched him, still confused about what was going to happen next.

"Seatbelt on." Smith put the car into gear.

Sammy didn't put his on and neither did the cop.

"Where do you live?"

Sammy took a deep breath, even though it hurt his ribs. He let it out slowly. "F-f-f-fifth."

"Not the gang's house. Yours. Where your mom and your baby brother are."

Sammy nodded with emphasis. He tried to sound more confident. "F-f-f-f-ifth S-s-street."

Smith drove toward Fifth. Once they reached the intersection, Sammy made a gesture indicating the direction of his house. With a measuring look at him, Smith turned onto Fifth in the direction

Sammy indicated. Once they had driven close enough to see it, Sammy pointed. Smith rolled to a stop in front of the house. He looked at the house for a minute and at the gang's crib a couple of doors down.

"Should I come in with you? I'd like to check on your family and talk to your mom about the gang and you getting mugged."

Sammy shook his head, panicking. "N-n-no!"

"I don't have to talk to her about the shoplifting. I just want to help out."

Sammy shook his head adamantly.

"It will get you in worse trouble if I come in?"

Sammy nodded.

Smith thought about it. "I'd like to come see you in a few days. See if we can get your family some help."

Sammy swallowed. He didn't think that there was anything Smith could do for them.

"If I wait a few days," Smith said, "they won't connect it with any trouble today."

Sammy looked down at the bag in his lap. Smith reached over and touched the can of baby formula. "Sam, if things are that bad, your family needs the help."

Sammy tried to swallow the lump in his throat. He was tough, but the cop's sympathy was more than he could handle. He rubbed his eyes with both palms.

"I can come back and pay a visit to your mom. She doesn't have to know that it's anything to do with you. There are programs. Resources."

Sammy wiped his nose with the back of his hand. He glanced down at it to make sure his nose wasn't still bleeding. Then he pulled the door handle and got out. Smith didn't say anything and didn't stop him. Holding the shopping bag tightly in his hand, Sammy walked quickly up the sidewalk. At the door, he stopped and looked over his shoulder at the police car. He waited.

Smith pulled out and drove off down the street.

Chapter Ten

JACOB PARKED HIS CYCLE and walked into Antonio's, looking for members of the gang. A few of them were hanging out. Jacob walked up to join them. They fell silent as his approach and sat looking at him.

Jacob looked at each boy's face in turn and stopped at Sarin's. Sarin stared at him with obvious hostility. Jacob swallowed and slid into a seat.

"What?" he asked, looking away from Sarin's bright eyes. "What's up?"

"Nice of you to join us," Sarin growled.

Jacob looked around. There were lots of other gang members who were not there. No meetings had been called. It wasn't like he'd missed something. He looked at the other faces for a clue as to what was going on. Hi-Top was always friendly, but even his eyes were wary. Travis sneered when Jacob looked at him. A couple of others just looked away.

"What'd I do?" Jacob asked. "Did I miss something?"

Sarin's eyebrow went up. "Well, you weren't exactly around when the cops busted up our little party the other day."

Jacob motioned for a drink from the waitress circulating through the diner. "I… heard them coming," he said uncomfortably. "Didn't think I'd stay around."

Sarin shook his head. "You never even got off your bike. Are you a Wildcat or aren't you?"

"*You* made me one," Jacob pushed back. "It wasn't my choice."

"Well, you are one now. Wildcats are loyal to each other. How are you showing your loyalty?"

Jacob was silent, pondering on this. He was handed his soft drink and took a long sip. "I told you Levi was a cop."

Sarin nodded. "Yeah, you did. And how did you know that? You didn't just notice a cop on our tail, you knew him by name. How do you know this cop?"

Jacob looked over at the other boys.

"You ain't been arrested, have you?" Sarin inquired. "You don't have a record. So how do you know this cop? You been ratting us out?"

Jacob shook his head. "No—never! I'd never!"

"Then I'm still waiting for an explanation. One that rings true," he warned.

Jacob gulped. He turned the cup in a slow circle on the table, his stomach twisted into such a tight knot that he didn't think he could swallow even one mouthful. "He… he's a friend of my dad."

Whatever Sarin had been expecting, it wasn't that. "A friend of your dad." His voice held a note of disbelief.

"I've… met him before… at my house… work parties…"

"Work?" Keith echoed. All eyes turned to him. "Where did your dad work with a cop?"

Like spectators at a tennis match, they turned back to Jacob for his reply. Jacob stared down at his cup.

"When did your dad work with this cop?" Sarin prodded.

"They've been undercover together," Jacob finally answered.

They all stared at him. Jacob felt the flush creeping up his face. He rubbed the space between his eyes with his fingertips, not looking at them.

"Your dad's an undercover cop?" Keith's voice rose in pitch.

"Sometimes he's undercover." Jacob swallowed. "Sometimes not."

"Your old man's a cop?" Sarin said.

Jacob nodded, still looking down.

"How come you never told me that before?"

Jacob scraped his thumb down the waxy coating on the cup. "You never asked."

Sarin obviously knew why Jacob had never told them. A cop's kid joining a motorcycle gang? The gang having to worry that Jacob might be informing on them or might let his father find something out by accident. It just wasn't compatible.

"A cop," Keith said. "What does he think of you being in the gang?"

Jacob gave him a look. "He doesn't know."

"Oh. Right. Well, sooner or later, he's gonna find out."

Jacob closed his eyes, shaking his head. That could not happen.

"How do you think you're going to prevent him from finding out?" Keith asked.

"I gotta try. I don't take my bike home. He doesn't work juvenile gangs."

"He doesn't wonder where you go?"

Jacob cleared his throat and shook his head. He hoped that someone would change the subject, but everyone still seemed intent on hearing his story, no matter how much he wanted to avoid telling it.

"He works long hours. Travels sometimes. I work, go to school… I don't spent a lot of time at home."

Travis gave a low whistle. "Cop's kid," he marveled. "Gonna be some fireworks if he ever figures it out."

Jacob took a sip of his pop. After a few comments, the conversation started to drift again, moving on to other issues.

Jacob looked up and saw Sarin still staring at him, eyes thoughtful.

It was only a couple more weeks until Duke's department Christmas party. He didn't forget that he wanted Jacob to go with him. As usual, Jacob acquiesced. The family Christmas party was a big deal, the social event of the year for all of the men and women who worked together in Duke's department. Jacob had gone to it every year for as long as he could remember. Lavish with gifts and alcohol, everyone was encouraged to have a good time. Duke was almost always blind drunk by the end of the night. This year, Jacob was sure, would be no different.

Duke eagerly took him around to introduce him to any the new cops in the department and re-introduce him to all of the old ones so that they could marvel at how big Jacob was; obviously a reflection of Duke's machismo. Jacob saw Thompson briefly. Thompson smiled up at Jacob pleasantly.

"Wow. What have you grown in the last year, Jake? Three inches? Six? Any plans to stop in the near future?"

Jacob looked from Thompson up to Duke and both cops laughed.

"You think he's going to catch up to you, Duke? Maybe even beat you?"

Duke chuckled. "We breed'em big in my family."

"Do you ever," Thompson obliged.

Duke grabbed at one of the other officers who was milling around, having a glass of punch and visiting. "Sherriway. Come meet my boy."

Sherriway looked for a youngster around Duke's waist level. Duke laughed.

"No, here. This is my son, Jake." He indicated Jacob.

Sherriway looked up at Jacob's face. "This is your son? How old is he?"

Duke glanced at Jacob. "Fifteen?"

Jacob nodded.

"Fifteen, and he tops everyone in the room but you," Sherriway pointed out, as if they might have missed the fact. "He's a monster!"

Duke took a gulp of his drink, probably to disguise a snicker at his milquetoast son being called a monster. "You bet he is," he agreed.

They continued to circulate and chat.

"Have a drink, Jake, loosen up," Duke pressed a cup of Christmas punch into Jacob's hand that Jacob knew hadn't come out of the kiddie bowl. Jacob took a swift glance around to make sure none of the other cops were paying any attention. "Oh, don't worry," Duke chuckled. "No one's going to give you any trouble. You can handle it better than any of them."

Jacob took a sip. Whoever had mixed the drink had been generous with the punch. "Someone could still report it or make a fuss."

"None of these guys would," Duke assured him.

Jacob wasn't sure how many drinks Duke had consumed so far, and he was drinking from the complimentary bar, not the punch bowl. He was right in that good place that Jacob liked him to be: contented and feeling no pain, but not yet to the point where he was slurring and mean.

Later into the evening, the families with young children had all departed, leaving the bachelors and older married men, and Duke with Jacob. Duke was past the pleasantly buzzed state, starting to grow raucous and rough. Sherriway had disappeared for part of the evening, but rematerialized now. He grabbed Duke by the elbow and was talking urgently with him. His face was flushed with drink and his manner nervous. A few times Duke tried to shake him off, but the man was persistent in whatever it was he was rambling on about.

"Jake. Come here. Listen to this," Duke commanded, spotting Jacob lurking around the door, hoping to be able to get out of there soon.

Jacob reluctantly joined them. He tried to concentrate on Sherriway's words. For a few minutes, the stream just flowed over him, but then he started to get the gist of what the officer was saying. He kept repeating declarations about what the Stars were doing and Jacob got the feeling he wasn't talking about TV or movie stars.

"Who are the Stars?" he asked, frowning in concentration.

"Listen, boy!" Duke cuffed Jacob. "Listen to what he's saying!"

"The Star Syndicate," Sherriway told Jacob, focusing in on him, his eyes wild and bloodshot. "Stay away from them, Jake. They're organized crime. Bigger than the mob. Bigger than any mafia. And totally off of anyone's radar yet. Nobody understands just how big they are, how they've swept the organized crime arena. It's all been covert. They have secret questions and codes, ways to identify each other. A whole symbolic language. They've infiltrated other organized crime groups, gangs, even the police force. They're actively recruiting and growing at an incredible rate!"

Jacob looked at Duke to see what his take was on this rant. Jacob had never even heard of the Stars before. How could they be so big or dangerous? Duke met his eyes and nodded back at Sherriway again, encouraging Jacob to pay attention.

"How do you know about them?" Jacob asked.

"I've been undercover. I've infiltrated right to the top level," Sherriway clutched at Jacob's arm. "Right to the boss of the gang; Shiny. Nobody else has gotten into the top level."

Jacob didn't know what to say. Sherriway seemed almost comical, he was so intense. But Duke didn't seem to think it was funny and that gave Jacob pause. Duke knew what went on in the department. He would know whether these Stars existed or not. He'd know where Sherriway had been undercover.

"When they meet you, they'll ask you, 'what do stars do?'" Sherriway said. "That's the entry level question. The answer is 'stars shine.'" He squeezed Jacob's arm, taking a glance around for anyone who might overhear. His eyes drilled into Jacob's. "Stars shine," he repeated urgently.

"Stars… shine," Jacob echoed.

Sherriway nodded. He continued expounding further code phrases, rituals, and procedures. He insisted that Jacob repeat them back, made sure he understood every piece of the puzzle. Goosebumps rose on Jacob's skin as Sherriway talked about brutal murders and the sociopathic behavior of Shiny, the gang's big boss, and his bloodthirsty 'run gang,' the top level of the syndicate.

Several times, Jacob tried to pull away from the conversation, his head reeling, not wanting to hear anything else. But Sherriway pursued him, held onto him, and Duke also insisted that he stay and listen. It grew late. Everyone was leaving. They were trying to clean up and put away the tables and chairs while Duke, Jacob, and Sherriway still stood there, deep in conversation.

At long last, Sherriway looked at his watch and indicated that he had to meet someone. Jacob saw his lips moving, as if he wanted to tell Jacob the details of that meeting too, but realized even in his drunken state that he couldn't reveal those last details. They parted at the door, going their separate ways.

Duke took Jacob home in silence, a frown line between his eyes. When they reached the house, Duke went straight to the fridge for a beer, but he didn't even get it open before passing out in the living room.

Jacob awoke early the next morning to the phone ringing incessantly. He eventually shed his blankets and staggered to his feet. He went to track down the wireless handset. It stopped ringing, but ten seconds later, started again. Jacob pushed the talk button and raised it to his ear.

"Hello?"

"Donell?" a male voice demanded urgently.

"This is Jacob."

"Jacob? Where's Duke? Is he there?"

Rubbing his eyes, Jacob looked in Duke's bedroom and then in the living room, where Duke was still snoring in his recliner. "Yeah. He's sleeping."

"Get him up. It's Larkin, Jacob. This is very urgent."

Larkin was Duke's boss. The snap in his voice told Jacob more than his words that this phone call was serious. Jacob looked at Duke and took a deep breath. He went over to Duke's chair and gave Duke a tentative shake of the shoulder. "Dad. Dad, it's the phone. Dad!"

Duke struck out, trying to hit Jacob.

Jacob pushed the phone to Duke's face. "Dad. It's Larkin, your boss. He's on the phone."

Duke blinked at him blearily. "Jake...?"

"Larkin's on the phone."

Duke focused on the phone. He gripped it and held it to his ear. "Donell," he grunted.

Jacob could hear Larkin's voice on the other end, speaking rapidly. He moved away to give Duke privacy but Duke made a motion for him to stay put. Jacob hesitated. Duke asked a few questions. Eventually, he hung up the phone, his face pale and tense. He looked at Jacob.

"What is it?" Jacob asked.

"Sherriway. He… was killed last night."

Jacob gasped for breath. He steadied himself on the back of the couch. "Killed? What happened? Was he driving?"

"Looks like a mugging… but…" Duke looked around him and found the beer that he had taken from the fridge the previous night. He twisted off the top and took a swallow.

"You don't think it was?"

"Jake… Sherriway was under deep cover until the Christmas party. He hadn't even been debriefed yet. They pulled him because he was in too much danger." Duke took another drink and cleared his throat. "He wasn't mugged."

"You think the St—you think someone killed him?"

Duke didn't answer. He drank, not looking at Jacob. Jacob waited for a minute then turned to go back to the bedroom to take care of Nicholas.

"Jake…?"

Jacob stopped and looked back at Duke.

"Did Sherriway say anything last night? About the Stars? The investigation?"

Jacob shivered. He hesitated. With the amount of alcohol that he had consumed, Duke obviously remembered nothing of the long conversation. "A little," Jacob hedged.

A shadow crossed Duke's face. He pressed the beer bottle to his forehead, even though it wasn't cold anymore. "Jake… you don't breathe a word of it. Not to anyone. No one can know anything he said."

Jacob wondered fleetingly about the fact that Sherriway hadn't yet been debriefed. If Jacob didn't report what Sherriway had said, all of that intelligence would be lost. All of the work that he had done, the danger that he had put himself in would be for nothing. He had known all the passwords, all the details of how the syndicate operated.

Duke stared at Jacob, his brows drawn down. "Not a word, Jake. Not to anyone," he warned again.

Jacob nodded. "Okay, Dad."

Chapter Eleven

D EKE WAS PLAYING CARDS in the visitor room. Not because he was expecting any visitors, but because that was the only place to do anything other than sit on his bunk and stare at the wall. He saw the guard bring in a tall woman in a skirt. The guard pointed in Deke's direction.

There weren't a lot of Wildcats left in custody, but Keith was a 'no fixed address' as well, and like Deke, was still being held. Keith saw Deke's eyes follow the severe-looking woman coming across the room toward them and gave a sly grin.

"Visit from your girlfriend, Deke?" he teased.

Deke snorted. "I think I can do a bit better than that!"

Keith raised his eyebrows and puckered his mouth doubtfully.

The woman approached the card table and looked around at the boys. "Which one of you is Taurus?"

Deke leaned his chair back on two legs and Keith pointed to him.

"You're Taurus?"

"That's me."

"Mary Cooke. I've been assigned to your case by DCFS." She looked around and nodded to an empty visitor table. "Why don't we go have a talk?"

Deke sighed in a long exhale. "Sure, why not?" He let the chair settle back onto all four legs and stood up, stretching his limbs lazily.

He fist-bumped with Keith and followed Mary Cooke to the empty table. They sat down facing each other.

"Can I call you Richard?" Mary Cooke asked, with a plastic smile. She set a thin file folder on the table in front of her.

"No," Deke said immediately. "Don't go by that. Deke."

"What?"

"Call me Deke."

She looked at him for a minute, then opened the folder and made a notation. "Deke, then." She met his eyes. "How are you doing, Deke? Are they treating you all right here?"

"Sure. Ain't my favorite place to be, but I got no troubles."

"Good. They called DCFS because you're a minor, no parents in the picture, no fixed address."

Deke nodded. "Yep."

"Where are your parents? You're a runaway?"

"I suppose. My mom was killed when I was just little. Old man… well, he got remarried but he was never really around much. I left a couple of years ago. I manage just fine on my own."

"You manage. Where have you been living?"

"With the gang. They're my family now. Don't need a guardian when you've got your brothers at your back."

"Well, your brothers, as you call them, don't seem to be the best influence on you. How are they watching your back when you're doing things like assaulting an officer of the law?"

"We didn't assault him," Deke argued, shaking his head. "He was in his car the whole time. We didn't lay a finger on him."

"I'm not your lawyer. I'm not here to argue about the charges. I'm here to evaluate whether you need to be taken into care and what we're going to do with you."

"I do just fine on my own," Deke maintained.

"You've had other charges. You have outstanding warrants for failing to appear."

"Yeah, that happens when you don't get served the court papers."

"That's what happens when you don't have an address," Cooke pointed out. "How can you be served if you have no fixed address?"

Deke shrugged. "They could find me if they really wanted to."

She folded her hands together and tapped them against her chin thoughtfully. "What happened to your mother?"

Deke took a deep breath and let it out. "What's it matter what happened to my mom? That was a long time ago."

"Fill me in. I have to decide what to do with your case."

"She was killed. Murdered. I was... six or seven. I don't really remember her."

"Murdered by who? What happened? Was it domestic?"

Deke shifted uncomfortably and looked around the big, bare room. Other juvies talked with their families, lawyers, or whoever else came to visit them. Or painstakingly put together puzzles with pieces missing or played a game of cards together in the corner. Deke didn't like talking about his mom. About the past.

"This guy she was seeing. He killed her. Him and my brother."

"Your brother was killed too?" she asked in surprise.

"No." Deke cleared his throat and corrected her. "My brother helped to kill her."

"Oh." Cooke's mouth formed a round 'O' that stayed there after she spoke. "Well." She didn't know what to say to this. "That must have been very traumatic for you. So your brother is... no longer in the picture."

"No," Deke agreed dryly.

"Your father remarried, but you ran away from him? Was there abuse?"

Deke looked at the woman's thin folder. Obviously there was not much about his background in there. It seemed like all she had was the intake report from the police. He ran his fingers along the edge of the table.

"The old man ain't so bad. But I guess he likes women... that control him."

"I see. And they probably don't stop at trying to control *him*."

Deke nodded. "Yeah. I know it probably ain't easy to try to take over a house full of boys. You can't blame her. But I couldn't deal with it anymore."

"You wouldn't consider going back?"

Deke pushed his chair back slightly from the table. "Nuh-uh. Don't even suggest it."

"Any other family members? Aunties that might keep an eye on you for a bit?"

"Some older brothers. I dunno where they all are. I don't remember any aunties or grammies."

She tapped the end of her pen on the folder.

"I'm fine with the gang," Deke said. "That's the best place. There ain't any point trying to put me anywhere else."

"What about a foster home?" Cooke asked. "Or maybe a group home."

"The gang is like a group home." Deke grinned. "Come on. I'm not one of your hard-luck cases. I'm not looking for a break to go back to school. I'm fine where I am. You don't have to save me."

"I'm guessing you would like to get out of here, though."

"Sooner or later. Most of the boys have been sprung already. But it always takes longer for the no-fixed-addresses."

"So let's get you an address."

Deke sat back with his arms folded across his chest. "My only address is the gang. You just tell them that you talked to me and I'm okay so they will let me go. I got my lawyer and my court date, that's all I need."

"And if you fail to appear again? That's a black mark against my name."

"You know where to find me."

She looked at him, considering. The system was full of kids who needed help. The foster care system was overloaded. All of the halfway houses and institutions. Everything was overfilled. Her only job was to make sure that he didn't need a placement. She could see that Deke would just run if she tried to place him somewhere else. It was a waste of time.

"You'll stay there, where I can find you?"

"Sure," Deke said. "Where else am I gonna go?"

"Fine." Mary Cooke scribbled notes in the file and then closed it and slid it into her valise. She thumbed through the other files nestled there.

"Would Keith Kenney be one of your friends over there?"

Deke grinned. "Yeah. You land him too?"

"Yes, I did."

"I'll send him over."

The wheels of justice moved slowly, but in a few more days, Deke was back out and at the Kittens headquarters again. He sat near the entrance, watching gang members coming and going, having a smoke and feeling glad to be home. Black walked in, taking his helmet off and holding it at his side.

"Hey little brother," Deke greeted.

Black's head snapped around. He scowled at Deke. "What?"

"Hey, we're brothers now, right?" Deke pointed out. "And you're only fifteen—"

"Sixteen," Black corrected.

"Sixteen now. So you're my little brother."

Black didn't look like he thought much of the idea.

"Because you're so *little*," Deke prodded, grinning. Waiting for Black to smile at the joke. But the bigger boy just stared off into the distance, seeing something that Deke couldn't. Deke studied his face.

"You got brothers of your own?"

Black stepped closer to Deke to talk. His voice was low. "I used to have an older brother," Black said reluctantly. "When I was little…" His face was pale. He let his long bangs fall over his eyes, obscuring them from view. Hiding. "Now… he's locked in."

Deke nodded understandingly. Brothers in prison he understood. He was surprised to hear that Black had a brother on the inside. Sarin had apparently not discovered the fact when he was considering Black for the gang.

"In the pen?" he acknowledged. "How long until he gets out?"

Black shook his head. "Never."

"Lifer, huh? Tough luck, man. See, that's why you need a big brother like me around, watching your back."

"How about you?" Black said, redirecting the conversation. "You got any brothers?"

"Loads of them," Deke said. "Or I used to. You know, before I left. I'm about the baby of the family. Just one younger and I don't know where he is. He ran away… never been able to track him down."

"What about your older brothers?"

"One in prison… the other two… I'm not really sure. They were out of the picture a long time ago. Drugs, homeless, I dunno. They had problems."

Black nodded.

"Old man got married again after my mom was killed. So there's little ones too, half-siblings. But I never really counted them."

"All boys?" Black asked.

Deke took a long drag on his cigarette. "Yeah. No girls, even with the second wife. Just a house full of boys."

They were both silent, considering their stories.

"The gang's my family now," Deke pointed out. "We got lots of brothers here."

"Yeah."

Chapter Twelve

PEOPLE HAD BEEN IN and out of the kitchen already, but Sammy kept his blanket wrapped around him, cuddled up on the opposite side of the room from the coffee maker. He continued to doze as people came and went. Hector hadn't shown up the night before so Sammy hadn't been kicked awake and he took every advantage of the extra time. He was still recovering from the beating Hicks had given him during the mugging. Although his ribs didn't take kindly to sleeping on the hard kitchen floor, his body was exhausted and needed more sleep to heal.

The doorbell rang several times, but nobody answered it. The visitor took to pounding on the door and Sammy eventually roused himself, unable to continue sleeping through it. He answered the door and saw the cop, Smith, standing there. Smith looked him over.

"That's looking lovely," he observed.

Sammy had looked at his face in the mirror the day before. He had purple and yellow bruises, some of them tinged green now.

He dropped his eyes, looking away from Smith.

"I'd like to see your mom," Smith said.

Sammy chewed on his lip, trying to figure out if there was a way to head Smith off. Inviting cops in could only lead to trouble.

"Come on, Sammy," Smith encouraged. "I can come in and look around on my own or you can just take me to her. What's it going to be?"

Sammy conceded. Best not to let a cop wander around on his own. He jerked his head at Smith and led him into the house. They went up the stairs to the bedroom. Sammy stood outside the door, awkward. He looked over his shoulder at Smith. Finally, he raised his hand and knocked on the door.

"What is it?" his mom's voice demanded.

Sammy opened the door tentatively, peeking in. His mother was sitting on the bed and saw him first. She scowled. "What is it, Sammy? Come in."

He opened the door further and she saw Smith. She drew her ragged housecoat around her. "What is this? What are you doing here?"

"Hello, ma'am. My name is Smith."

He stepped into the room and offered his hand to her to shake. But she just pulled her housecoat tighter and didn't take it. Smith took a slow look around the room. Sammy's mother sat on the low, bowed double-bed, with several layers of blankets but no fitted sheet. The carpet on the floor had frayed holes. There was the broken dresser. Bunny's pile of blankets on the floor made Sammy heartsick, wondering what had happened to her. The baby was wrapped in a blanket, lying in a cardboard box for a crib.

"What do you want?"

"I didn't catch your name, ma'am? Mrs. King, is it…?"

She looked at Sammy, eyes narrowed, then back at Smith. "Marisol King."

"Marisol That's a very pretty name. I'm just checking in to see how everything is. How are you folks doing?"

She looked at Sammy again. "Is this about the boy? Is he in trouble for something?"

"He's not in trouble. Though you know, we would like to see what we can do about his association with the gang."

"I've told him to stay away from them." Marisol looked away from them with her lips pressed tightly together.

"Sometimes that's not enough. Maybe we could get him in some after-school programs that would help to keep him from being bored and getting into mischief."

Sammy shifted uncomfortably. Most of the time he couldn't even make it to school and they thought boredom was the problem?

"He's a smart boy," his mother answered. "He should stay away from the gang. Just look at his face."

Smith nodded, looking at Sammy again. "I agree. We need to work on that, see what we can do. I'm wondering what else you might need. Everything okay with the baby?" He looked at the small form wrapped up in a blanket in the box. "Do you qualify for food stamps?"

"We get food stamps, but they don't go far enough," Her eyes went to Sammy and then back around the room. "I don't mind going hungry, but the little ones…"

Sammy stared at Bunny's abandoned nest of blankets. The little ones? Sammy wasn't little anymore and Bunny and the others were gone. There was only one little one left. How much did she really care?

"There are programs that provide formula for babies." Smith thumbed through the papers in the portfolio he'd been holding under his arm as if he had to search for the one for formula. As if he hadn't known that was the one that he would need. He pulled out a brochure clipped to an application form. "Here, this one. If you qualify for food stamps, you qualify for this program."

She took it from him reluctantly and her eyes flicked over the papers. Sammy knew she didn't like filling out forms. He went over to have a look at the baby.

"If you take it to the Social Services office, they'll help you to get it all completed and submitted," Smith said, apparently sensing Marisol's reluctance.

Sammy pulled the blanket back from the baby's face. He was sleeping peacefully. His cheeks were plump and there were no dark shadows under his eyes. He looked like the little cherub babies on Valentines cards, all rosy-cheeked. That was good. When Sammy stood back up, Smith looked at him questioningly. Sammy nodded.

"Now, what else can we help with?" Smith asked.

Marisol's eyes were dark with suspicion. "Why are you here?"

"Just routine, ma'am. The police force is part of the community and we are involved as much as we can be in community outreach, making sure that families like yours get the services that you deserve."

"You've never done that before. It's always been about Sammy, or Hector, or DCFS."

"Well, I'm here now."

Towering over Marisol while she sat on the bed, Smith looked around as if wishing that there was somewhere he could sit down. He had to settle for leaning down toward her, his hands on his knees, trying to get closer to her level to gain her trust.

"Is there any abuse, Marisol?" he asked in a confidential tone. "We can help you. Your husband…?"

"Hector." She shook her head. "Hector doesn't hit me."

Smith glanced at Sammy. Sammy just looked down at the sleeping baby, feeling his face flush.

"And the children? Does he get upset with them?"

"He got bruised like that from the gang," she asserted, gesturing at Sammy. "Not from Hector."

"Hector doesn't hurt them? Get frustrated?"

Sammy didn't need to look up to see her shake her head. He stared fiercely down at the baby, shutting everything else out.

"Now how about housing? This situation…"

"It's not illegal," Marisol protested. "We just share the rent."

"I'm not making a judgment," Smith soothed. "But I think we could find a better situation, where you have some more space. Independence."

"You don't know what we can afford. You think we would be here if we could afford something better? It's better than being on the street, sleeping under a bridge somewhere."

"Sure. I just think… there's subsidies, other social programs that maybe could help you out."

"We don't need any more charity," she snapped. She threw down the papers about the baby formula. "We don't need any more of your pity! I take care of my babies. Just go away and leave us alone."

"I'd like to help—"

"We don't want your help."

Smith straightened up. He looked helplessly at Sammy.

Marisol mistook the look. "You tell him to stay away from that gang. I can't control him. You put him in whatever program you want to keep him out of there."

Smith sighed. "Come with me, Sammy."

He turned and headed back out of the room. They stopped at the bottom of the stairs. Smith looked at Sammy.

"The baby looked okay?" he asked.

Sammy nodded. "A-s-s-sleep."

"Where do you sleep?"

Sammy shrugged.

"Her husband, Hector. Does he hit her?"

Sammy swallowed and looked down.

"Is that a yes?"

Sammy didn't respond.

"What about you? Does he hurt you?"

He didn't respond to that either.

"Sammy."

Sammy refused to look at Smith.

"All right… so what are we going to do about you and the gang?"

Sammy glanced in Smith's direction. They couldn't do anything about him being in the gang. He didn't want to be in the gang, but the choice wasn't his. The gang had already recruited him. He wasn't allowed to decline.

Smith was looking through his portfolio of brochures again. "Here, this one…"

He held out a glossy flyer. Happy-looking kids conversing around a table. YMCA. "They do lots of cool stuff. Outings, camping trips, all kinds of interesting things. They meet at the YMCA to talk, or hear speakers, or do indoor crafts and activities. And they also go out to different places: museums, movies; and like I said, camping."

Sammy nodded.

"Sound interesting?" Smith prompted.

Sammy wasn't sure how that would keep him out of the gang. He expected there was a catch. There was always a catch. He shrugged.

"It's kids your age," Smith pointed out. "Not older, like the gang. You could hang out with kids your own age, do fun things."

Sammy nodded.

Smith studied his face. "Let's get you signed up."

Smith sat down on the second stair from the bottom and spread the application form out with the portfolio providing a hard surface behind it. He uncapped a pen and started to fill in Sammy's details. He got down to the address and phone number.

"What's the address here? I didn't look at the house number."

Sammy took the brochure from him and carefully filled in the information, which was easier than trying to say it out loud. Looking over the form, he added his birth date. Smith took it back and signed it.

"I'll get this submitted. And then you'll have something productive to do with your time. Meet some other kids your age."

Sammy picked up his school backpack from the kitchen. Smith waited for him and walked down the sidewalk with him. "Off to school?"

Sammy shrugged. He broke away from Smith and walked off down the street as if he was heading for school. In front of the gang's crib, Maury came out the door and hurried after him.

"Sammy, my boy. Hold on. Got a job for you."

Sammy didn't let Maury grab his arm, but pulled back, avoiding him.

"What's with you? How come you've been so jumpy lately?" Maury demanded.

Sammy didn't say that he knew Maury was the one who had set him up, who had told Hicks that Sammy had money for the taking. He didn't say anything. But he looked over his shoulder at Smith's squad car. Maury followed his gaze and swore.

"What're the heat on us for?" he squawked.

He grabbed at Sammy's arm to pull him into the house. Sammy shook his head and avoided his grasp.

"Come on," Maury prompted. "Come inside, so we can talk."

He managed to catch Sammy and hauled him up the sidewalk. Sammy looked back at Smith, allowing himself to be pulled into the house.

Chapter Thirteen

JUGGLING A GIRLFRIEND WHILE he was in the gang was not easy. Jacob had never had much time to give Megan, even before. When he'd started to hang out with the Kittens, he'd been sure that she would dump him, tired of being ignored.

But she hadn't dumped him. He saw her at school when he could; in the hallways, between classes, over lunch. Occasionally, he managed to find some time for her after school or in the evening, but it was rare. Instead of being angry with him for not spending enough time with her, she seemed even more interested in him.

Megan had always been one of the prettiest girls at school. She always had boys chasing her, fawning over her. And she went through them like Skittles. Until Jacob. Jacob didn't know what attracted her to him, as he wasn't one of the guys who had chased her. Maybe that was the whole point. Maybe she wanted someone who wasn't so easy to get. Jacob didn't see himself as particularly good-looking; his hair longish and dark rather than the short bleach-blond hair of the popular boys. Too big and awkward. Too many scars. But if a girl was looking for big and muscled, Jacob fit the bill.

She really seemed to be interested in Jacob, always listening to what he had to say, even though he was quiet and shy. She was always free when he was looking to spend time with her. Jacob treated her with respect, more interested in talk than intimacy, and she seemed okay with that too. It had been nice to have a girl to share his time with sometimes, friendly and undemanding.

But that was over now. He could see by the look in her eyes when she asked if they could go somewhere after school. Something had changed. He was supposed to be out with the gang, but decided that he could be late for them for once.

"Jacob…?"

Jacob tried to focus on what Megan was saying. It was easier to just let his mind drift, to block it out and pretend that it wasn't happening. But he made the effort to look at her.

"Jacob…"

She reached behind her neck to unhook her necklace. The chain that she always wore threaded through Jacob's ring. It was stupid and sappy, he knew, but he loved to see her wearing his ring. He watched her take the ring off and slide it partway across the table toward him.

"I'm sorry. It's… I still really like you…"

Jacob stared down at the ring, avoiding her face. It hurt to breathe. He closed his eyes, forcing himself to take a deeper breath. He'd never expected the relationship to go anywhere. Right from the time that she started to show interest in him, he had assumed that she would get bored with him, that something would make her change her mind. It hadn't bothered her when he joined the gang and started hanging around with real hoods. It hadn't bothered her that he hadn't had the time for her that he should. Instead…?

"It's… well, it's my dad…" Megan trailed off.

Her dad had found out that his daughter was seeing a gang banger. A street thug. He wanted her away from Jacob's bad influence. And Megan was that one-in-a-million girl who, instead of rebelling against his strictures, was actually going to honor his wishes without an argument.

"Okay," Jacob nodded jerkily. "I get it."

He glanced at her face fleetingly, then back down at the table. Her eyes glistened with tears. But she was still breaking up with him. "It's… he says… he says your dad is a cop. A… a dirty cop."

Jacob's heart throbbed hard. Duke. This wasn't even about Jacob, it was about his dad. He supposed it was fitting that Duke would take this away from him too. He ruined everything else that mattered to Jacob.

"Yeah, okay…" He broke off and was silent, and so was Megan. A tear tracked down her face.

"I'm so sorry," she apologized again. "You never… you never said anything about your family…"

What made her think that he was going to start now?

"Is he…?" Megan started.

"Yes." Jacob's voice was much harsher than he intended it to be. Megan stopped speaking, the tears just running down her cheeks. "Yeah, he's a cop." He looked at her challengingly, daring her to ask more.

She said nothing. Jacob's chest ached. He wanted to reassure her, to stop her from crying. But it wasn't okay. It wasn't fine for her to dump him because her dad didn't like who his dad was. And they couldn't still be friends. He swallowed hard and stood up from the table. He turned to go.

"Your ring…" Megan started.

"I don't want it." It was an expensive ring. He'd denied his own needs to have something to give her. He would never give it to someone else. "Trash it if you like."

She tried to protest, but Jacob just turned his back on her and left.

Chapter Fourteen

DEKE WAS ASSEMBLED ALONG with the rest of the Kittens, as they had been commanded by Sarin. Sarin was meeting with Saunders, the leader of the gang whose territory abutted theirs to the north. Saunders' boys were assembled as well and each gang watched the other warily, sizing the opposition up, watching for any potential dangers.

The two leaders approached one another looking strong and confident. Like they did this every day. Like nothing could possibly go wrong. The gang members shifted, ready for any reason to start a rumble. The two leaders clasped hands and released. Sarin had a challenging smirk. Saunders' expression was angry, full of malice.

"You've been off your turf too often." Saunders' face was hard, his teeth clenched.

"We're expanding," Sarin explained airily, with a wide movement.

Saunders didn't rise to the bait, nor did he back down. "Keep out of our territory and there won't be any trouble."

Sarin's smile widened. Deke shivered with anticipation. He reached into his pocket to finger his knife, knowing it was time to be ready.

"How about a deal?" Sarin offered.

"What kind of a deal?" Saunders' eyes moved restlessly.

"A two-man fight. Simple. One of mine and one of yours. Nothing messy: bare hands, no interference, go it until one can't fight any more."

There were a few seconds of silence while Saunders considered this suggestion. "Winner takes...?"

"New territory."

"How much?" Saunders was deadly serious, in no mood for games.

Sarin accommodated him. "Four blocks in, all the way along the line."

"That's a lot. Can you keep that kind of area?"

"Can you?" Sarin returned.

Saunders' eyes were showing interest. "Any two men?"

"Seventeen or younger."

Saunders ran a practiced eye over the Kittens watching, measuring the strength of each one. He already knew who his best men were. "When?"

"Today, in half an hour."

"Here?"

"Your choice."

Saunders nodded. "Yes, then."

"Deal?"

"Deal."

They clasped hands again, and each went back to their waiting gangs. Saunders was confident. Deke wondered why Saunders had agreed so quickly. He didn't seem to suspect that it could be a trap. He'd looked over the Kittens and seen nothing to be worried about.

Sarin's eyes kept straying back to his wrist, watching the countdown to the fight. His forehead was starting to bead with sweat. Deke looked over his fellow Kittens, weighing which one Sarin was likely to pit against Saunders' fighter. Something was not going according to Sarin's plan. He was getting nervous as the time for the fight drew nearer.

All eyes raised at the sound of an approaching cycle. Deke watched the lone rider pull his bike a little closer to the group than the rest of the cycles were parked. They all recognized him and immediately started whispering to each other.

Sarin walked over to the rider. "Hello, Black. Little late, aren't you?"

Black raised his face shield. "Had some business." He looked at the two groups. "Personal. What's happening?"

Sarin didn't answer immediately. Black removed his helmet and brushed the hair back from his eyes. "You're just in time for a two-man fight," Sarin said. "Winning gang takes more territory."

"Who——?" Black started and then cut himself off when he saw the answer in Sarin's eyes. "No."

"You're gonna do it, Black. It's all arranged."

Deke watched Saunders slide in behind Sarin, craning his neck to see who had arrived. Saunders' teeth clenched and he looked back at his boys again, obviously reconsidering his plan. Deke imagined that Saunders was plenty worried after seeing how young the hulking rider was. Now he knew Sarin's ploy. He had to find a way to counter it.

"Don't do this, Sarin."

"The deal's been made. You're the one who's gonna fight for us."

"No."

"You don't and we lose territory." Sarin pointed out.

Black still shook his head.

"As a Wildcat, you will." Sarin's voice was hard, exercising his authority.

Black's jaw was set as he dismounted from his bike. He limped stiffly to stand between the two gangs. He looked back at Sarin. Sarin followed him, satisfied that Black wouldn't let him down.

"What are the rules?" Black demanded.

"No weapons, no interference."

Black nodded and waited. A boy almost his size emerged from the other gang.

"Forget it, man," Sarin told Saunders dryly, "we know Gary's at least nineteen."

Saunders grinned, motioning Gary back. It had been worth a try. By now he had had the time to select another boy. He was quite a bit smaller, but Saunders had obviously picked him for his speed and agility because of Black's limp.

Black removed his leather jacket and handed it to Sarin. His well-developed muscles bulged under his tight black t-shirt. Deke gave a low whistle between his teeth, impressed at the sight.

"The gloves too," Saunders instructed.

"No need," Sarin retorted.

"No weapons, you said. How do I know they ain't loaded?"

"My word. He's clean."

Black stripped off his gloves and stuck them in his back pocket. The other boy came at him fast, without warning and without a starting signal. Black responded with a punch to the boy's jaw. Gentle for Black, it was enough to knock the boy unceremoniously to the ground, seriously injuring his pride. In a flash, he was up again. Deke saw the sun glint on steel as he pulled a knife. Black's second punch was harder. It rang out with a vicious crack and the boy fell like a log. Black caught him, stripped him of the switchblade, and lowered him to the ground. A flick of his wrist buried the blade in the ground an inch from Saunders' foot.

Without a word, Black pulled his gloves back on and took his jacket from Sarin.

"Good job," Sarin said smugly, noting Saunders' discomfort. "I knew I could count on you." Sarin had hardly even glanced at Black.

"I said not to force me," Black said.

His third punch of the afternoon left Sarin sprawled on the ground. There was a collective gasp of shock. Black strapped his helmet back on and left. Deke looked at the Kittens around him. Their eyes were all wide with shock.

"Bloody hell," Keith murmured.

There was no official change of leadership over the Kittens.

Sarin made an attempt to laugh off the fact that Black had knocked him down without Sarin being able to retaliate. Like Black was just a hotheaded child whose tantrums were cute rather than a challenge to Sarin's authority.

But Deke and the others knew better. Sarin had been dropped on his butt. His rep was destroyed. Try as he might to subtly discredit Black, he couldn't regain the confidence of the Kittens. They looked to Black for leadership. He was now the alpha dog, whether he sought to be or not.

Things were going to be different now.

Chapter Fifteen

JACOB WENT OVER TO Antonio's after getting out of work. He glanced around as he entered. Several members of the gang were up at the counter. Deke noticed him at the doorway and waved him over. Jacob hesitated for a moment then limped over to them. There was only a small group. Sarin had a girl beside him who Jacob didn't recognize. She had straight dark hair and brown eyes so dark they were almost black. She was thin and sunburned and looked about fifteen or sixteen.

"This is Angel," Sarin said. "She's visiting town and will be hanging around for a while."

Jacob didn't know what to think of this. He let his hair fall in front of his eyes and mumbled a greeting.

"Man, are you ever shy." Angel laughed. Her voice was low and a little hoarse. "You got a name, mister?"

"Black," Sarin supplied.

Jacob sat down at the counter on the vacant stool next to Angel. He studied her carefully a moment while she wasn't looking, and looked away when she threw a glance in his direction. He only half-listened to her soft voice and the answers and laughter of the gang. After some time, the group rose and headed for the door. Jacob slid off his stool and limped after them.

Angel was doubling with Sarin. Jacob watched her for a moment without saying anything. She was close enough to hear him when he called her name softly.

"Yeah?"

Jacob tossed her his helmet. "Wear my helmet."

"I hate helmets. You wear it."

"You could get hurt."

Jacob tied a doo-rag around his own head, tucking away his long hair. He was really nervous about her riding without protection. He never rode without his helmet and leather. Neither did most of the gang. A person could really get messed up in a bike accident. Sarin turned around and glared at Jacob.

"Lay off her, Black, she doesn't have to. Besides, it's me she's doubling with, not you. Nothing is gonna happen."

Sarin grinned smugly. Angel tossed the helmet back to Jacob. Without another word, he strapped it on and rode off. The gang followed and caught up with him at the first intersection.

A few miles down the road they picked up a cop. Jacob saw the lights in his mirror first, then heard the siren. Sarin floored it and everyone followed suit. The game was 'lose the cop,' and they knew all the moves. The cop didn't shake easily. Jacob checked over his shoulder. It wasn't someone he recognized. Probably a rookie. New cops tended to be that way, always playing by the book, they didn't give up easily. Older cops often chased the gang just for the moves but broke off once they were tired of it or got another call.

Most likely, he had picked them up because Angel wasn't wearing a helmet. Some of the guys had been ticketed for that before—when they were traveling alone. A cop had to have some kind of nerve to chase the whole group without any backup.

They took the winding road up a steep hill. Jacob glanced at his speedometer. He knew this part of the road, knew how often there were accidents at the blind intersection at the top. Jacob sped up and pulled alongside the group to slow them down. Sarin was leading the chase and was way up ahead, already rounding the next-to-last curve to the top. Jacob cut across in front of the rest of the group to slow them down, trying to catch up to Sarin. As Jacob rounded the curve, he saw Sarin mounting the crest of the hill. He had swerved into the other lane right into the path of a semi coming up the other side.

Sarin's reflexes were too slow—perhaps he was blinded by the sun on the semi's windshield. He wrenched the handlebars around just as the bike hit the semi. The bike and rig hit at an angle and the cycle was thrown across the road and spun on its side in the gravel. The rig put on its brakes and jack-knifed across the road, rocking for a moment like it was going to turn over.

The other bikes were just coming around the bend behind Jacob. He pulled his bike to the shoulder and dismounted, running up to the bike, Sarin, and Angel.

Sarin had been thrown into the ditch but was on his feet, scrambling up the embankment to the road. Angel was still tangled up with the motorcycle. Jacob hauled the mangled bike out of the way and turned Angel onto her back. Her face was white and she was unconscious. There was blood on her face and clothes, but it didn't look as bad as Jacob had expected. She was all in one piece, with no exposed bones or gushing arteries.

The cop had caught up to them and gotten out of his car. He stood there, frozen. Everyone seemed to be stuck; slow to react. Jacob looked over his shoulder. "Call an ambulance—a couple of ambulances."

The dazed cop pressed the button on the radio on his shoulder and did so, fumbling for words but eventually getting the ambulances dispatched.

"Travis, give Sarin a hand. See if he's all right."

The policeman was still just standing there. Jacob was impatient. "You got first aid lessons. What do we do now?"

Looking at Angel's blood-covered face, torn clothing and arms, Jacob was at a loss as to what to do next. The cop knelt down beside them, his face white and drawn. Jacob pulled off his doo-rag and tied it tightly around the worst wound on Angel's arm, which was leaking blood at an alarming rate.

"She breathing okay?" he asked.

The cop clumsily checked and nodded. He seemed to be able to think more clearly now and felt Angel's wrist for a pulse. "She should be kept warm."

Jacob stripped off his jacket and laid it carefully over her. Sarin came up beside them. His jacket was torn and he had a wide gash in his arm, but otherwise he seemed unhurt.

"Man… " He swore softly under his breath. "She gonna be okay?"

"I don't know," the cop answered tensely, coming to life. "Why wasn't she at least wearing a helmet?" He wiped some of the blood off of her face.

Sarin looked away guiltily. "She wouldn't wear one." He was shaking and his face was gray.

"Sarin, sit down. Put your head between your knees," Jacob told him. Sarin obeyed the order. Angel made a noise and shivered. Her eyes opened and she lay dazed without moving.

"Angel," Jacob called softly.

Her eyes focused on him, then she saw the cop and jolted as if receiving a shock. She sat up. With wild eyes, she flipped out a switchblade. Jacob put his hand over hers.

"Get him back," he ordered. A few members of the gang pulled the cop away. Jacob slowly took the switchblade from Angel and closed it.

"Help me stand up," Angel said.

Jacob wasn't sure about her moving around, but he put his arm around her and assisted her to a standing position. She leaned heavily on him, breathing raggedly.

Sirens sounded in the distance and Angel stiffened.

"It's the ambulance," Jacob said. She relaxed.

The ambulances pulled up. An attendant took Angel from him, asking her questions.

Jacob and the others waited in the emergency room with Sarin. A doctor hurried in and talked in a low voice to the nurse at the desk. He glanced over his shoulder at the boys, then approached.

"You guys come in with the girl? Er… Angel?"

"Yeah, that's right. She okay?" Sarin asked.

"Well... er—see, we left her in an exam room, after taking care of some of the superficial injuries... anyway—we... uh—we came back and she was gone." He was obviously rattled.

"You mean you don't know where she is?"

"Did she come back through here?"

"No."

The doctor turned tail and retreated back to the warren of exam rooms.

"Sarin," Jacob started. "Did she say where she's staying? I mean, if we could call there...?"

Sarin shook his head. "She didn't say."

They waited. The time crawled by and Jacob listened to the nurse who was answering phones.

"General Hospital, emergency room... yes sir, one moment, please... Angel?" she skimmed down a paper and went on. "Yes, she was brought in from a motorbike accident—yes, I can transfer you to a doctor, who can give you more information... yes, she definitely needs to be brought back in. Thank you..."

Jacob and Sarin exchanged glances.

The time crawled by. Sarin was taken out to have his arm stitched up and then returned, waiting for x-ray. Jacob looked at the clock again and walked slowly across the room and back restlessly. Sarin watched him pace.

"What's'amatter, Black, your old man getting home early?"

Jacob hesitated. "Yeah."

"Go home, then. The others will wait."

He heard the sneer—the others were more faithful than Jacob was. Jacob wanted to go home to avoid any trouble with Duke, but he also wanted to make sure Angel was safe. He felt responsible for her.

"You think Angel's coming back?"

"You heard the phone call. She's on her way."

"How long will it take?"

"Hey man, cool it. I don't know where they called from. Either sit down and wait or go home."

Jacob looked out the window into the darkening night. "You gonna wait?"

"Of course I am. I wouldn't desert a lady in distress now, would I?"

"Especially when it's you who put her in distress," joked Talet with a snicker.

Sarin got up angrily and moved towards him. Talet wasn't prepared to face off against Sarin, even if he was injured. Talet put his hands up defensively, stepping back.

"Hey—I'm kidding, Sarin, just joshin' ya. I'm just kidding, I swear."

"You just drop it," Sarin growled. "You know it wasn't my fault."

"No way man—stupid cop acting all crazy—bad luck, plain bad luck—right Black?" he queried, trying to bounce Sarin's attention back to Jacob.

"Sure," Jacob answered vaguely, remembering how Sarin had sneered at Jacob's offer of his helmet to Angel.

"You don't sound sure," Sarin said sharply.

Jacob stared out the window. Sarin walked slowly across the room. "What's got into you? You dissin' me?"

Jacob shook his head.

Just then, a policeman walked in supporting Angel. She was bruising up and walked tenderly, leaning on the cop.

Thompson. One of Duke's closest friends.

Angel looked so roughed up that Jacob wondered how she had managed to get anywhere on her own. Thompson talked to the doctor for a minute, then the doctor took Angel toward the examining rooms. Thompson spotted the members of the gang standing around and headed towards them.

"You the guys riding with her?"

"That's right," Sarin answered coolly.

Jacob turned around and tried to look interested in the magazines. He was painfully aware that his movement had attracted both Thompson's and Sarin's attention.

"Yeah. She was on the same bike as me…" Sarin diverted Thompson's attention. It seemed like hours before the conversation was finally terminated and Jacob heard Thompson walk away towards the other cop, the one who had chased them. Jacob let out a breath of relief.

Sarin stood at Jacob's side, talking in a low voice. "What's up, Black? You know him?"

Jacob nodded. "Yeah, I know him."

"Like, how closely?"

"He's close friends with my dad. Comes over to the house… known him since I was little."

"Yeah? Angel's staying with him."

Jacob tried to swallow a big lump in his throat. "She's part of Dad's case." And that wasn't all. It was only a few days ago that Jacob had read a story to Nicholas from the newspaper about a juvenile named Angel. He gathered from what Duke had said over the past few days, that she was a Star. Part of the gang that Sherriway had been undercover with. The gang that had killed Sherriway.

Angel was a Star.

"If he's getting home early," Sarin said abruptly, "shouldn't you be getting out of here?"

"Yeah… but Thompson will see me," Jacob glanced quickly over his shoulder at the cops. "Even if he doesn't see my face, I'm sort of hard to miss, and with my limp and all… he'll know me."

Sarin shrugged. "Your old man, not mine."

"If he finds out I'm in a gang, he'll kill me."

Sarin turned away from Jacob to survey the room. Jacob looked at Thompson. He was still in conversation with the other cop. Maybe he wouldn't even notice Jacob if Jacob didn't do anything to attract attention. He started across the room, moving slowly, trying to control his limp, keeping other people between himself and Thompson if he could. But Thompson had seen him and left the company of the other cop to intercept Jacob. Jacob picked up speed to try to get to the door before Thompson could catch up.

"Excuse me, I'd like to talk to you!" Thompson called out, right behind him.

"I'm already late. Talk to Sarin."

"I see." Thompson stopped the pursuit, but Jacob could still hear his raised voice. "Well, say 'hi' to Duke for me, Jake."

Jacob swore angrily under his breath, slamming through the doors to go get his bike.

* * *

Chapter Sixteen

DISMOUNTING FROM HIS CYCLE, Deke took off his helmet and shook out his hair. He went into Antonio's and took a look around. At first he didn't see Sarin. He was in a corner booth instead of at the counter. Alone. Deke went over to join him.

"Hey, Sarin. 'S'up?"

Sarin motioned impatiently for Deke to sit. He leaned forward toward Deke. "So? You find anything out?"

Deke shifted uncomfortably. He didn't like the position that Sarin had put him in. Sarin demanded his loyalty to the gang, but Deke didn't feel loyal. He felt like a traitor.

"I'll tell you, he's a big guy, but he's not the easiest guy to shadow," Deke warned. "He almost caught me a few times. I'm still not sure… he might have seen me and just not done anything about it."

"Then he doesn't care that you were watching him. So spill."

"He doesn't go a lot of places. The school, his job, and home. Out with the gang."

"I already know about all of those things. But he's been disappearing lately. He's not going to school or work in the middle of the night, so if he's not with the gang, not at home, where is he?"

Deke rubbed his bristly chin, wincing as if squealing on Black caused him physical pain. It really rubbed him the wrong way.

"You remember that girl?" he asked. "The one who was on your bike, in that accident?"

Sarin scowled at him. "It wasn't that long ago, Deke. I think I can remember a couple weeks ago." He ran his fingers along the pink, healing scar on his beefy arm. "It was sort of a memorable occasion."

"Yeah. Well, Black's been taking off visiting her."

Sarin's jaw dropped. "What?"

Deke shrugged uncomfortably. "It looks like it's just friendly. You know, talking together and all. I don't think they're…" he raised his hands uncomfortably. "They don't get much privacy, you know."

"Why would I care?" Sarin growled. "How is he seeing her? Where?"

"That cop's house where she's staying. Black rides over there and she comes out. Sits on the front steps with him in the dark, talking."

Sarin shook his head. "Don't ask me what chicks see in that pup. Shy as all get-out, but he's got no trouble getting girls."

"And she was in hospital, he saw her there too." Deke wanted to be sure to include everything in his report.

"I know she was in hospital. I…" Sarin trailed off.

Deke resisted the urge to finish the sentence: "You put her there." Instead, he just nodded and kept his mouth shut.

"She was back there again, though. Just got back out."

"She was back in hospital again?" Sarin frowned. "What for?"

"Well… I couldn't exactly ask Black, could I? I dunno. Probably complications from the cycle accident."

Sarin straightened, sitting back in his seat.

"So he's going to see a girl," he summarized. "If there's one thing that can pull a boy away from a gang, it's a girl. At least… least we know he's not spending time squealing to the cops."

Deke shook his head. "From what I've seen of Black, he stays as far away from the cops as possible. Except for visiting Angel, that is."

Sarin shrugged. Deke stood up. He paused, his fingertips resting lightly on the top of the table. "What is it about this girl?"

Sarin's brows drew down and he looked at Deke, shaking his head. "What do you mean?"

Deke tried to put the feeling into words. "Stuff just doesn't make sense. Like, since when does a cop take a perp into his own home? And still keep her, even when she takes off and starts riding with a bike gang? And Black...? What does he know?"

"Know?"

"Well, even that first day, he seemed like he already knew her. He'd never met her before? How'd they get so close so fast?"

Sarin regarded Deke with a thoughtful expression but didn't answer.

Deke was practicing knife throws at a target with Keith and Travis when Talet came in. He obviously had news.

"What's up?" Travis asked.

"You oughtta check out the TV," Talet offered, gesturing back toward the sort of common room where they had run stolen power and cable, hooked up to a big screen that played most of the day and night. Deke stretched out his shoulders.

"Why, what's on?" Keith asked, narrowing his eyes at Talet.

"Come and see."

They exchanged looks with each other, but it was only the next room. They could take a break from their game if it was that important. Deke was the first through the door and looked at the TV. In the corner of the screen was a picture that was undoubtedly Angel. The reporter was saying 'armed and dangerous, do not approach,' and Thompson, the cop who had been at the hospital was beside her.

"...Extremely dangerous," Thompson said. "She might look like a harmless kid, but we would warn the public not to approach her. If you see her, please call nine-one-one."

"Whoa," Deke said. "That's pretty heavy."

"Dangerous?" Talet scoffed. "That little thing? Who are they kidding?"

Deke glanced around to see if Sarin was there and saw Black sitting at the back of the room, a shadow falling across his face. Black was watching the screen intently and didn't notice Deke's look.

"She could be," Deke pointed out. "You don't know."

"If she was dangerous," Talet said, "she wouldn't have been babysat at a cop's house instead of behind bars. They're just trying to make it sound like a big story."

Deke looked at Black. Black met his eyes and didn't agree or disagree. Deke could tell that Black didn't side with Lanny Talet. He knew something. Something he wasn't sharing with anyone.

* * *

Chapter Seventeen

DUKE HAD BEEN AWAY, undercover, for a few weeks. So when Jacob walked into the house, he was relaxed, not worried about running into Duke in a foul mood looking for someone to beat on. He threw his jacket over a chair in the kitchen and reached for the light. Strong hands grabbed him from behind and Jacob immediately fought back, throwing back an elbow, trying to twist out of the grip. He tried to wrench himself free, but there were more of them. Not just one man lurking waiting for him in the dark, but a whole group.

A hard rod hit him in the ribs and pressed against them.

"You know what that is, kid? You want to get your guts sprayed all over the room?"

Jacob stopped fighting.

"Don't move a muscle."

Without even thinking about it, Jacob turned his head to look at the man who spoke and one of the men threw a hard punch into Jacob's middle, knocking the wind out of him.

"You're looking to get yourself hurt bad, kid."

"Let's go," another voice urged. "Sticking around here ain't gonna improve the situation."

"Okay. Move nice and slow and don't do anything stupid, kid. No funny stuff, you got that?"

Jacob just stood there frozen, not saying or doing anything.

"Let's let the boss know we've got him."

A couple of tugs and Jacob went with the men toward the back hall. He pulled back, not wanting them to go into the bedroom and see Nicholas. But they kept him going, a feeling of sick horror growing in his belly, straight to the bedroom. There was another shape silhouetted in front of the moonlit window, the end of a cigarette glowing in front of his mouth. He shone a bright flashlight in Jacob's face, making him squint and pull back.

"Got the other kid, huh?"

He moved the light away and angry red afterimages floated in space before Jacob's eyes. The flashlight turned toward Nicholas. The man didn't shine it directly at Nicholas's face like he had at Jacob's but lit it him up well enough for Jacob to see Nicholas's wide, terrified eyes. He tried to take a step toward Nicholas to comfort him, but the men held him back.

"Bring him out," the boss said. "Johnny's supposed to be keeping watch, but I don't trust him for long."

When they got outside, the man made no attempt to conceal himself like the others did. He watched everything piercingly and dispassionately. His features were sharp and wary. He was tall and lean and well-disciplined, like a soldier standing at attention.

"March, kid. Out to the lane. There's a car waiting. You climb in and sit tight," the man instructed, his words clipped and precise. "Unless you want your brother getting hurt, you do exactly what you're told."

Jacob had no choice but to obey. He was so scared he was shaking. He felt like throwing up. He got into the car, with a man sitting on either side of him. One of them had a gun on him and Jacob turned to look at him. The man moved fast, bringing the butt of the gun down hard on the back of his neck and skull, stunning him, almost knocking him out. Stars danced in front of Jacob's eyes, everything around him seeming to dissolve into fragments.

"You watch it, kiddo. Just keep your eyes straight ahead."

The man on the other side wrestled a grip on both Jacob's wrists, bringing them around behind his back. He began to tie them with a length of rope.

The boss was sitting in the front, looking back. He laughed softly. "Look at you, you stupid fool! Letting a kid like that fool you! Let me."

The man forced Jacob to lean far forward, his chest on his knees, and he pulled on the rope viciously, sending pain shooting through Jacob's arms and shoulders. He pulled the rope so tightly it bit deep into Jacob's skin so Jacob couldn't move or press outwards against the rope as he had been doing. The man let go of the rope after tying the knot well and pushed Jacob back upright.

The man beside Jacob, the one without the gun, brought his hand into Jacob's view. Pale, thick fingers, laced with brass knuckles.

"Know what these are, son? Know what these are for?"

Jacob couldn't say a word. The gun was eased off his ribs and the gunman put a blindfold over Jacob's eyes.

"You know, a set of knuckles can make an awful mess of a guy," the man went on. Jacob felt the cold metal trace a path along his jaw and down his neck, making him shudder and break out sweating. He sat there, blind, waiting for them to tell him what they wanted of him.

"So," the man started conversationally. "Where's your daddy?"

Jacob felt his jaw drop and hang open, thunderstruck. Where was Duke? Duke was undercover. There was no way for Jacob to know where he was. There was no way for him to tell these men anything if that was what they had come for. No matter how much he wanted to comply with their threats, he could do nothing.

"Maybe you didn't hear me. I asked where your daddy is."

"I—I don't know," Jacob managed to croak out.

"So he can talk," the boss up front said in amusement. "But that ain't good enough. I want to hear him sing."

"Where is he?" the man with the brass knuckles repeated.

"I don't know."

The fistful of brass slammed into his ribs without warning and Jacob gasped in pain. The gun, pressed into his other side, jerked away and the gunman swore loudly and fiercely.

"Warn me before you do that! This kid almost had his guts spread all over the inside of the car! I've got a sensitive trigger—"

"Shut up," the brass-knuckles-man snapped.

"You guys get blood on the upholstery, you get it cleaned," the driver, Johnny, warned coolly.

"Oh, you keep your mouth shut!" the boss ordered Johnny. "Now, I think we should get a few things straight here first. What's your name, kid?"

"Jacob." He could barely whisper.

"What? Jacob? You know who we are, Jacob?"

Jacob had seen enough, he just hadn't had the time to put it all together yet. The silence was deafening and Jacob tried to gather his wits to put together all of the clues. They didn't give him a lot of time.

"Do you?" the boss prodded.

"Stars," Jacob answered quietly.

There hadn't been a lot of light, nor a lot of time to see and to figure out what he was seeing. But they had rings. They had the ruby rings that Sherriway had described. Ruby rings like the one that Angel had worn, that Jacob had gotten used to seeing on her hand until she had escaped Thompson's custody.

The man's next question sounded mildly surprised and infinitely more menacing.

"Well… do you know what Stars do?"

Of course Jacob knew the answer to that question. How could he ever forget? "Stars… shine."

All of the coded questions and passwords, rituals and procedures flooded back into Jacob's mind. As if any of that could save him now.

The Stars hadn't expected him to know the answer to their query, even though it was only an entry-level password. There was a stunned silence. Jacob imagined the eyes of all three men meeting as they considered the impact of Jacob knowing a Star passcode.

"Where's your daddy?" the boss questioned again.

They weren't going to be stopped just because Jacob knew a low-level response. And they weren't going to pursue it further to find out how many levels he knew. If they didn't ask, they could claim ignorance. They didn't know that he could give them the codes right up to Shiny's intimate circle. No one could fault them for not knowing if they didn't ask.

"I don't know where he is," Jacob whispered.

The man with the brass knuckles slugged him across the jaw. Jacob felt the metal tear at his flesh, and there was numbness for a few moments followed by a fiery pain.

"Sure you do, kid."

The next few days were a jumble of impressions, disjointed and confused. They kept the blindfold on Jacob and when he wasn't being questioned, a gag in his mouth. His wrists and ankles were tied tightly with rope, cutting off the circulation, impossible to free himself from. None of the tricks that Duke had ever talked about for getting free even came close to working. Perhaps Jacob was doing them wrong. For the interrogations, he tried to blank his mind, to embrace the pain and swim into it mentally, so that he would pass out; rather than fighting against it. Unconsciousness was his friend. They couldn't question him when he passed out.

Jacob was housed in a basement. There had been stairs that they had thrown him down when he arrived. The tiles were cold. He had no clue of the passage of day and night; he couldn't see anything around his blindfold, and he suspected that even if he could, there was nothing to see in the basement. It echoed and was cold and Jacob suspected that it didn't have any windows. There were no meals. He was hungry off and on for the first day or two, then his hunger abated. Or maybe he just couldn't feel it anymore through the pain.

There were several men. Jacob wasn't sure what the boss was called. No one ever mentioned him by name, simply lowering their voices and referring to Him. Jacob supposed it was probably Shiny, the head boss of the Star Syndicate.

One of the men who took the most pleasure in beating him when the boss questioned him was Sid. He was a cruel and vicious man who delighted in finding new methods of torture and frequently had to be reined in by the boss.

Jacob didn't suppose that he was being held for ransom. Who would they even call to make a ransom demand? They would have to find Duke, and Duke was not to be found. Jacob had a feeling they knew more about where Duke was and what he was doing than Jacob did.

The days and nights passed in a blur. When he wasn't being interrogated or beaten, he tried to sleep. Lying on the cold, hard floor, he tried to convince his brain that it was better if he was not conscious.

It was best to just block it all out until his body gave out and he died.

Jacob had been semi-conscious, vaguely aware of what was going on around him, for a long time. He heard raised voices nearby and then the door to the room he was being held it opened, and the blindfold he wore let in blinding rays of light around the edges. Jacob didn't move, hoping that if he showed no sign of being aware, they wouldn't bother him. His head throbbed. He concentrated on that, trying to block everything else out, hoping to pass out again.

"Black," a voice said softly. A female voice, young, but roughened by cigarettes or bronchitis.

"Black? Why would you call him that?"

Jacob shuddered. That voice he recognized. That was Sid.

"That's how he was introduced to me."

Her voice was so familiar, Jacob could almost hold onto it, could almost identify it. But not quite. It was beyond his reach.

Maybe he would fall back asleep, and when he woke up again, he would remember.

"He prob'ly saved my life," the girl's voice continued.

Sid was silent. Jacob's head whirled. He had saved her life? It made no sense to him.

"What do ya want from him?"

"Information on his father."

"Why not just use the Star network?"

Sid didn't answer. Jacob remained frozen, hoping that neither one would realize that he was conscious.

"Not official then," the girl observed. "Well, Shiny's coming in tonight. He'll be down to see ya."

"Why would he come down here?" Sid asked.

Jacob puzzled through this the best that his scattered, traumatized brain would let him. If Shiny was coming in tonight and didn't know anything about what was going on, then he wasn't the boss that had been giving Sid orders. That boss must be further down the totem-pole.

"He will. And I'll be with'im. Get Black cleaned up and ready to talk to."

Jacob listened to her retreating footsteps, out the door and then up the stairs. Sid remained behind, kicking Jacob to release his frustration. Mercifully, Jacob blacked out again after the first few blows.

For a long time, Jacob had been floating in darkness. He didn't know how long it had been when he heard the girl's footsteps again, as well as Sid's. This time, she was accompanied by a man whose feet barely whispered along the floor as he walked. Jacob was groggy. He tried to force himself back into the blackness, but it didn't work. He was awake and his body wanted him to stay that way. Maybe this was his chance to escape. But somehow, he didn't think so.

"Give him the whiskey and leave us alone," instructed a smooth voice Jacob didn't recognize.

"Here kid, drink up," Sid muttered, his thick fingers lifting Jacob's chin and pressing a glass to his lips. Pain and nausea flooded over Jacob, his head spinning at even this small movement. He swallowed a couple mouthfuls of the burning liquid, then choked on it. The rest dripped down the fresh shirt Sid had put on him in an effort to clean him up for Shiny. Sid laughed shortly at Jacob's efforts, then he shuffled out of the room, leaving Jacob with the smooth-voiced man and the girl who seemed familiar. The girl's gentle fingers worked at the blindfold across Jacob's eyes and the man pulled at the knots digging into Jacob's wrists and ankles.

The blindfold came off his eyes. The light of the room was blinding. Jacob's eyes squeezed shut. He couldn't force them to stay open. Tears ran out of the corners of his eyes and down his cheeks. The man's strong hands were rough. Jacob shied away once or twice involuntarily. They got the ropes off. The girl rubbed Jacob's hands with her smaller, soft ones, to restore the circulation.

"First of all, it ain't official," she told Shiny. "It's just his own personal thing. He coulda just got the information through the network. Easy." Managing to crack his eyes open just a fraction, Jacob could see her shake her head. "He ain't even doin' it right."

Jacob tried to focus on her words, to try to place her.

"Tell me some about the kid," Shiny said.

"Black—I don't know his real name—he's shy as a pup. Looks big'n tough and all, but he's real gentle. He's the one I told you about. I can hardly get two sentences from him at a time. Sid woulda made a better hit man."

"Thanks for the suggestion." Shiny's voice was dry.

There was silence. Shiny lit a cigarette. Jacob's eyes gradually got used to the light and he could see them. He realized all at once who the girl was. Angel. He should have figured it out a lot sooner. But he was hurt and tired. His brain wasn't working properly. Shiny sat back on his heels, watching Jacob. Jacob looked back and forth between the two of them, not moving.

"How bad's he been roughed up?"

"Busted ribs, starvin', maybe hurt inside. He should have a doctor soon…"

"Let him go, you're saying," Shiny said flatly.

"I didn't tell ya before… he knows at least to fourth level."

"At least?" Shiny's voice was surprised, his tone rising slightly.

"I only checked that far. Figured if he knows that much, someone high up is protectin' him."

"Sounds like it. How many leaks above fourth level in the last couple years?"

"Only one. Sherriway."

"So either one of us is looking out for him, or it was Sherriway. Well, that guy had style, I respect him for that."

"Tonight, Shiny?"

"Sure thing, Angel. Mind if I talk to him a little?"

"If he's in condition to talk." Angel shrugged. "I'll see'ya later."

She stood up, dusting off her knees, and left Jacob and Shiny alone. They listened to her footsteps fade away.

"How're you doing, Jacob?" Shiny asked.

Jacob was startled; Angel couldn't have told Shiny his real name. She didn't know it herself. But Shiny would certainly have checked to see what was going on and would have all of the answers, in spite of acting like he didn't know anything when he spoke to Angel.

"Still alive," Jacob managed to whisper after a few moments gathering his strength.

"I'll get you another drink in a while. It'll help you get your strength back. What's Sid been asking you about?"

"Duke. My dad."

"And what do you know?"

"Nothing."

Shiny stared into Jacob's eyes, looking for the truth. He sat back a little, drawing on his cigarette again. "You know, no one's looking for you."

"Wouldn't doubt it," Jacob admitted softly.

"No?"

"Probably don't know I'm gone."

"That bad, huh?" the man was sympathetic.

"Yeah."

The room was spinning. Jacob let his head drop slowly to his chest again, fading into the gray areas of unconsciousness.

"Sid," Shiny intoned, with not much more volume than he had used while talking to Jacob. "Bring me the bottle of Scotch from my cabinet."

There was silence for a moment.

"Yes, sir."

Sid must have been right behind the door listening.

"We're gonna get you back on your feet," Shiny told Jacob, sounding determined. A couple minutes later, Sid brought a bottle and handed it to Shiny. Shiny waited for Sid to leave and opened it. He slapped Jacob's cheeks lightly to bring him back around again. Jacob tried to keep himself away from reality, but Shiny patiently administered the Scotch and rubbed Jacob's arms and hands until Jacob knew he was back and couldn't avoid it.

Shiny guzzled down a few gulps of the Scotch himself and set the bottle aside. Standing up and wedging himself behind Jacob, he hooked his hands across Jacob's middle and heaved him to his feet. Jacob's broken ribs didn't like this treatment. He moaned in protest.

"You're okay," Shiny soothed, shifting his grip. Jacob tried to take some of his weight on his own feet, struggling to stay balanced and keep the room still.

"Attaboy," encouraged Shiny, half-dragging Jacob to a chair and setting him down. Jacob finally passed out again and didn't reawaken.

Chapter Eighteen

SAMMY WAS WAITING FOR Marcos to give him an assignment when the squad car pulled up beside them. Marcos and the other Sixer with them, Cal, didn't run. They didn't make any sign that they were concerned. They knew that the cops had nothing on them. Sammy bit his lip, looking to see the driver, knowing whose face he'd see. Smith sat in the driver's seat. He rolled down the window.

"Sammy."

Sammy felt his face get hot. He looked at Marcos for guidance, shifting uncertainly. Marcos looked at him and looked over at Smith. Then he nodded for Sammy to go talk to the cop. Sammy took a few steps over toward the car. He heard Marcos' voice behind him, answering Cal's low murmur.

"The kid can barely speak. You think he's going to sing?" he snickered.

Sammy's face got hotter still. He stood a couple of steps away from the car and looked at Smith, waiting for him to say what he wanted.

"That YMCA group that we signed you up for meets now. Why don't you hop in and I'll take you over?"

Sammy looked back at Marcos and Cal.

"What'cha harassing the kid for?" Marcos demanded. "He doesn't have to go with you."

"No," Smith agreed. "And he doesn't have to go with you, either. This is something he wanted to do; I'm just giving him a ride."

"Hey, I'm just taking care of the kid," Marcos spread his hands wide in an innocent shrug. "He's gotta have someone speaking up for him."

Smith eyed Marcos. He motioned for Sammy to get in. Sammy looked at Marcos one last time, waiting to be told to stop. When Marcos didn't object, Sammy went around the car to the passenger side and got in. He pulled the door shut and Smith drove away. Sammy watched the Sixers until they were out of sight, then finally turned back to look at Smith.

"You're okay. It's okay to tell them no. It's okay to make your own choices instead of just following the gang. Got it?"

Sammy leaned back against the seat and didn't say anything.

Smith drove him to an old building Sammy recognized as housing Social Services. For a moment he panicked, thinking that Smith was trying to pull something over on him. Maybe Sammy was being apprehended and put into a foster family. Or worse. But then Sammy saw the YMCA logo on one of the ground-floor office fronts. He tried to relax again. Smith was only doing what he'd said he would. Finding Sammy something else to do after school instead of hanging around with the gang. Smith opened his door.

"Come on. I'll walk you in and introduce you."

Sammy trailed behind him, into the YMCA office space. There were other kids around. Some he recognized from school or around the neighborhood, and others that he didn't recognize. They were looking at books, talking and texting with each other, or talking to the adults. The meeting or activity didn't appear to have started yet.

Smith put his hand behind Sammy's shoulder and guided him over to a woman who was sorting through some binders.

"Anne."

She looked up and smiled. "Hello, Phil. How's it going?"

Smith returned her warm smile and didn't answer immediately. Then he looked down at Sammy. "This is my friend, Sammy King. He's just signed up for the program."

Anne turned her smile on Sammy. "Hi, there. Nice to meet you, Sammy."

Sammy nodded and didn't say anything.

"He's the one I told you about," Smith said significantly. Sammy glanced at Smith, wondering what he had told her. He didn't like that Smith had spoken to her behind his back instead of in front of him. Smith looked down at him again. "He's a good kid, but he needs some help staying away from his neighborhood gang."

Anne nodded, not seeming upset by this information. "I'm very glad to meet you, Sammy. Why don't you come with me and I'll introduce you to some of the others?"

She started to circulate around the room with him, introducing Sammy to other kids and leaders. The man was Ron. He looked very much like Anne and stood very close to Anne like they were boyfriend and girlfriend. Most of the kids just nodded and said 'hi.' A few of them already knew Sammy by name.

One girl about his age, Becky, looked at Sammy and then commented to Anne: "I know him. He's really stupid."

Sammy felt his face flush and his mouth tighten into a scowl.

Anne gave Becky a look. "What have we said about talking about other people like that, Becky?"

"Well, he is," Becky insisted. "I've seen him at school. He can hardly even talk and he never knows the answers. He doesn't even come to school anymore. I thought he dropped out or was sent to the handicapped school."

"You're being very rude. You need to apologize to Sammy. He's a person with feelings just like you. You wouldn't like it if someone called you stupid."

Becky looked down her nose at Sammy. "Well, I'm not."

"Becky…"

Becky sighed noisily. "Fine," she snapped. "I guess I'm sorry."

Anne pressed Sammy's shoulder to move him around the room to the next person. "I'm sorry about Becky. She has her own issues and we're working on them, but it's slow going. You kind of get used to her after a while, but I'm sorry she was so hurtful."

Sammy pulled away from Anne's touch. He looked around the room, pinning down the exit. He should just leave. There wasn't really anything there for him. Smith had been wrong.

"Hang on," Anne suggested. "At least stay for one activity. I think you'll enjoy it once you get into it."

She had correctly interpreted his glance at the door. Sammy looked over his shoulder at her, pressing his lips together. Letting his breath out, he decided he'd stay. He'd already escaped his gang duties, he might as well enjoy being away from them for a while. As soon as he ventured back out into the neighborhood on his own, they'd be on his case again.

"Okay, everybody listen up." Another woman rang a silver bell and the room fell quiet. "I think we're ready to start. Today we have some drama games. It's going to be a lot of fun. Let's start out by walking around the room. Move your arms and your legs in big movements, take up lots of space, but watch out and don't run into anyone else, please…"

Everyone started to mill around the room, mostly walking in a circle clockwise around the space. A couple of people walked against everyone else or zig-zagged around the room in a random pattern. Sammy stood back watching everyone else.

"Come on, Sammy," Anne encouraged. "You too. No special skills required for this exercise. Just start walking around. Make yourself big."

He wasn't sure about participating. He wanted to just watch what everyone else was doing. He didn't really belong. Everybody else knew each other and Sammy was the newbie. He didn't want to perform in front of anyone. He felt exposed making himself big, when usually he tried to be invisible.

"Come on," she encouraged again. "I'll walk with you. Let's go."

Reluctantly, Sammy joined in on the activity.

After the YMCA activity, Sammy headed for home, but of course he had to pass the gang's house on the way. Zed was out on the steps smoking.

"Sammy," he called out. "Come over here, man. I was looking for you."

Sammy hesitated. He remembered Smith saying that Sammy could say no to the gang, but he didn't think that he actually could. If he tried to just go home without obeying Zed's invitation, the older Sixer would come after him and probably beat the tar out of him. So instead, Sammy turned up the front sidewalk and approached Zed.

Zed's eyes were dark and seemed small on his face. He had a bristly beard and he had lots of black tattoos on his deeply tanned arms. Sammy had been terrified of him at first. Everyone in the neighborhood knew that he was tough, good with a gun, and wouldn't hesitate to kill someone to get his own way. But so far, Zed had been pretty good to Sammy. He didn't make fun of Sammy's speech or rough him up and he usually seemed to be in a good mood.

"Siddown," Zed invited.

Sammy didn't sit down immediately. Zed motioned to the stairs next to him. Sammy glanced around to make sure there were no cops close by and sat down next to the big man. Zed continued to smoke and didn't say anything to Sammy right away. Sammy looked at him, wondering what he wanted. Zed looked back at him. His mouth was turned down.

"Who did the number on your face?" Zed asked.

Sammy looked away, biting his lip.

Zed waited. "Your old man?"

Sammy shook his head.

"Step?"

He shook it again. Zed continued to smoke.

"No reason to let anyone beat on you," Zed said. "Somebody's bothering you, you tell me. The gang will take care of it."

Unless it was someone *in* the gang that was beating on him.

Zed jabbed his finger into Sammy's ribs and Sammy jumped and gasped, fire racing through his ribs and belly. Before he could compose himself, tears rolled down his face. He wiped at them, trying to catch his breath. Zed looked at him dispassionately.

"That's about what I figured. How bad did he beat you?"

Sammy rubbed his ribs tenderly, trying to calm his breathing and force back the tears. "S-s-s-okay."

"Who? I don't hold with anyone beatin' on my boys. You give me a name."

Sammy swallowed.

"Tell me," Zed insisted.

Sammy breathed in. He held his breath for a minute. "H-h-hicks." He let the air out in a little puff.

Zed stared at him. "Hicks?" he repeated in disbelief. His heavy brows pushed down over his glittering eyes. "*My boy* Hicks?"

Sammy nodded.

Zed sat and smoked. "Why?"

Sammy looked at him.

"How come Hicks hit you?"

Sammy stared down at the sidewalk. "M-m-m-mon-ney."

"Money? Since when do you have money?"

Sammy didn't say anything.

"What, the money I gave you?" Zed's face suddenly flushed dark red under his beard. "I give you money to feed your baby brother and he beat you up for it?"

Sammy couldn't look at him or answer. He just swallowed, trying to deal with the pulsing pain and his emotions. Zed ground out his cigarette on the concrete step and went into the house without another word to him. Sammy sat there for a few minutes, wondering if he was supposed to wait for Zed to come back and give him a job. Eventually, Sammy got up and went back home.

Chapter Nineteen

NICHOLAS AWOKE AT THE sound of the front door opening. He sat listening, his head spinning, sweating with fever, hurting all over.

The smells of the room were putrid. Rot and infection and bodily fluids; his sensitive nose picked up all of them.

He listened, straining his ears, his heart racing uncomfortably fast. They had taken Jacob. Had they now come back to take him too? But as he listened, he recognized the familiar sounds of the housekeeper. The woman that Duke hired to do some minimal cleaning every week, to keep things from falling apart.

Nicholas listened to her rattling her equipment and working her way haphazardly through the house, dusting this and vacuuming that. She poured Pine Sol in the toilet, the sharp, sweet smell making Nicholas's eyes water. And eventually, she blundered into the bedroom. Usually, she didn't do much in the bedroom. Maybe touched the dust on the top of the dresser. But she was nervous being around Nicholas, spooked by his silence and his eyes. She didn't really look at him at first, hurrying in with her duster with a purposeful look. She walked past Nicholas, swinging the duster. The dust flying into the air tickled his nose. But in a moment, she was turning around. She must have sensed that something was wrong. Something was different. Nicholas felt her gaze wash over him like a warm cloth and then she started to shriek.

Somewhere in between the hysteria, she managed to call for an ambulance. The medical technicians carefully took stock of Nicholas; tubes leaking, infection raging, weeping bedsores, skeletal appearance.

"What is his name?"

"Nicholas. Nicholas Donell."

"Can he communicate?"

"No, no. He's been like this since he was a child. He can't move or speak."

"Where is his caregiver?" one paramedic asked the housekeeper.

"I'll call his father. I don't know what happened. The other boy usually takes care of him."

They examined Nicholas more closely, taking his vitals and looking for any other problems.

"We're going to move you, Nicholas," one technician spoke soothingly. "It's going to be okay."

They gently moved him to a gurney and covered him with a couple of blankets. Nicholas closed his eyes, finally able to lie down and rest his body. It still hurt. The fever still raged. He was still starving. But at least he could lie down.

The technician stroked his hair. "There you go. Just rest. It will be okay. The hospital will get you all fixed up."

The world was full of sound and motion that Jacob didn't want to wake up to. The hand that shook him sent him hurtling through space and he couldn't control it. And there was noise, loud and gritty and so overpowering that he couldn't make it out to begin with. The ground he was lying on sent hot nails of pain through him. He prayed desperately for the blackness to come and take him again, but it wouldn't. He was awake; horribly, painfully awake.

"Come on, kid. Get up and get going, before I decide to get mean and bust you."

A cop. He'd been left lying in an alleyway and had been discovered by a beat cop. Jacob didn't move. He kept his eyes shut, trying to keep the light from the street lights out, and wished the cop would just turn a blind eye and walk away. Just leave him to die. The cop kicked him heavily to persuade him to get moving, but Jacob only shut his eyes more tightly. Kicking didn't hurt now. Not like the gravel and glass in his eyes and face, rubbing into the raw wounds in his stomach. The cop grunted impatiently, grabbed Jacob by the shoulder and pulled him onto his back.

He had probably thought Jacob was drunk or stoned. Jacob saw him for a moment through slitted eyes, saw his mouth open in horror. The man clamped his mouth shut, straightened up, and looked around. Jacob heard him unsnap his gun. He slid over to the wall of the closest building and pulled out his radio. He gave a garbled, nervous message. His eyes were drawn back to Jacob even though he tried to look around and be aware of his surroundings.

"Stay where you are, officer," came back a reply after a moment. "We're sending you some backup to check the situation. Do you copy? Stay where you are."

"I copy," the officer answered back mechanically. He stood there staring.

Jacob couldn't judge how much time passed as he drifted in and out of consciousness before the squad car pulled up, lights flashing and siren blaring. It was loud and bright, filling his head with pain and nausea. Another officer jumped out of the car and went over to the first. Jacob lay in the shadows of the dark alley and wasn't immediately visible. The second cop saw him and shone a flashlight over him. Then he went quickly back to his car. He turned the car spotlight on Jacob so that the medics could see him as soon as they arrived, which wasn't long.

Jacob opened his eyes a slit and he saw the first EMT when he came up to see what he was to deal with. The paramedic turned away, closing his eyes. His partner swore and they jumped to work.

Jacob kept his eyes shut even though he was awake. He didn't pass out again. Jacob didn't want them to know he was awake.

After the torture of the last few days, the mere fact that anyone knew where he was or that he was still coherent terrified him. Blows and questions could begin to fall at any moment when he least expected it if anyone knew that he was aware.

In the ambulance, Jacob wasn't sure whether he was awake or if he had passed out again. He remembered Sid and the other men dragging him out of the car with great clarity. Every punch and kick was branded in his brain. Every cut and twist of the knife. Every movement and every sound he had seen or heard was impressed forever. The boss—not Sid or Shiny, but the tall, soldierly one—had been there. He had watched as if he was planning each cut and blow personally and Sid and his buddies were merely administering the carefully planned beating. The same driver, too, was there. Cool and quiet Johnny, who the boss didn't trust, who stayed behind in the car waiting for it all to be over.

"Shiny wants the kid put in hospital. Think you can handle that, Sid?" the boss had taunted, his voice tight with anger. His fury over his operation being thwarted radiated off of him like steam.

Jacob thought he was floating above the medics in the ambulance, that he had mercifully escaped all of the pain and torment and left himself behind. He watched as the medics stripped off what was left of his shirt and pressed electrified pads to his bloody chest.

With a jolt, Jacob was brought back to his body, back to the fiery pain and the torment. A scream of anguish caught in his throat and escaped even as he tried to silence it. He started to sob, halfway between the light and the darkness, caught between his desire to escape and his body's instinct to survive. He sobbed and sobbed and then started to swear. It was then the medics realized that he was conscious.

"Easy there, easy," one of them soothed softly. "I'm going to give you something to put you back to sleep. Just relax, you're gonna be okay."

Finally, Jacob was allowed to leave it all behind and slip into the soothing warm blackness.

Chapter Twenty

SAMMY WAS CROUCHED DOWN by the box that the baby slept in, making faces and cooing at his little brother, who was no longer asleep. Marisol sat on the bed nearby smoking a cigarette. They weren't supposed to smoke in their rooms, so the window was wide open to try to prevent anyone from smelling it. The baby held tightly to Sammy's finger, his eyes intent on Sammy's face.

There was a loud rap on the door. They all jumped. Marisol looked at Sammy and then at the closed door.

"Who's there?" she demanded, without opening it.

The visitor didn't bother to answer, just threw the door open and walked in. It was Jade, one of the girls in the Sixth. She chomped on a wad of gum, glancing around the room and focusing on Sammy.

"You. You're wanted. Come on."

Sammy looked at his mother, waiting for her to object, to get after him and say that he shouldn't go. She was the one who kept saying that he should just tell the gang 'no.' But she stared at the thin, straggly-haired girl and didn't tell her 'no.' Sammy rose from his crouch and with a little finger-wave at the baby, he followed Jade out of the room. He could hear the baby start to cry as he walked out.

Jade didn't look at Sammy. She just led the way back down the stairs, outside and over to the gang's crib. Sammy followed her with an uneasy knot in his stomach. Usually they just kept an eye out for him and called him when he happened to be out. It was the first time that they had actually entered his house to come and get him. The gang was encroaching more and more on his personal space, letting him know that he wasn't his own person anymore. He was theirs to do with as they pleased.

When he entered the front door of the house, it was obvious that something was up. The front room and entryway, usually quiet other than a guard or whoever gave Sammy his assignment, were full of gang members talking and milling around, their eyes excited and faces animated. Sammy stopped, looking around. Jade looked back, and seeing him lagging, grabbed his arm and dragged him forward. Right up to Zed, who was looking murderous. Zed's face was flushed red, almost purple, his dark eyes were hard and intense. His long, greasy hair looked messy and disordered like he'd been running his hands through it. Jade let go of Sammy. Sammy stood there, terrified of what was going to happen next. Zed put his hand on Sammy's shoulder, turning him so that they were both facing the room of gang members, Zed standing behind Sammy, holding onto him.

"I can't believe I gotta say this," Zed growled.

The room was instantly silent, everyone tense and listening.

"There ain't no stealing from your brothers and sisters in the Sixth. There ain't no bullying on members who are younger or weaker than you. And you sure as hell don't beat on a brother to steal the dough I just gave to him."

Everyone stood, mouths slightly open, looking at Sammy and the multi-colored bruises on his face. Sammy had nowhere to hide. He just stood there hanging his head, blushing furiously, wishing for a way to get out of the spotlight. Members of the gang were whispering to each other. Those who didn't know what was going on were trying to find out from the others.

There was a scuffle towards the door and a few of the older Sixers collared Hicks and brought him up to Zed and Sammy. Zed's eyes traveled over the rest of the gang, looking for any other trouble.

Hicks tried to pull away from the boys holding him. His eyes blazed with anger and indignation. "I didn't do nothing wrong!"

"You do this by yourself?" Zed nodded toward Sammy.

"I don't know what you're talking about!"

Zed hit him. Sammy heard the crack of the blow and saw Hicks' head snap back. Blood began to stream from the boy's nose.

"I asked if you did this yourself."

"I din't do nuffin' wrong!"

"You wanna scrap with someone your own age or size, or bigger than you, you go right ahead," Zed said. "I got no problem with that. But this guy?" he gestured at Sammy. "He can't defend himself. He's your little brother; you protect him."

Hicks made an animal growl of protest. Zed buried a fist in his stomach. Sammy winced at the dull thud and the grunt and puff of air that escaped Hicks' lips.

"You did it yourself?" Zed questioned. "You want the whole beating?"

Hicks shook his head, but was winded and not able to speak. Zed waited for him to get his breath back.

"Who helped you?"

Hicks' words were strangled. "Stewie and Boozer." Hicks coughed, his face twisting in pain.

Zed ignored the ensuing struggle at the other end of the room, punching Hicks again in the face with a crack that burst his nose open. Sammy looked away from the gore, feeling sick. Another punch in the stomach and Hicks hit the floor, let go by the boys who had been holding him still. Zed left him there and headed for the other side of the room. He wiped his big hands on his pants, leaving long bloody streaks.

The observers moved quickly out of Zed's way, the crowd parting before him. Stewie and Boozer awaited him at the other side of the room, but not by choice. The boys who had been so quick to take Hicks' orders and helped him to beat Sammy, were not nearly as keen on sharing the punishment for the violation. The crowd closed back up behind Zed, so Sammy could no longer see what was going on. He didn't want to. He had no interest in seeing them punished for his sake. He could hear the blows and scuffling feet. He closed his eyes, trying not to picture what was happening to them.

When Sammy opened his eyes, all that he could see was Hicks lying on the floor in front of him. His face was a horrible mess, with the busted, laid-open nose. Sammy wanted to throw up at the sight of the cartilage in the midst of the blood and torn flesh. Hicks lay there groaning and wheezing, his breath making a wet sucking noise like he'd inhaled water at the swimming pool. Hicks' eyes opened and focused on Sammy. Sammy didn't know what to do or say. He wanted to apologize, to explain that Zed wasn't doing this at Sammy's request. He hadn't wanted to rat Hicks out.

"I-I-I…" he couldn't get any words out.

The sounds of the beating at the other end of the room petered out and the crowd started to thin once the show was over. Zed walked back over to Sammy wiping his hands on a rag. He studied Sammy.

"You wanna kick him? He had you held so that he could beat you and steal your money. You go right ahead."

Sammy shook his head. Zed shifted his gaze to Hicks, maybe wondering what Sammy saw when he looked at his former attacker.

"He's gonna drown," Zed observed. He reached down and grabbed Hicks by the shirt, pulling him up and propping him against the wall in a sitting position. He delved into Hicks' pockets and tossed something toward Sammy. Sammy caught the small package and looked down at it. A thick wad of cash held together with a money clip.

"That's yours," Zed said.

"N-n-n-no…" Sammy held it back out to Zed, but Zed didn't make any move to take it back.

"It's yours."

Hicks started to gag and snort, his arms going out rigidly. Zed shifted Hicks' position again so that he was leaning slightly forward, his head bent down instead of back. Blood gushed from his nose and his breathing eased.

"D-d-d-doc…?" Sammy suggested.

Zed shrugged. "He beat you up. He was willing to let your baby brother starve to death. What do you care if he lives or dies? He oughtta suffer for a while."

Zed gazed down at the money in Sammy's hand. Then he frowned in sudden realization. "Maury! Damn that boy! After I gave him a second chance!" Zed looked around for the young guard, but he was nowhere in sight. If Maury was smart, he had run while he had the chance and would never return. Zed swore angrily. He marched off to look for Maury or talk to someone else. Sammy was left alone, staring at Hicks.

Zed said that he should just let Hicks suffer. Hicks deserved it. He'd left Sammy alone in the alley, crying and bleeding. But Sammy couldn't sit there watching Hicks choke to death on his own blood. The gore made him feel sick. He tried to think of what to do. Creeping up to Hicks to see if he was conscious, Sammy breathed shallowly, feeling like his own breathing was as labored as Hicks'. As he touched Hicks' shoulder to look in his face, Hicks choked and coughed again, spraying blood. Sammy wiped his face and moved back from him.

Sammy thought he should go get help, but his feet felt nailed to the floor. He tried to move, but it was like moving through concrete. Set concrete. He got closer to the door and had to navigate around the other two boys. They didn't appear as bad off as Hicks, propping themselves up on their elbows and groaning, eyes following Sammy as he tried to get around them. They didn't try to stop him or trip him up, but he was sure they would, given the chance.

He was relieved to get outside the door, out into the fresh air. He took several deep breaths to clear the smell of blood from his nostrils. But breathing deeply hurt his bruised ribs so he stopped. He walked down to the city sidewalk. To his irritation, a police car slowed down, dogging him. He looked at the driver, expecting it to be Smith. But it wasn't. It was another cop; older, heavyset.

Sammy stood there, unsure what to do. If it had been Smith, Sammy might have been able to do something. Might have been able to try to talk to him. But he didn't know this other cop, not well enough to try to talk to him.

The squad car stopped and the fat cop got out of the driver's seat and approached him. Sammy shifted, trying to decide whether to run. But his hesitation kept him from acting, and the cop stood in front of him.

"What's going on in there?" The cop nodded toward the house.

Sammy shrugged, looking for an escape route. The cop was talking into his radio, but it was all code and Sammy couldn't decipher it. He tried to inch away, but the cop reached out and caught him by the shoulder.

"Don't try to go anywhere. Are you hurt?"

Sammy shook his head, then looked down at his shirt where the cop was looking. Fine speckles of blood covered his shirt.

"That looks like back-spatter. Was someone shot?"

Sammy shook his head. "N-n-n-no."

The cop made more calls on his radio. Sammy looked at his name badge. This one was harder to sort out. Nunez. Sammy tried to pull out of his grip. But Nunez didn't let him go. Other police cars started to pull up. The cops called back and forth to each other, obviously considering a raid on the gang's house. Smith was one of the cops who came. He got in close to Sammy.

"Sammy, what's going on?" he asked. "Are you okay?"

Sammy nodded.

"Is this your blood? You got beaten up again?"

"N-n-no."

"What happened?"

Sammy made a motion toward the house.

"Who got hurt?" Smith pressed.

Sammy couldn't answer.

"Did someone get shot?"

Sammy shook his head.

"Sammy…" Smith got down to Sammy's level, his eyes intense. "I need you to talk to me. You can do that, can't you?"

"Y-y-yeah."

"We're going to go in there. Somebody needs medical attention, right?"

Sammy nodded.

"They weren't shot, though?"

"N-n-no."

"Do we need an ambulance? Need to get someone to the hospital?"

Sammy held up three fingers.

"Three people?"

Sammy nodded.

"Okay. Can we get in there? We'd rather not have to get a whole tactical team and chance a firefight. Can you get me in there without a confrontation?"

Sammy looked up the sidewalk to the house. He swallowed and nodded.

"Great," Smith said. "Let's go in, take care of this."

Smith gave Nunez a nervous glance and he and Sammy started up the walk. The other cops sheltered behind their vehicles, making Sammy feel exposed to the house. But he'd been in and out of the house plenty of times and had never been in any danger before. Sammy led the way back up to the house and opened the door with a big lump in his throat.

To begin with, Smith saw Stewie and Boozer on the floor and moved toward them. But Sammy tugged on his elbow, pointing to Hicks propped up against the wall. With a quick look around the room, Smith went over to Hicks. Sammy followed anxiously behind him. Hicks had started to slide down the wall and his breathing was again rattling wetly. Smith moved in and checked him over, talking quietly into his radio to check on the arrival of the ambulance.

There was the noise of approaching footsteps, and Sammy and Smith both tensed and turned.

"Sammy, hey, I'm glad you're here," Pinky said, seeing him before noticing the cop leaning over Hicks.

Jade was beside him, still chewing and popping her gum. Sammy shook his head and indicated Smith.

Pinky looked him over and his eyes narrowed. "What are you doing here, cop? You can't come in here without a warrant."

"Sammy let me in," Smith said. "I'm just here to help out with your injured." Smith looked around at the three boys on the floor. "Seems like they ran into some kind of trouble. Sammy let me in so that we could leave the rest of the officers outside."

Pinky went over to the window and looked out between the cracks of the newspapers taped over it. He swore under his breath at all of the police cars.

"Just take them out of here," he indicated the injured boys with a brief motion. "We don't need that kind of trouble."

He frowned, watching Smith tend to Hicks. Then his eyes were drawn to Sammy's bloodstained t- shirt. "You can't walk around looking like that," he pointed out in exasperation. "Sheesh, kid. Get a shirt from someone else before you wander around like that. Lucky we didn't get the whole force down on us."

Sammy looked down at the shirt, cheeks hot. He turned away and pretended to be helping Smith.

"Why don't one of you get the door for the EMTs?" Smith suggested.

Pinky raised an eyebrow at Jade. Rolling her eyes, Jade went to the door and opened it. The first set of EMTs brought in a stretcher.

Chapter Twenty-One

SOME OF THE BOYS were watching a movie on the big screen when Larry dropped by the gang's headquarters. The older Wildcats put on an occasional appearance there, but mostly they hung out at each other's apartments or whatever bar or nightclub was currently popular.

"Flip over to the news," Larry told Talet, who had the remote control.

"We're in the middle of a movie," Talet argued, not taking his eyes off of the screen.

"There's a kid that's all over the news. I want you guys to have a look at him."

Deke looked at Larry, frowning. Why would Larry care about a kid on the news? The older boy caught his inquiring gaze and raised an eyebrow at him.

"What kid?" Deke questioned.

"He's been on all day. You haven't seen?"

"Who watches the news?" Keith scoffed. "It ain't like we have to take a current events test."

Larry walked over to Talet to take the remote from him. Talet pulled it back, his body tightening. He was much smaller than Larry, slim, with wiry muscles that were nothing next to Larry's big, hardened ones, shaped by years of construction site work.

"Change the channel or I'll do it myself," Larry warned.

Knowing that he wouldn't be able to win in a fight against Larry, Talet sullenly flipped over to a news channel.

They all watched, waiting for the clip that Larry was referring to. After various spots on the weather and traffic throughout the city, a woman anchor was shown, standing in front of the hospital. She related the story of a mystery boy who had been discovered the previous evening, tortured and beaten nearly to death, in an alleyway. He hadn't been identified yet. There was no missing persons report out on him. His face was so battered and swollen that no one would be able to identify him that way. The camera showed a distance shot of the boy in bed, hooked up to various machines and monitors, face and torso heavily bandaged. The cameraman obviously hadn't been allowed to get any closer. He panned the full length of the body, big feet hanging well off the end of the mattress.

Deke sat up, riveted to the screen. "Whoa."

"You said a kid," Talet pointed out.

"He is," Larry said. "They're estimating he's sixteen."

As the shot of the boy ended and the newscast cut back to the anchorwoman, Deke pulled his eyes away from the TV and looked at Larry. "Who is that?"

Larry rubbed his chin. "I wanted to see if anyone else had the same suspicion."

"It ain't Black," Deke asserted.

"No? Where's Black been the last week?"

Deke considered, looking around at the other guys, waiting for one of them to jump in and discredit the theory. "It couldn't be him. How could anyone beat him up? You guys have seen him fight. No one could do that to him."

"Anyone can be beat up with handcuffs on and a gun to his head," Talet pointed out.

"Black hasn't been at work for a week," Larry said. "I can see him skipping out on some Wildcats activities, but he never misses work. A day here or there if he's in bad shape, but then he calls in. Just not showing up for a week... that's never happened before."

"But who would do that?" Deke demanded, trying to imagine it. None of the gangs would kidnap a rival and torture him for a week. They might beat down a Kitten who wandered into their territory or challenged them, but what had happened to the boy in the hospital, that was different. Deke's skin broke out in goosebumps and he shuddered. "That wasn't Saunders' boys. What happened?"

Larry shook his head. "I dunno. Can't figure it out. But that's gotta be Black."

Deke took a quick glance around the room and lowered his voice. "You don't think Sarin had something to do with it, do you?"

Larry raised his brows. "What?"

"It's just that, since the fight, you know… Sarin and Black…" Deke trailed off.

Larry shook his head. He waved at the TV screen. "This wasn't politics. This is… some seriously bad karma."

There were nods from some of the others. Deke looked around. "You really think it's Black?" he asked. "So what do we do?"

"I guess we make a phone call," Larry said.

"To his old man? Why hasn't *he* reported Black missing? They said there's no missing persons report."

Larry's brows drew down. "No—call the TV station," he gestured impatiently at the TV. "Who'd want to talk to his old man?"

"If that's Black," Deke persisted, "then how come his Dad didn't report it? He lives here. He'd know he was gone. That's gotta be some homeless kid; not Black."

"Maybe his old man's undercover," Keith suggested. "He wouldn't even know Black's been gone."

They all nodded, looking at each other.

"Yeah," Deke admitted. "Yeah, maybe you'd better call the TV station."

Chapter Twenty-Two

SAMMY WAITED FOR A long time for the cops to leave what they considered to be the crime scene. Smith spoke to Sammy at great length, with infinite patience, trying to get him to relate what he had seen. But Sammy's loose lips had resulted in enough violence already; he wasn't about to open his mouth and cause any more. The others in the gang whom the police managed to question were equally closed-mouthed and the police didn't get anywhere in their investigation. They eventually disbanded and some of them went to the hospital to see if they could get any kind of statement out of the victims.

Sammy stood on the front steps of the gang's house, looking down the street at his own building. It was dark out now and although he would be safe running a couple of doors down to his own house, he wasn't sure he wanted to. If Hector had come home, then Sammy would be in trouble for staying out so late already. Or if Hector were already in bed, then Sammy would get his whipping in the morning.

A big hand clapped over his shoulder, making Sammy jump wildly. He gasped as the pain in his ribs radiated through his whole body.

"You can stay here the night," Zed said.

Sammy looked up at him. Stay at the gang house? He knew a lot of the Sixers did. Some of them didn't have anywhere else to live. Others only stayed there part-time. Sammy had never thought about staying there, with his house being so close at hand. He looked down at his t- shirt, which he still hadn't changed. If his mom saw him all bloody again, she was going to freak out.

"Do you want to?" Zed persisted.

Sammy nodded.

"Stay, then. You can crash wherever. And someone can give you a shirt that ain't bloody before you go out again. We take care of our own, eh?"

Sammy looked briefly at Zed's face. He was horrified by the earlier show of violence, seeing how Zed had beaten all three boys; particularly Hicks. But at the same time, Zed was being kind to Sammy, and Sammy couldn't be that afraid of him.

Zed looked down at Sammy and smiled. "You got nothin' to worry about, kid."

Sammy was used to sleeping on the hard kitchen floor, so crashing at the gang's crib was a luxury rather than a hardship. He was able to snag an easy chair. He curled up with a blanket and slept there all night in comfort. His ribs were feeling a lot better when he awoke the next morning. And he wasn't kicked awake. He just awakened gradually as he became aware of the activity and voices around him.

Sammy peered around with his lids just barely cracked open, observing as much as he could before letting anyone know that he was conscious. Everything seemed safe, so eventually he opened his eyes the rest of the way. When no one was paying any attention, he made his exit.

Creeping silently into his house, Sammy went first to the kitchen to see what time it was and if Tiny was up. He found Tiny sitting up on the floor, his blanket still wrapped around him and his hands cradling a hot mug of coffee. Tiny looked up and gave him a little smile. A couple of the others were still lying asleep, wrapped up in whatever blankets they could find. Sammy crept into the room and approached Tiny.

"Hector?" he whispered. "H-h-he g-gone?"

Tiny's eyes flitted around, then settled on Sammy again. "He came home last night. Didn't stay overnight, though. Had a fight with your mom and left."

Sammy helped himself to half a cup of coffee and sipped it in silence for a few minutes before going upstairs. Tiny didn't say anything else. He just sat watching Sammy.

Once Sammy drained his cup he put it down in the sink and headed up to their room. When he opened the door, he found his mother still in bed. He pulled the blankets away from her face.

"M-m-mom?"

She stirred, reaching up to rub her eyes. She winced and pulled her hand away when she touched the tender, swollen bruises. Sammy pushed her hair back from her face.

"Mom?"

She squinted at him. Both eyes were blackened and he wasn't sure whether she didn't open them wider because she didn't want to wake up yet or because they were too swollen.

"Sammy? What are you doing here? Where were you yesterday? You didn't come home!"

"Y-you okay?"

She groaned, readjusting her position. "See to your brother; he was crying last night."

Sammy left her side and crouched over the baby in the box. He pulled the blankets back to uncover him. With dismay, he found blood on the blanket. Sammy examined the baby's face and found dried blood in and around his nose as well. There was a crescent-shaped bruise under his right eye. He squawked and made noises as Sammy picked him up. His eyes opened and he stared at Sammy.

"Keep him quiet," Marisol moaned, pulling the blanket back up to her face.

Sammy sat on the edge of the bed and held the baby close as he found a bottle and prepared the formula. While the baby sucked greedily on the bottle, Sammy attempted to clean the dried blood away from his nose.

The baby stared up at Sammy.

Sammy took the baby over to the bed and tucked him in beside his mother. She seemed irritated, pushing the baby a few inches away. Sammy pushed her hair back from her face again.

"M-m-mom!"

"What is it, Sammy?"

"T-t-take c-c-care…"

"I always take care of him," she growled. "I spend all day every day taking care of him."

"H-h-hurt."

"I don't hurt him."

"H-h-he's hurt."

She squinted at Sammy. "There's nothing wrong with him."

Sammy took the cash out of his pocket and held it in front of her face.

"What's that? Where did that come from?"

"T-take c-care…"

She propped herself up on her elbow and swiftly took the roll away from him. Her eyes brightened as she shuffled through it. She sat up and nudged the baby toward the edge of the bed.

"You take him. I have to go shopping. You're not going to school anyway, are you?"

Sammy caught the baby up in his arms before she could push him right off the bed. He pulled the blanket off, allowing the baby to stretch his limbs. Sammy could feel the heaviness of the sodden diaper and put his brother on the floor to change his diaper and get some clothes on him. He kept his eyes on the baby, averted from his mother, as Marisol got dressed to go to the store. At least she wasn't likely to get rolled on the way to the store like Sammy had been. The gangs generally left mamas alone, as long as they kept to their own business. Sammy spread zinc cream in a thick layer over the baby's diaper rash.

Sammy finished putting pants and a shirt on his brother and picked him back up. The baby gripped him like a little monkey, clinging to him. Sammy gave him a reassuring squeeze. He looked at his mother to see if she really wanted him to take the baby. She flipped a hand toward him.

"You can keep him. Just don't stay away overnight. You bring him back after supper."

Sammy nodded his understanding. He grabbed his school backpack and one-handedly loaded it up with diapers and formula and other necessities. Marisol put on a pair of sunglasses and flitted out the door without saying goodbye. Sammy hefted the backpack onto one shoulder and followed a few steps behind her. They separated at the door. Sammy wasn't sure where to go. He only knew that he couldn't go to school now that he had the baby to take care of. And he didn't want to stay in the room. The baby should get some fresh air. Sammy went back to the gang house and sat on the front steps.

After a while, Marcos came up the walk, his arm around a tired and disheveled-looking Jade. He looked at Sammy, raising his eyebrows.

"Well, what have we got here? Looks like Sammy is training an apprentice."

Sammy grinned at this. Jade pulled away from Marcos and dug through her pockets for a cigarette, spitting her wad of gum out into the middle of the yard.

Marcos bent down to ruffle the baby's thin curls. "So, has he got the makings of a messenger boy in him?"

Sammy shrugged, his face heating up.

"Let's see him." Marcos held both hands out.

Jade rolled her eyes and smoked. She slouched there, puffing on the cigarette and looking bored. Sammy reluctantly handed his baby brother over to Marcos. Marcos held him out and weighed him in his hands, then brought him in to his body and held the baby on his hip.

"He's a wiry one, isn't he?" he observed. "Muscly little guy."

Sammy nodded. "S-strong."

"What's his name?"

"H-h-hector. J-junior."

"Hector Junior?" Marcos shook his head, looking at the baby. "He's way too white for a Hector." He ran his finger through the baby's dirty blond curls. "We're gonna have to come up with something better."

The baby started to squirm and Marcos patted his diapered bottom a couple of times, then handed him back to Sammy. The baby grasped onto Sammy, clinging tightly. Sammy let go of the baby for an instant to show Marcos that he could hold his own weight, then held him close again.

"He's like one of those monkeys," Marcos laughed. "A spider monkey or capuchin or something."

"C-capu…" Sammy couldn't quite get the word out.

"Capo," Marcos suggested. "Why don't we call him Capo? Because he's the boss, eh?"

Sammy smiled. "Capo." He looked the baby in the eye. "Capo? C-capo?"

Capo stared back at him, eyes big and intense.

"Looks like Capo's already a brawler." Marcos touched the bruise under the baby's eye.

"Yeah." Sammy sighed.

"Are you gonna go in?" Jade demanded of Marcos.

Marcos shrugged. "Go in if you want. I gotta give Sammy a message, here."

She huffed and went into the house. Marcos blinked at the slam of the door and rolled his eyes at Sammy. "Women." He worked a notepad out of his back pocket and pulled out the short pencil that was jammed into the coil. "Need you to get this to Dionne. He's over at Pinky's. And he's gonna have a package for you, so you wait."

Sammy looked anxiously at Capo. He couldn't exactly leave the baby there alone while he ran messages. And he had a feeling Jade and the other girls were not in the mood for babysitting.

"Take him with you." Marcos advised. "Who's gonna think you're on business with a baby?"

"S-sure?"

"Yeah, why not?"

Dionne's package had been jammed down into the backpack all day, wedged between diapers. There were other deliveries and Marcos had been sent off on some mission for Zed, so Sammy hadn't been able to deliver it. Sammy was on his way back to the house to see if Marcos was back when a police car nosed up beside him. Sammy's heart started racing. He knew it would not be good news if he were caught with that package on him. He kept walking, ignoring it.

"Sammy. Hey, Sammy!"

Swallowing, Sammy turned his head to see Smith looking out the lowered window at him. Sammy readjusted his grip on the baby.

"You going to the YMCA group, Sammy?" Smith asked.

Sammy shook his head. Smith put the car in park and got out. He adjusted his peaked cap and bent to look at the baby. "This is the baby brother?"

Sammy nodded. Smith looked Capo over. "How did he hurt his face?"

Sammy pulled back from Smith slightly, turning away. "F-fell down."

"Really." Smith attempted to make eye contact with Sammy. "Are you sure it wasn't your mom or her boyfriend?"

Sammy pretended to be playing with Capo, making faces at him and letting the baby wrap his fingers around Sammy's. He shook his head without looking at Smith.

"Is that the only place he's hurt?" Smith reached over and pulled up Capo's shirt. Sammy was startled and didn't pull it back down immediately. They both looked at Capo's exposed white tummy. Smith frowned at the pink scars around Capo's belly button.

"What happened there?"

Sammy ran his finger over the puckered scars. "B-b-born w-w-with…" Sammy struggled with how to pronounce the medical word for Capo's defect, then shook his head. "…P-p-p-problem."

Capo squirmed and chortled at Sammy's touch. Sammy tickled him and then pulled his shirt back down.

"He was born with some kind of birth defect?" Smith filled in.

Sammy nodded.

"He looks pretty normal, now. Any lasting effects?"

Sammy shook his head. "He's p-p-p-pretty good."

Smith patted Capo on the back. "Good. Must have been difficult handling medical bills in your family's circumstances."

Sammy didn't try to give him any of the details.

"You want to take care of him. Keep him safe," Smith said. "If anyone is hurting him… you can talk to me about it."

Sammy gave a quick shake of his head.

Smith was silent at first, letting him think about it. When Sammy didn't jump in to change his answer, Smith went on. "Well… what I stopped you about is the YMCA group. You can bring him along."

"B-b-b-bring him?" Sammy repeated.

He had hoped that having Capo with him would discourage Smith from making him go to the activity. He wanted to get the package from Dionne out of his backpack. It was worrying him, weighing him down.

"They won't mind. And he'll get lots of attention. It's a safe place."

Sammy just stood there, uncertain.

"I can't drive you over today. I don't have an infant seat in the car. But you know where it is, and you can still get there in time."

Sammy considered. Going was probably the only way to get Smith off his back. If he didn't go, Smith was going to keep looking at him, trying to sort him out. And he might decide to check out the contents of Sammy's backpack, in the same way that he had just pulled Capo's shirt up without warning or permission. Sammy nodded.

"Great," Smith approved. "I'll check back later to make sure that you got there."

Which meant that Sammy really had to go, he couldn't just fake it. Sammy sighed and started walking.

Chapter Twenty-Three

JACOB OPENED HIS EYES and watched the nurse on the other side of the room tending to another patient. She slowly made her rounds and when she got to Jacob's bed, her eyes brightened.

"Well, you're awake! How are you feeling?"

Jacob didn't answer, looking first at her face and then letting his eyes wander around the room. He knew where he was, of course. He wasn't a stranger to hospitals. But the events that had led him there were still vague and shadowy. He felt exposed, as if he was in danger. He sought to go back to sleep, to recede back into the darkness where no one could find him.

"Jacob?" The nurse shook his arm gently and took his pulse. She stood there for a moment as if she wasn't sure what to do, then made her notations on his chart and continued on her way.

It was a couple of hours later that she walked back in with the doctor. Jacob closed his eyes. Better that they thought he was unconscious. They couldn't expect him to answer questions then.

"He was awake," the nurse said. "I'm sure of it."

The doctor checked Jacob's vitals briefly. "Jacob… open your eyes. There's time for sleep later."

Jacob didn't move, hoping they would both go away.

"I know you're awake, son."

Reluctantly, Jacob opened his eyes. He was so frightened, afraid of further beatings and torture. Whenever he awoke, they beat him more.

"That's better. How are we feeling?" the doctor asked gently.

Jacob shrugged painfully.

"Need anything?"

His voice was pleasant, but he watched Jacob with sharp eyes, diagnosing every movement Jacob made or didn't make. Jacob knew he should answer aloud and that they'd give him whatever he asked for, but he couldn't. He couldn't find his voice. He couldn't answer other than to stare helplessly back and finally shake his head. Soothingly, the doctor continued to check him over.

"You're having some trouble breathing because of broken ribs," he explained. "And you won't be able to eat normally for some time. You're doing remarkably well, but it will take some time to completely heal from the punishment you took."

He gazed into Jacob's eyes. Jacob looked away, closing his eyes again. Hiding.

"Just rest," the doctor said. "There will be plenty of time for questions later."

Of course, Jacob knew that sooner or later the police would be there to question him. They left him to sleep for a few more hours and then an officer materialized at his bedside. Jacob saw him and turned away, closing his eyes again.

"Jacob, I'm here to ask you some questions. Turn around and talk to me and this won't take long."

Jacob kept his eyes tightly shut.

"Come on, son. I need to hear your story. We need to catch these perps. You don't want them to hurt someone else like this, do you?"

Jacob didn't comply. The cop touched him lightly on the shoulder. "Jacob. Do you remember me?"

He waited in silence. Eventually, Jacob turned back around to look at him. The man's face was familiar. Jacob searched his memory for a name. Young fellow. Not one of Duke's pals, but Jacob had met him once or twice. Newton.

He nodded, a tiny movement. Newton nodded back approvingly. "That's right. I know you've been through a tough time, Jacob. A horrific experience. But you need to talk to me. Tell me everything that you can so we can catch these guys."

Jacob shook his head and closed his eyes again.

"Do you know who did this to you?" Newton asked.

Jacob just kept still, as if he were sleeping. Newton breathed a loud sigh of exasperation.

"Come on, Jacob." He put his hand on Jacob's arm and the heart monitor sped. "You know how this works. We can't do anything without a cooperative witness. These guys could hurt you again. They could hurt your family. Other innocent people. You can't let people like this roam the streets."

Jacob pulled his arm away. The monitor was beeping rapidly and started shrilling some kind of alarm.

"Do you want to talk to your dad?" Newton demanded. "Will you tell him?"

Jacob's chest was seized with pain, making him gasp and cough. The cough set everything else on fire. Jacob's body convulsed, every muscle clenched in pain.

A nurse hurried in at the sound of the alarms. She laid a hand on Jacob's forehead.

"There now. Are you in pain?"

She reached over and hit the button on the morphine machine. A wave of cold rolled over Jacob's body, deadening some of the pain. He tried to control his breathing, not to sob aloud. The nurse stroked his hair and watched his face. The pain in Jacob's chest eased slightly, but still squeezed his wildly racing heart.

The nurse prepared a needle and injected it into the IV. Jacob's head spun and his vision started to blur.

"You'll have to go," the nurse told Newton. "Come back some other time. He'll be more stable in a day or two."

When Jacob next surfaced through the nausea and pain, becoming conscious of the outside world, he found Duke sitting next to his bed. Sitting in the hospital visitor chair, Duke looked like an adult sitting in a kid's playhouse chair. He dwarfed it.

"You awake, Jake?" he asked.

Jacob blinked. His vision was blurred and his eyes sticky. Duke watched him, scowling, his eyebrows drawn down and close together. He appeared to be entirely sober, which wasn't necessarily good news.

"I didn't even know you were gone," Duke said. "Where were you? What happened to you?"

Jacob just concentrated on breathing. Even that hurt his ribs and his chest. It was going to be a while before he was up on his feet again. Duke stared at him fiercely.

"Don't ignore me, Jake. When I ask a question, I expect it to be answered."

"Uh, sir… sir?" One of the nurses making her rounds tried to get Duke's attention. "Could I talk to you for a minute, in the hall? Out here?"

Duke was surprised by the interruption and looked the nurse up and down before deciding to see what it was she wanted. He got carefully up from the small chair and let her lead him out into the hallway. She was not a tall lady. He towered over her like she was a child. Jacob closed his eyes. He could still hear most of their conversation in the hall.

"He hasn't said a word since he woke up," the nurse explained to Duke. "What he's been through is very traumatic and the doctors think that it is probably psychological rather than any kind of brain damage. You just need to give him some time."

"I don't baby my son. Everyone is too concerned these days about hurting kids' feelings. Well, if you want them to grow up to be able to function in the real world, you can't go pussyfooting around them all the time. Jacob is tough. I'm not going to treat him like he's damaged."

"I don't know if you understand the extent of his injuries. How much he's been through."

"Jake's tough," Duke reiterated. "Nobody's telling me that I can't talk to my own boy."

"No… but he might not be able to talk to you yet. He's been through a significant—"

"I know my son," Duke snapped. "You don't."

She tried a couple more times to appeal to him to be sensitive to Jacob's feelings, then eventually gave up. Duke returned to the room. He shook his head, clearly irritated now. The nurse hadn't done Jacob any favors by getting Duke riled up.

"You think I'm going to treat you like a baby like everyone else has apparently been doing around here?" Duke bent in closer to Jacob.

Jacob swallowed and shook his head. He tried to raise his voice to answer, but nothing came out. He cleared his throat and looked at Duke helplessly. Duke pulled the visitor chair closer than it had been before and sat down just inches from Jacob.

"I know you've been hurt, Jake. And I want to know who did it."

Jacob nodded. He licked his lips. "Dad…" it came out in the barest whisper, but Duke heard him and leaned in closer.

Jacob tried to sit up a bit, feeling vulnerable lying flat on his back. Duke helped him readjust his pillow. "…the Stars…" Jacob whispered.

The angry flush drained from Duke's cheeks. His eyes got wider. "Stars," he repeated. He didn't say anything else right away.

Jacob let his eyes shut when Duke didn't speak or move. The drugs formed a fog in his brain. The machines humming and beeping made him drowsy.

"Jake," Duke roused him. "Jake, you're sure it was the Stars?"

Jacob nodded.

"Did you see him? Shiny?"

Jacob swallowed, remembering the man who had come to see him. Remembering the things Sherriway had told him about Shiny. He tried to answer but couldn't get the words out. Duke saw the answer in his face. He drew his hand down his face, wiping sweat away and smoothing fine lines of fatigue. He swore under his breath. Jacob saw something in Duke's face that he had rarely seen there before. Duke was bigger and stronger than anyone. It took a lot to scare him. But he knew enough about Shiny and the Stars to be scared.

"Why? Why did they take you? Was it…?" he halted.

Jacob gazed at him.

"Why?" Duke repeated.

"They… wanted you…"

Duke swore more loudly this time, viciously. He stood up abruptly. His whole body coiled. Jacob cringed, preparing himself. The heart monitor started to race. Duke's face was hard and white. He swung one of his huge fists with all of his power behind it. Jacob squeezed his eyes closed.

There was an explosion as Duke smashed his fist into the wall. Drywall dust and debris rained down on Jacob. The heart monitor alarm was trilling and there was a frightened yelp from the man in the next bed. There was a rush of voices and footsteps and the room was overrun by nurses, interns, orderlies, and security guards. Jacob squinted at the confused group between his fingers, still expecting a blow from Duke at any instant.

Jacob thought it would take all of them to control Duke and get him out of the room. If he'd fought them, it would have taken at least that many. But Duke wasn't angry and he wasn't drunk and he didn't fight them. He let the security guard point him toward the door and let the nurse squeeze in to check on Jacob's vitals. Jacob put his arm over his face to try to block out all of the noise and chaos.

Whether on his own or from something the nurse injected into his IV, he soon slid back into unconsciousness.

Chapter Twenty-Four

ANNE SAW SAMMY COME in the door and made her way over to greet him with a smile.

"Hi, Sammy. How's it going today?"

Sammy looked around to see who else was there and what they were doing.

"No baby today?"

"N-n-no."

"He was sure a sweetie. What did you call him again?"

"C-c-capo."

"That's right, Capo. Cute name. How is he this week, everything going good?"

Sammy nodded. His mom had stocked up on supplies from the money that Zed had given him. There was enough formula and diapers for a good long time now. And food for the rest of the family. Even some fresh fruit, which Marisol didn't normally get because it was expensive and went bad too fast, especially with no fridge to keep it cold.

Hector had freaked out when he got home and saw everything that she had bought. He acted like it was his own money that she had spent instead of Sammy's. Sammy took Capo downstairs with him and slept with the baby cuddled in his arms, the blanket wrapped around both of them. Tiny and the others didn't like babies in the kitchen, but they could hear the screaming and fighting going on in Sammy's family's room upstairs and they didn't censure him for bringing Capo down.

Sammy had awakened several times in the night to the sound of sirens and each time cuddled Capo to him protectively, afraid that the police were coming to break up the fight between Marisol and Hector. They would arrest them both and call Child Services to take Capo away. And once they took Capo away, Sammy would never see him again.

"Sammy?"

Sammy brought his attention back to Anne. "Huh?"

"Capo? Everything is okay?"

"Y-yeah. Fine."

"Good. You're a good brother. Very responsible."

Sammy shrugged, his face warming. Anne tried to pat him on the back, but he veered away from her, avoiding her touch.

"You've got about ten minutes for visiting, then we'll start," Anne advised.

Sammy wandered further into the room where the others were gathering. Darla, one of the girls that he knew from school and the previous couple of meetings, watched him walk up.

"Where's your baby today?"

"H-h-home."

"Too bad," Darla said. "He was really cute. You should bring him again."

Sammy eyed her, wondering if she was making fun of him. She didn't laugh or try to get anyone else's attention, so he had to assume that she was serious. He raised his hands in another shrug.

"You don't talk much, do you?" she observed.

Sammy's face heated up and he knew he was blushing. He swallowed and shook his head.

"He's stupid," Becky intoned, intruding on the conversation.

"*You're* stupid!" Darla shot back. "You should just shut up!"

Sammy glanced from one girl to the other, not sure what to think or how to react.

"*You* shut up!" Becky returned, her voice rising.

"You quit making fun of Sammy! Just because he doesn't talk, that doesn't make him stupid!"

"He is stupid!" Becky shouted back. "I know he is! He never knows the answers to the questions! He never even comes to school anymore!"

"That's not because he's stupid," Darla argued.

Anne and one of the other helpers, Janet, moved in on the girls, shushing them and trying to move them apart.

"Girls, girls! You know how to be nice to each other. We don't talk to each other that way here. This is a safe place. No one gets made fun of or talked down to."

"Darla has a crush on stupid Sammy!" Becky sneered. "I guess she likes dumb boys, because he's a moron!"

"Shhh," Janet murmured, moving Becky away. "Just settle down, Becky. Darla's not doing anything to hurt you. Just stay out of it. She can like who she wants to like and talk to who she likes. It doesn't hurt you."

"You think I like Sammy?" Becky demanded. "I don't like him! I don't care if she talks to him!"

"Then what's the big deal if Darla likes him?" Janet pointed out reasonably.

Sammy looked back at Darla. Anne was whispering in her ear, talking low enough for Becky not to hear her. Sammy's face and ears flamed. Darla shook her head at Anne, her mouth a straight line.

"I know," she insisted. She gave Anne a little push to make her go away. She looked back at Sammy, rolling her eyes and shaking her head. "I don't think you're stupid. Just because you have trouble talking, that's not because you're stupid."

The heat spread from Sammy's face and ears to the rest of his body. His skin burned. Looking down at his arms, he saw that the skin was bright pink and puffing out into irregular white welts. He rubbed his nails over the itchy marks. Darla looked down at his arms.

"Did you get bites? Are those from mosquitos?"

Sammy shook his head, scratching harder. He could feel the weals breaking out all over his body. He scratched at his neck.

"Um… Miss Janet?" Darla called uncertainly. "Miss Janet, I think something's wrong."

Janet looked up from her conversation with Becky, a frown line between her eyebrows.

"Darla, I'm trying to handle this," she protested.

"But… Sammy…" Darla looked at Sammy, gesturing to him.

Janet looked at Sammy and her brows shot up. "Oh! What happened?" She left Becky and hurried over to Sammy. Her eyes flicked over his face, neck, and arms. "Are you okay, Sammy? Did you eat or touch something you're allergic to?"

Sammy shook his head. His entire skin was hot and itchy. Everyone's eyes were on him, making him more embarrassed, which just made everything worse.

"Let me get you some Benadryl. You don't know what you got into?"

Sammy couldn't explain to her that he hadn't touched anything. It was just a stress reaction. He just stood there while she went to her office. She came back a few moments later with a couple of pink pills and a glass of water. Sammy swallowed them down. He tried to avoid all of the eyes on him, wishing that people would just go back to what they had been doing before. Janet winced, watching him scratch.

"You're going to end up scratching your skin all up. How about some cool cloths? Would that help?"

"M-m-m-maybe."

In a few minutes, she had cool, damp cloths for him. Sammy dabbed at his skin, trying to cool it down and keep from scratching. Anne hovered nearby.

"We should be getting started," she said apologetically. "Do you mind if we start, Sammy? Are you okay?"

He nodded, hoping that she would distract everyone's attention back away from him. He dabbed his forehead and neck, wishing that the hives would just disappear. Or that *he* could.

Anne went to the front of the group to get the activity started.

Chapter Twenty-Five

THE WEEKS AT THE hospital were long and tedious. Jacob had to go through lots of testing and rehab, being examined and poked and prodded in between long stretches of boredom and sleep. The hospital was never quiet and once he started to heal and wasn't in so much pain or on such high doses of painkillers, he found it hard to sleep at night. There was a police guard outside his door who denied access to any visitors, so even if members of the gang did come by to see him, Jacob couldn't see them. At least the police kept the media away so that Jacob wasn't bothered by reporters. Eventually, the novelty of the 'mystery boy' wore off and they stopped trying.

Duke quickly tired of taking care of Nicholas, who had already been released and harassed the hospital daily to pronounce Jacob well enough to go home. At long last, the doctors and nurses agreed that he was healed enough to be up and around and eat a more normal diet. Duke signed him out. He dropped Jacob off at the house before heading off to work.

Jacob walked in the front door of the house, locked the door behind him, and just stood there, leaning against it. His heart was pounding hard. He tried to calm himself down. Nothing was going to happen. The Stars were not going to be there again. He would be safe in his own house. Steeling himself, he walked the rest of the way in, carefully checking for any unwanted visitors in the kitchen or living room before heading to the bedroom.

Nicholas was lying in bed. Duke obviously couldn't be bothered to move him to his chair during the day. After Jacob's extended stay in the hospital, Jacob understood even better what it must be like for Nicholas to lie there day after day, unable to move, with no one to talk or visit with, nothing to do, just trapped inside his own brain.

Jacob moved in close to Nicholas and smiled at him. "Hey," he said softly, "I'm back."

Nicky's eyes widened slightly and he gazed at Jacob intently. Jacob choked up a bit.

"Hey, Nicky."

He bent over and scooped Nicholas up. For a few minutes, he just held Nicholas close. He couldn't hold back the tears. His body shuddered and jerked with sobs. Duke had shown no joy in Jacob's release. He just wanted Jacob out of the hospital, taking care of Nicholas and making meals, and not reminding Duke of the impossibility of protecting his family from the Stars. But Nicholas… Nicky's eyes shone with his joy over the return of his baby brother. Jacob had lain in bed for days worrying about Nicholas and how he was doing. Nicholas had been Jacob's responsibility for years and he knew that Duke wouldn't provide him with the same level of care.

He gave Nicholas another gentle squeeze and carefully put him down in his wheelchair and strapped him in. He saw the liquid antibiotics on the dresser.

"You okay?" He ran his fingers over Nicky's tangled hair.

They stared into each other's eyes, doing their best to read each other's thoughts. Nicky's eyes narrowed at the corners, turning down slightly.

"I'm okay," Jacob assured him. "Don't you worry about me."

He picked up the comb from the dresser and carefully worked on Nicky's hair, infinitely gentle and careful not to pull it in spite of the tangled knots. When he finished Nicky's hair, he pushed the wheelchair into the bathroom. He ran some warm water and gave him a sponge bath. There were bruises and bedsores all over Nicky's body. His skin was so fragile and Duke's big hands were not well-suited to the tasks that Nicholas needed to be done. Try as he might to be careful, he simply didn't have the coordination or the patience to attend to Nicky's needs without hurting him.

"It's okay now…" Jacob crooned. "Everything is okay…"

Jacob repeated it over and over. He didn't know whether it was to soothe Nicholas or himself. It didn't really matter, they were part of each other. Their lives were intertwined and Jacob couldn't tell which of them needed to be calmed more.

He stayed with Nicholas on through the afternoon, sitting with him, talking to him about the events of the past weeks and just being with him. Nicholas never demanded anything more from him.

Eventually, Jacob had to attend to other matters and he said goodbye to Nicholas to go to his job site.

It felt strange going back to the construction site. Both familiar and foreign at the same time. Jacob tracked down his boss.

"Still got my job?" Jacob asked Billy shyly.

"Well, kid…" Billy lit up a cigarette. "There's lots of guys out there looking for jobs, and uh… you just disappearing like that— well, we needed someone for the job. You know how it is. We got someone else."

Jacob's heart thumped hard. His stomach tied in knots. He needed that job. "Are there any openings at all?"

"Times are hard, boy. There ain't nothing."

"What am I going to do? You don't know where I could get a job, do you?"

"No… most places won't take a kid young as you—hamburger joint, maybe."

Jacob limped off across the construction site slowly. How was he supposed to support himself now? And not only himself, but Nicholas too, and Duke if he spent all of his paycheck on women and drink.

Jacob jumped wildly when a hand fell on his left shoulder.

"Sorry, kid, didn't mean to startle you. Walk you off the site?"

Jacob realized it was Larry and tried to relax. His nerves were shattered; he jumped at the least thing. He blew out his breath noisily.

"I can't see on that side," he told Larry, gesturing. "I got… they hurt it… too much damage…"

"Sorry," Larry apologized again. "I didn't know."

They walked toward the gate off the construction site.

"Sorry to hear Billy let you go," Larry said. "You are a good worker, better than a most of the other guys."

"Thanks."

"You gonna be okay?"

Jacob shook his head. "I just don't know what I'm gonna do for a job."

"You going to stay in construction? You've been working here for what, two and a half years?"

"Yeah. I dunno. I haven't done much else and I don't have training for anything else."

"Well, listen, I'll tell you if I hear something, okay?"

"Yeah, thanks."

Larry slapped Jacob on the back and Jacob went on to get his bike.

Hearing a bike engine, Deke looked up the street as he strapped on his helmet. The rider was immediately recognizable.

"Black!"

The others turned around and looked. Sarin shrugged. "Yeah, heard he was out."

"Heard he was out? Who told you?" Deke demanded. "I thought it would be all over the news again."

"Nah. The only reason people cared to begin with was because no one knew who it was. Mystery boy… that gets people's attention. Some down-and-out kid from the hood… not so much."

Deke supposed that was probably true. He finished putting on his helmet and watched Black's approach.

"Larry," Sarin said.

"Huh?"

Sarin raised an eyebrow. "Larry told me he was out," he explained. He put on his own helmet.

"Oh, yeah."

Black pulled his cycle alongside and flipped up his helmet, looking them over.

"Hey, Black! Welcome back!" Deke greeted eagerly. "How's it going, man? You feeling okay?"

Sarin gave Deke a sour look. But Deke and the others had sorely missed Black during his long absence. He was part of their family.

Jacob's shoulder lifted and fell again. He was pale. His expression was guarded and wary. "Yeah, I'm on my feet again," he acknowledged.

"Let's celebrate!" Keith suggested. "Come on. What do you want to do?"

Black looked past them at the gang's headquarters. "I just thought…"

"No, man," Deke protested. "We can't just hang out here tonight. It's a celebration. Celebrating your release. We gotta go somewhere."

Black scowled and looked down at his bike, considering. Deke could understand that he was probably still feeling pretty rough and just wanted to take things easy. But the gang had been impatiently awaiting his release and they weren't going to be satisfied with sitting around the TV tonight.

"Drinks," Keith suggested.

"Maybe Black ain't up for it," Talet interposed with a sneer. "I mean, he ain't lookin' too good. Maybe we'd better just let him lay down for a nap."

Black's eyes flicked over to Talet and then back to Deke and Keith. He didn't once look at Sarin.

"A drink sounds good," he admitted. "But I ain't gonna be staying all night. I got things to do."

He didn't say that he had to be home before his old man, even though they all knew that was what he meant. Deke looked over at Talet to see if he was going to pick a fight over it. If he were going to best Black physically, it would have to be now, while Black was still sick and injured, barely out of his hospital bed. But Deke saw Talet size up Black and decide that he still couldn't beat him in a fight, even in this condition. So Talet didn't push it any further. Black looked them all over again, wary, then nodded.

"Let's ride."

The club was hopping and the gang was having a blast. Aside from Sarin, who was in a morose mood and seemed to be trying without success to drink Black under the table. Maybe he thought that in Black's weakened condition, he'd have a lower tolerance for alcohol and this would be Sarin's chance to show that his own machismo was stronger than Black's. But Sarin's throat was flushing red from drink and Black seemed unaffected so far.

"Set'em up again," Sarin ordered the barman.

Black stretched gingerly and stepped off of his stool.

"Where are you going?" Sarin demanded. "You done? You've hardly had a thing."

Deke hadn't been counting Black's drinks, but he'd certainly had more than Deke could have stomached. Not 'hardly a thing' by a long shot. But Black was unfazed by Sarin's question.

"If I'm gonna drink any more, I'm gonna have to get rid of the last few first." He headed for the men's room.

Deke looked back at Sarin for his reaction. The bartender set out more drinks for Sarin, Black, and the others at the counter who were in need of refills. Sarin glanced around and thinking himself unobserved, pulled Black's glass over to himself. Deke frowned and elbowed Keith, nodding for him to watch Sarin. They both watched as Sarin dropped something into the drink and gave it a swirl. He pushed it back over in front of Black's empty stool.

"That rat!" Keith breathed.

"What are we gonna do?"

Both of them just sat there, looking at each other, as Black returned from the restroom and sat down. He picked up his drink.

Deke thought he should do something. Let Black know that Sarin had spiked his drink. Tell him not to drink it. But that would be an open declaration of mutiny against Sarin, who was still the official leader of the Kittens. And Deke couldn't fight Sarin or stand up to the rest of the full-fledged Wildcats who he would have to explain himself to and possibly fight to the death. Not a pleasant thought. So he just sat there, frozen, unable to think of a way out. And they just watched Black down the glass, Mickey and all.

Keith swore.

He looked sickly green under the club's flashing lights.

Chapter Twenty-Six

DUKE WAS HOME BEFORE Jacob, and Nicholas was worried. Had it been too early for Jacob to be released? Had he ruptured something picking Nicholas up when he was still in such a weakened state? Was he lying by the road somewhere, bleeding internally, and nobody knew anything was wrong?

Duke let himself into the house and Nicholas could hear his heavy footsteps as he walked through the house looking for Jacob. Duke came down the hallway. He looked around the bedroom, scowling.

"Not here." He studied Nicholas for a moment, deep in thought. "You're not down for bed," he observed, "so he planned to be back."

Duke looked around the small bedroom, but there was nothing else to look at. No clue as to where Jacob might be.

"Nothing's happened," he muttered to himself. "He hasn't been kidnapped again. He's just out enjoying himself. What do you expect after he's been cooped up in the hospital for weeks?"

He walked out of the room, automatically flipping off the light switch as he went.

It was another hour before Jacob got home. Duke had waited for him, sitting in front of the TV, trying to distract himself from his worry that Jacob might be hurt or kidnapped again.

Nicholas heard Jacob stumble over the doorstep on the way in and heard him rub up against the wall trying to hold himself steady.

"About time you got home," Duke growled. "Where have you been?"

Jacob belched. He took a couple more unsteady steps into the house. Duke got up out of his chair. "Are you hurt?" he asked. "Or just drunk?"

Nicholas could hear Jacob shifting his feet, trying to keep up with the tilting universe without falling on his face. "Guess I had too much," he said in a surprised tone. "I'll… make you dinner."

"Whoa, there," Duke prevented Jacob from going into the kitchen. "You're just going to burn yourself. Or burn the house down. You'd better go sleep it off."

They made slow progress down the hall. Nicholas wondered how Jacob had managed to ride his motorcycle or walk the rest of the way home after parking it when he was so impaired. Duke brought Jacob into the room and flipped on the light to guide Jacob toward his blankets in the corner. Jacob's head snapped up and he stared at the light as if he'd never seen it before.

"Why is it doing that?" he asked, in an awed voice.

Duke's mouth formed a long, flat line. He grasped Jacob's chin and pulled his face around to look into his eyes. He swore and slapped Jacob across the head. Jacob let out a surprised yelp and then he reached out his hands as if to catch the stars dancing in front of his eyes.

Shaking his head, Duke took out a pair of handcuffs and pulled Jacob's hands behind his back.

Chapter Twenty-Seven

SAMMY HAD A DELIVERY for Pinky and tracked him down at the gang's crib after checking several other likely places first. Pinky held out his hand impatiently and took the brick-shaped package from him.

"From Marcos?" he questioned sharply.

Sammy nodded. "M-m-m-marcos."

"About time. Where've you been?"

Sammy frowned. It wasn't like he'd been slacking off. "L-l-l-ooking f-f-for… y-you."

"Looking for me. Well, here I am. Here's where I've been all day. Look a little harder the next time."

Sammy looked down at the floor biting his lip.

"What's the matter with your face?"

Sammy felt his face flush again in embarrassment and hoped that it wouldn't make the hives any worse.

"You look like you got into poison ivy or something." Pinky studied him with fascination.

Sammy stared at Pinky's hands, focusing on the big rings on his smallest fingers, and the one finger that jogged to the side, obviously broken at one time or another. Pinky's fingers were thick and the knuckles scarred. He wore a lot of jewelry.

"H-h-hives," he tried to explain.

"I hope it's not catching," Pinky took a step back from him and then looked at the package he held in his hands as if it might be contaminated.

Sammy shook his head. "N-no."

"Huh." Pinky motioned to the stairs, where the sounds of raucous laughter and loud music emanated. "You should go down. Get something to eat. They ordered in."

Spicy, succulent smells floated up with the heavy beat of the music. Sammy thought he should probably go home to eat so that his mother wouldn't worry and he could check on Capo, but his stomach started rumbling at the smell.

"Go on," Pinky told him. "You're too skinny. You could use some meat on your bones."

Sammy gave in and went down the stairs to the big common room where everyone was partying. There were lots of open liquor bottles and takeout boxes were scattered over the tables and counters around the room. The music blared, party lights strobed, and the big screen TV was on, though Sammy had no idea what they were watching. He helped himself to some kind of chicken or pork in a nearby box and almost groaned aloud over how good it tasted. Supper at home would be something from a package. Dry cereal or crackers, juice boxes, maybe some spreadable cheese. Nothing that could even compare with hot, juicy chicken.

"Hey, Sammy!"

He looked up and saw Angie, one of the boys only a couple of years older than him, waving to get Sammy's attention. He and some of the other younger kids who were in the gang were congregated in a corner. Sammy went over to join them. Angie did a double-take when he saw Sammy's face close up.

"What the hell happened to you?"

Sammy focused on his food. "It's n-nothing."

"Someone hittin' you or what is that?"

Sammy shifted uncomfortably. "H-h-hives."

"Hives? What's that? From, like bees? You got stung?"

Sammy rolled his eyes and shook his head. "J-j-just s-s-st-stress."

"Stress?" repeated Casper, joining in on the conversation. "Stress about what? Come party with us, we'll cure that!"

Sammy munched on the food, but it was getting spicy and he looked around for a drink. One of the girls passed him a bottle. He couldn't remember what her name was and blushed a little, looking away from her as he accepted it from her. He took a swig straight from the bottle and grimaced at the bitterness. It burned all the way down his throat. Sammy chased it with another bite of the chicken to get the taste out of his mouth. He put down the bottle and looked for something sweeter.

"You wanna relax," Casper continued, "try one of these." He held out his hand, with a couple of small, hand-rolled cigarettes on his palm.

Sammy wrinkled his nose and shook his head. "N-n-no."

"Come on, man. I'm offering to share. No cost. Don't tell me you've never tried weed before."

Sammy shook his head. "N-no."

"You gotta try," Angie piped up. "It'll take away all that stress. Seriously."

Sammy looked away, looking at the various open bottles on the tables and picking up a red-colored cooler. He took a gulp and found it much more palatable than the first drink.

"Come'ere," Casper invited. "Sit over here. We'll share one."

Sammy hesitated. He should be going home. He couldn't go home smelling like pot. The house had strict rules about drugs. Get caught and get kicked out. They might even eject his whole family, not just Sammy himself.

Casper tugged on his arm, and Sammy followed, not sure what else to do. They sat down together. Angie pushed his way in too. Casper pulled out a lighter and lit up one of the roaches. He took a drag on the joint and passed it over to Sammy. Sammy moved to pass it on to Angie and both boys punched him lightly in objection.

"Take a pull," Angie ordered, not taking it from him.

Sammy looked from one to the other and reluctantly put it to his lips. He took a shallow breath, not wanting to choke on the smoke as he'd seen other first-time smokers do. He kept most of the smoke in his mouth instead of breathing it down to his lungs and released it after a moment. Both boys indicated their approval.

"Not bad, man. You're smooth," Casper complimented him.

Sammy felt a little light-headed but noticed no other effects. He leaned back and watched the others take their turns before the joint was passed back to him again.

Chapter Twenty-Eight

DEKE LOOKED AROUND, ALERT for any trouble as he and Sarin approached Black's door. Neither of them had ever been there before. None of the gang had ever been to Black's house.

The lawn, what there was of it, looked sad and neglected. The house itself was old, small, and run down. But it didn't stand out from the rest of the neighborhood and who was Deke to judge? He didn't have a house at all.

Sarin rang the doorbell, leaning over the rail along the steps to peer into the kitchen and living room windows. Deke glanced up and down the street.

"Doesn't look like he's home."

"Just 'cause he doesn't answer, that doesn't mean he ain't home," Sarin pointed out.

"I don't see his bike. There's no garage. So he must not be home."

"He doesn't park it at home. His old man doesn't know he's in a bike gang and he's trying to keep it that way."

Deke remembered something of the kind being mentioned before. He shoved his hands into his pockets. "Well…?"

Sarin tried the door handle, and it wasn't locked. "Come on."

"I'll just keep a lookout…" Deke suggested, not wanting to invade Black's space. Black might be a gentle giant most of the time, but Deke knew he could break either one of them in half. He wasn't about to cross into Black's territory and chance it.

Sarin grabbed Deke's arm and pulled him into the house, then pushed Deke ahead of himself, so that Deke was in the lead. Deke looked around the living room. Cigarette butts and empty bottles just laying around the rooms, garbage and filth everywhere. Sarin bent down to pick up a couple magazines and admire the centerfolds, then jerked his head for Deke to continue on. Deke poked his head into the kitchen, stacked high with unwashed dishes. There were beer cans and other junk all over the place. Deke led Sarin first to what appeared to be the master bedroom, then a cold, empty room, and then the last bedroom.

Deke stopped in the doorway, going no further. Sarin shouldered his way past and took a glance around the room. He froze upon seeing the boy in the wheelchair. Then he adopted a deliberately casual, relaxed stance.

"Hey, Black."

Black was standing in front of the window looking out into the back yard. He didn't even twitch at their entrance. Deke took a slow look around the small bedroom. There wasn't much to see. There was a bed on one side and a makeshift bedroll and blankets on the other. There was a small dresser and the boy in the wheelchair. With Sarin and Black both in the room, there wasn't much space left. Deke stayed in the doorway, out of the way.

"Hi, Sarin," Black said.

"Nice place you've got here."

This was answered with silence from Black.

"You ain't been around," Sarin commented. "Thought maybe you been avoiding us."

Black finally turned around. His eyes went first to Sarin, then to Deke in the hallway, carefully weighing and measuring all the details. Deke felt his jaw drop. Black was wearing a t- shirt. It was either old and he'd outgrown it, or he wore it small to show off his well-muscled chest. But along his throat was a deep slash, swollen and discolored, obviously infected.

"Man," Sarin said, shaking his head. "What the hell happened to you?"

If he hadn't known better, Deke would have assumed that it had happened as part of the beating that Black had sustained, the one that put him in hospital. But he'd seen Black a week ago when he got out of hospital. It hadn't been there then.

Black's shoulders lifted and fell in a shrug. "My dad," he explained.

"That needs stitches," Deke told him, though Black must already know that. "And it's real infected."

"I… can't…"

Sarin shook his head. "Can't? How come you can't?"

"He said… I'm not supposed to leave the room… I'm grounded."

Sarin gave a bark of laughter. "You're grounded? What are you, ten? He can't stop you."

"He… I…" Black shook his head helplessly. "I can't."

"Black, what kind of yellow are you? I've seen you fight. Your old man can't keep you here. You're just being—"

Black hauled off and hit Sarin clean across the jaw. Not particularly hard, considering he probably could have shattered Sarin's jaw without exerting himself. Sarin was knocked to the floor by the blow and didn't move for a moment, dazed. He recovered, jumped up, and charged Black. Black hit him again, harder. When Sarin got up this time, his only goal was to get back at Black. He rushed Black and was hit again. This time, he stayed down. Black's eyes went to Deke, waiting for him to take action. Deke put up both hands defensively, showing he had no intention of joining Sarin in any attack, verbal or physical.

"He'll never get it," Black's dark eyes were bleak and hopeless. "He's just never going to understand, is he?"

Deke swallowed. He licked his lips and tried to raise his voice. "Uh… understand what?" he croaked.

Black stared at him. Almost as if he was looking through Deke. Deke shifted nervously. After a few moments of silence, Black looked away from him and turned away to open a drawer of the dresser. Deke watched Black's face as he looked through a handful of photographs. His expression was grim. Sarin started to stir. He sat up groggily, rubbing his jaw. He groaned, stumbling clumsily to his feet. He and Black stood looking at each other.

"Don't you think I'd handle my dad like that if I could?" Black asked.

Sarin nodded and felt his jaw gingerly. Black handed him one of the snapshots.

"Me and Dad at last year's Christmas celebration," he explained.

Sarin held it up in front of his eyes, rolling his neck stiffly. Deke cautiously took a couple of steps into the room behind Sarin to get a look at the photo. A big man had his arm thrown around Black's shoulders like they were best of friends. He was a head taller and considerably broader than Black, with massive muscles bulging under his shirt.

"Man, how big is he?" Sarin said in astonishment. "Must be seven feet tall!"

"Yeah." Black handed Sarin another photo. "When I was a kid."

It was an old picture of the entire family. Black's mother and father, the two boys held in their arms. His mother was tall; she came up to just over his father's shoulder, and she was very thin. Black was two or three years old, held in his father's arms, wide-eyed. His arms and face were riddled with bruises. His brother was being held by their mother.

"Where's your mom now?" Sarin asked.

"She's dead. Long time ago."

"And that's…" Sarin motioned towards the boy in the wheelchair awkwardly, "…your brother?"

"Yeah. This is Nicholas."

"Born that way?"

"No. He was… had an accident. He had… a head injury and a stroke."

"Oh," Sarin studied Nicholas. "Can he understand us?"

"Yeah, sure." Black swallowed, looking at his helpless brother. He took a long, shuddering breath. "I gotta get out of here." He put his hand on Nicholas' shoulder. "I gotta get us both out of here. Somehow."

Black pulled his leather jacket on, his expression hard and grim. The jacket covered up the gash in Black's neck and Deke winced, imagining the leather rubbing into the raw wound.

"Where are you going to go?" Deke asked.

Black looked at Deke as if he'd forgotten that he was there. Black shook his head. He left the room, brushing past Deke. Sarin followed, cocking an eyebrow at Deke. Sarin looked back over his shoulder at Nicholas. The boy didn't move. Sarin and Deke followed Black. Their bikes were parked in front of the house, but as Deke had noted, Black's wasn't in sight. Sarin straddled his bike and put on his helmet, watching Black's brisk progress down the street. Deke followed suit. As Black turned the corner, Sarin started his engine and followed at a respectful distance, giving Black his space. Black's long legs and his desperation meant that he moved at a quick pace, and they reached his bike before long.

"You wanna go for drinks?" Sarin suggested as Black got on his bike.

Black gave him a hostile look before pulling his helmet on. "So you can spike mine again?"

Sarin's mouth fell open. He looked over at Deke, making a choking sound of protest. But Deke knew that Sarin had been the one to drug Black's drink and didn't back him up. He couldn't deny what he'd seen with his own eyes. Sarin looked back at Black.

"What makes you think that?"

"Went home blitzed. Got arrested by my own dad." Black's visor was up and he gave Sarin a long, hard look. "What kind of 'brother' does that?"

"If your drink was Mickied, what makes you think it was me? Why would I mess with your drink?" Sarin blustered.

It was a good act, but Black didn't believe a word of it. He looked at Deke, assessing him. Deke wasn't sure what Black read there, but the other boy nodded, apparently satisfied. He flipped down his visor and pulled out on his cycle.

Sarin revved his engine and followed Black. Deke pulled in behind. He wasn't sure where any of them was going but apparently Black was leading the way. After being cooped up at home, Black was ready to lay some tracks. Once off of the residential streets, he opened the throttle and they roared over cloverleafs and throughways as if the devil was on his tail. And it wasn't long before they picked up a real live tail. A siren wailed over the sounds of their engines. For once, Black's sixth sense for cops in the vicinity had failed him.

They all turned their heads to look at each other and slowed down, pulling over to the shoulder. The police car pulled in beside them, boxing them in. The cop got out of his car, face grim, one hand on his weapon. Sarin and Deke flipped up their visors.

"What's the big hurry?" the cop snarled. He was young, hardly more than a rookie. "You trying to get yourselves or someone else killed?" He favored them each with a glare. "Licenses and registration, all of you."

Sarin worked his wallet out of his back pocket and handed it over. Deke's license was loose in his pocket and his registration was in one of his saddlebags. He turned and bent over to reach for the registration and the cop had his gun out of its holster in a flash.

"Get away from those bags!" he snapped.

Deke froze, his hand out. He looked at the cop's white face and pinched expression, and swallowed hard. He slowly raised his hands.

"I'm not doing anything," he promised. "I was just going for my papers."

The cop eyed each of them, the gun in his hand moving from one to the other. He was outnumbered. Deke, who might have a weapon in one of his bags, Black, who still hadn't raised his visor or removed his helmet and was as big as an ape, and Sarin, an obviously well-experienced juvie, whether or not the cop knew he was the leader of the Kittens.

"Chill, man," Sarin soothed, not about to get shot up over a stupid traffic stop. "We're all cooperating. Nobody's gonna try nothin'."

The cop still wasn't sure. But he didn't call for backup. Deke wondered whether he already had, or if it had just completely escaped his mind that he should be getting some help instead of handling the three of them all by himself. He seemed inexperienced and out of his depth. He shouldn't be all by himself, without a senior partner in the car.

"My papers are in the left-hand bag," Deke said. "The outside pocket."

He wanted to tell the cop that he didn't have a gun in there. but he was worried that even just using the word might convince the cop that there was and push him over the edge. So Deke bit his tongue and kept his mouth shut. He just sat there, half-turned-around on his bike, hands in the air. Cars were slowing down as they passed the scene, drivers gawking over the three toughs facing down the law.

For a few minutes, they all stood there, frozen. The cop finally started to move. He approached Deke slowly. With the gun zeroed in on Deke's chest, he approached the motorcycle. Crossing his left hand over his body, he reached for the saddlebag that Deke had indicated. The gun wavered as he bent over to check. The cop gave him a warning look. Deke didn't move. His heart was thumping hard and fast. It would all be so funny, if he didn't have a gun aimed at his chest, with a nervous, hyped-up young cop on the other end.

The policeman pulled Deke's registration papers out of the bag, glancing down at them briefly. He lowered the gun slowly, his eyes darting to Sarin and to Black. No one moved. The cop jerked his gun toward Black.

"What about you?"

Black didn't answer.

"I want your license and registration, punk. I'm running out of patience."

Sarin's head turned toward Black, looking to see how he would respond. Deke was getting anxious about the cop. He didn't have the calm, soothing manner of a seasoned officer. You couldn't rattle those guys. They were just cool and mellow no matter what. But this guy, *he* was rattled. He had no backup. He was scared. He saw Black as a threat, not a kid who was at the end of his rope and needed help.

"Hey Black, you know this guy?" Deke asked with a tight grin. "He one of your dad's buddies?"

None of them moved or looked at each other. Finally, Black spoke, still not lifting his visor to show his face.

"He's just traffic. Not a detective."

The cop frowned at this.

"Black's old man is a cop," Deke informed him. "Big dude— what's his name, Black? I bet everyone knows who he is."

"Donell."

"The Duke?" the young policeman's expression brightened and the nose of the gun tipped down. His eyes ran over Black's shape, obviously comparing it to his father's. "Sure, everyone knows Duke. What's your name?"

Black hesitated before answering. "Jacob."

"Put up your visor and let me see your ID."

Black didn't move at first. Deke wondered if he'd been hoping for a confrontation. Suicide by cop. If so, Deke had just ruined his plans. Finally, Black moved, pushing up his visor. His eyes were bruised hollows. Deke hadn't noticed them in the dimness of the house, but they were stark in the sunlight. He looked bad. Desperate. The cop's grip tightened on his gun.

"Look, he's had a bad day," Deke explained. He invented wildly. "He got some bad news. You know how it is; girls and their crap. She wasn't good for him, but…"

Sarin was staring at Deke, frowning. Baffled about just what Deke was up to. Deke raised his eyebrows at him and rolled his eyes toward the cop, inviting Sarin to pitch in.

"Just give him your card, Black," Sarin ordered. "Then we can all go for a drink. Drown your sorrows."

It was the wrong thing to say. Black's face flashed anger, undoubtedly remembering how Sarin had spiked his drink and gotten him into so much trouble in the first place. Deke got off of his bike abruptly, not even caring when the gun swung around to him again. Black was going to get them all killed if Deke couldn't get things calmed down.

"Stay where you are!" the officer's voice was high-pitched, near breaking point.

Deke ignored him and covered the pavement between his bike and Black's quickly. "Come on, man," he urged with a laugh that he hoped didn't sound as forced as it was. "Quit teasing this poor cop and help a brother out. Just get out your driver's so we can ride on."

Black frowned at Deke, eyes dark and pained, then reached into his inside pocket and brought out his wallet. Deke snatched it out of Black's hand and passed it over to the officer.

"There you go. You see? Your buddy Duke's son. Now… don't you think you can give him a break? He's just upset. We'll go somewhere to cool down. You know how the Duke is! He'll be grateful for your help," he bluffed wildly, suppressing panic.

The policeman considered this, looking down at Black's license and back up at his face again. Some of the tension was draining from his face.

"You guys need to take it easy, all right?" he said earnestly. "I can't let you put others in danger. Go have a few drinks with your buddies and forget about her. A girl's not worth having an accident over."

He holstered his gun and Deke breathed a deep sigh of relief. He felt like he'd been holding his breath for the whole encounter. The cop handed all of the papers to Deke and Deke distributed them appropriately.

"Thanks, man," Deke said sincerely. "You're really helpin' a guy out."

"You boys take it a little slower." The cop's eyes lingered on Black. "He'll be okay?"

"We'll take care of him. He'll be all right."

The cop went back to his car. The boys revved their engines and rode on. They turned off onto a quieter road, and Sarin motioned for them to pull over. Visor up, he stretched his neck and rubbed his forehead.

"That was close," he breathed.

Deke grinned. Now that they were out of danger and they hadn't even been ticketed, he was just feeling the adrenaline. Heart thumping, he felt exhilarated at the narrow escape. Sarin shook his head at Deke in amusement.

Black's face was, if anything, bleaker. "Dad's gonna find out I'm a Wildcat, now."

Deke sobered up quickly. He realized that while his ploy had gotten them out of immediate trouble with the traffic cop, it hadn't made things any better for Black.

"He was gonna find out sooner or later," Sarin raised his hands in a shrug. "Maybe Deke did you a favor outing you now."

Black didn't say anything.

"Why don't we go pick up some of the boys?" Sarin suggested. "We'll go out."

Black shook his head. "I gotta… figure out… what to do."

"You can figure that out there as well as here."

"Why don't you just stay at HQ?" Deke said. "That's where I hang my hat. It ain't bad."

"What about Nicholas? I gotta find somewhere safe for him."

Sarin rolled his eyes. Deke couldn't even think of where to begin with that one. "There's gotta be places for people like him," Sarin said. "Institutions. You can't take care of him."

"I do take care of him," Black snapped back hotly. "I always take care of him! He doesn't belong in one of those places."

"*That* was taking care of him?" Sarin motioned the direction they had come from. "Tryin' to get yourself shot by a cop? That's taking care of your brother?"

Black bit his lip and looked down at the ground. "I wasn't..." he mumbled. "I was just... trying to think how to get out of it."

Sarin glanced over at Deke and divined that Deke doubted, as Sarin did, if that was the whole truth.

"If you ain't gonna go home and you ain't gonna stay at HQ, you're gonna have to find somewhere else," Sarin pointed out. "You wanna find a place, come talk to the boys. They know all the places to go."

Black considered that, then nodded, looking defeated. "Yeah. I guess."

They headed back in.

Black was hunched over on one of the couches, his head hanging down, a beer clutched in one hand, and the other hand over his eyes. Deke looked at him for a moment, then continued to whisper to the other boys who were there, telling them all about the events at Black's house and on the road. They each tried discretely to see the cut on his throat, but it was well-covered by his black jacket.

"So we gotta think of something," Deke explained. "Somewhere he can crash, where they'd take this brother of his too."

"Was he paralyzed?" Andrews asked. "Like, a quad? Or just in a wheelchair 'cause of his legs?"

"A quad, I guess," Deke raised his eyebrows and shrugged slightly. "I didn't ask. He can't talk or move or nothing. Black said he had an accident. Hurt his head."

"He's a quad, then," Andrews said with certainty. He shook his head. "No shelter's gonna take a quad."

Hi-Top wrinkled his nose. "How's Black take care of him?" he asked. "Does he, like, have to change his diapers and everything?" He gave a shudder. "Man, send him to an old folks home. Let the nurses do it."

"I guess, I dunno what Black's gotta do, but he says he takes care of him. Doesn't want an institution. He still wants to look after him, just not at his place anymore."

"Cops might know somewhere," Andrews said. "Beat cop who knows the shelters and all…?"

"He can't go to the cops," Deke pointed out in exasperation. "His old man's a cop. They'd just rat him out."

"Social worker?"

"They'll put him in an institution. Quick as a wink."

Keith had been sitting quietly, thinking about it. "I know a priest," he said slowly. "He knows some of the shelters and halfway houses."

"A priest?" Travis laughed. "How do you know a priest, loser?"

Keith just looked at him for a moment. Then he looked back at Deke to see what he thought.

Deke considered the suggestion and shrugged. "Why not? It's the best idea I've heard so far. I mean, I know some places you can go, but what's a soup kitchen gonna do for a guy like that?"

"How does he even eat?" Hi-Top mused. They all looked at him. Hi-Top flushed red. "I don't know!" He squirmed. "I was just wondering! Does Black spoon-feed him?"

Deke rolled his eyes. He jerked his head at Keith. "Come on, we'll see what Black thinks."

Keith glanced over at Black and got up reluctantly. "Doesn't exactly look like he wants company."

Deke grinned. "He won't bite."

"Don't think I want to get close enough to find out."

Black looked up as the boys approached and sat down closer to him. He rubbed his eyes, took a long breath through his nose, and looked at them.

"What's up?"

Deke nodded to Keith. "Keith knows a guy."

Black's eyes turned to him.

"I know a priest," Keith said. "He's a good guy. Helps a lot of street kids. Never made any trouble for them."

Black considered. "I'm not… religious…"

"You don't gotta be. You don't gotta go to church or be part of one. He'll help anybody."

"You think he could help? With Nicky?"

"Maybe. I dunno. He's the only one I could think of that might be able to."

Black sighed and rested his forehead in both hands for a few minutes as if it was too heavy to hold up. He took several long, deep breaths. Scrubbing his eyes again, he sat up. "When can I see him?"

Keith looked at his watch. "We can try now. If you want."

Black nodded. "Yeah, I guess."

Keith looked at Deke. "You coming too?"

"Yeah. Nothin' better to do. Maybe—" Deke cut himself off.

Keith gave him a look. "What?"

"I just—nothing."

He couldn't quite bring himself to talk to them about his own brothers. Maybe a priest who helped out a lot of street kids would know something about Deke's little brother. But the chances of that were slim.

Deke and Keith were not the only Wildcats who joined Black on his quest to see whether the priest could help him out. Sarin was there as well. Talet was there to see what trouble he could make. Hi-Top straggled along.

They all traipsed into the church past the long, empty pews, and into the offices. Black towered over all of them, his helmet still on, visor up, the straps hanging loosely at his throat. They stopped at the reception desk outside the priest's office.

"Can I help you?" the girl asked nervously.

"We want to see the preacher," Sarin informed her coolly.

"I'm afraid he's busy right now..."

"So I guess he should hurry up, huh? We don't like to wait."

She stared at Sarin, obviously anxious, trying to decide what was going on and what to do about it.

"Hey, Marta," Keith greeted, grinning down at her.

She looked startled and transferred her attention to him. "Oh—Keith." She smiled weakly.

Keith introduced the others. "My friends Talet, Sarin, Deke, Hi-Top and Black."

Black paced across the small room restlessly, like a panther penned up at a zoo.

"So what's up with Father TJ?" Keith questioned.

The receptionist looked at the other boys, Black pacing, and tried to sort out an answer. "Why did you bring these guys?"

"Black needs help. Can't talk to the cops, of course," he teased.

She looked at his face. "Is that some kind of joke?"

Keith tried to get serious. "He needs help, all right? Maybe the Father can suggest something."

"What do you mean he can't talk to the police? Why did you say that?"

"I can't really tell you…"

"And what's with all the others?"

"Moral support."

"I don't think he wants it," Marta observed.

Keith looked over his shoulder at Black. He paced up and down the room, looking at the door all too often for Sarin's nerves. As they watched, Sarin came up beside Black, slapping him lightly on the shoulder as he spoke to him. Black jumped and turned quickly toward him. Sarin pointed him to a seat and persuaded him sit down. Sarin returned to talk to the others and Black stayed slouched in his chair, cradling his head in his hands again.

"Why don't you go talk to him?" Keith teased Marta.

"No, thanks!"

"You afraid of him?"

"Sort of," Marta admitted.

Keith giggled. "Black wouldn't hurt a fly."

"He's so big," Marta shuddered. "Just look at his hands!"

Jacob's black-gloved hands were big. And they were as strong as they looked.

The door clicked open and the priest and another man were standing in the doorway. The other man cut through the room and was gone. The silver-haired clergyman stood there for a moment, looking at the visitors apprehensively.

"When's... when is my next appointment, Marta?"

"Not until two-thirty."

"I'm going out for lunch... I'll be back in time for it."

Sarin stepped in his way. "We're waiting for you, man."

"Do you have an appointment?"

"Love thy fellow man," Keith quipped, "by appointment only."

The priest flushed and tried to push past Sarin. Sarin shoved him back.

"Careful, Sarin," Keith warned.

"Listen, padre," Sarin spit. "We didn't come here looking for trouble, but if you're gonna give it to us we're happy to oblige."

Talet gave a little whoop.

"I'll call the police," the priest countered.

"Just forget it, Sarin," Black said with a deep sigh. "I got a better idea." He headed towards the door.

"What's your idea?" Sarin was obviously irritated that after all of the day's drama, Black was just going to walk out on him.

"I know the combination to Dad's gun safe."

He disappeared out the door. They all looked at the priest, stunned.

"Well, that's that," Deke said, a lump in his throat and a strange, hollow feeling in his stomach.

"What exactly did he mean?"

"What do you think he meant?" Sarin asked. "He's gonna play Russian Roulette with six bullets, that's what."

The priest looked alarmed. "What? Why?"

"'Why not?' would be a shorter list."

"But you've got to stop him!"

"Me?" Sarin threw up his hands in exasperation. "Why should I stop him?"

"You're his friend!"

Sarin laughed. "You wouldn't say that if you knew half the things I done to him!"

The priest looked at the door, concern plain on his face. "I'm going after him," he announced.

Keith breathed a sigh of relief. "Let's go. I'll see ya, Marta."

"Bye."

"Good luck!" Sarin laughed. "When he sees he's bein' followed, he'll lose you in the cloverleaf in no time flat."

They went anyway. The bikes headed out first, followed by the priest in a long, black car. Sarin was right. As soon as Black spotted his pursuers, he drove into the complex tangle of cloverleafs and started weaving in and out of traffic, making tight turns and complex figures through the twisting roads. The priest was easy to lose. The other bikes were more difficult, but Black was well-practiced and eventually managed to shake his pursuers.

Leaving the last interchange, Black slowed as he approached a stalled motorist.

It was the priest. Heeding Sarin's warning, he had chosen an exit and prayed Black would take it. Black gave in and pulled over. But he didn't get off the bike or put up the visor on his helmet to talk.

"I'm sorry for the way I acted back there. I was afraid," Father TJ confessed.

Black's shoulders raised and fell in a tired shrug. He looked behind him and watched Sarin and Deke pull out of the cloverleaf and join them.

"I was just asking how I could help," the priest explained.

"Take off your helmet, Black," Sarin ordered.

Black sat on his bike, unmoving. They waited. Slowly, he unbuckled the strap and pulled his helmet off. He turned away from them, wiping at his eyes and composing himself. He turned back to face them, his Adam's apple bobbing as he struggled to remain composed.

"Show him."

Again, Black moved on a delay. He was slow to reach up and pull his jacket away from his throat to expose the raw, festering wound. The priest was as white as a sheet. Black closed his jacket again, staring down at the pavement.

"His dear old daddy," Sarin explained. "Black's biggest problem."

Father TJ looked at Black, who didn't explain any further.

"He also lost his job and got busted, so things aren't going so great. But his old man's the biggest problem."

"Is there nothing you can do to reconcile with your father?" the priest asked. "Surely there's something you could do for the peace of your home…"

Black raised his eyes and looked at the priest straight on. "I'm getting us out of there. One way or another. We gotta get out of there."

"I know of several facilities in the community where you can get a meal and bed," Father TJ admitted, "someone to talk to…" his voice trailed off. "Some are church-run, but not all of them require you to be any particular faith."

"That's what he needs," Deke agreed, nodding vigorously.

Black raised his hand, preventing them from congratulating themselves too quickly. "What about Nicholas?"

Father TJ raised his brows questioningly. "Nicholas?"

"My brother."

"You… have a younger brother that you want to take out of the home too?" The priest shook his head slowly. "We have to be really careful. If he—"

"It's gotta be somewhere he can come too," Black didn't let the man finish. "I'm not leavin' him alone with Dad. He'll be in the hospital again."

"Space can be tight. I'm not sure who might have two openings right now—"

"He's in a wheelchair," Black fired at him. "It has to be ground floor, accessible."

Father TJ looked stupefied. "A wheelchair."

"Kids in wheelchairs need help too. There must be somewhere…"

Father TJ frowned, thinking about it. "There's Sunset…" he said slowly, "they have a couple main floor bedrooms. But I'm not sure if it's *fully* accessible… bathrooms and all…"

"That's okay. That'll do," Black nodded.

"We can see if they have space."

"One thing," Sarin cautioned. "You can't tell anyone about this. The cops might be around. Half the force knows him, so they'll be looking real hard. Don't say anything."

"I can't lie."

"If you don't, you'll be pushing Black right back home and his old man's liable to kill him if he doesn't do himself in first. Things might not be so cool in your life, either."

The man swallowed with difficulty. "I'll check on whether there's any space."

Sarin smiled and slapped Jacob on the back. "Follow the preacher, Black. We'll see you around."

Deke lingered as Sarin got back on his bike. "Hey Black," he said in a low voice.

Black turned and looked at him. "Listen… you'll let me know if you run into any other Tauruses, huh?"

Black gave him a half-smile. "Sure, Deke."

"Okay. See-ya later. Come by the crib once you're settled."

Chapter Twenty-Nine

SUNSET HOME WAS A huge old ramshackle house, added onto many times before being converted to a youth shelter. The priest pulled in front of the building and got slowly out of the car. Jacob flipped up his visor and dismounted and trailed along behind the priest without a word. They were met by an older, thinly smiling woman who greeted the priest warmly. She was slim and blonde, dressed conservatively in a blouse and dark pants.

"Good afternoon, Father TJ. Another boy for us?"

He nodded. "Yes, if it works. This is…" he trailed off.

"Jake Donovan," Jacob supplied, hoping not to be traced too easily.

"Nice to meet you, Jake."

"There are some complications…" Father TJ warned.

She ignored his token protest, waving it aside. "I think it will work out. We had one leave last week, and another is just transitioning out, so you'll fill the gap for us, Jake."

That meant there would be two vacancies. Enough space for Nicholas too. The woman put her hand on Jacob's shoulder and he startled violently. She withdrew her hand and turned her attention back to Father TJ, giving him a chance to calm back down.

"Won't you stay for lunch, Father? It's being served in the dining room and I'm sure the children will enjoy seeing you. I'll take Jake up to his room."

The priest assented.

"Come on, Jake," the woman urged. Jacob followed her up the stairs and down a hall into one of the bedrooms. "Here you go. Left side is yours. Craig will be leaving in a few days and then you'll have the room to yourself until we get another boy. It isn't much, but…"

Jacob looked around. For him, it was a lot. A bed to sleep on, after all these years. Carpet. He hadn't had anything more than his blankets on the floor since he was five or six. There was a dresser to put clothes in. If nothing else, somewhere clean and neat to take a break. Jacob walked over to the window and looked out. He had a view of the street at the side of the building.

"You can put your stuff in the drawers and closet—" she started, and then she stopped herself, seeing he had brought nothing with him. "If you haven't got anything, we'll remedy that as soon as we can. Someone can go out with you after supper to get what you need. Lunch will be in about half an hour. You're welcome to explore the rest of the place, meet the others… one of us will go over the rules with you when you're ready."

Jacob nodded and didn't turn around.

"My name is Lynn and later on you'll meet Teresa as well. She helps run the home. We don't always agree and you may find her a little… hard-nosed, but her family contributes a lot of money to the home, so she has a big say in what goes on. We just try to live with her. As for the other kids, you'll meet them all in time. Keep an open mind, we've all got our problems."

"Yes, ma'am," he agreed. He turned around, but he didn't know what else to say. It was happening so fast, he didn't know how to tell her about Nicholas. And Father TJ hadn't gotten around to telling her that part. Maybe Father TJ would discuss it with her over lunch, tell her the rest of the story. And then Lynn would decide whether it was okay for Jacob to stay.

"Take the helmet off and stay a while." She smiled. Jacob reached up and took it off. "That's better. You can stay up here if you want, or explore."

Jacob nodded and she left, shutting the door quietly behind her. He stared out the window, trying to decide if he'd made the right choice.

Nicholas heard Duke arrive home. He had Thompson with him. It was probably a good thing he wasn't alone when he realized that Jake was gone. He rarely had anything to do with Nicholas, but he had been known to throw a few punches in Nicky's direction when he got angry and there was nowhere else to vent his rage. After settling Thompson in the front room, Duke went to the fridge to get a couple beers. He slammed the fridge shut and headed down the hallway toward the bedroom.

"Jake. I need you to—"

Duke stopped in the doorway, taking in the fact that only Nicholas was there. He made a growling noise and clenched his fists. "Fat lot of help *you* are," he muttered to Nicholas. "Where's Jacob?"

Thompson started coming down the hall. "Something wrong, Duke?"

Duke backed out of the room and shut the door before Thompson could see Nicholas and start asking questions.

"I'm out of beer," he explained levelly. "I was going to get Jacob to pick me up some more."

"Isn't he in?" Thompson asked.

Duke choked, but managed to answer calmly. "I don't know where he is. He should be home. We'll go out for drinks instead."

Chapter Thirty

JACOB WAS LYING ON the bed, his eyes closed, trying to work things out in his mind, when there was a tap on the door. It opened, making him jump. It was Lynn.

"It's time for supper, Jake. Come on down."

Jacob breathed slowly and evenly. Lynn waited for him and in the hallway put her hand lightly behind his back to guide him. He jerked sharply away from her touch.

In the dining room, several tables had been pushed together to accommodate the dozen or so youth that the home sheltered. The low buzz of conversation stopped when Jacob walked into the room. They all turned and looked at him curiously. Jacob headed for an empty chair, his eyes down.

"Take your jacket off before you sit down," Lynn said. "I can hang it up for you."

Jacob ignored this advice and sat down, reaching for the nearest serving dish. He hadn't had anything to eat since he'd gotten home from jail and been consigned to his room. The smells of the cooking supper had been driving him crazy.

"Jake," Lynn's voice was measured, "I don't like to repeat myself and I don't appreciate being ignored."

Jacob raised his eyes to hers, pleading with her mentally not to force him. But as he looked at her, he knew it was no use. There was silence around the table as the kids all watched him waiting for his response.

"Watch it, she'll take away your privileges," one boy warned through a mouthful of potato.

"Jake…" Lynn's tone indicated 'this is your last warning.'

Jacob hesitated one last time and then slowly removed his jacket. The cut on his throat was exposed to view and everyone gasped at its appearance. Some of them looked away and some of them stared at it. Jacob took a couple of bites of supper, knowing that she was going to insist on getting the cut treated right away and his chances at a meal were quickly fading.

"Come here and let's take a look," Lynn sighed.

Jacob pushed himself back from the table reluctantly. He grabbed a roll as he walked toward her. Lynn stood up and looked at the throbbing wound.

"Well, that's pretty ugly. You guys behave yourself for Teresa. I'm going to have to take Jake to the clinic."

Jacob put his jacket back on as they walked out of the dining room and out to Lynn's car. She unlocked the doors and Jacob slipped into the passenger seat. Lynn started the engine and pulled out. She glanced over at him as he munched on his bun.

"Is that a gang jacket?"

"Motorcycle jacket," Jacob said around a mouthful of bread.

It was true. He'd had it before he'd joined the gang and gotten their logo stitched on the back after. Lynn eyed him doubtfully and drove on.

"We don't want you attracting any trouble. There is a local gang, so I'd suggest leaving the motorcycle jacket at home."

Jacob tried to think of which gang's territory he was in. She was right, of course. It wouldn't do for him to be wandering around in another gang's territory wearing a Wildcats jacket.

"So how did you get that cut?" Lynn asked.

Jacob didn't answer. He stared out the window, trying to sort things out in his mind to compose an answer.

"Like I said before, Jake, I don't like being ignored. You may not feel like talking right now but I think you need to let a little out. You can't keep your feelings bottled up all the time." She was silent for a few minutes and then began again. "You're a big guy,

Jake. A lot of people would say that means you're tough and should be able to handle any problems by yourself, but that isn't so. Nobody can get along alone. It's obvious you've been in a fight. We don't condone fighting and we won't keep fighters. Who was it with?"

This time she waited longer, long enough for Jacob to go over things in his mind and decide what was safe to answer.

"My dad."

"What were you cut with?"

There was a long pause, but Lynn waited. Finally, Jacob decided he couldn't afford to tell her any details and shook his head, looking down. Lynn saw the movement out of the corner of her eye and glanced over at him.

"You'd better answer out loud, I can't be watching you when I'm driving in this traffic."

"Okay."

"You aren't going to tell me anything other than that you got cut in a fight with your dad?"

Jacob let his breath out, relieved that she wasn't going to force it further. "Yeah."

They pulled into the parking lot of the clinic, and Jacob followed Lynn in. It was the supper hour and there weren't many people in the waiting room. The doctor was quick and competent. After checking Jacob's wound, he shook his head.

"This should have been seen to a long time ago. We're going to stitch this up and do what we can to clean up the infection." He started the procedure, freezing the area so that he could put in the stitches. "If the medication I give you doesn't start to clear up the infection within a few days, we may have to hospitalize you."

Jacob was silent. Lynn watched the doctor clean and stitch the wound. When he was finished the stitching, the doctor wrote out a prescription.

"I'm prescribing a very strong antibiotic. Don't take it on an empty stomach." He glanced at Lynn significantly to make sure she caught this. "You've got to eat better. You won't stay healthy if you don't take care of yourself. Come back in a week and we'll look at the stitches. If you get a fever or the infection doesn't start to clear up, see a doctor. You're going to have a nasty scar that you wouldn't have had if you had gotten this looked at sooner."

Jacob nodded. The doctor handed the prescription to Lynn.

"Go on out to the car, Jake," Lynn handed him her keys. "I'll be right out."

Jacob was surprised, but took the keys and headed out to the vehicle. He'd been there less than a day, she knew he was in a gang, and she trusted him not to just steal her car? He sat in the passenger seat and put the keys in the ignition so that he could play the radio. Lynn was only a couple of minutes behind him.

Of course, dinner was over by the time they got back to Sunset and Jacob was famished. Lynn told him earlier that he was welcome to explore the house, so instead of going up to his room, he took a surreptitious detour into the spacious kitchen. Jacob made a quick circuit of the fridge and pantry cupboards. He stuffed several granola bars and other snacks into his pockets and grabbed a fork and a plastic container of spaghetti from the fridge to take with him to his bedroom.

Jacob listened for a moment to the sounds of the house around him. A television or two. Distant voices. Occasional footsteps overhead. Nothing that sounded dangerous. He took a slow, even breath, and headed out of the kitchen. He crept up the stairs, alert for any movement or threat. In the hallway upstairs, he got turned around, not sure which direction his bedroom was. He took his best guess and turned right. Two of the other residents were in the dim hall, standing close together, in intimate conversation. Embarrassed, Jacob froze and tried to sort out whether his room was down that hall or if he'd come the wrong way. His eyes took time to adjust to the dimness of the hall after the bright kitchen. One of the figures was an older boy, a dark-haired tough who looked like a drug dealer or gang banger. The other was a blond-haired girl, maybe twelve years old, short and slim. Her stance was defensive, her hands up in front of her chest, mouth turned down as she argued with him. The boy leaned in, hulking over her, leering. She tried to take a step back from him to establish her personal space but ran into the wall.

A door opened and Jacob turned toward it in relief, hoping to find that it was the door to his own room. But it wasn't the boy who had been introduced to him as Craig. Jacob didn't know the names of the others. The new boy, blond, slim, with lines of fatigue around his eyes, glanced at Jacob, but his attention went immediately to the couple further down the hall.

"Leave her alone," he growled, taking a few steps closer to them.

The dark boy's head turned and he looked the blond one over.

"Get lost, Pal. This is none of your business."

"Cassy doesn't want anything to do with you, David. So leave her be."

"We're just having a little conversation." David gave Pal a suggestive smile. "I haven't laid a finger on her."

Pal motioned to the girl. "Cassy, go on, go to your room. It's okay."

Cassy shifted to make her escape and David's hand shot out, closing around her arm. "I don't think so."

"You said you weren't bugging her. So why can't she just go if she wants to?"

"Why don't you just go back in your room and get stoned? Stick to your strengths."

Pal took another step forward, shoving David without effect. "Leave her alone!"

David pulled Cassy closer to him and wrapped his other arm around her to force her face closer to his. Jacob's inertia disappeared and he took a few steps toward them. He didn't bother arguing with David; that obviously wasn't the way to get through to him. He shoved David back and being a lot bigger and stronger than Pal, his push was more effective. David stumbled back, letting Cassy go. He faced off against Jacob.

"Oh, newbie wants some action," he sneered. "You think this is any of your business? I'd think again if I was you. Maybe you'd like your throat split all the way around this time!"

Jacob stood balanced on the balls of his feet, waiting to see if David was going to attack. Cassy moved past Jacob, sheltering behind him or retreating to the safety of her own room. Jacob was relieved that she was out of the way.

David sized Jacob up and was reluctant to attack.

"Just leave her alone," Jacob warned. "Like Pal said."

"Who do you think you are to give me orders?"

Jacob raised his eyebrows. David was rapidly proving himself a coward, eager to threaten or bully those who were younger but not prepared to take Jacob on physically. "Maybe we should just talk to Lynn," Jacob suggested. "Or one of the other leaders."

David fell back, still glaring at Jacob. "You're making a mistake, newbie. You're going to regret crossing me."

Jacob waited, silent. David retreated down the hall and turned at the end, disappearing from sight. Jacob watched to see if David was going to come back once he figured Jacob's guard was down. A door shut, followed by silence. Jacob waited a few more long seconds. He turned back around to face Pal and Cassy.

"You okay?" he asked Cassy.

Cassy put her arms around Jacob in an impulsive hug. He looked down at her, his heart racing, not sure how to deal with this new problem. He looked at Pal for help or advice. Pal's face flushed a bright red. He forced a smile that looked as angry as his scowl at David.

"Thanks, man. Always helps to have a giant on your side when dealing with a creep like that."

"Should I have stayed out of it?" Jacob was uncertain of the vibe he was getting off of Pal.

"I can't beat David. But I figured he'd at least have to let go of Cassy to fight me."

Jacob admired Pal's guts, protecting Cassy when he knew that he'd be beaten. He looked down at Cassy, who finally loosened her grip and smiled up at him. She was a pretty girl. She'd be gorgeous when she was older, but now had only an innocent, pretty face, framed by feathery blond hair. Her eyes were green or blue and sparkled when she smiled.

"Thank you. Thank you so much!"

Jacob shrugged, feeling his face flush. He looked down, letting the fringe of his long hair obscure his expression. "It's nothing."

He looked at Pal, who was shifting uncomfortably and looking back over his shoulder. "I'm Jake." He offered his hand to the smaller boy.

"Pal."

They shook, Jacob keeping his grip firm and friendly. Not so hard that it would be taken as a challenge.

Pal let go slowly. "Thanks for helping out."

Jacob nodded. He examined the closed doors along the hallway. "I'm… sort of lost. I don't know where my room is."

Pal looked at the plastic container in Jacob's hand and smirked. Jacob hadn't even thought to put it down or drop it before challenging David. "Yeah. You're not down here."

"I'll show you," Cassy offered. She put her left hand into Jacob's right and gave it a squeeze. "Come on." She tugged.

Jacob shrugged at Pal and let Cassy lead him out of the hallway, back past the top of the stairs and into another.

"It's been built onto a few times," Cassy explained. "So it can get confusing. You'll figure it out."

"Yeah. It'll just take a few days."

"I'm glad you went down the wrong one."

"Yeah… me too. Are you going to tell Lynn that David's bugging you?"

"I… don't want to make waves." Cassy's bottom lip tightened. "I've been in foster homes, in other places… You don't want to make waves."

Jacob's brows pressed closer together. "Will you be okay? I don't want you getting hurt…"

"I don't think he'll be at Sunset for long. He's had two warnings already. Three strikes…"

"But you won't tell them."

"Let someone else get him in trouble."

Cassy led Jacob to a door and opened it. The room was empty, Craig nowhere in sight. Jacob let go of Cassy's hand, but she followed him in through the door. She closed it behind her and then sat cross-legged on Craig's bed. Jacob looked down at the spaghetti bowl in his hand.

"Go ahead!" Cassy encouraged. "Eat! You missed supper."

Jacob sat down on his bed and opened the dish. Even cold, the spaghetti smelled heavenly. He felt like he hadn't eaten in a week. With another encouraging nod from Cassy, he started to eat.

When Thompson came into work in the morning, he found Duke sitting in his chair, waiting for him.

"Duke! Hey, what's up?"

Duke shifted his weight, making the chair creak in protest. Thompson eyed it, wondering whether it would stand up to the punishment.

"I want you to take on a missing persons case," Duke said.

Thompson frowned. "I rarely do missing persons. Who's disappeared?"

Duke frowned at him as if Thompson was being dense and should already know. "Jacob."

"Your son?" Thompson stared at Duke.

Looking more closely at Duke, he started to notice things he hadn't before. Duke was paler than usual, his hands clenched around the arms of the chair and the veins on his arms standing out. His jaw was dark with five o'clock shadow after putting in a late shift. Thompson got a cup of coffee for each of them and leaned against the desk watching Duke sip it.

"What happened last night?"

"Nothing," Duke said blankly, "he didn't come home." He looked around the room, frowning.

"You don't think he's been abducted again, do you?" Thompson asked.

Duke thought about it and shook his head. "No… they would have just killed him the first time. I think he's split. Run away."

"Have you reported it yet?"

"Not officially, I guess. Listen, Jack—I want you to take the case. I could pull a few strings…"

"It's not my field," Thompson protested. "I've only done missing persons a couple of times before."

"Sure, but you know Jake."

"Half the force knows him, Duke."

"But you know him best. I want you on it," Duke said bullishly.

Thompson didn't say anything for a moment. He knew that once Duke Donell had decided something, there was little use trying to change his mind. And he had decided he wanted Thompson on the case.

"All right," Thompson said finally. "I'll need all his files and you have to be totally honest with me."

"Have I ever not been?" Duke stood up. "I'll get you on the case. Who's your partner?"

"Don Jaslow."

Duke nodded and started to turn away. He paused. "Thanks, Jack. It means a lot to me."

The next day, Teresa entered Jacob's room without knocking or invitation. She was the opposite of Lynn, dark instead of blond, her clothes showy rather than conservative. She had on a fluffy red blouse with a deep neckline that made Jacob blush and look away from her.

"I think it's time that we had a talk, don't you, Jake?" she asked, sitting down on the bed too close to him.

Jacob shifted uneasily away. "Okay."

"Come here," she patted the bed next to her and opened up her leather bifold clipboard. "So we can look at this together."

Jacob was already uncomfortably close to her. When he didn't move over, she moved toward him, her hip nudging his. He looked down at the paper in the clipboard, hoping to get through the interview quickly. Teresa put one arm around him to pull him closer.

"Here we go. We'll start by going through some of the house rules."

Jacob nodded.

"This is not a comprehensive list. There are other rules too. But this will give you a good outline, to start out with."

"Okay."

She looked up at his face for a moment, then back at the list of rules. "No drugs, alcohol, or smoking inside the house. Do you use drugs, Jake?"

Jacob shook his head. "No."

"Drink? Smoke?"

He shook his head again. It wasn't a lie. He wouldn't drink while he was at Sunset. He wasn't an alcoholic. He drank when he was with the gang and he sometimes drank at home with Duke or to numb the pain. But he didn't need alcohol to get by.

"No?" Teresa studied him, her eyes sharp.

Jacob looked away, shaking his head.

"If you are found with drugs or alcohol or if you are under the influence while you are at the house, you will be expelled. We have zero tolerance."

"Yeah. Okay."

"We also have zero tolerance for weapons, any kind of violence in the house, or any backtalk or disrespect toward the staff."

"Uh-huh."

She nodded toward his hands, scarred across the knuckles. "Those look like lethal weapons, but I don't suppose we can ask you to leave them behind," she teased.

Jacob attempted a laugh but it just came out as a choking sound. She rubbed his back and tightened her grip on him. "No need to be so nervous. I don't think you're going to have any trouble with these rules, do you?"

"No, ma'am."

"No sex."

He swallowed. "Okay."

"No girls in your room, even other residents. Do you have a girlfriend, Jake? I'm sure you must, with that physique."

"Not right now."

"You're straight, right? Sometimes Father TJ doesn't ask, but we only take straight teens here. I know there are lots of kids who are kicked out because they are gay, but we can't take them here. It's against our charter."

Jacob could feel himself blushing again. "Yes."

"But no girlfriend…?"

Jacob shook his head.

"You're playing the field, huh? You have to be careful doing that…"

He looked down at the clipboard to read off the next rule. "Nine o'clock curfew." He raised his brows. "Nine o'clock?"

"We don't want our kids staying out late. Get in off of the street and stay out of trouble. We don't want them staying out drinking and chasing around being stupid. We'll put on a movie for the evening or have a pizza party. Lots of fun things happening around here."

That was going to severely limit Jacob's ability to see the gang. But maybe that was a good thing. He'd have a valid excuse to give Sarin for not being able to participate in any gang activity.

"That sounds fun."

Teresa gave him a brilliant smile. "It is. That's been one of my contributions to the House." She looked back down at the paper. "All residents must either be going to school or, if sixteen or older, working full time." She looked at him, raising her brows.

"I… I work, but I lost my job…"

"So you're not working right now?"

"No… I'm looking for something."

"Well, you'd better step it up. We don't offer any free ride at Sunset House. School or full-time work. Those are the only two options."

"I'll find something. I'm a good worker. I just… I was in hospital and I lost my job… because I was sick."

"I'll be expecting to see proof of employment as soon as possible."

"Okay." Jacob nodded, trying to convince her that he was going to be able to find something.

"Let's get you registered." Teresa moved the checklist to the other side of her clipboard, revealing a registration form. "Do you have some identification?"

"Uh…" Jacob had his driver's license on him, but it wasn't in the name Jake Donovan. And he wasn't going to register using his real name. "No… do I have to?"

"We do need something… Do you have anyone to vouch for your identity?"

Jacob shook his head.

"Hmm. Well, let's fill out the form, anyway." She filled in his assumed name and asked him his birthday.

As they got past the usual basics and Jacob scanned further down the page, he started to get more anxious. There were numerous lines that he was supposed to sign, declaring that he would follow each of the rules of Sunset House. How was he going to get Nicholas registered at Sunset? Neither of them could use their own names and Nicholas couldn't go to school or work. Jacob would somehow have to provide enough for both of them. Teresa said there were no exceptions. But surely when she saw Nicholas, she'd understand.

"You need to sign each of these," Teresa pointed to the lines. "No one can become a resident until they've agreed to all the conditions. Just like we discussed: no drugs or alcohol, weapons or violence, sex, curfew…"

Swallowing, Jacob took the pen Teresa proffered and signed each line, focusing on not signing his real name.

Thompson looked through the stacks of files. "Looks like we got Child Services, school, medical—and a police jacket! I didn't know Jacob had a record!"

Jaslow's dark eyes were sharp. His brows drew down. "What's he got?"

Thompson opened the file and checked. "Drugs. Released on probation three days ago."

"He's run away," Jaslow said with certainty.

"Looks that way, all right… but where would he go?"

"Read the files."

Jaslow was the senior partner and he rarely read the paperwork except as a last resort. He understood criminals in his gut. That's the way he liked to work. He could grind through the files as well as any officer when he had to, but he rarely did.

"I'm interested in his thick medical file," Thompson said. "Let's see how it looks."

"Go ahead, I'm listening."

Jaslow leaned back in his chair, hands behind his head, and shut his eyes. Sharp-eyed, Thompson scanned the pages.

"Born at the General. Came back at four months, with internal injuries and hemorrhaging typical of abuse. Charges were laid for abuse and dropped provided the mother take some counseling. Next time he was a year and a half old; scalding injuries. Overheated bathwater. No charges. After that, he was brought in by Duke with a broken hip and femur. Numerous bruises also noted at the time. I remember Duke mentioning that—said the boy was hurt while he was out of town. The hip was shattered and didn't heal properly." Jaslow nodded and Thompson read on. "Charges were laid for abuse and gross negligence and dropped—"

"Why were they dropped?"

"It doesn't say."

"Hmm." Jaslow thought about that for a minute. "Go on."

"Next time brought in by ambulance when Duke called in. Broken collar bone and shoulder, minor back injuries and a couple broken ribs. He was three at the time. This time it says the charges were overridden."

"By whom?"

"Doesn't say." Jaslow was silent, so Thompson went on. "Broken ribs and fractured jaw, his mother brought him in. No charges… stitches… concussion… next major incident, he was about ten. He came in with double pneumonia in an advanced stage. Charges were laid for neglect and overridden again. In a few times after that... stitches, broken bones... after about twelve, the only major incident was the abduction. You know the story. The doctor notes that he had a lot of scars, remodeled bones from fractures that were never treated..."

"Nice."

"You think he was abused?" Thompson looked up.

"I think that's pretty obvious," Jaslow said dryly.

"Another good reason for running away."

Jaslow frowned, rubbing his forehead. "You've been over to Duke's place, haven't you?"

"Sure. A number of times."

"You were never suspicious? Never saw anything?"

Thompson shook his head slowly. "Not that I can think of. Duke's always been very good with him... No, there was one time, the first time I was there... Jacob was maybe six or seven. Duke smacked him and I stopped him. He showed remorse, said it had never happened before... Jacob often has bruises, black eyes... I always just figured he had trouble at school. Big kid, gets in fights... like father, like son. Duke never shies from a fight."

"What's the boy like?"

"Hmm. Quiet; a little withdrawn, maybe. With his family background—his parents' breakup and his mother's death, and all, that's normal. I don't know if we've ever really spoken to each other, other than just hellos."

"What's his police record?"

Thompson opened the file and flipped through it more quickly than he had the medical file. "A few charges of assault, but they were all ruled self-defense. The only charge that stuck was the last one. Tested positive for LSD. It doesn't mention he's in a gang, but he is."

"Which one?"

"Motorcycle gang. The Wildcats."

"How long's he been with them?"

"I don't know. He was with them at the time of Angel's accident, that's all I know for sure."

"I can't picture Duke allowing that."

"I can't either. He must not know about it. Hunt, his probation officer, might be able to tell us more."

The boy had been standing there for ten minutes without fidgeting, which was something many grown men couldn't do. He was also there early and had asked politely for the boss, quietly refusing to talk to anyone else. Pat looked up from his paperwork and studied the boy. Big, broad shoulders, well-built. And quite young. He had a nasty-looking gash across his throat and a black eye to finish it off. His face masked any emotion.

"Well?" demanded Pat.

"I'm looking for a job, sir," he answered, adding a short list of duties he'd filled on a construction site before. There were a lot of hazards on a construction site and some of the jobs he described were ones that no one in his right mind would give a kid of the boy's age.

"How old are you?"

"Sixteen," he admitted after a moment's hesitation.

One point in his favor, he didn't lie about being under-age. But that wouldn't help him if he fibbed about his experience. "You're lying. No sixteen-year-old would ever get those jobs."

"Sir, I've worked since I was twelve. Been in construction since I was fourteen, full-time as soon as I turned sixteen," he said slowly, calmly. Pat was impressed at his self-control after being called a liar straight to his face. If he had had a fit, he would have blown all his chances of getting a position.

"Where've you worked?"

"Billy's Construction. Small company. I can find you the phone number if you like."

"I know it. Why aren't you still there?"

"I was in hospital a while ago and someone had to cover the job. He let me go."

"Take off your jacket."

He was wearing a windbreaker that couldn't be his; the sleeves too short by three inches and the back stretched tightly over his shoulders. He removed it without asking for an explanation. Pat studied the boy closely. He sure wasn't carrying any extra weight around. If anything, he was undernourished, but built like a bull. His tight black shirt showed every muscle.

"What were you in hospital for?"

"Personal."

"Is that where you got the stitches?"

"No, sir. Got those yesterday."

"You're a fighter?"

"Not if I can help it."

It seemed like the perfect opportunity. If Pat didn't hire him, the competition was bound to grab the chance. The kid appeared to be competent and had the experience he needed. He'd be cheap labor.

"Where are you living?"

Something like anger flashed through his eyes for a moment and then was controlled. "Sunset Home."

"The shelter?"

"Yes, sir."

He wanted the job badly. Pat divined that he wanted to be independent and he'd work hard for it. "Any trouble with the police?"

"No, sir."

Pat studied him closely and didn't detect any sign of dishonesty. He sighed and straightened his papers. Unless he found a catch, it was a chance he didn't like to refuse. He deliberately didn't commit to a salary.

"How soon can you start?"

"I got some things to clear up today."

"I'll take you around the site tomorrow. No lates or you're out."

"Thank you, sir."

The boy slipped on his jacket and left. He didn't slam the door. Pat reached for the phone and it wasn't until he'd been connected with Billy that he realized he didn't even know the boy's name.

"Billy? Pat Cowell here… I had a kid in here looking for a job, said he was an ex-employee of yours. I didn't catch the name. Young kid. Tall, good build… yeah… how was his work?"

After completing some initial interviews, Thompson and Jaslow sat down together again to review progress on the file and work through the next steps in the investigation.

"How was the interview with the probation officer? Hunt?" Jaslow settled into his chair and took a sip of coffee.

"No luck. He's never met with Jacob."

"How long did you say he's been on probation?"

"Since two days before his disappearance. So, four days now. Hunt says he made the appointments, but things came up and he canceled out."

"The kid canceled?"

"No, Hunt did."

Jaslow grimaced. "He hasn't talked to Jacob at all?"

"Not really. For a couple minutes on the phone Wednesday, but not enough to discover any problems."

"Not Thursday?"

"Nope."

"So we don't know what happened Thursday."

"No. Hunt called a few times but didn't reach Jacob."

"Donell says he saw Jacob last on Wednesday night. That's our last positive contact."

Thompson marked it down in his notes.

"Did you have any luck with the gang?" Thompson asked.

"Not yet. They're lying low. No one wants to talk and we've got nothing to compel them. I'm having Sarin Mace's house watched in case Jacob shows up there. We have to talk with Mace too."

"Mace is the leader?"

"Only of the younger guys. The gang is split into two age groups. The older ones don't have a leader, they're one-for-all and all-for-one. Hard to get anything out of any of them."

"So which group would have the best information?"

"I'm not entirely sure. The younger set, the Kittens, will know Jacob better, but the older Cats will know what's happening better. We need Mace, he's the key. He's got a foot in both camps."

"Do we know where Jacob works? I haven't been able to find out from the files."

"No. Not many people really know him. I've asked around at a lot of the hangouts, but they only recognize him in passing. What have you managed to pull from the files?"

Thompson took out his notes and stared at them for a moment without saying anything. "This is very difficult, knowing Duke the way I do," he explained.

"Well, we're on the case now. Pretend it's someone you don't know. What've you got?"

Thompson cleared his throat and started reading his report slowly and unemotionally.

"Jacob Donell lives in an older, lower-class area. Child Services says they never found enough evidence to prove that Jacob was abused by his father, but after reading his file, it's pretty obvious that he is. His mother was originally charged with the abuse and denied custody, but the incidents didn't stop when she stopped seeing him. She was allowed visiting privileges until he disappeared for at least a week during an unauthorized camping trip."

"At least?"

"The investigating officers were pretty sure that he'd been gone for some time before he was reported missing."

"What kind of shape was he in when he was found?"

"Not bad. A sprained ankle and a few scratches, but he wasn't starving."

Jaslow swore.

"What is it?" Thompson asked.

"You're telling me the kid's bush-smart as well as street-smart? He could just take that cycle of his out to the woods and we'd never find him."

"I hadn't thought about that." Thompson considered. He nodded, eyebrows raised. "I guess he could."

Jaslow swore again. "Go on."

"Well, after he turned six, we've got his school files to go on. He was frequently truant. When officers looked into it, they usually found him sick in bed. He's worked casually from the time he was eight or nine, wherever he could get it. Sometimes photocopying papers for the school. Mowing lawns. Whatever. He remained truant a lot of the time and at ten he was charged for the first time with assault by the parents of a twelve-year-old who had apparently picked a fight with Jacob and lost. The boy ended up with a broken arm and concussion."

"Was Duke ever in the army?"

"Special forces. He still gets time off to upgrade his training. Why?"

"It sounds like Jacob is a little too good at unarmed combat."

"Yes… I'll ask Duke about it."

"The more I hear, the less I like this. He's a big kid, right?"

"Six-six or more, now. Built like Duke."

"We've got a big, street-smart, bush-smart kid out there, probably trained in unarmed combat, reconnaissance, and weaponry. A kid right on the edge. If he doesn't want to be caught, we're going to have a real hard time getting our hands on him."

"And going by his record and past experience, he may also be running with a gang and high as a kite."

Jaslow swore flatly. "Anything about his mother?"

"When Jacob was young, she was separated from Duke. Her boyfriend went to jail for abuse and bodily harm when he crippled her first child. Then she went back to Duke for a while… it's a bit of a mess, trying to figure it all out."

"There's a child before Jacob?"

"Yeah, another boy. I'm not clear whether he was Duke's or not."

"Could Jacob have gone to her?"

"She died when he was six or seven."

"Died of what?"

"Murder, never solved. She was with the boyfriend when he got out of jail and a while after that showed up on Duke's doorstep again. Apparently, they had fought and she went to Duke for protection. She later left him again and was killed."

"She just couldn't keep away from these guys, could she?"

"Apparently not."

"How badly was the other child hurt?"

"He was in a persistent vegetative state. It doesn't say on the file anywhere that he died, but I suspect he did or he's in some institution in care of state somewhere. Duke's never mentioned him."

"Where was her boyfriend at the time of the murder?"

"He disappeared. Must have taken a new name, because we can't track him down."

Jaslow closed his eyes, leaning back. "So where do you think Jacob would go?"

"I really don't know. He doesn't have any relatives aside from Duke or friends other than the Wildcats. Maybe if Hunt had gotten a hold of him, he would have had one touch-point. But he didn't."

"I'll bet you anything Mace knows something. But we can't sit around waiting for things to happen. Have we arranged a search of Donell's house? I don't like waiting around for Duke to wipe out any clues he may have left."

"We've got one for tomorrow."

"Good."

Chapter Thirty-One

SAMMY SAT PLAYING WITH Capo, waiting for the YMCA
activity to start. Darla was cooing and hanging over Capo,
trying to get him to laugh. The baby watched her with wide
eyes, and waved his hands and squealed, but she couldn't get him
to smile or laugh. But whenever Sammy leaned in close to him or
blew in his face or made a noise, Capo was all smiles. Great big,
slurpy, gummy smiles.

There was a new male voice over the clamor and Sammy
looked around warily to see who it was. Officer Smith was
standing inside the room, talking to Anne. Ron, who Sammy had
figured out by now was Anne's brother, not her boyfriend,
moved in closer to talk to the two of them. Smith was looking
around the room. When his eyes met Sammy's, he smiled and
gave a little wave. Sammy had actually gone to the activity without
Smith having to remind him or herd him there. Sammy turned
back to Capo and rubbed his curly head.

"Why won't he smile for me?" Darla pouted.

"D-d-doesn't kn-n-now you."

"But I'm not scary. I can always make babies laugh. Watch
this!"

She leaned closer and made a silly face, then flopped her head
all around like a broken puppet. Capo didn't smile. His eyes went
to Sammy instead, seeking a connection with him. Sammy smiled,
and Capo gave him another wide-mouthed grin.

Smith approached Sammy. "Got the little guy again today, huh?"

Sammy nodded. Smith tickled Capo's belly, but rather than laughing, Capo went rigid at Smith's touch.

"Shhh," Sammy calmed, cuddling Capo closer to him and kissing his forehead. "Shhhh."

"Did I scare him? Sorry."

Sammy held Capo to himself. "S-s-okay," he murmured.

"So why have you got him today? Everything okay with your mom?"

Sammy glanced at Darla and felt himself blushing. "Sh-she's okay."

Smith looked at Darla, then back at Sammy, and raised his eyebrows. "Oooh… okay. Good. Nice of you to take him off her hands for a little while."

Sammy grinned and nodded.

Smith looked at his watch. "I'd better scram. I'll see you later."

As Smith walked away, Ron whistled through his teeth to get everyone's attention.

"Okay, crew. We're going to go over the camping equipment list today. Did everyone remember to bring their permission forms?"

There were some groans around the room.

"If you didn't bring it today, you're going to have to make an extra trip and bring it to me tomorrow. After that, it's too late. You can't go if you don't have your form. But it's this weekend, people, so it needs to be in now. Everybody grab a list," he handed out a couple of piles to be passed around the room. "There's nothing too hard here. You don't have to go out and buy a bunch of camping gear. The YMCA supplies all of that stuff. What you need to bring is things like clothes, a backpack, a flashlight, and toilet paper for the outhouses. If you don't have something on the list, let one of us know right away so that we can make sure you are supplied. Understood?"

There were a few nods around the room. Sammy looked down at the list, working through the words carefully and checking off in his head whether he had or could get his hands on each item. A flashlight would be a problem. A personal first-aid kit. Most of the rest seemed straightforward.

"You're coming, right?" Darla whispered.

Sammy nodded.

"Becky's not! Her mom won't let her."

Sammy raised his eyebrows. That was the best news yet. A few days camping in the wilderness, away from all of the gang and family troubles, and no Becky. It was almost like a real vacation.

"I bet it's because she still wets the bed." Darla giggled.

Sammy looked down at Capo, trying to swallow a lump in his throat. He didn't like Becky, but hearing others made fun of always made him feel queasy. He played with Capo's hair and looked over the equipment list instead of at Darla.

Chapter Thirty-Two

JASLOW AND THOMPSON STEPPED into the house and looked around. It was completely silent. They apparently didn't need to worry about Duke wiping away clues; he hadn't bothered to throw away his garbage or wash any dishes. Jaslow glanced through a stack of magazines by the easy chair, then walked slowly around the front room, looking for anything out of place or of possible interest. There were beer bottles piled in several places around the room and a liberal carpeting of newspapers beside the couch.

"Notice anything out of place?" he asked Thompson.

"It isn't usually this bad," Thompson said apologetically. He hadn't come any further than the doorway to the kitchen beside the front room. There he had stopped, shocked at the state it was in.

"Probably the kid does the housekeeping. Come on, give me a tour."

Thompson was hesitant. "This is the front room... the kitchen's in there. The bedrooms are at the back of the house."

Thompson led the way to the back hall, and down the hall to the bedroom on the end. They walked in and looked around. Thompson gasped and just stood there staring at the boy lying in the bed. Jaslow moved close and put his fingers lightly on the boy's throat for a moment.

"It's not Jacob," Thompson finally said.

"I guess not," Jaslow agreed. He looked around the rest of the room and his sharp eyes caught the corner of one of Jacobs photographs that Duke had kicked under the bed. He bent over and picked it up. He found the other loose pictures and the envelope with the rest in it. Jaslow looked at them slowly. "So this is the older brother who was hurt."

Thompson nodded.

"What's his name, do you remember?"

Thompson mentally reached for the name, just out of his grasp. He'd read the whole story, made notes of it. "Um… Nick? Nicholas, I think… Is he okay?"

Jaslow didn't say anything at first, considering. "I think we should have him removed. I know you may not like the idea, but… the boy's feverish. A person like this is very prone to infection." He pulled back the thin sheet that covered Nicholas, dispassionately surveying the bare form beneath. "Duke hasn't been able to keep his hands off of him, either."

Thompson looked at Nicholas' skin, mottled with bruises. He nodded slowly. "I guess you're right. Though I don't understand why he would keep the boy here, if he wasn't prepared to take good care of him."

"It doesn't always work that way."

"What will Duke say?"

"We're doing what's best for the boys."

"I'll… call someone about it."

Thompson stood there for a moment longer and then turned away as he made the call. Jaslow pulled the sheet back over Nicholas gently and stood looking at him.

"You must be cold." He picked up one of Jacob's blankets from the corner and spread it over the older boy. He picked up the photographs again and studied them until Thompson got back. "Keep these, I want to look at them later."

Thompson took them and tucked them into his notepad. "Someone will be by to pick him up soon."

"Good. Let's take a look around while we're waiting."

Thompson opened the closet to see what was in there. Jaslow pulled the other blankets back and folded them up. He picked up the pillow and stripped off the pillowcase, showing it to Thompson.

"He's been hurt sometime lately." There were bloodstains on the pillowcase. Jaslow indicated the pictures he'd given to Thompson. "He was looking at pictures of his family, he may have been upset. I don't like it, this is the stuff suicides are made of."

"Do you want to check the rest of the house?"

Jaslow motioned for Thompson to lead the way.

After checking out the junk yard of a basement, they climbed the stairs to the kitchen and Jaslow looked around uneasily. "We're missing something here… Something's out of place."

Thompson looked around, frowning. "Other than that somebody's got a lot of dishes to do, I don't see anything."

Jaslow blinked. "There are too many. One man doesn't go through that many dishes in two or three days. Especially not when he only eats one or two meals at home."

"There's Nicholas, too."

"Nicholas doesn't eat. He has a gastric tube."

Jaslow went over to the sink and began to sort through all the dishes and arrange them on the table, stove, and counter. "Way too many. Duke doesn't eat eight-course meals. Why didn't Jacob do the dishes the days between his probation and running away?"

"Maybe he's been gone longer than Duke realizes. Maybe he left the day he got off probation."

"Possible." Jaslow sorted through the dishes and held up a knife, looking at the edge.

"There's blood on that," he showed it to Thompson.

"It's a butcher knife. He had steak and used it to trim the meat."

Jaslow studied the blade and shook his head. "I'm not so sure. There's blood on the boy's pillow. It would explain Jacob not doing any dishes since he got out on probation."

Thompson looked skeptical.

"It could also explain his disappearance," Jaslow said.

"You mean he ran away because he got into a fight with Duke."

"That's not what I meant," Jaslow raised his eyebrows.

Thompson laughed. "That's ridiculous. If Duke got rid of Jacob—like you're inferring—he wouldn't be so stupid as to leave the murder weapon in the kitchen sink! He *has* worked on a few murder investigations in his time!"

"I'm not jumping to any conclusions. I'm just speculating. You've got to admit it's a possibility. The boy must have been getting harder and harder to handle the more he grew up."

"It's ridiculous."

"It's unlikely. But it's a possibility. I'll have the lab take a look at the blood and identify whether it's human or animal. It's probably beef but I'm not going to assume that blindly."

The doorbell rang and Thompson went to answer it. It was the ambulance that had arrived to transport Nicholas. Thompson escorted them to the bedroom where they looked Nicholas over. In a few minutes, Nicholas was on a gurney and ready to go. One of the attendants asked the officers for the paperwork.

"We haven't got anything," Thompson said.

"You can't have him moved without the proper permission."

"We have the authority to take abused children into temporary custody," Jaslow said firmly.

"Is he a child? I haven't even seen any identity papers."

"He's…" Thompson stopped to figure it out and turned to Jaslow. "He's eighteen or nineteen. He's an adult."

"He's mentally incapacitated. That's the same as a child."

"No, it's not—" the woman disagreed.

"Look, we have reason to believe that he's being abused. He can't remove himself from the situation, so we're making him a temporary ward until all the technicalities have been worked out."

"Do you have the authority to do that?"

"What papers do you need signed?"

She got appropriate forms from the ambulance. After reading them over, Jaslow filled in all the signature lines and passed it back.

"Okay? Your papers have been signed. Get him out of here."

Chapter Thirty-Three

THOMPSON HAD BEEN QUESTIONING Sarin Mace for a while but wasn't getting anywhere with him. Mace had on a pseudo-friendly attitude. He acted as if he wanted to help with the investigation but smirked every time he answered a question. The door slammed open and both Sarin and Thompson jumped. Thompson turned around as Duke strode into the room. He towered over Mace, making him look like a child by comparison. Mace had been tipping his chair back on two legs, but it landed abruptly on Duke's entrance. Mace's composure shattered like glass, the smirk disappearing. Duke grabbed him by the front of the collar, pulling him up off of his chair just slightly.

"Where's Jacob?"

"I dunno—honest, man, I dunno where he is!"

Duke wasn't satisfied. He threw Mace back into the seat. He leaned in close, his face inches from Mace's. "When did you last see him?"

"S-see him?" Mace tried to pull back, to regain some personal space. "Thursday… in the morning."

"Where?"

"His place."

"Did you see anyone else there? Anyone hanging around? Suspicious?"

"No."

"Where's Jacob?" Duke shouted. He slammed his hand down on the table.

"I don't know!" Sarin's voice cracked. His hands clenched into fists. "I swear man, I don't know where he went. I ain't seen him since Thursday. Nobody has!"

Duke turned to Thompson. "What can you get him for?"

"Unlicensed weapon."

"Search his place. Keep him as long as you can. He'll talk to me. Cool him a day or two and see how he feels."

Duke withdrew, turning slightly sideways and ducking to slip out the door. Thompson heard a sigh of relief from Mace as the door shut behind Duke. He turned and looked at the boy. All of the bravado was gone and he sat shaking in his seat.

"You really want to spend much time talking to him?" Thompson asked reasonably.

Mace shook his head. "I don't know nothing. Donell ain't been around. I dunno where to find him."

Lynn checked on Jacob at the end of the day to see how he was doing. She paused before she left again.

"Is there anything we can do to help you settle in, Jake?"

"Ma'am…" Jacob started shyly.

"Just call me Lynn, that's what the others do."

Jacob stood there tongue-tied, shifting his feet nervously.

She waited. "Well?"

"I have a brother…"

She saw what was coming. "If I were you, I'd really think about it before I invited him to stay here, Jake. It could really cause problems with your father. It might not be the right thing for your brother. It's always best to try your hardest to work your problems out before you decide to run away from them."

Jacob nodded.

"However, if you decided that it was the best thing and your brother wanted to join you here, I wouldn't prevent it. You two could share a room. We have another vacancy, as you know."

Craig had departed earlier in the day.

"Yes, ma'am… there's one thing, though."

"What is it?"

"He… he's in a wheelchair."

Lynn raised her eyebrows in surprise. She considered it. "We could shuffle people around and work out a room on the main floor. Though there isn't good access to a washroom…"

"Oh," Jacob felt his face heat up. He looked away. "He doesn't need it."

Lynn studied him. "Jake, why don't you sit down and tell me about your brother?"

"Yes, ma'am…" He sat and shifted around, anxious. "What do you want me to tell you?"

"How handicapped is he?"

"He's… he's like a quadriplegic… he wouldn't be able to work. But I'd put up for him and I'm used to taking care of him."

"Wouldn't he need special medical care?"

"Not if I was taking care of him."

"What arrangement is he in right now?"

"I guess Dad is… but last time Dad took care of him, he ended up in hospital."

"Does he have any control of himself? Can he communicate?"

"I… I guess not. They say he's a vegetable." Jacob saw her look and hurried on. "There's nothing wrong with his mind, he's as smart as I am. He's just… stuck in a body that doesn't work."

"He can't communicate?"

"Well, not like you do… but I can tell, I know what he wants."

"He can't talk?"

"No, ma'am."

"Does he signal? Do you have some kind of system worked out?"

Jacob hesitated, trying to give an honest answer. He and Nicholas communicated, but there wasn't a system. No code. He could just tell.

"Um… no, not really."

"I think he would be better off in the care of some other institution."

Jacob couldn't believe it. That was why he had come here, on Father TJ's suggestion that they would be able to take in Nicholas. Jacob put his face in his hands, trying to hold the emotions in. Lynn didn't say anything for a while.

"Jake, I said I wouldn't prevent you from bringing him and I won't. You know what kind of responsibility his care entails, what cost, and how your family functions far better than I could. If you feel that it's the best thing, I won't stop you. But please think it through. You wouldn't be here all day; what if something went wrong while you were gone?"

"It wouldn't… He's alone all day at home."

"Not completely alone, surely."

Jacob nodded. "I'm the only one who takes care of him, usually."

"I can't imagine how you could have left."

"I… I just couldn't stay."

As they refilled their coffee cups, Thompson saw Jaslow focus suddenly at something beyond the bullpen. "Looks like trouble."

Thompson turned to see what he was talking about. Duke was barreling towards them. And he was not happy. "Where is he?"

"Where's who?" Jaslow raised an eyebrow. He took a drink of his coffee.

"Don't play games with me! The other boy! Nicholas. What gives you any right to take him away like that?"

"He was sick. Had some good bruises, too. Did you give him those?"

"Bruises?" Spittle flew from Duke's mouth. "He's so sensitive a fly landing on him would bruise him. Where is he?"

Jaslow opened his mouth to speak. Thompson held up a hand and shook his head, taking over. "Duke… why don't we go sit down—"

"I'll stand. You tell me what's going on here, Jack—I thought you were a friend! I trusted you!"

Thompson kept his voice calm, trying not to betray his nervousness at what Duke might do if pushed too far. But they were in the middle of the police station. There were plenty of people around to help if Duke blew.

"Duke… both boys were being abused."

"What are you talking about?" Duke demanded.

"I'm talking about hitting them, slapping them around, even breaking bones! I'm talking about Jacob in the dead of winter coatless, catching pneumonia. Nicholas lying in bed with only a sheet on, covered with bruises. What do you think I'm talking about?"

"I'm surprised at you," Duke growled. "I thought you had more sense."

"I've read those files. They paint a pretty bleak picture. You want to know why Jacob ran away? You're an abusive parent."

Duke's face was flushed red with anger, but he struggled to control himself. He kept his voice to a low growl. "I never gave Jake anything he didn't deserve. And as for his brother—the only time I ever touched him in my life was to feed and clean him!"

"Sorry, Duke. You won't be getting either of those kids back."

"Oh, won't I? To think I trusted you, Thompson! I trusted you with my kids. I never trusted anyone with even knowing about Nicholas before! And you do this to me! I'll get them back, both of them. Those kids are all I have. They're the only thing left of Sandra, and I'll have them, whether you like it or not!"

"Did you know there was a knife in your sink, Donell?" Jaslow inquired.

Duke looked at him, his brows drawing down. "So what if there was? A man's entitled to utensils when he eats, isn't he?"

"A butcher knife."

"What about it?"

"One with blood on it, human blood. Jacob's type."

Duke did a double-take. He shrugged, eyes narrow. "So maybe he cut himself."

"You're not getting those boys back, Donell."

"Just watch me," Duke growled.

He walked away.

Cassy was stretched out on the bed that used to be Craig's. Jacob was nervous, listening to the sounds of the house. She wasn't supposed to be in his room. That was against the rules.

"I worry about people," Cassy commented.

Jacob looked at her, not sure where she was going with this. "Who?"

"Oh… everybody." Jacob waited. *Everybody* was a pretty big target and since Cassy had brought the subject up, he assumed that she had someone more specific in mind. "Pal, I guess…"

Jacob nodded his encouragement. "What about Pal?"

"Nothing. Just…"

Jacob looked away from Cassy, out the window. It was too intense looking at her eyes, her fair, innocent face.

"Did you know… he takes drugs?"

Jacob looked back at her. He shook his head. "No. But… lots of people do."

"My daddy did."

"Did your dad die? Is that why you're here?"

"No. He's in prison. He stole and did drugs… and other stuff. He's in prison where he can't hurt anybody or do any of those things…"

"Oh. I'm sorry."

"Yeah. Me too. But Pal… he doesn't hurt anyone… except himself."

"Because he takes drugs?"

Cassy got up and paced restlessly across the room. "He said it doesn't hurt anybody. But it's not good for him. And… he's getting worse…"

"You should tell someone," Jacob suggested.

"I don't want to get him in trouble. And it's not like it's crack. That stuff is bad. He just takes uppers. Because they make him feel better. Not so depressed."

Jacob thought about the worn, tired look that Pal perpetually wore. He certainly was not a happy-looking person. Jacob wondered what his story was. "If he went to a doctor about it, they could give him some kind of antidepressant. Instead of street drugs. That would be better."

Cassy shook her head. "He says he's tried all that before. Nothing ever worked. He says they put him on a lot of different stuff when he was in school. But it just messed him up."

Jacob frowned. "Isn't he still going to school?"

Miss Teresa had indicated that everybody had to go to school or earn their keep. Most of the kids went to school. Jacob was pretty sure Pal didn't work. He headed off at the same time as everybody else who went to school.

Cassy chewed on her lip. "That's what they think."

"But he doesn't? Where does he go, then?"

She sat back on the bed, chewing on her thumbnail. "Just... around... not everybody goes to school."

"You don't either?" Jacob guessed. He didn't like the idea of her hanging out all day with an older boy, a dope user at that. She was going to get hurt. "You should, Cassy. Get an education."

Cassy shrugged. "You don't."

"I did until I turned sixteen. And I've got a job. What would they say?"

"Who?"

"Lynn... Teresa..."

"Well, Teresa wouldn't like it. But who cares?" She stopped chewing her nail and looked at it. "I'm worried about Pal."

"Yeah. Is that why you hang around with him?"

"What do you do about it? You can't talk people out of taking drugs."

"No... I'm not sure what you can do. If he's depressed and won't take a prescription... what else can you suggest?"

Cassy nodded and flopped down on the bed again.

Jacob hesitated at the door. There was a knot in his stomach, a premonition that something bad was going to happen. It was a cold day, so he was wearing his Wildcat jacket. He needed his jacket to get to work and he couldn't be late for work. He'd just have to go and hope that none of the Blackbirds gang were around. He had seen some of them in the neighborhood and they had left him alone—but that was when he wasn't proclaiming himself a member of another gang. He'd just have to hope that none of them were still out in the early morning, following their late-night revelries.

He was less than a block from the construction site when he saw the black-jacketed figure up ahead. His muscles tensed and he looked for a way to avoid the confrontation. It was obvious the boy saw Jacob, he was clearly walking straight towards him. In glancing around, he saw, out of the corner of his eye, another shape coming towards him from the right. It was not a chance confrontation with one gang member, he was being jumped by several. They'd probably been tailing him for blocks. Jacob hurried more quickly towards the boy approaching from the front in order to be done with him before the others reached him.

"I think you're off your turf," the Blackbird said when they were close enough.

"I'm not here as a Wildcat," Jacob returned evenly. He didn't figure he'd be able to talk it out, and he didn't want to delay until the other boy reached him, but he had to try.

"You're out of your territory."

The boy on his right must have run partway because suddenly he was there beside them. "Trouble?" he said casually, as if it was a chance meeting.

"This cat's here to cause trouble," the first remarked.

"That true, cat?"

"I'm working at the Daventry site, just bridging over 'til I find somewhere to settle. I'm just going to work."

"You're wearing your jacket."

"Only one I got," Jacob stripped it off, even though he knew it would solve nothing at this point. He didn't want it restricting his movements while he was fighting. He let his breath out slowly, watching the vapor form in the crisp air, and waited.

"You're still a Wildcat."

"I ain't lookin' for trouble."

"Sure you are, cat, or you wouldn't be here."

In spite of knowing it was a set-up, he didn't expect what happened next. They must have panicked, decided that they might not be able to overcome him by sheer muscle. There was a loud crack like a backfire and a sudden, cold numbness in Jacob's shoulder, followed by a flare of pain.

Jacob whirled around to locate the shooter. He had approached from the left, Jacob's blind side.

In a few seconds, he reached the third boy. He wrenched the gun out of the other boy's hand and hit him across the jaw with it in one motion, then whirled back around to face the other two—the other three, for they had been joined by yet another Blackbird.

As Jacob moved for the closest one, another jumped on his back, trying to get a hold around his neck; Jacob flipped him off and he hit the pavement with enough force to knock him unconscious. Jacob reached for the other boy again.

A knife flashed in the sun and Jacob knocked him down before he could do any damage. The last boy didn't need a further demonstration of Jacob's fighting ability and bolted. Jacob looked around carefully for any other Blackbirds and picked up his jacket. He walked onto the construction site and headed into the trailer.

"Heard shots," Pat commented, not looking up to see who it was. "Any excitement?"

"You got a first aid kit?" Jacob asked quietly.

Pat looked up in surprise. Jacob's arm was bloody. He fingered the hole in his shirt. He stripped it off, and touched a surface cut across his stomach gingerly. The boy with the knife had managed to touch him. But it was not deep, hardly even bleeding. Pat stood up and motioned Jacob into a chair as he got the first aid kit.

"Bullet still in there?"

Jacob craned his neck, trying to inspect the injury.

"I think it went through."

He tried to help Pat bandage the injuries, holding the gauze pads in place and waiting for the bleeding to stop. Pat remained silent for a while, his eyes taking in the many other scars Jacob sported.

"I thought you said you didn't fight."

"Met up with the locals," Jacob explained, gesturing to his jacket. Pat looked puzzled for a moment, then nodded his understanding.

"I see." Pat shifted, trying to keep steady pressure on the shoulder wound, which was still oozing blood. "I'll have someone run you up to the hospital."

Jacob shook his head. He suddenly caught sight of the clock above the desk. "I gotta get to work, I'm late clocking in."

"You can't work like that!"

"Why not?"

Pat was shocked. "You're hurt!"

"I've worked with worse... I—I don't wanna lose this job," he pleaded.

"Listen, Jake, take a holiday. Come back in three weeks when that's healed up. There will still be a job here for you."

Jacob's head spun.

It was happening again. He was going to lose another job. Teresa at Sunset had made it clear that he was expected to hold down a job or stay in school, or he'd be kicked out.

He had to have a place to bring Nicholas.

A lump in his throat, Jacob stood up and struggled to pull his t- shirt on again. Pat helped him. He pulled on the jacket in spite of the danger of running into more Blackbirds on the way home. He was already shivering with cold that started deep down in his middle.

Jacob walked out without another word.

Thompson looked up as Jaslow approached his desk and sat down.

Jaslow noticed his frustrated expression. "What's wrong?"

"Nicholas has already been returned to Duke."

Jaslow shook his head in disbelief. "How did that happen?"

"Somewhere up the chain of command, like always. Somebody gave an order and it was followed." Thompson's lips pressed together into a thin line. "Duke was by to say that he was giving us another chance with Jacob, but that if anything happened, we'd be off the case."

Jaslow sat down and sipped his coffee, passing a second cup across to Thompson. "I suppose they could take us off the case. But they can't control what we do outside work time."

"That would mean working double-time. I couldn't do it for long."

"You haven't taken your vacation yet."

Thompson opened his mouth to protest, then closed it and nodded. "If it comes to that."

Jaslow tipped his chair back slightly, making the springs squeak. "By the way, Mace was released yesterday. He lawyered up and they couldn't hold him any longer on the weapons charge."

"Yeah. Duke mentioned it."

Jacob walked back towards Sunset slowly to get his bike. He kept his eyes open for any further Blackbirds but didn't see any. What was he going to do? He wasn't going to be able to stay at Sunset unless he had a job. He had to support not only himself, but Nicholas as well. He'd promised that Sunset wouldn't have any extra expenses because of him and he knew that Nicky's food and medical supplies could get expensive. Not to mention any emergency care if he had a crisis.

The dressing on his shoulder felt soggy. Jacob had thought the bleeding had stopped, but it obviously hadn't. It felt like it was soaking into his shirt as well.

Larry might know of a job opening. Even if Billy didn't have anything, Larry might know about some other sites that Jacob could check out. Jacob had been at Larry's with the gang several times. He reached his bike and pulled on his helmet.

On top of everything else whirling around his head, it seemed like there was something wrong with his motorcycle. Jacob couldn't seem to keep it straight, it kept pulling off to the side, making him weave back and forth.

By the time he got to Larry's street, Jacob was dangerously weak and dizzy. He pulled into the driveway back behind the apartment, put down the kickstand, and steadied himself on the handlebars, waiting for a wave of nausea and vertigo to pass.

That's how Larry's neighbor discovered Jacob. Slumped over the handlebars, with blood soaking his shirt and jacket, dripping down the chrome of the bike. Hank, the neighbor, wasn't a Wildcat, but he knew Larry was. Jacob was too big for Hank to move by himself. He called Larry at work. Larry explained to Billy that there was an emergency and he'd be back as soon as he could. Larry was steady, Billy knew he wasn't the kind to leave at the drop of a hat, so he let Larry go.

Larry and Hank managed to lift Jacob between them. They got him into the apartment and onto the couch. Between them and Maggie, Larry's girlfriend, they held an around-the-clock vigil watching him. Not a gang chick, Maggie was a nurse at the hospital, which came in handy when a Wildcat needed medical care.

Chapter Thirty-Four

Jacob woke slowly and for a while he was restless and hot and uncertain where he was. A hand grasped his arm and Jacob jerked back in a panic.

"Shh, easy man," a voice said gently.

Jacob didn't move. The hand grasped his wrist and held him. Jacob opened his eyes. They were sticky and blurred for a few minutes, and then his vision started to clear.

"Larry?" His voice was hoarse.

"Hey buddy, you okay?"

"I made it."

"Yeah." Larry was sitting on a chair next to the couch. He leaned over, feeling Jacob's forehead. "How're you feeling?"

"Okay."

"Want some grub?"

Jacob thought about it. He didn't feel exactly hungry. He felt weak and empty, like an engine on its last fumes of gas. But there was no nausea.

"Sure, I guess."

Larry left Jacob to get him something. Maggie and Hank were both around. Jacob kept his eyes down, trying to avoid talking to them. Larry was back a few minutes later with a warmed-up bowl of canned soup. He sat down on the edge of the bed and watched Jacob take it shakily.

"What happened? How'd you manage to get yourself shot?"

"Blackbirds." Jacob recounted what had happened.

Larry nodded. "There were cops asking about you at work. You won't be safe here once they find out I'm a Wildcat. They've already checked out Sarin and some of the other guys."

"I gotta go anyway," Jacob agreed.

He stopped talking as Maggie approached the bed. She smiled and exchanged glances with Larry. "Glad your fever broke. You must have had real wild dreams," she commented, "you were delirious."

Jacob looked at Larry. "Did I... say anything?"

"A lot more than you're saying now," Maggie teased. At Jacob's look, she hastened to reassure him. "Most of the time we couldn't tell what you were saying... you talked some about your mom and dad."

"Some about the beating that put you into hospital, too," Larry supplied.

Jacob gulped. Duke had warned him never to talk about the Stars and he didn't intend to. But if he gave something away while he was delirious...

"I was off my head," he warned. "Just a bunch of crazy talk."

Larry raised an eyebrow and didn't comment.

When Larry had gone to bed and Hank had gone home, Jacob got up and put on his now-clean shirt and jacket. As he went through the kitchen, Larry's phone vibrated on the counter where it was plugged in. Jacob looked over at it to see Sarin's name and a text message displayed on the screen before going black again.

Going to find some excitement in Maplewood. Taking some of the guys.

Jacob wondered briefly how the tough motorcycle gang would do at roughing it without the conveniences of the city. He wrote a note of thanks to Larry on the back of a utility bill envelope, hesitated a moment before signing it, then quietly let himself out.

Larry woke up in the morning with a severe hangover. He had drunk far too much the night before, celebrating Jacob's recovery. He squinted in the bright sunlight. Maggie was long gone to the hospital. He shook his head to stop it from pounding. It didn't stop. It took a few more crashes to realize that there was someone at the door. Larry got up and headed for the door. It sounded like someone was ready to break right through.

"Open up, Enrik, we know you're in there!"

Larry unbolted the door slowly, wondering thickly who the 'we' was. When the bolt clicked back, the door flew open and men swarmed in.

A warrant was shoved in front of his face and Larry realized belatedly what was going on—they were there looking for Black. He followed one of the cops into the living room. Everything was in place and there was no sign of Black or that he had ever been there. No untidy blanket. No bloodstained bandages.

Larry sighed with relief and went back into the kitchen. He went to the fridge and took out a bottle of beer. There was a note on the back of an envelope underneath the cell phone. Larry picked it up, but one of the cops snatched it from his hand before he could read it. The policeman read it and handed it back.

Thanks for everything. Sorry I had to leave. BJ

Larry grinned. B for Black and J for Jacob. It made perfect sense to Larry, but wouldn't clue in the cops.

"Who's BJ?" the cop questioned.

"A friend," Larry was hoarse. He took another swallow of the beer. Normally, he would have considered it too early to start drinking, but it was a day off and he needed something to steady his nerves. He watched the proceedings with interest.

One of the cops saw Larry grinning. "What is it you find so amusing?" he snarled.

"What exactly are you looking for?"

"Jacob Donell. When did he leave here?"

"Donell? I don't know if I know a—"

"Cut the games. Jacob Donell. You work with him. He's a Wildcat—a Kitten."

"Donell… oh, yeah." Larry faked remembering. "Big, dark-haired kid, right? But Billy fired him almost three weeks ago. He hasn't been around. What'd he do?"

"Runaway."

"Runaways always get this much attention?" Larry inquired.

"Listen, you do your job, and leave us to do ours."

Jaslow sat down at his desk and thumped down a stack of papers.

"Nothing," he muttered, staring at the stack. "I was sure we'd get something from Mace or Enrik. But Mace has dropped out of sight. Enrik… there wasn't even anything at his apartment that we could hold him on. I was sure Jacob would be there—when we realized he was a Wildcat and worked with Jacob…" He snorted, leaning back in his chair. "Everywhere we look it's a dead end."

"Do you still think he's a runaway?" Thompson asked.

"I'm beginning to wonder. He tells no one where he's going, takes nothing with him, and there's no trace of him, no trail."

"But there's no ransom note, no sign of foul play."

At that point, Duke walked up to the desk and laid down a traffic violations ticket.

"I got that in the mail today. It was so bizarre, I thought you should see it."

It was a photo radar ticket of a motorcycle license plate that must be Jacob's. Thompson realized that Duke didn't know his son had a motorcycle.

"Pull up a chair."

Duke looked at Thompson for a moment, brows drawn down, then sat. The chair squealed in protest.

"Have you ever heard of the Wildcats?" Thompson asked.

"Sure, a motorcycle gang. Busted them in vice a few times."

"Jacob is in that gang. This is his motorcycle." Thompson tapped the ticket.

"Since when does he have a bike?" Duke was incredulous.

"We'd have to check the registration date."

Duke stared at Thompson in disbelief.

"What's the date of the ticket?" Jaslow asked.

Duke looked at it. "Last Thursday. The day he disappeared."

Jaslow opened his notebook and wrote it down. "I'll tell you if we find anything."

"How long has he been in that gang?"

"We're not sure. Like I said, we'll tell you if there's a lead."

Duke scowled and stomped off. Thompson sighed, knowing that if they ever did catch up with Jacob, the boy was going to be in deep trouble.

Chapter Thirty-Five

SAMMY WOKE UP, HIS head hazy and confused. He blinked his eyes and looked around, finding himself not on the kitchen floor with his blanket, but at the gang's crib. He couldn't remember going to sleep the night before. Had something happened, or had he just fallen asleep at the end of a long, busy day? Sammy stretched and rubbed his eyes, trying to remember what day it was and what had happened the previous day.

He was stiff with cold and had no blanket, which suggested that he had not intended to fall asleep in the chair. When he turned around in the chair and put his feet to the floor, he realized with a shock that he had bare feet. He pulled his feet back up onto the chair and looked at them, frowning. No shoes. No socks. The rest of his clothes were all in place. What could he have done with his shoes?

Sammy scanned the room, looking for his missing shoes. The remains of the gang's latest revelries lay around the floor. Discarded bottles and food containers, various bits of clothing, and even some of the gang members themselves lay every which way around the room. Sammy got quietly to his feet and made a slow circuit, looking for his shoes. Still no luck. Sammy was getting frantic as awareness continued to trickle into his consciousness. He was supposed to be going on the YMCA camp. He couldn't go on the camp if he had no shoes. He'd packed his school backpack the day before so that everything would be ready to go. Marisol had even given him a couple of granola bars.

Zed was on one of the couches. He awakened and watched Sammy. "What's up, little man?"

Sammy looked at him, the panic welling up from his guts, tears threatening to fall from his eyes. "M-m-my sh-shoes," he gestured at his feet.

"What shoes?" Zed laughed.

"Th-th-they're gone!"

"Yep, I'd say you're right about that."

"I n-n-need sh-shoes!" Sammy insisted.

"I don't think mine are gonna fit you," Zed said unhelpfully.

Zed closed his eyes again. Sammy went back to the chair that he had slept in and looked again for his shoes, though he knew there was no point. They weren't there or he would have found them the first time.

Unsure what to do, Sammy headed for home. Maybe he had left his shoes there for some reason. He picked his way down the sidewalk, avoiding as much of the gravel and broken glass as he could, but still ending up getting bits embedded in his skin. He stopped a few times to brush the debris off. When he got in the front door, he looked around for his shoes. They generally did not leave their shoes at the door, but it was a possibility. Sammy's shoes were not there. He glanced in the kitchen. Everyone was still asleep. No coffee on yet. Sammy took a quick look at everyone's feet, to make sure that none of the other kids had taken his shoes. Or maybe he'd given them to someone. He couldn't remember.

Sammy went upstairs to their room. He knocked on the door before going in and poked his head through the doorway. Marisol stirred sleepily. Sammy saw with a sinking feeling in his stomach that Hector was there too.

"Sammy?" His mother groaned, shifting and looking at him before closing her eyes again. "What's wrong? Are you sick?"

"He didn't come home again last night," Hector pointed out. He squinted at Sammy. "You just getting in now?"

Sammy shifted his feet and looked down at them. They were dirty from the dust of the street.

"It's that camp today," Marisol said. "What time is it? Are you leaving already?"

Sammy sniffled and swallowed, his nose starting to leak. "M-m-my sh-shoes." His throat was tight and hot, his voice rising in tone.

Hector sat up, swinging his feet over the side of the bed. He looked grumpily at Sammy, a 'V' forming between his eyebrows. Sammy took a step back, ready to run. Though how far could he run without shoes…? Hector looked down at his feet.

"Where are your shoes?"

Sammy sniffled again.

Marisol sat up, rubbing her eyes. "What?" She looked at his bare feet and shook her head. "What happened to your shoes?"

Sammy shrugged his shoulders. "D-don't kn-now."

"How can you not know what happened to your shoes?" Hector barked. "Are you drunk?"

Sammy shook his head.

Marisol looked at the clock. "You're supposed to be at the YMCA in an hour. Have you got all your stuff ready to go?"

Sammy just stared at her. How was he supposed to go anywhere without shoes?

Hector got out of bed and walked toward Sammy scratching his chest, matted with hair as thick and curly as a monkey's. Sammy took another step back. Hector stopped at the closet and pushed clothes out of the way to look at the floor.

"You've got old shoes in here. You can wear those."

Sammy stepped a little closer to see what shoes were there. Amongst the mess of Hector's and Marisol's shoes, with a pair or two of Bunny's thrown in, he found an old pair of Spiderman sneakers from the year before.

"T-t-too s-small."

"Well, there's nothing else here for you to wear. You've got to have something. There's no time or money to get you new ones."

"B-b-b…" Sammy tried to swallow his tears and not let any leak from his eyes. He couldn't even *fit* into last year's shoes. They looked tiny.

"Sit down and stop your blubbering," Hector ordered.

Sammy obediently sat down on the floor, gulping. He tried bravely to keep his emotions contained. Hector picked up the Spiderman shoes and loosened the laces. He looked determinedly at Sammy's feet.

"No point in putting socks on, they'll just make the shoes tighter."

Sammy looked at the old shoes. They were cheap canvas sneakers. Maybe they would stretch a little with Sammy's feet. Hector grabbed Sammy's right foot and slipped the shoe on over his toes. Then he started to pull on the back of the shoe to force it on over Sammy's foot. Sammy jerked back.

"Ow!"

Hector grabbed his foot again and held onto it more tightly as he pulled on the back edges of the shoe and tried to stretch it all the way around Sammy's foot. Sammy's toes were cramped against the end of the shoe and Hector's rough fingers chafed at Sammy's heel, trying to tuck it into the back. Finally, it was on. Sammy reached for it.

"Ow, it h-hurts!"

"Shut up," Hector ordered. "And leave it on."

He grabbed Sammy's left foot, and proceeded to repeat the process, mashing Sammy's too-big foot into the tiny shoe. When he succeeded in getting the second one on, Hector sat back on his heels, looking pleased with himself.

"There. That will do you."

"N-no."

Hector clapped him across the side of the head. "Don't talk back to me! You guys are taking the bus to your campsite. These will be just fine. We'll see what else we can get you when you get back."

The tears were falling down Sammy's cheeks now, his ear ringing from the blow.

"Tie them up," Hector ordered.

"P-p-please!"

"What, you think there's time to go shopping before you have to be there? You'd better grab your bag and get on your way."

Sammy bent over to tie the laces, tears dripping onto his hands.

Marisol was looking down at Sammy's feet doubtfully. "Don't you think you could drive him?" she suggested. "He'd better not do too much walking in those. They're pretty small."

Hector glowered at her. "You baby the boy too much. He's got to toughen up." He shook his head at Sammy. "Listen to him blubbering over having to wear old shoes."

Sammy sniffled and snorted, trying to quell his tears.

Hector looked at the clock. "I've got to get dressed. If you want me to drive you over, you go get the coffee started."

Sammy got to his feet. Standing was even worse than sitting with the shoes on. They pinched so badly Sammy half-expected them to burst open with the pressure of his feet on the inside.

"They'll stretch," Hector said. "Walk around in them a bit to break them in. Go on now. My coffee."

Sammy wobbled out of the room and minced down the stairs, holding onto the rail all the way down. None of the others who slept on the kitchen floor were stirring yet, so Sammy moved around them as carefully as he could, starting the coffee brewing. Even his quiet movements awakened Tiny, and he sat up against the wall yawning without covering his mouth, showing off a fine view of his tonsils.

"What's'amatter?"

Sammy was still trying to stop sniffling and every step hurt. He looked down at the old sneakers.

"L-l-lost my sh-shoes."

Tiny stared at his feet, then looked up at Sammy's face, watching him shift tenderly from one foot to the other waiting for the coffee to brew. Tiny took a long sniff and wiped his nose with the back of his hand.

"Phew. Your ma smoking up there? You smell like weed."

Sammy pulled his shirt up to his nose and took a whiff. He coughed. He could probably get high just from smelling his clothing. Sammy couldn't remember what had happened the night before, but obviously he had either been smoking or hanging around while others were. Maybe that had something to do with why he couldn't remember.

It was too late to go up to the room and change. Hector would be coming down the stairs any minute for his coffee. Sammy motioned to Tiny.

"T-trade m-me?"

Tiny paused only an instant before shucking off his shirt and tossing it to Sammy. Sammy pulled his off and threw it at Tiny. Hector's heavy footsteps were on the stairs. Sammy pulled the warm shirt on as quickly as he could, jamming a finger as he missed an arm-hole. Tiny pulled Sammy's shirt inside his cocoon, pulling the blanket back up to his neck. He put on a sleepy, bleary-eyed expression, and didn't move as Sammy finished struggling into Tiny's shirt and Hector made it into the kitchen.

Sammy pulled the pot out from under the machine, even though it hadn't finished dripping yet, and filled a big mug for Hector. Hector took the cup and cuffed Sammy's ear, his nose wrinkling at the smell of the coffee dripping onto the hot plate.

"You're burning it, stupid! You pulled it out before it was done."

Blinking rapidly, Sammy put the pot back onto the hot plate to catch the rest of the coffee as it dripped.

"Moron," Hector scoffed. "Get in the car if you want me to drive you."

Chapter Thirty-Six

J ACOB LOOKED AT THE house for a few minutes before going up to it. Duke's car was not there, so the house should be empty, but he wanted to be sure. He went to the door and slid his key into the lock. He opened the door and slipped into the house and looked around. It was possible Duke could have left a girlfriend behind. Or the housekeeper might be there. But he checked the front room and Duke's bedroom and there didn't appear to be anyone there. He went into his bedroom and picked Nicholas up off the bed.

"We're getting out of here, buddy. I've got a place we can stay, they said you could come. We'll never come back here."

He looked into Nicky's shining eyes and smiled.

"You know I wouldn't leave you here."

Jacob laid Nicholas back down to clean and change him. He looked at the hospital bracelet still attached to Nicky's arm. "You were in hospital again? I'm sorry…"

Jacob cut the bracelet off and strapped Nicholas into the wheelchair. He grabbed a duffle bag from Duke's closet and dumped out his gym gear in order to fill it with Nicky's necessary medical equipment. He stroked Nicky's hair, hardly believing that he was actually going to take Nicholas out of there. To go and never come back. Neither of them would ever have to put up with Duke's abuse again.

He looked into Nicky's eyes. "It's okay, isn't it? You don't want to stay?" He studied Nicky's face until he was sure what he saw there, then breathed out. "Yeah. Let's go."

Jacob retrieved several more items to add to the duffle bag. Wrestling the wheelchair down the front steps wasn't usually such an ordeal, but Jacob's barely-healing shoulder presented problems and he worried he was going to reopen the wound. Clenching his teeth, he lowered the wheelchair down one step at a time, until they were at the bottom.

Jacob called a taxi to pick them up a few blocks from the house and drop them off a little way away from Sunset. He wheeled Nicholas slowly up the walk. It was early morning and Jacob tried to enter quietly. It wasn't that he was trying to sneak in; he just didn't want to disturb anyone. If he'd wanted to sneak in, he wouldn't have waited so late.

Jacob was stiff from the cool morning air and his limp was very pronounced. His shoulder and arm were throbbing and he had a hard time steering the chair straight. But finally he was in the door. They were safe.

One of the boys came bounding down the stairs with a football under his arm. "Jake's back!" he shouted over his shoulder.

Lynn heard and came out to see him. "Jake, where've you been?"

"I was sick," Jacob said. "Didn't want to bother you."

Lynn's eyes lingered on Nicholas. "I moved the girls up to your room to leave the one down here for you if you decided to bring your brother."

"Thanks."

"You aren't looking very good. Lie down and rest for a while. We'll get things straightened out later."

Jacob went into the new downstairs bedroom and put Nicholas by the window in the sun. He was tired and worn out and Lynn's suggestion to lie down was a good one. He stretched out on the bed and started telling Nicholas about all that had happened since he'd left with Sarin. He was asleep before he could finish the account.

Teresa was heading towards the bedroom when Lynn caught her. "Leave Jake alone for a while. He's not feeling well and he's brought his brother with him."

"He brought his *brother*?" Teresa's cheeks flushed a dusky red and her penciled eyebrows rose.

"That's right. We talked about it before and I told him that if he felt it was the right thing, he could."

"He's just using us," Teresa said.

"No, I don't think he is. He's working and trying to look after his brother. He's not just relying on us to take care of him. Please leave him alone for a while."

"All right." Teresa sulked.

"I'll ask Jake about his brother later on and we'll introduce him to the others. He's handicapped, but Jake says he can take care of Nicholas himself, so don't bother him about it."

Teresa shrugged and walked off the other direction, an ugly scowl on her face.

Cassy poked her head in Pal's door. "Hey. Are you okay?"

Pal startled and looked at her. "Yeah… fine. Why?"

Cassy stepped into the room. "I don't know… you just seem like you're really down this week… even more than usual."

He stared out the window, which looked across the alley to the back of the brick building behind Sunset House. Not a very inspiring view.

"Pal?"

He turned and looked back at her, forcing a tired smile. "I'm fine, Cassy."

"What's wrong?" she asked, not believing it for a minute.

Pal rubbed his temples. "Nothing, I said I'm fine."

"But you're not. Do you want me to get Lynn? You could tell her what's wrong."

"No!" Pal held up his hand. "Don't get her. I can handle it myself."

Cassy raised her brows.

"I'm just… I'm tired, that's all," Pal said.

"No, you're not. You're upset about something… you're really down. Right?"

Pal shrugged, sighing in exasperation. "Yeah, I am. And I don't want to talk about it. So just leave me alone."

"What are you down about? What's going on?"

"It's just my life, Cass. You can't change that. I'm just… tired of living this life. No family. No home. I miss… what my life shoulda been like. Even if it never was."

Cassy wandered over to sit on the bed. "I miss my daddy," she offered.

"Yeah. I know."

"Do you miss your daddy?"

"No… not really… he wasn't… he wasn't ever there for us. And my mom died when I was just little. I don't really remember her. Then… my brothers." He paused, eyes distant. "It's my brothers I miss. But I had to get out of there."

"Yeah…" Cassy nodded. "I wish I had brothers. What were they like?"

"They looked after me, since I had no mom and my dad didn't care, they were the ones who looked after me, making sure that I got fed and went to school dressed for the weather and all. They looked out for me."

"How long has it been…?"

"Years," Pal admitted. "I probably don't remember the way it really was anymore. It's probably more a fairy tale memory than the way it really happened."

"If they looked after you, why did you run away?"

"I had to get out. I just… they couldn't protect me all the time and they had to go away… and I just had to get out of there."

"And you don't know where they are now?"

"No. They wouldn't even remember me if they saw me."

"I bet they would," Cassy argued.

Pal shrugged. He picked at a hole in his jeans. They could hear voices on the floor below, coming up through the air vents.

"Did you hear Jake came back?" Pal asked Cassy.

"Jake's back?" Cassy's face lit up. "No, I didn't know. I'll go see him!"

She left, pulling the door shut again behind her. Pal was left feeling even emptier than he had been to begin with.

There was a quiet knock on the door and Jacob roused himself to answer it, heart pounding. He got up and put his hand on his throbbing shoulder, trying to quiet it before answering the door. He glanced at Nicholas and then opened the door. It was Cassy. Jacob let her in.

"I missed you, Jake! Where were you?"

Jacob smiled a little, shy. "Thanks, Cassy. Say, uh… do they keep a first aid kit here?"

Cassy frowned and went to get it. She got back and handed it to Jake and sat on the empty bed. She gazed at Nicholas and back at Jacob.

"This is my brother."

"What's his name?"

"Nicholas."

"Hi, Nicholas," Cassy greeted.

"He can understand you, but he can't answer," Jacob explained.

"Oh."

Cassy looked awkward, unsure of what to do or say. Jacob tried to make things more comfortable for her. "Anything interesting happening lately?" He went over to the door to shut it.

"Well, the day you left, there was some shooting—that gang got into a fight and a couple of them got picked up by the cops."

Jacob didn't look up as he stripped his shirt off and tenderly peeled back his bandages to re-dress the wound. Cassy stared at him open-mouthed.

"That's from a bullet!"

"Yeah." Jacob looked briefly at her, wondering about her immediate recognition of a bullet wound.

"What from?" Cassy asked.

"You just said."

"No, I mean how did you get shot?"

"You just said."

"That gang?"

"Yeah."

"Does it hurt much?" Cassy got up to look at it, her voice sounding high and worried.

"Not much. Cassy—you won't tell anyone, will you?"

"But Jake…"

"Please, Cassy."

She didn't say anything for a while. "Okay," she said finally, "I won't."

Jacob finished bandaging the wounds and pulled a fresh shirt out of the dresser and put it on. He picked up the other one and considered the hole in it.

"Do you think anyone would realize this is a bullet hole?"

"They probably won't even notice. Teresa was mad when you didn't show up. What do you think she'll say?"

"I dunno."

Jacob sat down on the bed and sighed, rubbing tired eyes. "I don't know anymore, Cass. I'm just so tired…"

"You better rest now; then you can think better later."

She slipped out of the room, shutting the door behind her. Jacob lay down again, one hand pressed against his throbbing shoulder.

"She's nice," he said softly to Nicholas. "I like her a lot."

Thompson was awakened by the ringing phone. Janie stirred beside him, groaning. He picked it up and stumbled out of the room so that he wouldn't disturb her any further.

"Where is he?" Duke growled in Thompson's ear, without preamble.

"We haven't found him yet, Duke," Thompson said foggily, not understanding.

"I told you he was staying with me. You can't keep taking him out of my house or I'll have you fired!"

"What?"

"Nicholas! Where is he this time?"

Thompson rubbed his eyes, trying to focus on the conversation. "Nicholas. Nicholas is at home with you."

"You took him again!"

"I didn't, Duke."

"There are only so many places to put someone like him. How long do you think it will take me to find him?"

"*Nicholas* is missing now?"

"Yes! Because you took him!"

"No. We didn't. I'll send a crew out to the house to check for evidence."

Duke was silent, finally winding down. "You didn't take him?" he asked doubtfully.

"No."

"Then where is he?"

Teresa came in while Jacob was sitting on the edge of the bed talking to Nicholas.

"Well, Jake," she said immediately, "it was nice of you to inform us of your departure ahead of time." Her voice was heavy with sarcasm.

Jacob swallowed and looked at her with a sinking feeling in his stomach. He had obviously done something wrong. And now she was there to exact her retribution.

"It was kind of sudden," he said, shifting away from her, measuring her distance from Nicholas.

"Well, you know our rules." She stood over him, looking down at him as if he was a child or a naughty pet. "What do you think would be a suitable punishment?"

Jacob stared at her blankly. Whatever punishment Teresa thought he deserved, Jacob expected it immediately. He didn't expect her to discuss it.

There was a sound at the door and Jacob turned quickly to identify it. Lynn entered the room. She smiled reassuringly, but Jacob felt worse rather than better. Now it was two against one. Logically, he knew he was big enough to hurt them physically, to protect himself against them, but his heart beat wildly. He couldn't face any more torture and abuse. And Nicholas was there. He had to protect Nicholas and that meant that he couldn't run away. He wanted to get up and stand in front of Nicholas, to guard him, but Lynn and Teresa flanked him on either side.

"Why don't you tell us the whole story, Jake?" Lynn suggested.

"I was sick. I didn't want to bother you," Jacob explained. Acid rose in his throat. He felt like he was going to throw up.

"And…?"

"I… stayed with a friend a while… 'til I was a little better."

"I think he's telling the truth," Lynn assured Teresa. "You know he has been sick."

Jacob guessed that Lynn was the good cop in their good cop-bad cop ruse. She was there to make Jacob think that someone was on his side. To put him at ease, to persuade him to confide in her. And when he did, she would turn on him, attacking where he was most vulnerable. Jacob knew how it worked.

"I know no such thing!" Teresa snapped. "And it doesn't matter, he was supposed to tell us! He can't just take off like that. Skip curfew. Just disappear for days, making us worry about him. He's not working, he's not going to school. He's just trying to get a free ride."

"I'll work," Jacob protested. "They told me to go home… because I was sick. I still have a job."

Teresa sniffed, looking at him with narrowed eyes, projecting her belief that he was lying. "I think we should just turn him over to the police," Teresa said, her breath hissing through her teeth. "He's a malingerer. Incorrigible. If we search this room, we'd probably find drugs. Maybe stolen property. Who knows what else?"

Jacob looked around the room, panicking. The police? She didn't have anything to charge him with. But if she searched the room… she'd find the things he'd taken from home… she'd kick him out. She'd kick both of them out on the street. Even if she couldn't find anything to charge him with.

"Teresa," Lynn said in a cautioning tone.

Jacob's eyes jumped back to Lynn. She was the one that he had to watch out for. Teresa made it clear where she stood and what she planned to do. But Lynn… she pretended to be nice and then would move in with the attack when he turned his back on her. She was the one who would fake being nice and then sneak into his room and attack him while he slept.

"You don't know anything about this boy," Teresa pointed out. "He's got no history. No ID. No one to vouch for him. We don't have any idea where he has come from. What he did before he came here."

"I didn't do anything," Jacob said. His voice was cracking and he cleared his throat and tried to keep it even, like he was calm. Like he didn't have anything to hide. He knew it was a lie. They didn't know that he was on probation. That he'd been arrested for taking drugs. They didn't know that he was part of a motorcycle gang. If they found out any of those things, they would kick him out. They'd never let him stay.

"You're grounded," Teresa told Jacob in a growl. "Until I decide what to do and how to handle you, you will not leave this room. Is that understood? You leave it and I'll call the police. They know me. They won't put up with any nonsense."

With that done, she whirled around and stomped out the door. Jacob looked at Lynn, his heart practically bounding out of his chest it was beating so hard. He swallowed, tears prickling his eyes.

Lynn raised her eyebrows and shook her head. "I'll try to straighten it out," she sighed. "Until I do, please stay here to avoid any trouble. I don't think you're well enough to be running around yet anyway." She gave him a faint smile.

Jacob didn't know what to do or to say. He just stared at her. He was right back where he had started out. Duke had grounded him, had ordered him to stay in his room. And Jacob had run away. But he'd just run right back to the same situation. Again, he was trapped. Unable to go to work, to fend for himself. Unable to protect himself and Nicholas from Lynn and Teresa and the other house residents. One call to the police and he'd be dragged off to jail. Duke would have Nicholas again and would probably kill him within a couple of weeks.

"Just rest," Lynn advised in her soft voice. A voice that tried to camouflage the danger that Jacob was in. "We'll work it out. Teresa does tend to get a bit carried away sometimes."

She attempted to touch Jacob on the shoulder and he flinched away. It took all of his strength to keep his hands down and to not hit her, not to protect himself before she could hurt him. Lynn sighed and walked out of the room, closing the door behind her.

Jacob collapsed onto his bed, putting his face in his hands and sobbing, trying to catch his breath and calm himself down before the emotion could carry him away. He breathed hard, trying to stay strong. He couldn't give in to emotion and let down his guard. He couldn't be vulnerable. He had to stay in control. He wiped away the tears that had escaped his eyes and stood up.

"It was supposed to be safe," he told Nicholas, shaking his head. "This was supposed to be a safe place. But they're going to call the cops. And then Duke will come..."

Nicky's eyes were wide, alarmed.

Jacob opened the drawers of his dresser and pulled out his clothes. He stuffed them into his duffle bag. He carefully packed the other items that he had brought from the house. This was the end. He was running and he knew that it wasn't going to end well. He could see how he was just going to keep running from one trap into another.

There was no escape. There was no safe place. Not for him.

"I thought it was going to be okay here… I thought it would be all right… I'll find the Wildcats. Hide out as long as I can… They'll take care of you here. They'll make sure you don't get sick. If I'm not here, they won't call the police and Dad won't find you. He won't know where to look. He doesn't know about this place."

The door opened softly, without a knock. Jacob whipped around, panicked. "Oh—Cassy."

She walked slowly into the room, frowning. "Are you going somewhere, Jake?"

Jake glanced down at his bag and put it down on the dresser. He zipped it up to prevent her from seeing the contents, biting his lip to keep it from trembling. "I have to go, Cassy."

"Why? You just got back!"

"I just can't stay. It's not safe here."

"You're safe. Everyone is safe here."

Jacob shook his head. "I have to, Cass."

"What are you going to do?" Her brow wrinkled. Her eyes shone like she was going to cry.

"I can't tell you." He was silent for a moment, just breathing and trying to keep calm and think things through logically. "Cassy, I can't take Nicholas… you'll make sure they take care of him, won't you?"

"I'll try…"

"And you'll talk to him, won't you? He gets lonely when he doesn't have anyone to talk to him." Jacob couldn't keep his voice from cracking and rising a few notes.

"But… he can't talk, can he?" Cassy asked.

"No, but he understands. He still needs people to talk to him."

"Okay. I'll try…"

Neither of them said anything for a while.

"Are you going home?" Cassy asked at last.

"Never!" Jacob said vehemently. "I'll die before I go back there."

"When are you going?"

"Tonight." He looked down at his backpack.

"Where?"

"Maybe to the mountains." Jacob rubbed his eyes. "I haven't really figured it out yet. That's where the others are… maybe they'll know what to do."

"I'll… miss you."

"I'll miss you too."

Cassy threw her arms around Jacob and held on tightly. Jacob winced and started to sweat at the pain in his shoulder. After a moment, he pushed her gently away.

"I'll… see you later."

"Okay, Jake. Okay."

Cassy turned away from him, her lips quivering, and left the room. Jacob leaned back against the wall and groaned.

"I guess I'll go meet Sarin and the guys," he said at length, in a calm voice. "They'll take care of you here. It'll be okay. I'll come back… when I figure out what to do."

When it was dark and everything was still, Jacob finished feeding Nicholas his evening meal.

He hugged Nicholas and said goodbye with a lump in his throat.

Chapter Thirty-Seven

THOMPSON HANDED JASLOW A cup of coffee and they sat down. Thompson knew better than to say anything when Jaslow was doing paperwork—it meant things were getting desperate. After a few minutes, Jaslow looked up. He sighed and leaned his chair back.

"Okay. Square one, a kid disappears. What do we do first?"

"See if there's any reason for an abduction, homicide, or runaway," Thompson said promptly.

"Right. Now, abduction—his father's enemies. Homicide—the same, or someone doesn't want him to talk. Or Duke kills him in a rage or by accident. He's in a gang, vulnerable to street violence. Runaway—he's having a bad time at home, is fresh out of hospital, lost his job, and is on probation. Suicide also becomes a possibility. Now what?"

"Find out when he was last seen, check to see if he took anything. Ask around."

"No one knows anything."

"But then there's the bloody knife," Thompson pointed out. "And Nicholas disappearing."

The phone rang and Jaslow scowled. Then he answered it. "Hello… speaking, who's this?" His brows went up. "Uh-huh… yes, great. Where can I reach this man?" He grabbed a pen and scribbled a number and address down on the side of one of the documents he was reading. "Right… got it, thank you." He hung up and took a deep breath. "We just got a lead."

"Who was that?"

"Jacob's old boss. We turned him up a couple of days ago, but he couldn't give us anything. Anyway. He remembered just today that one of his buddies who heads another site phoned him about a boy he was thinking about hiring. A boy answering to Jacob's description. He is not exactly easy to mistake."

"How long ago did his friend call him?"

"Last Friday, he thinks."

"Great." Thompson looked at his watch. "I've got to head home. We'll pick this up first thing tomorrow?"

Jaslow nodded and pushed his papers to the side.

Thompson knocked on the trailer door and he and Jaslow entered. Pat looked up when the door opened.

"What can I do for you?"

"We're looking for a boy whom you may have employed here," Thompson said.

"His name?"

"Jacob Donell."

Pat pulled out a list of employees and ran his finger down the list. "Nope, no Donell."

"He may be going by another name."

"I don't do all the hiring here. I get a lot of men from other sites that I never even see. If you don't have the name he was hired under, I can't help you."

"He would have come on not very long ago and he used to be at Billy's Construction."

"Like I say, we have a large turnover here. What kind of work does he do?"

"He's sixteen. Big guy."

"Ah… Jake. Donovan," Pat supplied.

Thompson looked at Jaslow. "Donovan was his mother's name."

Jaslow displayed Jacob's mugshot to Pat. "Is this him?"

"Yeah, for sure. That's him. What do you want him for?"

"He's a runaway. Also broke probation."

"I see. He told me he wasn't in any trouble with the police, but… I'll get him for you." He looked at his employment list to see where Jacob was working and picked up a walkie-talkie. "Joey? Send Donovan over here if he's not busy."

There was a moment of radio silence and then the reply came back. "You gave him some time off, boss. What do you need?"

"Sorry, I forgot. I don't need anything. Thanks." He hung up and looked back at the officers. "I sent him off for a few weeks to recuperate from a gunshot wound."

"Oh?" Jaslow inquired.

"The shoulder was pretty bad, but it looked like he's been hurt worse before."

"What do you mean?"

"The kid's covered with scars. Bad gash across his throat and he said he'd just gotten out of hospital." Pat looked over his paperwork. "If you need him, he's staying at the Sunset Home. It's on Third Ave, just a few blocks west of here. You can't miss it."

"Thanks for your co-operation," Thompson acknowledged. They left to find Jacob.

A slim, blond woman answered the door at the big, rambling Sunset House. She raised her eyebrows, looking at them.

"Yes? Can I help you?"

"We're looking for Jake Donovan," Thompson told her.

"Jake…? What's this all about?"

"Is he here?" Jaslow questioned, stepping in through the door without being asked.

The woman stepped back slightly. "I'm Lynn Travers," she said, holding out her thin fingers to shake. Her eyes went from one to the other.

Thompson shook her hand. Firm and dry. But Jaslow was impatient with her stalling. "We need to see him, please. This is a police investigation."

"Jake hasn't done anything, has he? He seems like such a good kid…" Her eyes grew troubled, her eyebrows drawing down. "It's not because of his brother, is it? Charging Jake with kidnapping for bringing him here…?"

"Is Nicholas here?" Thompson asked, relieved to have found him, but also worried about the boy being sent right back to Duke, who was obviously not properly equipped to handle him.

"I believe both those boys were abused and neglected," Lynn went on. "Jacob may have taken Nicholas without permission, but he was trying to do the right thing to protect him."

"We need to see him now," Jaslow growled, "before he figures out we're here and makes a run for it."

Lynn was pale. Her mouth tightened and she nodded. She led them through the house to a main floor bedroom. She raised her hand to knock on the door and Jaslow nudged her aside, shaking his head. With his hand on the doorknob, he made eye contact with Thompson. They both drew their sidearms. Lynn gasped, her eyes growing wider. Standing to the side of the door, Jaslow turned the handle and pushed it open with a whoosh of air. Thompson knew Jacob was gone before he even breached the room. He took a quick glance around to verify his instinct and hurried to the window, holstering his gun and looking for some sign of Jacob's fleeing form.

"He's long gone," Jaslow advised. "The room wouldn't be this cold without the window being open all night. We've missed him."

Thompson swore, venting his frustration. Just when they caught up with Jacob he was gone again, slipping through their fingers. Lynn poked her head in the door. "Is it okay? Can I come in?"

Thompson motioned with his fingers for her to come in. Jaslow had holstered his service weapon and bent over the boy in the bed, checking his pulse. "Hello again, Nicholas," he said softly.

"He can't have left," Lynn protested, looking around the room. "We just talked to him last night. He was asked to stay here while we sorted things out…"

"What things?" Jaslow questioned. He pulled back Nicholas' blankets and Thompson saw that the boy was neatly dressed in flannel pajamas. "Close the window, Jack."

Thompson did. Jaslow covered Nicholas back up.

"Well, just… he'd broken some rules, missing curfew and disappearing for a few days… and then when he came back, he had Nicholas… Teresa had some concerns. But I don't think Jake had really done anything wrong…"

Jaslow nodded and started a search of the room. He poked through the wastepaper basket and made a slight nod at it for Thompson to look. Beneath the wrappings from Nicholas' formula feeding, Thompson could see a package that was immediately identifiable as one of the big-name brands of ammunition. The same kind favored by the police force. Thompson's chest tightened. That was not good news.

Jaslow moved to the small chest of drawers. The items in the drawers were mostly for Nicholas' care. Formula, medical tubing, gloves, diapers. Under a stack of clothing, Jaslow discovered a stash of granola bars and other food.

"Kids who have been neglected often hoard food," Lynn observed quietly. "Jake was awfully skinny."

"He hasn't left anything else of his behind," Jaslow observed, checking the closet as well. "Only the things for Nicholas."

"He didn't really come with anything," Lynn said. "We managed to get him a change of clothes, some toiletries, but he didn't have anything else."

"He went back to the house to get Nicholas. He could have grabbed anything he wanted."

"Well… I don't know what he might have grabbed. I didn't see anything."

"We'll need to talk to the other residents. Was he close to anyone?"

"No, not really. He'd only been here a short time. They're all at school…"

"We'll need to get them back here." Jaslow glanced back at the wastepaper basket grimly. "Before anything happens."

While they were waiting for the other kids to get home, Jaslow and Thompson made some inquiries and went to visit Father TJ.

"Do you know the boy in this picture?" Jaslow questioned, holding it up for the man to see.

"No."

Jaslow frowned. "Take a good look."

"No," the priest insisted. "I never saw him in my life."

"You took him to Sunset, didn't you?"

The man hesitated. "I take a lot of kids to a lot of shelters. I don't remember."

"He's disappeared from the home. We need information about when he came to you. Now, are you going to help us out?"

"I'm sorry… I can't tell you anything."

Jaslow studied him. Thompson looked on, frowning. "He didn't come by himself, did he?" Jaslow asked.

The preacher paled and shook his head. "A lot of them… half a dozen… they said—if I said anything…"

"We can get you police protection. You don't have to worry about anything."

"I don't want any trouble…"

"Of course not." Jaslow's eyes were narrow and fiery.

"They came in here," Father TJ confided. "They wouldn't let me leave. This boy—the one in the picture…?"

"Jacob," Thompson told him.

"He walked out, told the boy in charge that he was going to kill himself—I couldn't just stand by!"

"No," Thompson agreed. "It's all right. No one is saying you did anything wrong. What exactly did Jacob say, do you remember?"

"He said… his father had a gun and he'd use it."

Thompson exchanged glances with his partner. "Then what happened?"

"He left. We followed him. I intercepted him coming off the cloverleaf. Then the other guy caught up and made him take off his helmet and show me his cut—"

"What cut?" Jaslow questioned, remembering that Pat too had mentioned it.

"A deep one, across his throat. It was horrible. He said his father did it. How could I refuse to help him?"

"What else did Jacob have to say?"

"He didn't do much talking… He was quite upset. It wasn't him I was afraid of. Not really. He wasn't like the others."

"Who was it that threatened you?"

"The leader, he had a strange name. And then when I came back here after, there were some of them waiting for me…"

"Sarin Mace?"

"Sarin, yes, that was it."

"We'll nail him. How about the others? Did you hear any other names?"

"No, I don't think so."

"We'll show you some pictures. Do we know where Mace is right now, Jack?" Jaslow asked.

Thompson swallowed. "He and some of the others are apparently camping out."

Their eyes met. They both knew finding Jacob was not going to be easy if he had retreated into the wilderness.

Jacob pulled in beside the other motorcycles and flicked up his visor to view the camp. A few guys from the gang came into view.

"Hey Sarin, it's Black!" one of them yelled into the trees.

"What's back?" Sarin came into view a few moments later with two guys Jacob didn't recognize. "Oh. Hey, Black. What're you doing here?"

Jacob wasn't sure of that himself. He shrugged, trying to look casual. "Just thought I'd stop by."

"All right." Sarin hesitated a moment, then spoke again, in a low undertone that the others wouldn't hear. "Hey, I met your old man the other day. He's… really something else, isn't he?"

"Yeah."

Sarin shrugged. "Well, hey, you don't know Hanley and Carlos, do you? They got busted just before we took you on."

The boys smiled and clasped hands with Jacob. One of them slapped him on the shoulder as he shook hands and Jacob winced.

"Careful," he murmured. "I took a bullet a few days ago."

"Yeah? Where from?"

"A Blackbird."

The boy nodded. "Cool."

The other boy was eyeing the rifle in the holster on Jacob's bike covetously. "You got much ammo for that beauty?"

"Yeah."

"You didn't bring a lot of gear," observed Sarin, looking over Jacob's pack. "You planning on staying around a while?"

"Yeah… I travel light."

"Good. We could use another man. We're thinking of heating things up for a hiking expedition coming through here. Carlos' idea."

Thompson and Jaslow questioned the Sunset Home residents in Jacob's and Nicholas' bedroom. They finished questioning Pal and had to wait a few minutes for the last resident on their list. Thompson saw the young blond through the open bedroom door as she conversed with Pal. She obviously wasn't keen to come and talk to them. After several encouraging motions from Pal, she finally made her way down the hall and stood in the doorway.

"Come in," Thompson invited.

She took a couple of reluctant steps into the room.

"Well then, you must be Cassandra," Jaslow said.

"Cassy. Yeah."

She had on a white blouse and blue jeans. On studying her, Jaslow noted her eyes were slightly red. "What do you know about Jake, Cassy?"

"He just came a little while ago… he's quiet, but really nice."

"When did you last see him?"

"I'm not sure. A few days ago."

"And how was he feeling?"

"Not very good… he had the 'flu." Cassy's eyes wandered over to Nicholas, strapped in his chair.

Jaslow didn't say anything at first, letting the silence draw out. Then he spoke. "You're lying to us, Cassandra. You were the last one to see Jake last night. And he didn't have the 'flu, he had a bullet wound."

She was startled and for a moment stared at him with her mouth open. "He didn't want anyone to know." Tears started in her eyes.

"Did he threaten you?" Jaslow asked.

"No, no. He'd never do that! But he asked me not to say anything… he said he just wanted to be safe."

"He would be safe with us. You don't need to worry about that. His family is very worried about him. His father arranged for us to take the case, since Jack has known Jacob since he was six or seven."

Cassy looked at Thompson through the tears. "He said he'd never go home. He said he'd sooner die."

Thompson couldn't think of anything to say to that. He swallowed. "Do you know where he's headed?"

"I don't know. He didn't know for sure. He said 'maybe to the mountains', but he didn't know."

"Did he say anything about meeting up with his gang?"

"No. He wanted to go away to somewhere he was safe. Maybe the mountains. That's all."

"If there's anything else you know, you'd better tell us," Jaslow warned.

She stood there chewing on her lip. Thompson had been expecting an immediate denial. He exchanged glances with

Jaslow. She knew something more. Maybe she didn't want to share it, but there was more.

"What is it, Cassy?" Thompson prodded.

She looked over at him, a tear making its way down her cheek. She sniffled and swallowed. "When I came in, he was packing his bag…"

Thompson nodded encouragingly.

"He closed it, so I wouldn't see."

"But you did, didn't you?"

She nodded. "He had guns."

"We thought that he might. What kind of guns, do you know?"

"A rifle. Short. Black. I'm not sure what else. A Colt M1911."

Jaslow raised his brows at Thompson, then looked back at Cassy. "You're sure?"

Cassy considered. She shook her head. "I only caught a glimpse of them. But… that's what I thought."

"Did you ask him about them?"

"No. I didn't tell him I saw."

"Thank you for letting us know. Is there anything else we should know?"

Trying to hold back the tears, Cassy shook her head. Thompson moved to pat her on the back, but she shied away from him and left the room sobbing.

Chapter Thirty-Eight

JACOB LOOKED THROUGH THE telescopic sight on his rifle, focusing on the distant group.

"They're just kids!"

"YMCA children's camping trip," Sarin informed him, "ages six to twelve. There are fifteen kids and three leaders."

Jacob studied them, keeping his eyes averted from Sarin. "Why?"

"It's good sport, that's why. And no one to stop us out here. We can handle three adults easy. You could handle them all by yourself."

Jacob was disgusted. But he didn't have to have any part in it. He was free to do what he liked, and not even Sarin could stop him. Duke had taken Jacob along to survivalist training just about every year; sometimes more than once. Even when he was little, Jacob had quickly learned how to take care of himself.

No one could even find him.

Thompson and Jaslow were both standing by the table with the map spread out between them, trying to organize a systematic search of the wilderness area Jacob was supposedly hiding out in with the gang. It was not proving to be an easy task.

The phone rang and Thompson picked it up. "Yeah?" he answered, his eyes still intent on the map. He straightened up, listening. "Oh, no… yeah, we'll be there right away… okay." He hung up quickly and tapped Jaslow on the shoulder. "There's been some trouble at Father TJ's chapel."

Jaslow straightened, his eyes blazing. "Let's go."

They drove in silence and were admitted past the police barricades. Thompson approached one of the officials he knew. "What happened?"

"Well, the priest was under guard at your request. The officers guarding him went to investigate gunshots outside the building. A boy opened fire on the congregation once they were gone and in the confusion, someone got to the priest and he was knifed."

Jaslow swore.

"Have you got the culprits?" Thompson asked.

"We got the guy that fired on the congregation and no one got out of the church, so the guy with the knife is still in there. We have the area barricaded, so we hope to be able to get the guys who fired shots outside too."

"How many were hurt?"

"Two in the congregation were winged. The priest's condition is serious but stable."

Thompson spoke to Jaslow. "Why don't you help them out inside, and I'll talk to the guy they got?"

The officer in charge nodded. "That's fine. The kid's over there in a squad car."

Thompson went over to the cars and Jaslow went into the church. The gunman was seventeen or so, and was sitting in the car with a smirk on his face. At Thompson's request, he was pulled out of the car to talk. "I'm Officer Thompson. Why don't you tell me what went on in there?"

"Why should I?"

"I think it'll make things a lot easier on you if you do. What's your name?"

"Lanny."

"Talet?"

"That's right."

"I've heard a lot about you, Talet. You lookin' to do hard time?"

"I won't do any time."

"Assault with a deadly weapon—you injured two people in there. Also, conspiracy to commit murder."

"You can't prove anything."

"Who else was in on it?"

"I ain't tellin' you nothin'."

"Give me a name."

"Not a chance."

"You've got a long record, Talet. You're known as a troublemaker. They aren't going to go easy on you."

"You don't know anything," he sneered.

"Tell me about it, then."

"My old mom. She's sick. Gonna croak one of these days and I'm the only one taking care of her. If they gave me time, she'd buy it for sure, 'cause no one would take care of her. If she didn't die of a broken heart first."

"It's not going to work this time, Talet. You being a murderer yourself, she'd probably be feeling a lot better if you weren't taking care of her. Maybe she'd recover completely, huh?"

"Doctors say she's gonna die, can't have any stress."

"I'm telling you how it is, Talet. They're not going to let you off on account of your ailing mother this time. 'Fess up, tell me what was going on in there, and maybe I'll put in a good word for you."

"You got nothing on me."

"Give it up. The whole congregation saw you. You've got plenty of witnesses. You haven't got a chance of beating the rap this time."

Lanny looked uncertain for a moment and then masked it. "We're just protectin' a friend, man. A friend who's gettin' a lotta unfair rap from his old man, happens to be a cop. We can prove that cop was beatin' on him all the time. What jury's gonna believe any of his stupid cop friends? Who would put away a guy for just protecting a friend?"

"How were you protecting anybody?"

"Well, the priest talked, didn't he? We warned'im if he talked, he'd get hurt."

"How do you know Father TJ said anything?"

"About Donell? What else would he be talkin' to you guys about? You guys are looking for Donell, but you ain't never gonna find him."

"Why is that?"

"You just ain't. Because you're stupid, that's why. So much for protectin' your priest, huh? You couldn't stop us."

"Maybe not, but we're going to have the satisfaction of finally seeing you in the slammer." Thompson walked away.

Three boys were being hauled out of the church. Two of them went with only the usual amount of protest, but the third was struggling wildly and protesting loudly and with vigor.

The boy caught sight of a policeman he knew and yelled out to him. "Officer Chapman! It's me—I didn't do it! You know I wouldn't do that to the Father!" The officers putting him under arrest halted. "Please! Please, you know I wouldn't hurt no one! Tell them I didn't do it! Please…!"

The cop he was talking to walked over slowly, looking puzzled. "Keith? What are you doing here?"

"I always come here to hear the sermons! Won't somebody listen to me?"

"Let him go," Chapman said with a nod.

"He's part of the gang that master-minded this thing," one of the officers objected, giving Keith's arm an extra twist. "He's as guilty as they all are."

"Keith, do you have any weapons on you?"

"I'm clean, I swear it—I'm clean!"

"Of course he's clean. They all are. Would you keep carrying around a bloody knife? No, you'd chuck it first chance you got."

"Please—" Keith started again.

"Okay, cool it. Did you have anything to do with this? Anything at all?"

"No! I didn't know or I would of warned the Father! I would of said something!"

"Let him go," Chapman told the others again. "I'll take him in for questioning myself."

They finally let him go and Keith sighed in relief. He looked at Chapman gratefully. "I swear, I didn't know anything about it."

"I believe you, Keith. Do you mind me taking you in?"

"No, man, that's cool. Man, that scared me," he took a deep breath and let it out slowly. "It never bothered me when I'd done something and I knew it. But I'd never hurt Father TJ."

"You're okay now. I probably won't be the one questioning you, but I'll be around. Make sure you tell the officer everything you know."

"I will."

Keith wasn't looking too comfortable when he sat in the interrogation room with Jaslow and Thompson.

Jaslow sipped his coffee. "Tell us what happened when Jacob went to Father TJ."

Keith looked nervous. "I guess his being there was kind of my doing. Sarin, he asked if any of us could help Jacob."

"And what was it Jacob needed help with?"

"He'd had another bout with his dad and couldn't take the heat anymore. He needed to get away from it all."

"And why did you think of Father TJ?"

"Well… I go to his sermon pretty regularly. He helps out with a lot of street kids, getting them straightened out, finding 'em places to stay and all. I didn't know the boys would do anything like this!"

"Who was it that threatened the priest?"

"Threatened him? It wasn't me! I don't know who. Maybe Sarin. I wasn't there with them both the whole time."

"And when did you hear about the plan to attack him today?"

"I never heard anything! I would have stopped them!"

"You expect us to believe that your friends didn't mention anything of this to you? That you just happened to be there by chance when it happened?" Jaslow's voice was heavy with sarcasm.

"I didn't know anything about it! I always go to his sermons!"

"No one in the congregation spoke up for you, did they now?"

"I go in late and leave early. I stand in the back."

"Sure."

"I don't exactly look like I belong, do I?" Keith pointed out. "So I don't like to be obvious."

Thompson looked over Keith's ripped jeans, too-tight shirt, and gang jacket. They were cleaner and neater than would be expected, and his long hair was clean and carefully slicked back. A gold cross hung around his neck, but crosses were nothing new among JD's. Mentally, Thompson compared him to the picture on his file. His mug shots showed your typical low-class punk; long, greasy, unkempt hair, grubby, disorderly clothes, his shirt open at the chest to show off a detailed tattoo.

"I don't recall your file saying you're religious," Jaslow said.

"It's in there somewhere. My PO used it to 'prove my character' and get me a lighter sentence a while back."

"Maybe next time we have a warrant on you, we should check the church," Jaslow scoffed. Keith's shoulders dipped and he breathed out, relaxing a little. He recognized that Jaslow was easing off.

"My best hide-out," he returned, with a mock-sulk.

Jaslow didn't smile, but he didn't scowl either. "If the others support your story, you're off the hook. But if we find out you're just stringing us…"

"I swear it's the truth, man. Father TJ's a pretty decent guy. He helps out a lotta kids. I wouldn't want anything to happen to him."

"How much involvement have you had with Father TJ personally?"

Keith hesitated. Jaslow waited and Keith eventually spoke up.

"My folks kicked me out when I started stayin' out late and gettin' in trouble with the police. I go back every now and then to see them and they don't mind me staying so much now. But to begin with, I was just a kid and I didn't have anyplace to go. I wasn't in the gang yet. I got rolled by a couple of guys walkin' downtown. The cops, when they found me, they took me to the hospital to get patched up and then took me to Father TJ. I stayed at one of the shelters for a while, 'til I got into the gang."

"Your file says you're living at home."

"Yeah, well, they gotta have somewhere to send court notices. I only go home once every few months to visit. I don't live there."

"Where do you live?"

He shrugged. "With the guys."

"Wildcats?"

"Yeah."

"What shelter did you stay at?"

"It's called Trinity House. They wouldn't have sent Jacob there, though, 'cause he's not actually religious."

"And you are religious."

"Hey, man, give me a break! I know I got a record and I'm in with a gang. You think I'm no good. But you ain't seein' it all. Maybe I smoke and drink and stay up late at wild parties. So what? So do a lotta people, a lotta adults who got clean records. So do a lotta kids their parents think are straight arrows. I'm just worse 'cause I been on the street on my own a few years."

Jaslow shook his head. "You could go straight if that's what you really wanted."

Keith swore. "How? How am I supposed to go straight? I'm tryin' to finish school, so I don't got a job that'll give me enough money for rent. No one's gonna foster me, 'cause I'm too old. Even at the shelter I was still gettin' beat up every week! I'm with the gang for protection and I couch surf or stay at the crib so I don't have to pay rent. I still gotta pay for my food and drinks and where am I supposed to get the money? No one will hire me, 'cause I don't have any experience and I look like a hood. If I didn't look like a hood, how long do you think I'd last on the streets? If I don't look like I'm gonna stick the next guy in the gut, I'm the one who's gonna get split. So how am I supposed to go straight?"

"You'd find a way if that was what you wanted," Jaslow said firmly.

Keith swore again.

Jaslow stood up to leave. "If I don't talk to you again before you leave, take my advice; stick around town in case we're looking for you. And keep away from church."

"I've had enough preaching to last me a long time," Keith sneered.

Jaslow left, jerking his head for Thompson to follow.

Jacob scrutinized the gang's camp set-up in silence. The packs of food were dumped beside the fire pit, begging for wildlife to invade the camp. The tents were clumsily set up in full view of any searchers who happened to come in the right direction. Tools were left about for anyone to trip over or slice a foot on.

"What'd'ya think?" asked Hanley, who was standing beside him.

Jacob shook his head. "It's a disaster."

"Aw, it'll do all right until the brats get here. It's not like we're gonna get hurt 'cause we're a little messy."

Jacob didn't say anything. Hanley changed the subject abruptly, turning to look at him. "Do you gamble?"

"Not really. Why?"

"Just wonderin' if the name 'Black-Jack' would suit you."

Jacob raised his eyebrows. "You're putting Black and Jake or Jacob together, huh?"

"You got it. It would make more sense if you were a compulsive gambler."

"Well," Jacob said after a moment, "life's a gamble, isn't it?"

Hanley grinned. "Hey, that's good. All the chances and beating the odds and all that, right? The way the chips fall... you make the best of your hand... I like it, man."

They stood there a few minutes longer, Hanley sizing Jacob up and nodding. "Black-Jack. It's beautiful, man."

Sammy was shuffling slowly along the path, his head down and hands in his jacket pockets. He had lost sight of the rest of the YMCA group. In a few minutes, Anne came jogging along the trail back toward him.

"Come on, Sammy! Let's pick up the pace!"

Sammy nodded, his face getting hot.

"You've got to stay with the group, Sammy. This is no place for a kid to be alone. Pick up your pace a little and stay with us."

Sammy quickened his pace ever-so-slightly. It was as much as he could manage.

Anne went ahead of him, back to where the others were waiting. "I don't know what to do with him," she complained to Janet. "Every time I turn around, he's further behind."

"He'll learn. Once he loses us by enough, he'll panic and catch up as fast as his short legs will carry him."

Sammy caught up, and they moved on again. Ron left his group and dropped back to talk to Anne. "You doing okay, sis'?"

"You bet. I've just got a kid that isn't keeping up."

Ron glanced over his shoulder. "Sammy? He is going pretty slow. Maybe I can convince him to move it."

He grinned and dropped back to Sammy's side. "Hi, Sammy. How's it going?"

Sammy didn't look up. He stared at his Spiderman shoes, putting one foot in front of the other. He was already doing the best he could. Why couldn't they just leave him alone?

"If we want to reach the camp by noon, you gotta keep up, buddy. Then you can rest. Do you think you can do that?"

Sammy shrugged. Ron touched his chin to make him look up. Sammy jerked away from his touch and retreated to the far side of the trail.

"Hey, stay to the middle of the trail," Ron said sharply. The trail was on the edge of a steep drop. Ron moved towards him. Sammy took another step backward and the dirt beneath his foot started to slide. Ron froze. Sammy felt a surge of panic and struggled to get back onto solid ground. He teetered and scrambled on the edge for a few moments, his stomach feeling like it had already gone over. Then he made it back to safe ground and stood still, trying to catch his breath.

"Be careful," Ron told him. "You guys have been told there are dangerous places up here! Stay back from the edge."

Sammy kept his distance from Ron, watching his hands, wary of punishment. Ron moved to the inside of the path. "I want you right against this side," he touched the rock wall beside him. "I want you touching this side. And I'm going to walk on the other side."

Ron slowly moved to the outside edge of the trail and Sammy mirrored his movements, switching to the inside. Sammy touched the rock tentatively, looking up at Ron. They walked like that for a while and Sammy started to relax and breathe normally again.

"Speed it up a bit, we've already lost the others," Ron commented.

Sammy couldn't possibly move any faster.

"Do I have to carry you?" Ron asked with a laugh. He considered Sammy for a moment. Sammy froze, not liking the look in Ron's eye. The man grabbed him and ran to catch up with the group. He ran right past them. Sammy kicked and squirmed wildly, trying to escape his grasp. When Ron put him down, Sammy stood there frozen.

"Hey, it's okay," Ron soothed.

Sammy's heart pounded wildly. He couldn't move. Couldn't talk and couldn't go on. He couldn't seem to get enough oxygen when he breathed in. The other children had stopped to stare at him. Anne came forward.

"What's wrong?" she asked Ron.

"I don't know—guess I startled him."

Anne put her arms around Sammy in an attempt to comfort him. "It's okay, Sammy. Ron didn't mean to scare you."

Sammy's whole body shook. He pushed her away.

"Let's just move on," Janet urged. "Another half hour and we'll be there."

The YMCA group had arrived and the leaders pointed out to Sarin that the gang had camped in their reserved location. Deke watched the action with interest.

"Oh sure," Sarin said in an exaggerated tone of friendliness. "We'd be delighted to break camp, wouldn't we guys?"

The sneers and mutters from the rest of the boys weren't the least bit comforting to the YMCA group.

"See? No problem. You want to camp here? Fine. Your privilege." Sarin looked around at the rest of the Wildcats. "Okay guys," he said sharply, suddenly authoritative, "take down the tents and get the gear together. Hop to it! Ten yards east to the next clearing. Let's go!"

The Kittens weren't impressed with having to take down and set up their gear again. They had all thought that Sarin would stand up to the YMCA group and make them move. But apparently that wasn't what Sarin had in mind. The Wildcats camp was dismantled and the equipment loaded onto the bikes. Sarin watched the gang with sharp eyes.

Deke had already moved his tent and approached Sarin. "Hey, Sarin. Where's Black-Jack?"

Sarin looked quickly around the clearing. He saw one of the women in the YMCA camp watching him and listening too closely. He grabbed Deke to move a little further away.

"I ain't seen him lately and I don't see him now. His bike's gone too." Sarin swore. "If he's pulled out on me already..."

"He's got to be close by," Deke placated. "We would have heard his engine if he left. I'll look around."

"Be careful. He may not be in the best mood, and besides his fists he's loaded with arsenal this time."

Deke raised his brows, thinking about that. He'd never seen Black use a weapon before. His fists had always been enough. Did he even have any experience with firearms?

"I don't know what he's up to," Sarin said. "He may have decided he doesn't want to stick around. He coulda left to tell someone what's goin' on." Sarin shrugged. "It could be nothing. He could be out pickin' daisies. Maybe even plannin' a game of

Russian roulette. But he could also be holed up just waitin' for someone to make the wrong move."

Deke nodded. "I'll be careful."

Chapter Thirty-Nine

SAMMY STOOD WATCHING THE leaders set the tents up. He leaned against a tree, completely worn out. After a while, Janet saw him and motioned to him. "Come here, Sammy," she invited.

Sammy approached, unsure what kind of trouble he was in. He sat down on the log she indicated. Without comment, Janet unlaced Sammy's shoes, loosened the tongue, and tried to pull them off. Sammy had to hold onto the log to keep from being pulled right off. It took several tries, but Janet finally got them free. Sammy was relieved. He'd been afraid they'd have to be cut off, with how badly his feet had swollen. He looked down at his mangled, bloody feet. His feet and ankles were black and blue with bruises, swollen, and blistered.

Janet filled a bucket with cold water from the pump and gently dipped Sammy's feet into the bucket. Sammy relaxed as the pain turned into cold numbness. Looking at the shoes, Sammy couldn't believe that his feet had actually been forced into them. It looked physically impossible. One ankle was badly swollen. Janet looked around at the other leaders.

"Anne, come over here."

Anne approached and saw Sammy's feet. "How in the world did that happen?" she asked in amazement.

"He can't hike in these, that's for sure," Janet indicated the shoes. "And he's going to have problems walking anywhere for the next little while."

"So I see. Well, we'll have to work something out. You just take it easy, Sammy. We'll have something to eat soon." Anne went back over to continue unpacking.

Janet flushed the sores with antiseptic and looked Sammy in the eye. "Why didn't you say something to someone about this, Sammy? It would have been better for you to hike in your bare feet than to go on like this."

"S-s-sorry." Sammy stared down at the ground.

Janet studied his face and said nothing more.

Jacob was sitting, reclining with his back against a tree, some distance away from the others. Sarin's order to move the camp 'ten yards east' wasn't much of an exaggeration. The camps were practically on top of each other, making the YMCA group nervous. After a brief search, the gang had given up on finding Jacob, so he had time to himself. They would have a hard time finding him even if they got the whole gang out looking. He had learned his lessons well. If he walked out of his camp now, someone coming through it wouldn't even know he had been there. His bike was hidden away in such a manner that only a professional could find it.

Jacob's mind went back to the absent-minded trooper who had quite literally stumbled over him in the half-light of dusk ten years ago. He smiled to himself. It would take more luck than that to discover him this time.

The loud laughter of the gang had faded out several minutes ago and suddenly the campfire songs of the YMCA camp stopped. Jacob stood up and circled the area. He didn't want them to see him before he could see them. His soft sneakers made no sound.

"Are you saying you don't want us in your little sing-along?" Sarin questioned, his voice carrying in the silence, heavy with unspoken threats.

"This is a private camping trip," Anne explained quietly.

"Don't look too private to me, lady."

"Please leave us alone."

Sarin laughed and swore at her, calling her a name off-handedly that he had probably used on most of his girlfriends. Ron stepped up to Sarin, his eyes blazing and face red with anger. "You take that back."

Sarin looked surprised at his reaction. "Why would I do that?"

Ron swung at him, but he'd obviously never been taught the amenities of street-style fighting. Sarin hit him twice, coolly, and had him doubled up on the ground, fighting for breath. Sarin waited for him to get back up or try to trip him, but Ron just lay there groaning. Sarin looked down at him in disgust, then looked back up at Anne.

"He started it, lady. We didn't ask for no trouble. No hard feelings?"

"I hate you," Anne hissed.

"Because I whipped your boyfriend?" Sarin was incredulous. "Big deal."

"He's my brother."

"Thought he was a little young for you. Well, let's sing."

They stared at him in shock. Sarin started to sing. Laughing, the rest of the gang joined in. The children looked around at each other and gradually joined in. Janet bent over Ron, soothing him. She glared up at Sarin, calling him names under her breath. She got Ron sitting up again and gave him some coffee. He was still pale and shaky, glaring darkly at the others.

Darkness came swiftly and the firelight bathed the faces of the children. The supervisors were beginning to relax, seeing that no harm came if the gang was not provoked. The atmosphere grew less strained. Jacob drew in closer so that he could see them in the dimness.

The children's eyes were better than the supervisors' and one of them spotted Jacob and pointed him out to Janet. The song faded out and Sarin turned around to see what had distracted them.

"Well, if it isn't Black-Jack."

"Why don't you put your rifle down and stay a while," invited Carlos sarcastically.

Jacob didn't move. Janet gasped when she saw the gun at his side. Jacob leaned back against a tree and watched them, waiting for them to turn around again and go on with their singing. Sarin wouldn't let their attention stay on someone else for that long.

"Black-Jack ain't too friendly," Sarin informed the group with a faint smile. "They say he's pretty handy with his gun. He's out on probation right now."

"Come sing, Black-Jack," another of Wildcats called out.

Jacob turned and withdrew again into the trees.

Chapter Forty

SAMMY WATCHED ANNE CLEANING up after breakfast. "Let's move on today," she said to the other leaders. She glanced in the direction of the other camp. "I don't think it's wise to stay around here."

Sammy wasn't sure why they were so concerned about leaving. The gang hadn't seemed too threatening the night before. They left the campsite when they were asked and they sang songs around the fire. They didn't seem as tough as some of the bangers that Sammy normally saw around the neighborhood or had to deal with in the Sixth.

"Sammy's in no condition to hike," Janet reminded her.

Anne glanced over at Sammy, frowning.

"I could carry him on my shoulders, he's pretty light," offered Ron.

"Do you think he'd let you? After the way he reacted yesterday?" Anne asked.

"It was just too sudden yesterday. I startled him, that's all. I'm sure if he realized what was going on…"

Janet took a few steps toward Sammy, smiling at him and looking him in the eye. "We'd like to get away from those boys. If we go on today, would you let Ron carry you piggy-back or on his shoulders?"

Sammy shook his head. "N-n-no…" He took a step back, watching Ron warily in case he was planning on grabbing Sammy like he had the day before.

"It's okay," Anne soothed. "I guess… we'll see what else we can work out."

"Meanwhile," Ron told her, "I'm going to take these guys out swimming."

"You coming in?" Carlos asked.

Deke shook his head. "Nah, you go ahead. I'm just gonna get some sun."

Carlos looked at Deke with narrowed eyes. "I bet you can't even swim."

"Where would I learn how to swim on the street? The potholes?"

Carlos laughed and circled the edge of the lake. With a yell, he cannon-balled into the lake, splashing all the little kids as well as Ron, who stood on the shore in cut-offs and a t-shirt supervising. Ron protested good-naturedly and the children screamed with delight. Carlos horsed around for a while among the kids and took to dunking them.

Ron tensed and warned him to cut it out. Carlos ignored him. Most of the children squealed and submitted to being dunked. Until Carlos noticed the shy one called Sammy, nervous and carefully avoiding him. With a few strong strokes, Carlos reached Sammy and tried to dunk him. Sammy slipped away from his grasp, and in doing so, found himself in deep water. His face turned sheet-white. He flailed his arms desperately. Carlos swam out to him. Deke relaxed, thinking Carlos would bring Sammy back to shore.

But Carlos reached Sammy and dunked him, holding his head under the water for longer than he had the others. Sammy surfaced and gasped for air and Carlos pushed him under again, oblivious to Ron's shout of alarm. Another gasp for breath and Sammy went under again. Deke stood anxiously on the rocks, but there was nothing he could do. Ron jumped in and swam toward

Carlos and Sammy. He pulled Sammy out of Carlos' grasp and flung him towards the shallow water. In a rage, Carlos set on his foe. He was stronger and better skilled, a dirty street fighter. Gaining the upper hand, he held Ron's head under the water. After a few heart-stopping moments, Ron ceased his wild thrashing and was still. Deke struggled with himself, wanting to interfere, wanting to stop Carlos. But he knew he couldn't even put his feet in the water without choking up.

At that moment, Jacob appeared out of the bush. He took in the details in an instant and ran through the water to reach them. With one hand, he grabbed Carlos by the upper arm and threw him to the side. Then he bent over and grabbed Ron around the waist. He carried Ron to dry ground.

"Go find their nurse," he ordered.

Carlos cursed defiantly. "He jumped me, man!"

Jacob's face was pale as he tried to locate Ron's pulse. He put his rifle to his shoulder with the other hand. "Now!" he ordered.

Carlos didn't like looking down the barrel of Jacob's rifle. He ran for the camp.

He was back quickly, followed by Janet. She saw Jacob leaning over Ron and drew her own conclusions. Her eyes went wide and she dropped to her knees beside Ron.

Jacob withdrew and disappeared back into the trees.

"Hey Larry," the foreman called. "Billy wants you. Go ahead, but hurry back."

Larry wiped his face and checked the cables for stress, flashing back to Jacob's warning, 'did you check that cable...?' He'd been one of the best workers they'd had. It had been a bum move for Billy to let him go. Larry swung down and crossed the site to the trailer where Billy was.

He walked in and got a jolt. Two cops stood inside the door waiting. Casually, Larry put his foot on the chair and began tightening the laces on his boots. His eyes were fixed on Billy as he did so, but his mind was focused on the two cops and their positions.

"You wanted me, Billy?"

"These men want to ask you some questions."

"Yeah?"

One of the officers shifted warily, but from the position Larry was in, he could do little. Lazily, Larry pulled his foot down and put the other up.

"You're under arrest," the cop said, his voice smooth and cool. In a flash, Larry pulled out the knife sheathed at his ankle. He lunged for the door, but the cops were pros and had been expecting trouble. The second cop stepped in his path and together they managed to wrestle the knife away from Larry. It wouldn't have been so easy, had the quarters not been so cramped. Handcuffs closed over Larry's wrists.

"Stop fighting; you'll only get hurt," one of them growled.

They led him out behind the trailer where the squad car was parked, hidden from view. But they didn't get in.

"What am I under arrest for?" Larry demanded.

The tall one looked him over. "Obstruction of justice, harboring a fugitive."

There could only be one fugitive, but Larry played dumb. "For what?"

"Where's Jacob Donell?"

"How should I know?" Larry shot back.

The shorter one, jaw clenched, muscles standing out in his throat, slammed a fist into Larry's ribs. Larry grunted with the pain and continued to face them boldly. The smaller cop danced, ready for a fight. "Talk to us, stupid. Talk and you won't get hurt."

"I don't know—" Larry was forced to stop by a right cross to the jaw. He stepped back, spitting blood. The taller cop maneuvered behind him, grabbing his arms to keep him from moving away.

"Last time I saw him was when he got fired!"

Another belly blow, harder this time, with two more following in quick succession. Larry groaned and leaned back for support against the cop holding onto him.

"I don't got to tell you anything!"

He couldn't fight back. Couldn't do anything but stand there and take the punishment. A few more blows and blood was streaming down his face.

"What do you want to hear?" Larry finally asked.

"Now you're talking, big boy. I want to know where he is, how long he was at your pad, and how bad he's hurt."

Larry spit out the sharp corner of a broken tooth and cleared his throat. "I don't know where he is." His assailant kicked him heavily in the shins. "He was never at my place." A kick in the knees almost had Larry on the ground. "And if he's hurt, it wasn't bad enough for me to hear about it."

The cop backhanded him across the face, the slap ringing out like a gunshot. Larry could feel his face flushing, furious and humiliated.

"Unlock these chains and I'll fight you 'til I drop! Do this to me and you're gonna pay!"

He was silenced by a series of punches and the cop behind released him. Larry fell down and tried to get back up. Driven back to the ground by both cops' heavy kicks, Larry finally lay still. One officer bent down and unlocked the handcuffs. They stepped into their car and drove off.

Sammy wandered around the campsite restlessly. Others were resting, playing games, or talking. But Sammy was anxious, looking for something else to do. The atmosphere in the camp was tense. The children had to stay in the camp. Ron had been brought to his tent and seemed to be doing okay, tended to carefully by Janet. Anne kept a watch on the children and encouraged them to entertain themselves.

Janet came out of Ron's tent. Anne looked at her.

"I think it's time that we got some help. I'm going to see who I can get on the radio," Janet said.

She moved to the larger tent where most of the medical and emergency supplies were. Sammy shadowed her, peeking in the zippered doorway to watch her use the radio, a bit of a novelty over cellphones, which wouldn't work from the wilderness area.

On arrival, she found it smashed into bits. Janet ducked back through the tent flap and looked around. Finding one of the boys from the gang looking on with an amused expression, Janet swore, staring at him.

"Did you do this? How could you? We need to send an emergency message—"

"Ah, chill. Rats don't drown as easily as that."

"I want to talk to your leader."

"How sweet. He's busy."

"Planning more violence and sabotage? Maybe one of you would like to dig a knife into a couple of the kids, just for kicks!"

"I'll be sure to suggest it," he said, showing his teeth in a predatory grin. "Violence and sabotage, that's got a nice ring to it, doesn't it? You won't need your radio, lady, 'cause no one's leaving this camp."

Thompson was impatient as they waited for Enrik to answer the door. "I hope he didn't catch wind of us," he said to Jaslow.

The door opened slowly and a girl stood there. Her eyes travelled over their uniforms and narrowed. "What do you want?"

"We're looking for Larry Enrik," Jaslow said.

"He can't come to the door."

"Then we'll come in."

"No."

Jaslow forced the door open the rest of the way. "Where is he?"

"Please, not today! You've already done enough damage."

Jaslow raised his eyebrows. "We haven't been here since the search and no damage was done."

She laughed shortly but gave way a little. "If you hurt him..."

"We're just here to talk." Jaslow pushed her gently out of the way and she let him. She turned around and led them to the living room.

Enrik was lying on the couch, nursing two black eyes and a swollen face. His nose was obviously broken and he was badly bruised up. He squinted at the two officers and cursed under his breath. His fists clenched and he shifted to get up.

"Larry," protested the girl, "stay there. Don't move, please!"

Ignoring her, he rose to his feet. He swayed, then fell forward in a dead faint. The girl grabbed him but was only slowing his fall. Jaslow caught Larry and helped move him back to the couch. The girl sat down beside Larry, touching him gently.

"He can't get up. He has a bad concussion."

"What happened? Gang fight?"

"He also has broken ribs and teeth missing."

"What happened?" Jaslow repeated.

"A couple of cops went to the construction site to ask him questions—only they took him behind the trailer and beat him up when he wouldn't answer them!"

Jaslow scowled and glanced aside at Thompson, then back to the girlfriend. "What were they asking him about?"

"You know what they were asking about."

"Tell me."

"About Jacob Donell."

"What do *you* know about Jacob Donell?"

"You going to start on me now? Why don't you just leave us alone? Leave us in peace. We haven't done anything wrong!"

"No one is forcing anyone to do anything here," Jaslow said. "I'm asking you what you know."

"Go away." Tears started in her eyes. "Just go away and leave us alone. I've got enough work to do here! I've got to take care of him. I spent all night taking care of him. I missed work and I'll be lucky if I don't lose my job! Larry will be sure to lose his, just like Jacob did when he was hurt. You want to ruin us? You've done a pretty good job of it!"

"Ma'am…"

"Go away!" she screamed. "Get lost, just go away! Leave us alone!" The tears poured down her face in earnest now and

Jaslow didn't say anything. She swore a few times. "Why did you do that to Larry? Why?"

Thompson raised his brows questioningly. Jaslow nodded. Thompson called an ambulance for Larry and when they arrived, had the EMT's look at his hysterical girlfriend as well.

Sarin dumped out another backpack and poked through the supplies. The younger woman was standing close by, tears brimming in her eyes. "I don't understand…"

"Simple. No one leaves this camp. Not you, or your friends, or the brats."

"Haven't you done enough?" she choked out.

"I haven't done nothin'."

"What about the moron with the gun? He nearly killed Ron! And you said yourself he's trigger-happy!"

Sarin looked at Deke, making sure that he would keep his mouth shut. He shrugged at Anne. "That's not me, that's Black-Jack."

"Then there's the idiot who sabotaged—"

Sarin slapped her hard across the face. He grabbed her arm, twisting it up behind her back. "You watch how you talk about my boys." His voice was tight and threatening.

She didn't say anything and Sarin twisted harder. Anne cried out with the pain. "I won't—I won't, I'm sorry!"

Sarin relaxed his hold and pushed her away. Anne shook her head, her brows drawn down. Deke could understand her confusion. Sarin hadn't defended Black-Jack; he'd let her put him down. But his reaction to her slur toward Carlos was immediate. She shuddered, turning away from Sarin. Her eyes were wide with fear. Deke felt a little sorry for her.

"I got sentries out there," Sarin said, "so no bright ideas about leaving the campsite."

Sarin took a look at Deke before walking away, warning him to stay out of the way.

Deke entertained himself watching Anne and Janet performing their duties and chasing kids around, trying to keep them under control. Deke sympathized with the kids, who were bored and wanted to be off doing campy things instead of sitting around where it was safe.

There was the crack of a gun close by and everyone looked around quickly. Janet came out of her tent. They all looked towards the sound.

"Probably Black-Jack doing a bit of illegal game shooting," Deke suggested, even though he had no idea whether it was Black-Jack or someone unrelated to the Wildcats.

There was a high-pitched, piercing scream close at hand and a volley of shots even closer than before cut it off abruptly. Their faces went shock-white. Without considering the possible consequences, Deke and the YMCA leaders and the other Wildcats ran through the dense bush towards the sound.

The first thing Deke saw was Sammy, lying face down on the ground. Black-Jack stood a little further down the trail, with his back to them and the fancy black rifle in his hand. Janet pushed by and turned Sammy over. He was pale, frozen in fear, but there wasn't a mark on him. Deke looked around more carefully. He stood there dumbly, staring at the dark, hulking heap sprawled on the ground in front of Black. Blood was spotted all over the foliage and in a pool at his feet.

"I never killed anything before…" Black broke the silence, his voice sounding breathy and far away.

The torn undergrowth behind the bear showed how it had come charging straight towards Sammy, stopped only by the lead Black put into it, finally collapsing bare inches in front of him.

"Man," Deke said in amazement. "Good job, Black. You're lucky it didn't go for you."

Black's left hand was on a tree in front of him. He slowly pivoted around and leaned back against the tree for support.

"It did," responded Black unnecessarily, in the same blank, unbelieving voice.

His chest and stomach were torn open by deep slashes, bleeding profusely. Anne shrieked. Sarin stared and swore under his breath.

"There was a cub…" Black's eyes focused on Janet. "Where's your medical kit?"

There was silence for a moment, and Janet answered carefully. "You can't use it."

"What do you mean?" Sarin's voice was angry. "How long do you think he can hold out like that?"

"He can use the medical kit only if you'll stop harassing us and just leave us alone."

"No," Sarin said coldly.

Deke stared at Sarin. Black staggered through the bush towards the YMCA camp. The others followed. Janet rushed to her tent, blocking Black's path. He pushed his way past her impatiently. Fetching the kit and stripping off his tattered shirt, he rinsed his wounds freely with a bottle of antiseptic. He sat down on a stump and didn't move for a while.

"I ain't gonna last long like this," he said to Sarin. "You gotta stitch me up."

Sarin bent over the medical kit and opened a package of gauze. "Here."

Black pressed the bandage against the worst of his wounds, shutting his eyes tightly with the pain. Sarin fumbled with the small packages with shaking hands. Sterile needles and thread were included in the kit. By the time Sarin got them open and the needle threaded, Black appeared barely conscious. With trembling hands, Sarin touched the needle tentatively to Black's skin. Black bore it well for the first few stitches, then jumped involuntarily, and the needle ripped across his flesh. Sarin's face was gray.

"This ain't gonna work without freezing." He pressed bandages over the bleeding wounds, put Black's hand over it. With the order "hold it there," he walked off.

Nothing happened. Deke stood there. Sammy hovered nearby, his face still pale, looking at Black wide-eyed. Ten minutes later,

Carlos walked into the camp. He looked at Janet and jerked his thumb in Black's direction. "You: take care of Black-Jack."

"Take care of him yourself, I've already got patients," she retorted. "As long as you guys harass us, you don't get any help."

Deke looked anxiously on.

"Sarin says you'd better," Carlos said, "because no one else is going to."

"You're abandoning him?"

"All's fair in love and war." He shrugged.

"What if he dies?"

"Then it's your fault—you're the one that's got the training and the tools."

With this revelation, Carlos walked off.

Deke shifted anxiously, taking a couple of steps toward Black. "I'll help with what I can—but I don't know nothing about first aid."

Janet sighed. "I can try. But I can't do much. He needs a hospital."

Deke cast around for a solution. "The transmitter…? Can it be fixed?"

"Not a chance."

Chapter Forty-One

JASLOW SCRUTINIZED THE TWO officers in front of him. Parnell and Brooks were both big, well-muscled men. Young, though. Too hot-headed and inexperienced.

"Sit down," he ordered.

The men exchanged glances and sat down, smiling amicably. Jaslow threw three large, color glossies down on his desk. Three pictures of Enrik. A mugshot from his last arrest; bulging muscles, smirking at the camera. One at his apartment while the paramedics stripped him to the waist, revealing the dark bruises and reddish blotches covering his torso. The third in his hospital room, hooked up to IV, oxygen, and electronic monitoring equipment.

Jaslow said nothing and waited for their reactions. Parnell paled considerably and swallowed; the other raised his brows slightly, but otherwise registered no emotion.

"You're being charged with brutality on Larry Enrik," Jaslow informed them.

"Don't know what you're talking about," Brooks said.

"You went to the construction site he works at, took him out behind the trailer and gave him a beat-down when he wouldn't answer your questions."

"You can't prove any of that."

"Enrik got your squad car number and gave it and your descriptions to his girlfriend. One of the other guys at the site confirmed the description and his boss made a formal complaint at the end of the day and identified you both from your service pictures."

Parnell swore softly under his breath and turned another shade paler. "I didn't think it would go that far… but he wouldn't talk and I was thinking of Jacob…"

Jaslow considered. "Do you know Jacob?"

"Only in passing. Feel bad for the poor guy…"

"You realized, of course, when you were working Enrik over, that he was protecting Jacob? That he was trying to keep you from finding Jacob because Jacob doesn't want to be found?"

"We don't know that," the young man argued.

"Jacob said he'd die before he'd go back home."

Parnell looked shaken. "But Duke said… I just wanted to help Duke, to get Jacob back where he was safe."

Jaslow turned to Brooks. "How about you? Anything to say for yourself?"

"I'll say my bit in court. If it gets that far."

"I expect your reports on my desk within two hours. Complete reports. You're dismissed."

Brooks stood up and marched out without a word, but the younger officer lingered. "Sir?"

"What is it, Parnell?"

"What hospital is Enrik in?"

Jaslow raised an eyebrow. "General. Why?"

"I… uh… want to apologize to him."

"You can try. I doubt it will do much good."

"Thank you, sir." He turned to leave.

"Parnell."

"Yes, sir?" Parnell looked back.

"His girlfriend is there too, Madeleine Burke."

"As a patient?"

"She had a bit of a breakdown."

The boy shook his head slightly, eyes down. "Thank you, sir, I'll do what I can."

Thompson spread out the map for the chopper pilot.

"First, we want to make a sweep with the helicopter across here. That covers the most-used camp sites to begin with. Take lots of pictures and report anything you find suspicious. We're looking for amateurs. They won't be hidden. If that sweep doesn't pan out, we've got marked the reserved campsites. They may be hanging around there. There are ten to fifteen young adults and they've got motorbikes. If we still can't find anything, it may be because they've moved out of our jurisdiction or it may be because they're better hidden than we expect. We'll go to a ground search and get help from across the state line."

The pilot nodded.

"Any questions?"

"What are they wanted for?"

Thompson studied him. "Does it make any difference?"

"The more I know, the more I can help."

"What we've got here is a street gang. We're looking for one particular man. He's broken probation and wanted on several charges. Okay?"

"Fine."

"Here's his picture." Thompson handed a picture of Jacob it to him.

The pilot looked at it for a moment before putting it into a pocket.

A nurse bustled in and shook Larry gently. He opened his eyes groggily. "You have a visitor."

Beyond her stood a man whom Larry could just barely make out. The concussion was affecting his vision. The visitor moved closer and Larry saw that it was a cop. One of the cops who had put him in hospital. The policeman came up close to him, his face flushed, lips pressed together straight and thin.

"How are you feeling, Enrik?"

Larry sneered. "Come to admire your handiwork?"

"No... I came here to apologize. For what I did back there. It was wrong. I'm... I'm really sorry."

"Oh—let me finish for you. It was your partner's fault. He's the one who thought of it and he talked you into it. Right?"

Parnell stiffened. He chewed on his lip. "No. No one forced me into it. I was stupid and I let things get out of hand." Larry said nothing. Parnell tried to explain himself. "I had convinced myself I was acting in Jacob's best interests and you were hurting him by not answering."

Larry shut his eyes. "Yeah?"

"I realize I was wrong… you were his friend. You were protecting him the best you could."

"Great. You've apologized. Now you can leave and I'll be even happier."

"I'd like to ask you a few questions. Civilly. No pressure."

"You'd like to ask me some questions?" Larry repeated in disbelief.

"Not about where he is or was or anything like that. Just what kind of a guy he was."

"Like what? I knew him from work, that's it."

"I know. Was he good at what he did?"

"The best," Larry agreed, thawing a little. "He's a good learner, real quick. He's strong and he isn't afraid of heights. Billy wasn't sure at first how he'd do at heights, with his limp and all, but he's good. We worked together a lot."

"He'd been with the company a long time."

"For his age, yeah."

"And you've worked on a lot of the same sites."

"Yeah."

"He was a quiet kid."

"Do you know him?" Larry studied him with narrowed eyes.

"Hardly. I met him. Drank with his father a few times."

"His old man." Larry drew a painful breath. "I guess he's quite a piece of work."

"He's okay."

"If he was okay, Jacob wouldn't be running and I wouldn't be laying here. You know what he did this time?"

"No, actually."

"The guy beat'im up again, ended up slicing his throat with a butcher knife. That's the kind of great guy his old man is."

Parnell looked uncomfortable. "Nobody knew how he got that cut. How bad was it?"

"The thing was infected real bad, had to be stitched up."

"How was he recovering?"

"He's tough. It was healing okay when I—" Larry broke off.

"When you saw him," Parnell finished, nodding slowly. "After he took a bullet in an altercation with a rival gang."

"It won't help you," Larry shot back defensively.

A nurse poked her head in the door. "Finish up, you're over your limit," she warned.

Parnell nodded and she left again. "When did you see him last?"

Larry considered for several long moments. "He was only at my place a couple of days. I haven't seen him since."

"What was his condition when he came to you?"

"Bleedin' pretty bad, unconscious, fever. When the bleeding stopped and the fever broke, he was okay. He still wasn't in the best condition, but he could walk around."

"Where is he now?"

"Don't know where he went from my place."

"The gang should know, shouldn't they?"

"Jacob's quiet. He doesn't give out much personal information."

A different nurse came in and shooed Parnell out. Larry was pale and drawn. Parnell said goodbye and left.

Nicholas had been parked in front of the window where he could see part of the street and watch people coming and going, moving through the neighborhood. It was more entertaining than staring at the wall or ceiling, which was how he had previously spent his days.

Lynn escorted an unfamiliar woman into the room. The stranger smiled at him, placing herself squarely in front of him and looking him in the eye, something very few people did.

"Hi, Nicholas. My name is Brandy. I'm a communications specialist for people without a voice."

Nicholas studied her, reading everything he could from her face. People without a voice. Nothing like minimizing the greatest problem a person had. The woman gave him a reassuring smile and started unpacking her bags. Nicholas watched her mount a tablet on an articulating arm onto his wheelchair. She booted up the software.

"This is a system that responds to eye gaze, Nicholas. It analyzes where on the screen you are looking and lets you pick phrases or use the onscreen keyboard to spell out words. Then it speaks them out loud with a synthesized voice."

Nicholas' heart started beating faster. He repeated her words in his head, worried that he might have misunderstood her. The splash-screen came up on the tablet, then an input screen divided into sections.

"Now, if you just focus on one part of the screen…"

"Yes," the synthesized voice said, when Nicholas stared at the green button.

Brandy smiled. "Good. Now, I need to choose what interface will work best for you. The default screen requires the use of reading and spelling. Your file says that your accident happened when you were four. There are other interfaces that use pictures or symbols—"

"I… want… this."

Brandy laughed. "Well, I guess that answers the question of whether you can read."

It took time to spell out the words that were not on the frequently used words panel. "Jacob taught me."

"Jacob must have been a special friend, to take the time to do that."

"My brother."

"Oh, I see."

"I want to talk to… Cassy."

Brandy's brows drew down. "Oh. Is she one of the other children here?"

"Yes."

"I'll see if I can find her."

Brandy left the room and came back several minutes later. Cassy followed behind her. She looked at the new computer with interest. "Hi Nicholas," she greeted. "What's all this?" she asked, turning to look at Brandy.

"My voice. I need to talk to Thompson."

Cassy turned back and stared at Nicholas in shock. "Wow! Did you really do that? It's not just a trick?"

"No trick," Nicholas answered. "Call Thompson."

"Who?" Cassy asked.

"Cop. Please. Number from Lynn." Nicholas gave up on full sentences. He could get his message across without a lot of extra words.

"Oh. The ones who were here looking for Jake?"

"Yes. Now. Please."

Cassy hesitated, then left the room. She was back with Lynn a few minutes later.

"Cassy told me, but I can't believe you're already talking," Lynn said. She looked down at the computer.

"Call Thompson here now."

"Okay. Will do, Nicholas. You don't know how good it is to see you able to communicate."

Inwardly, Nicholas smiled. "You don't know how good it feels," he entered laboriously.

Lynn smiled. "I'll go make that call. You want him to come here?"

"Yes."

"Okay. I'll see if I can get a hold of him."

"Thank you."

Lynn showed Thompson and Jaslow into Nicholas' room. She had obviously explained the situation to them. They looked over the new equipment with interest but didn't ask what it was for.

"Something is wrong," Nicky's synthesized voice said.

"What do you mean?" Jaslow asked.

"Something happened to Jacob."

Jaslow sat on the bed across from Nicholas, watching his face carefully. "What's happened?"

"I don't know."

"Did he tell you something? Send you a message or communicate with you?"

"No."

"How do you know something has happened? Because he hasn't come back?"

"I can feel it. I know Jacob. I feel something is wrong."

"I see," Jaslow said slowly. "You're basing this on instinct."

Nicholas was relieved that Jaslow hadn't passed it off as imagination. Nicholas had lived with Jacob for years, he knew him, had a connection with him. He knew something had happened. Something was wrong. To a policeman like Jaslow, gut instinct meant just as much or more than what appeared to be solid facts. Thompson, who seemed more surprised than Jaslow by Nicholas' new ability to communicate, managed to gather his wits to ask some questions.

"What did Jacob say to you when he left? Did he give any indication of where he was going?"

"He was going to meet Sarin and the Kittens."

"In the mountains."

"Yes."

"Where exactly, do you know?"

"He didn't say."

"Did he know where they were or did he have to search for them?"

"I don't know."

"Nicholas… Father TJ suggested that Jacob might be suicidal. Our investigation supports that. What do you think?"

"He was… overwhelmed."

"He had a lot of things happen to him before he left home. And since then. The children said that he might have had a gun or guns with him."

"Yes. Guns."

"I see. Why would Jacob need guns if he was just going to meet the gang and camp?"

"I don't know."

"I'm not so sure of that, Nicholas."

Nicholas didn't say anything. After a lifetime of saying nothing it was an easy habit to fall back on.

"I want to know if he's gone AWOL on us," Jaslow said sharply.

"No."

"Then why the guns? Has he always armed himself like that?"

"No."

"Why now?"

"I don't know… different after the… kidnapping."

"Go on."

Nicholas had a hard time putting it into words. "Scared of being hurt or controlled."

"And if someone tried to hurt him or to control him, he intended to use a gun to make sure they didn't?"

"No. Just a threat."

"And if someone didn't listen to the threats? Didn't believe that he'd use the gun?" Jaslow persisted.

"He didn't want to hurt anyone."

"If he didn't want to hurt anyone, why the guns?"

"For protection. A warning. He didn't want to shoot anyone."

"What do you expect us to do now, Nicholas?"

"Find him!"

"But you don't know where he is."

"With Sarin. With the Kittens. In the mountains."

"It's a big area. We're already searching. We'll do our best. But if you can't tell us anything else, then we're already doing all we can."

Janet leaned over and searched for a pulse. She found it at last, faint and slow. Her eyes went to Black-Jack's thick, broad chest and flat stomach; covered with bloody bandages. Removing them, and mopping up the blood, Janet examined the wounds more carefully. Black-Jack had taken the bear's blow at an angle and the pad of its paw had smashed his ribs before the claws contacted. The force must have propelled him backward, saving him from the full intent of the claws. He was lucky; any other way and he would have been disemboweled. But maybe he wasn't so lucky. Maybe instant death would have been better than his suffering.

Her clumsy stitches were pulling apart already, his muscles straining under the skin. Skin seemed such a fragile thing. Janet hadn't pulled the stitches tight enough, afraid of causing more damage. As a result, the wounds were still bleeding too freely. Earlier, Black-Jack had been delirious. His eyes moved wildly. He muttered when he got enough breath. He was quiet now and she was afraid he was weakening.

She heard a helicopter and crawled quickly out of the tent. As she stood up, Sarin slipped up beside her. He slid his arm around her shoulders and pressed his gun to her ribs.

"Anyone tries to signal the whirly-bird and I'll blow her guts out," he shouted at the others. He looked up at the sky and pointed dramatically at the helicopter. "Wave to the helicopter, guys," he told the children who were standing around, frightened. "Wave at the helicopter and say hi!"

They waved, uncertainly at first and then more enthusiastically. Sarin watched the adults with sharp eyes. Janet caught the look and slowly turned her face to the helicopter and waved.

Sarin nodded approval. "Atta girl. Keep doing the right things and no one gets hurt."

The helicopter flew on. Sarin let go of Janet. Her face hot, Janet ducked back into the tent to tend to her patient.

Deke stood watching Janet rinse bloody bandages in the lake. They both watched the pink spread in the shallow water. When Deke shifted his position, a twig cracked under his foot and she turned her head quickly to look at him. Deke didn't move, staying back so he wouldn't scare her.

"How's he doing?"

Janet didn't answer at first, biting her lip and looking at him. "He's not getting any better."

Deke shifted, a tight knot in his stomach. "But he ain't gonna—die, or nothing—right?"

"What would you care if he did?" Janet snapped.

Deke opened his mouth, but the words didn't come to him. How could she think that he wouldn't care what happened to one of the boys in the gang? One of his brothers?

"I'm sorry," Janet said. "I know you helped out, so you must care. But yes… he could die. He's seriously injured."

Deke swore. He moved closer to her, looking at the bloody bandages that she was washing.

"You don't think he will, though, do you? Black, he's tough…" His voice cracked and Deke gulped, trying not to let her see his emotion.

"I don't have experience with trauma like this. He's not tough enough to last out here without proper treatment. He's still losing blood and his ribs are shattered; he's got bone fragments inside. His breathing's getting worse by the hour. One of those pieces of bone might have punctured a lung. I don't think he can last long."

Deke sat down on the pebbly shore, his legs suddenly weak and wobbly. He put his head between his knees, breathing through the wave of dizziness and nausea. "I'm going to try getting out," he said finally.

"What?"

"Sarin won't like it. He won't let me leave if he knows… how far to the next Ranger station or town?"

"By foot, three days… that's why we needed the radio. But on your bike—"

"I can't take the bike if I want to get a head start on Sarin. He'd hear me leave and be right behind me."

"Can't you just wheel it far enough away that he won't hear you…"

"The other guys are hanging out around the bikes. I'd never get away with it. I've got to walk."

Janet shook her head grimly. "I don't think he can hold out that long."

"He'd better." Deke took a deep breath. "I'll get going."

Chapter Forty-Two

THE HELICOPTER TOUCHED DOWN on the landing pad and wound to a stop. The chopper pilot stepped out. Jaslow went to meet him. The young man unzipped his jacket a few inches and wiped the sweat off his face.

"Anything?" Jaslow asked.

The man spat to the side and looked back at Jaslow. "Nope."

Jaslow watched him carefully. The aviator's eyes were wary and he obviously didn't like talking to Jaslow.

"Can I get you a drink?"

The man cast a glance in his direction and then away again. "I still got work to do and I might be flying again today. Maybe later."

His 'maybe later' was a very polite 'no.' He never intended to take up the invitation. He tapped the camera around his neck as he said 'work' and Jaslow remembered he was also their photographer and did his own developing. Thompson had said more, but Jaslow hadn't been paying much attention.

"Do you know where the lab is?"

"Yeah. I'll have these to you in an hour or so."

He parted from Jaslow abruptly. Jaslow went to find his partner. "What was it you said about our pilot?"

Thompson raised his brows. "Antony Taurus. Goes by 'Toni-toni.' He's just out of prison for fraud and murder."

The man hadn't looked much over eighteen.

"He's young."

"That he is. He was sixteen at the time of his arrest and was tried as an adult."

"What did he do?"

"Tampered with some bankbooks and fiddled some photos to give an alibi to the man who murdered his mother."

"Nice kid. When did he start flying?"

"I'm not sure. He got his license shortly after he got out of prison, as soon as he had his hours. Passed his test with flying colors."

Jaslow ignored the pun. "Did he plead?"

Thompson nodded. "Pled guilty. Said he'd do it again if he had the choice, even knowing he'd get caught."

"And this is the guy we're hiring to assist in an investigation?"

"We needed a pilot and a shutterbug. He's pro at both and cheaper as a package deal. Prison authorities said he was dependable, recommended him highly."

"Okay… as long as he doesn't fiddle our photos."

Toni-toni came back with the photos. He sat down on the chair and tipped his cap up slightly. He put the stack of blown-up black and white glossies on the desk. At Thompson's request, he started at the top and commented on each picture.

He hesitated when he got to one group of photos. "Something wrong with this camp?" Jaslow prompted.

"No-o-o…" Toni-toni trailed off.

"You aren't sure?"

"Just a feeling… it was a professional set-up, not amateur like you said. There were a lot of little kids. But… I just got a feeling something was wrong, out of place."

Jaslow looked up the coordinates of the camp on the map and compared it to a reservations table. "This one, right?"

"Yeah."

"It's a YMCA camp. They're authorized to be there."

Toni-toni nodded. "I know."

Jaslow didn't expect to find anything in the photos, but respecting the pilot's instinct, he flipped through the rest of the photos in the group carefully and studied the details of the reservation. "There are too many tents, and the YMCA kids are all inside the camp instead of out doing activities. Something's going on there…"

He stopped paging through the photos. "What's this?"

"It's a blow-up of the one before, their faces."

Jaslow studied it carefully, then handed the fuzzy enlargement to Thompson. "Tell me that's not Mace."

"Yeah… that's him. Jacob should be there," Thompson said.

"Uh-huh."

The pilot glanced down at his watch. "I've got to refuel before I can fly over there again. We won't be able to get there before dusk."

"We'll go tomorrow, then," Jaslow decided.

Deke tripped over another root and fell on his hands and knees. He was exhausted. Almost too weak and tired to go on. But he remembered Black-Jack. The nurse had said he might not make it another day. He forced himself to get back to his feet and run on.

Janet slept fitfully, waking every time Black-Jack moved or made a noise. Then she awoke to the noise of the tent zipper and sat up, panicking.

"What is it?"

The gang leader, Sarin, stuck his head through the flap. "Get out here. Now."

"What—what time is it?"

He had already withdrawn his head. Janet crawled out, feeling disoriented.

Sarin roused the adults and herded them to the center of camp. Ron was still too weak to put up a fight—or else he had learned his lesson—and everyone else went without a protest.

"Where's Deke?" Sarin demanded.

They all looked at him in bewilderment and Sarin repeated the question. When they still didn't answer, he yelled over his shoulder. "Carlos, come here."

Carlos made an appearance, scowling. "Yeah? What'd'ya want?"

"You think you can make these folks talk?"

Carlos' expression brightened. His eyes went from one face to the other and then around the camp. He went over to one of the tents, unzipped the front, and yanked Darla out. Carlos picked her up and she stared at him wide-eyed. Her hair was tousled, the thin nightgown clung to her, and she shivered in the cool morning air. Carlos drew his pistol from his pocket and pressed it against her side.

"They'll talk now," he assured Sarin with a big grin.

"Well?" Sarin tried again. "Where's Deke?"

There was silence for a moment and he studied their faces. Sarin looked grim. He looked over his shoulder to Carlos again and Janet broke down.

"Don't—don't hurt her. He's gone to get help."

"Help?"

"For your friend—Black-Jack—medical aid, because he can't hold out much longer."

Sarin laughed humorlessly. "Black-Jack is tougher than you imagine. Which way did Deke go, and when?"

"On the east trail, early this afternoon."

Sarin shrugged at Carlos, who put Darla down and pushed her back toward her tent. "Deke's gonna find out what happens to snitches," Sarin growled.

Toni-toni slouched in the pilot's seat and paid little attention to what Jaslow or Thompson was doing. He explored the underside of the panel with light fingers and checked the readings of all of the dials carefully. Jaslow frowned.

"What are you doing?"

"External checks," he said curtly. "I got enemies and I wanna make sure no one messes with my chopper."

He was more amiable to Thompson, who asked what kind of a chopper it was. "Revised rescue 'copter. Lots 'o' room and good control. Quieter, too."

"Revised how?" Jaslow demanded.

"Hey look," Toni-toni shot back, "if you don't trust me, get out now. I'm not flying you."

Jaslow settled back rigidly in his seat and said nothing more. Toni-toni finished checking the instruments and took off. Thompson kept up a casual conversation to begin with, but the airman was little disposed to talk and Thompson eventually left him alone.

After a while, they were flying over the thick forest. Toni-toni's eyes were intent on the scene below and his hands moved familiarly over the controls. "I don't know how far we're gonna get. We got a weather system coming in up ahead, low cloud cover and bad winds. I'll do what I can, but…"

He trailed off. There were three loud cracks below them and the ping of metal under the chopper. The helicopter pivoted sharply and the officers hung on.

"Are we hit?" Thompson shouted out.

"No, steady as she goes. This baby's reinforced, they couldn't harm us with a machine-gun."

"Those were gunshots," Jaslow said.

Toni-toni was lowering the helicopter. "Sure. And that was a heck of a distress signal." He pivoted the chopper again. "There he is," he said. He spoke to the officers. "There's still a rope with a harness right in the back. Toss it out after you open the door. Be ready to haul it up when I say." Toni-toni glanced over his shoulder at Jaslow, who was following his instructions. "It's attached to the crank to your left. Use that. Thompson… help him out."

Toni-toni focused on keeping the chopper steady, watching the figure below reach for the rope and sort out the straps. The boy tested his weight on the harness and waved. Toni-toni pulled the chopper straight up until the boy cleared the trees and signaled to the officers. When they heaved him up on board, Toni-toni hardly even glanced at him to admire his rescue job. He could hear the ragged gasps, and the exhaustion in the boy's voice as he panted out a few inarticulate words. There was a flask tucked beside Toni-toni's seat. He took it out and handed it back to Jaslow.

"Try a little of that on him. Just a little."

Jaslow handed it to the boy, who took it gratefully and gulped some down. He choked and looked at the flask, his eyes wide. Jaslow took it back and smelled it. He handed it back to Toni-toni, and the pilot guzzled a few mouthfuls down. With one hand, he screwed the cap back on and put it in its place.

"What's that?" Jaslow asked.

"None of your business. It helped, didn't it?"

Some of the color was coming back to Deke's face and his gasps were fading.

"I thought you weren't allowed to drink while flying."

Toni-toni grunted something indistinguishable. Jaslow turned his attention back to the matter at hand. He loosened the jacket that was tied around the boy's waist and pulled it off. "You're a Wildcat," he said, looking at the jacket.

Deke looked at him, looked at the jacket, and nodded. Toni-toni looked over his shoulder. When Jaslow lowered the coat, he saw the boy's face and swore under his breath. Jaslow turned and looked at him.

"You've got a job to do. Pay attention to your flying," he said.

Toni-toni turned around again to tend to his job. Deke continued to stare at the back of his head. Thompson took in their reactions. "Do you two know each other?"

Toni-toni didn't turn around again. Deke nodded dizzily. "He's—I'm… I'm Deke. Taurus."

It was a moment before it registered. "You two are related? Brothers?"

"Yeah… Toni-toni and me…" Deke stared at the pilot. "I ain't seen'im since he went to prison…"

"Well, sorry to have to break up the family reunion, but you have some explaining to do," Jaslow said firmly.

Deke suddenly remembered his errand. He leaned back and let his eyes shut a little, exhausted. "One of the guys, he got mauled by a bear... I came to get help."

"What happened?"

"You gotta get down there and help him. He's in pretty bad shape. I been running. Trying to get to help..." Deke trailed off. His eyes shut the rest of the way. "Man, it's good to sit down..."

Jaslow watched him for a moment. "Who was hurt?"

The boy didn't stir. Jaslow reached over to grab him by the shoulder and the helicopter hit a convenient air pocket, throwing Jaslow against the side.

"Leave him be," Toni-toni told him.

"He's going to answer some questions."

"Let him rest."

Toni-toni's voice was threatening. Jaslow looked at him. He backed off.

"Why don't you go sit with Thompson and leave the kid be?" Toni-toni suggested.

Jaslow obeyed and Toni-toni relaxed, focusing his attention back on the control panel.

"I don't want any trouble. You want to talk to Deke, wait 'til we're grounded and the kid's sobered up."

"Fair enough," Thompson agreed with a forced smile.

Toni-toni opened his flask again and took a sip. "You want some?"

"Knock-out drops?" Jaslow asked, looking at Deke, now unconscious to the world.

"Watch it, cop. If he's dehydrated and drinkin' that stuff on an empty stomach, it's no wonder he's out like a light." He stashed the bottle beside his seat again. "You may need it yet. I don't know if we're gonna make it to that campsite."

He was silent then, battling with growing winds and thickening clouds. Glancing in his mirror, he called out to the officers.

"Hey, Thompson? You wanna make sure the kid's okay?"

Thompson got up and went unsteadily to Deke. He felt the boy's wrist for a pulse and after a few seconds let it go again.

"He seems fine."

"Strap him in, then do the same with yourselves."

Thompson buckled Deke's seatbelt and went back to his own seat. "Did you know he was a Wildcat?"

"Sure. I been keeping tabs on him."

"Why didn't you tell us that when we were looking for them?" Jaslow asked.

"Why didn't you tell me you were looking for the Wildcats?" Toni-toni shot back. "You never mentioned what gang you were after."

Jaslow considered this and realized it was probably true.

"How long has he been with them?" Thompson asked.

"A while. Since before I got out of prison."

There was silence for a time. Toni-toni was sweating, concentrating hard on his flying but not making much headway against the weather system.

"We can't make it," he said finally. "We gotta go back."

"How long can this weather last?"

"Longer than my fuel and we're only on the edge of it. A few days, maybe."

Jaslow swore. "But we're so close!"

"We're too close to the trees and the mountains already and visibility's getting worse. Forget it. I can't fly through this safely."

The trip back to the city was without incident, but the atmosphere was grim. When they got back, the officers were hesitant to leave without talking to their witness.

"He'll be at my place tonight and I'll bring him around here tomorrow," Toni-toni assured them. "He came lookin' for help and you're the guys that can get it."

Jaslow opened his mouth to argue, then left it at that and went into the building with Thompson.

Janet went back into the tent, soaking wet from the rain. She sat and looked at her patient.

He was watching her. Not staring without seeing, not the wild and restless watching of his hallucinations, but watching her movements and seeming to take it all in.

"Hi," said Janet uncertainly.

Black's eyes flicked to each side, then back to her again. "Hi." His voice was hoarse.

"How are you feeling?"

He was a moment in answering. "I—I don't feel nothing. Nothing at all." Janet swallowed. She tried to appear unworried at this news, but Black obviously didn't buy it. "How—bad is it?"

"You're okay. You just need to rest."

Neither of them believed it.

"Where's Nicky?"

"Hush, you shouldn't be talking."

"I got to talk before it's too late…"

"Nonsense—" Janet said briskly, but she couldn't keep up the pretense. "I'm sorry…" she apologized, though she wasn't sure what for. He didn't say anything. "Where's who?" Janet asked after a moment, remembering his question.

"Nicholas," he said very softly. "But… he couldn't be, could he?"

"Is he in the gang?"

His eyes crinkled in the corner. "No… my brother."

"Nobody has been able to leave the camp, forget coming in. No, that's wrong. Your friend went to get help."

"Friend…?"

"Deke."

"Deke went to get help?" Black-Jack looked puzzled. "Sarin let him?"

"No. He left without telling Sarin. Lucky for you or he wouldn't have gotten far."

Black lowered his eyes, nodding his head slightly. "I'm not exactly on good terms with Sarin."

His thoughts were drifting. For a few minutes, he seemed to be mumbling to himself, but Janet couldn't tell what he was saying. Then his voice grew stronger again.

"I didn't want to cause trouble," he protested. "I never wanted to hurt no one… I just wanted to go somewhere safe… Sarin… he never understood…" his voice was getting faint again. "He's funny… sometimes he's decent, but…" Black muttered a few more remarks that Janet couldn't catch and then passed out again.

She sighed and checked on his bandages.

Jaslow was furious as he burst into the condo. He had trusted Toni-toni to bring Deke to the police station, but Toni-toni hadn't done so. Thompson had phoned, but there was no answer.

Jaslow strode up to the manager's desk, showed his badge, and demanded access to Antony Taurus' room. The woman there looked doubtful, but led the way, followed by Jaslow, Thompson in tow. After several knocks, the woman fit the master key in the lock and opened the door. It stuck at first but eventually gave, and the officers pushed their way past her. Toni-toni was sitting at the kitchen table, concentrating on some detailed area maps. His face was unshaven and his flask within easy reach. He appeared only vaguely curious as to why the officers were there and why the manager had let them in.

"Where's your brother?"

"Sleeping like a baby," Toni-toni responded, jerking his head towards the bedroom. "Don't wake him."

Jaslow checked the room and came back more relaxed, but still angry. "You didn't answer your phone."

"I don't usually. But it hasn't rung this morning. Sometimes it acts up."

Toni-toni pulled out his cell phone and looked at it, shaking his head. Jaslow watched as Toni-Toni shut it off and turned it back on again. Jaslow was starting to calm down. Looking around, he studied the suite more carefully. Everything was new, of course, since it had all been purchased since Toni-toni's release from prison. Surprisingly, though, the furnishings looked expensive. Not thrift store purchases by any means. Jaslow didn't see how it could be within a brand new pilot's price range. Especially a pilot who had apparently bought and modified his own helicopter.

"Any chance of flying in today?"

Toni-toni gestured to radio equipment on the counter. "No. I already checked. I'm looking over the maps, though. Maybe something can still be done, if we fly in another way."

Jaslow's eyes narrowed in suspicion. "You're doing more than you have to. What do you expect to get from all this?"

Toni-toni said nothing at first and didn't look up from his calculations. After a while, he laid aside his instruments with a sigh. "If it was that important to the kid, I'm not going to just stand by and let it go." Toni-toni paused, his face drawn and muscles tense. "You guys think I'm some kind of monster because of my mom's murder. But I wasn't going to stand by and let her hurt my kid brothers. So I helped cover for someone else who didn't like the things she was doing either."

"Who else of your family have you been in contact with recently?"

"No one. Deke's the first one I've talked to since I went to prison."

"No one else?"

"No. My dad got married again and has a new family now. Parley ran away. Deke's been living with the gang. My older brothers... I wasn't that close to them."

"And you haven't seen any of them in... how long?"

"I don't see what this has to do with anything. I haven't particularly wanted to, except for the kids."

Toni-toni's eyes darted to the side and in a few moments the officers heard Deke stirring in the bedroom. "Give'im a chance to waken up. And go easy on him," Toni-toni said in a low voice. "He came to get help."

Jaslow nodded.

Deke emerged from the hall, yawning. His eyes were tired and bruised-looking. He saw the officers and made no comment. He reached for Toni-toni's flask, but his brother caught him by the wrist. "Lay off the drinks this early in the mornin'."

"*You're* drinking."

"I been up for a lot longer and I don't gotta talk to the cops."

Deke moved to the cupboards in the kitchen. He fixed himself a bowl of cereal and ate it standing up, watching the officers warily. He put the dishes aside and sat down on a chair, turning it around to rest his arms and head on the back. "One of the guys in the gang is hurt bad. Real bad."

"What happened?" Thompson inquired. "Go slowly."

Thompson flipped open his notebook and waited, pencil poised. Deke took a deep breath, and staring at the woodgrain in the table, slowly explained it.

"We went up there to camp by this hiking group. Just to make them nervous or somethin', I don't know. Just something for a little fun. It was Carlo's idea—"

"Full name?"

"Uh, I don't know his first name. His last name is Don Carlos."

"Go on."

"See, Sarin ain't so bad himself, or even Carlos, really, it's just when they're together... I dunno, they egg each other on..."

"What happened?"

"Black-Jack got hurt protectin' one of the YMCA kids from a bear. Sarin didn't even care! Ever since Black knocked Sarin down in front of the gang, Sarin's been out to get him... Most of the guys have had enough, they're ready to bug out of there. But Sarin and Carlos won't quit and Black-Jack's hurt real bad—"

"Explain how he got hurt. What happened?"

"One of the little kids must have been wandering around where he wasn't supposed to. There was a bear around. Black said it had a cub. The kid must have got between them. Black-Jack was there and he got the kid out of the way, but he got hurt himself before he shot it. Or after. Before it died..."

"How bad are his injuries?"

Deke didn't answer for a moment. He toyed with his spoon and empty cereal bowl, thinking about it. "The YMCA nurse is takin' care of him. She... didn't think he could make it until I got help... He's hurt bad." Deke's eyes went longingly to Toni-toni's flask. He rubbed his temples. "Real bad."

"Do you know Black-Jack's real name?" Jaslow asked.

Deke had to concentrate to dredge it up.

"Jacob Donell."

Janet was surprised to find Black stirring again when she checked on him in the morning. She waited for a few minutes to see if he was going to wake up. He did. He saw her immediately and tried to move. He couldn't get up, and lay there for a moment stunned, not recognizing his surroundings. Slowly, understanding crept into his eyes. He whispered something and Janet leaned closer to hear what he was saying.

"Water…?"

"Hang on. I'll get some."

Janet crawled out of the tent and stood up. The storm had been stilled for a while, but everyone still seemed to be in their tents. A figure moved towards her and it was a moment before Janet realized with relief that it was Sammy.

"Hi, Sammy. Everything okay?"

Sammy's eyes went to Janet's tent. "H-h-he's h-hurt b-bad?"

Janet was surprised at first that Sammy would be inquiring after Black, but then remembered that it had been Sammy that Black had protected from the bear.

"Yes," she admitted. "He's hurt pretty bad."

"I s-s-s-see?"

Janet scratched the back of her head. Letting Sammy see anyone in that kind of shape didn't seem like a very good idea. And it was her instinct to keep the YMCA children as far away from the motorcycle gang as possible, even from Black-Jack. Maybe especially from Black-Jack.

"I don't think that's a good idea. Why don't you go on back to your own tent?"

Sammy just stood there and didn't say anything. Janet looked down at his bare feet, which must have been ice-cold on the damp ground.

"How are your feet?"

"B-b-b-better."

"Good. Maybe we can get on our way again pretty soon."

Janet said it as if she wasn't burdened down with a bigger responsibility. As if things were like they had been a couple of days ago, before she had to worry about Black and how to take care of him. And if he would survive.

"I have to go get some water," she told Sammy.

He nodded and Janet went on. When she got back to her tent with a canteen of drinking water, Janet found Sammy inside, sitting quietly, a blanket wrapped around him. He looked down at Black and didn't say anything to him or to Janet.

Janet filled a collapsible cup with water and held it to Black's lips. He got a couple of swallows down, but then he choked. The rest of the cup went down Black's chest, soaking into the bandages to mix with blood. Coughs racked Black's body and tears rolled down his cheeks. Bloody froth leaked out the corner of his mouth. Janet wiped it away with tears in her own eyes.

"It will be okay," she reassured him. "It's all right. Everything will be okay."

Black's coughs stopped abruptly. He lay still with his eyes shut. Janet checked his pulse. Black breathed for a few minutes, ragged and wet-sounding. He opened his eyes again and met hers.

"Ma'am…"

"Janet."

"Ma'am… I can't do it."

Janet stared at his wide brown eyes, then looked away. She had heard him described in varying degrees of frightening detail by the Wildcats, but they hadn't told her this. The helplessness, the acceptance, and the fear in his eyes didn't match up with the gang's description. Looking past the blood-soaked bandages, the gang jacket lying beside him with the guns on top, looking past the hard-muscled, scarred body, he could have been one of the children. She saw the same look mirrored in Sammy's eyes as he sat there watching. A terrified, helpless, abandoned look.

"Hold on," Janet told him. "Just a little longer and you'll be in a hospital, with professional help. You've made it this far. You can do it."

His eyes closed and opened again, in despair. "It's too hard."

"You have so much to live for. You're so young, you have so much of life ahead of you!"

"No…"

"Think about your family…" she urged.

Black's breath hissed out between his teeth. "My brother," he said, and his eyes wandered to Sammy. "Nicholas."

Chapter Forty-Three

THOMPSON LOOKED ACROSS HIS desk at Jaslow, who was scowling into the depths of his coffee cup. "We should tell Duke."

"That Jacob's been injured? Why? There's nothing he can do."

"He has a right to know what's happening. Especially when Jacob may be…"

"He half-killed the boy a dozen times himself," Jaslow growled. "What difference will it make to him?"

"He has to know."

"What I'm worried about is getting someone in there."

Thompson shook his head. "How? We can't fly in and I don't know that we could do much if we could. We're going to need a lot more personnel in there than just you and me. Getting them in and out is not going to be easy."

It didn't matter what Janet said to Sammy; he wouldn't leave the tent. Janet couldn't understand why he would choose to be there instead of playing with the other children in the YMCA group. He hadn't been with them for a long time, but she knew that he got along with a couple of the children.

But Sammy just sat there silently in her tent beside Black-Jack, watching him and listening to him with wide eyes.

Black-Jack was delirious most of the time now. Listening to him, Janet knew that the stories that the gang had been telling her and the others were not true. Most likely, they were invented by the gang members to frighten the YMCA group or to entertain themselves. Like ghost stories told around a campfire.

Black-Jack spoke tenderly of his brother, Nicholas, when he was conscious or closer to consciousness. And when his mind went to the darker, more deeply hidden parts of his mind, she learned about his father. About an abusive father who sometimes seemed to love him, and a frightened, helpless mother who let herself and her babies be abused. Working with the YMCA kids, Janet knew how common the story was. How many children were starving for affection, for just one kind word just once in a while. Janet looked at Sammy and sighed.

The tent flap opened and Ron put his head into the tent. He saw Black-Jack, propped up to try to keep his breathing easy and to keep blood from draining from the bandages onto his face. Black-Jack's face was gray. He was too weak to move, to do anything more than whisper when he could get the breath. Sweat slicked his face from the heat of his fever.

"He's going to die, isn't he?" Ron said. There was a kind of evil enjoyment on his face when he said it.

"I'm afraid…" she started, and trailed off, unable to express it.

"It's what he deserves," Ron hissed. "I'm glad it's slow. Pickin' on a guy, using that gun because he knows he's not strong enough, no matter how big he is. It's what he deserves!"

"Get out of here," Janet told Ron sharply. There was alcohol on his breath. The only way alcohol could have gotten into the camp was through the gang. So Ron was fraternizing with the enemy. And they had turned him against the one person who wasn't like them.

"I'll go where I please."

"Get out, and get out now!" she ordered and shoved him. His balance wasn't good and he tipped over backward, out of the tent. Janet crawled out after him, giving him another good shove as he tried to get up. A lot of the gang members were around. It was getting dark and Janet always got nervous as the gang started to get rowdier. Anne was sitting on a log by the fire. Janet spoke to her.

"Will you please look after your brother?"

Anne looked unconcerned. "Why, what's wrong with him?"

"He's drunk and he's making a fool of himself."

"He deserves to die!" Ron shouted.

"Shut up. Look after him Anne, I've got enough to worry about."

"And I don't?" Anne asked, motioning to the gang.

Janet looked around at the young men more closely. They were laughing, in high humor. Some of the children were playing around and being silly. Probably restless after being cooped up in the campsite for so long. Then Janet realized.

"Those kids are drunk! What are you doing, letting them give the kids alcohol?"

"You stop them," Anne suggested morosely. "I value my life and health."

Janet looked around. "Where's their leader? Sarin?"

"In their campsite, probably."

Janet stalked off, letting her fury carry her. She spotted Sarin. "If you call off your boys now, before this gets any more out of hand, I'll vouch for you when the cops get here. But if you let them continue, I'll charge you with everything I can think of!"

"Whoa, settle down, lady," he held up his hands defensively. "What're they doing?"

"What are they doing? They've got half the kids drunk! If anything happens to the children, I'll hold you responsible—"

"Take a chill pill, huh? A little booze won't hurt them."

"It won't hurt them? These are little kids we're talking about! Do you know how fast they can get alcohol poisoning? Do you know what it's doing to their nervous systems?"

"Cool it. I know a lot of guys who started drinkin' when they were kids. It won't harm them."

"Guys who lead any kind of normal life? Who have half a brain left to reason with? Come on, guys who have any smarts?"

Sarin considered. Then he shrugged and stood up. "I'll look after it."

She followed him to the YMCA campsite. Sarin grabbed a couple of his boys. "Clear out. Go back to your tents."

"Come on, Sarin. Watch the kids—"

"Get back there, or I'll paint the next mountain with your brains!" Sarin shouted. "Move it!"

They moved. The others in the gang saw what was happening and a few left of their own accord. Sarin kicked a couple of others out. Sarin looked around at the children, shaking his head in amusement.

Janet looked around for Ron. "Where's—"

Sarin froze and held his hand up to silence her. The hair rose on the back of Janet's neck at his alert posture. He looked around and his eyes focused on the tent Black-Jack was in. "One of those drunk kids picked up Black's gun," he whispered.

Janet felt the blood drain from her face. Sarin walked silently over to the tent and peered in the flap. He drew it back very slowly and Janet saw Ron's silhouette before Sarin's hand snaked out and the gun went off.

Janet covered her mouth and bit her hand, trying not to cry out. Sarin wrestled Ron out of the tent, disarming him. Ron was yelling in protest. "He deserves—"

Sarin landed a heavy blow across the back of Ron's neck with the gun. Ron fell to the ground in a heap and didn't move. Anne rushed over to her brother. Sarin tossed the gun back into the tent and went back over to Janet.

"You got a bullet in your sleeping bag somewhere, but he didn't hit anyone. Who let him booze it?"

"One of your devils."

Sarin grinned. He raised an eyebrow. "Listen, I'll shoo these kids into their beds, you go take a look at Black-Jack. I don't think he's doin' so good."

"Does that concern you?"

"Maybe it does. Maybe I just don't want a corpse stinkin' the place up. Just do like I tell you."

Janet went back into her tent to see to Black-Jack. His eyes were open and he watched her enter. "When did you wake up?" Janet asked.

His eyes were sad and worried-looking. "When he came in…"

"I'm so sorry…"

"…not your fault…" he whispered.

"There's no excuse for him to do something like that! I can't believe he would do that!"

"It's okay…"

Janet looked at Sammy, still sitting in the corner, his eyes wide and frightened. "It's all right, Sammy," Janet tried to reassure him.

When she put out her hand, he pulled back, staying out of reach. He pulled the blanket around him more securely and just watched her and Black silently.

Father TJ reluctantly turned off the light and paused for a moment before leaving the building and locking the door. He looked up and down the street but saw nothing unusual. Only the usual hopeless and homeless. No sign of gang activity. He sighed and tried to walk down the sidewalk casually. A figure stepped out of the shadows.

"Father?"

His heart raced and his stomach tightened. It was one of them. Long, greasy hair and dark glasses. Dark glasses and it was night time. Both his jacket and his shirt were open at the chest, showing off a huge, complicated tattoo. "Father TJ? It's just me."

Father TJ recognized the voice. The boy took off his dark glasses and shoved them in his pocket.

"Keith?"

Keith looked embarrassed. "Yeah. Look different in my street clothes, huh?"

The man nodded.

"Walk you to your car, Father?"

Father TJ hesitated. He knew Keith, and yet… "Well, if you like."

He actually did feel safer with Keith there, once they started walking. The shadows remained shadows, the street people were all street people he had seen before. Who slept there every day. "Keith—you didn't have anything to do with…"

"No, Father," he shook his head vigorously, "that's what I wanted to tell you. I didn't know. I would have warned you if I knew."

Father TJ looked into Keith's eyes and knew it was the truth. He unlocked his car and paused before getting in. "Do you need a ride anywhere, Keith?"

"No. You just drive safe to your own part of town."

"I will. Thank you."

Keith smiled and shut the door for Father TJ. "No problem."

Thompson and Jaslow went by Sunset House to let Nicholas know the developments in Jacob's case.

After telling him about the latest details gleaned from Deke, Nicholas said nothing. Both of the officers surreptitiously looked at his computer set-up, trying to determine if everything was properly positioned, or whether perhaps something had been bumped out of alignment so that it could no longer track his eyes. But it was obvious that Nicholas was looking away from the tablet screen, staring off into space.

"Nicholas, do you understand what we told you?" Thompson asked eventually.

It was unsettling to look into his blank face after what they had just told him about Jacob. And when Nicholas finally did switch his gaze to his computer and they heard the synthesized voice, it was flat and unemotional.

"I want to see Duke."

"I don't know if that's such a good idea," Thompson said.

"Yes. I want to see him. Social Services says I'm a competent adult. He can't ever have me back."

"I know he can't take you back. But I still don't think this is the time…"

"Please. I've never talked to Duke. I want him to hear me."

Thompson looked at Jaslow for his response.

"We can set it up," Jaslow agreed. "But you aren't to say anything to him about what's happened to Jacob since he left home. We are not letting Duke know any details until we can get into the camp and Jacob's condition can be evaluated. Duke needs to be kept out of this."

"OK," Nicholas agreed.

Jaslow and Thompson looked at each other, trying to evaluate whether they should allow the meeting to take place.

Officer Brooks pulled the squad car to a halt outside a fast food joint and turned to Parnell. "Just coffee?"

"Just coffee."

They didn't see or hear the motorcycles. The gang must have left them behind or beside the building. The doors were jerked open and a gun was shoved into Brooks' chest.

"Not a muscle," one of the black-jacketed figures growled. "Both of your hands on the dash. Nice and slow."

Parnell looked at the young man giving them the commands. "Listen, guys, put away the guns and we can talk. You can go away quietly and we won't ever mention this—"

"Shut up, Parnell. Hands on the dash, now!"

They obeyed slowly. Brooks gave it a try. "You'll only regret this."

"I don't think so. Put your hands on your head and step out of the car if you want to talk to us, Brooks."

He didn't move.

"I said get out of the car, Brooks."

Brooks moved to obey. His face was bright red. His movements were a little too quick and unschooled.

"Slow down. Don't try anything. Parnell, you sit tight and keep those hands steady."

Brooks straightened and gritted his teeth as one man took his gun from his holster. Another unclipped the handcuffs from Brooks' belt.

"Okay, Brooks. Hands behind your back."

He hesitated. They wrestled him into position.

Parnell looked toward the store, knowing that someone must be able to see what was going on. Surely they would call for help.

One of the gang reached for his wallet and was pushed back by the ringleader.

"This ain't no mugging. This here's payback and we all agreed on the rules."

"Okay, okay."

Brooks was taken out of Parnell's sight. Parnell's gun and handcuffs had been taken, but he was still seated in the car with his hands on the dash. Just waiting his turn, he assumed.

Enrik was standing guard at the car. He couldn't have been recovered from his beating or he would have been taking care of Brooks personally, leaving someone younger on guard duty.

"I said you guys would pay. Can't rely on the justice system. They don't even put you guys on administrative leave!"

Parnell swallowed. "So I'm after Brooks?"

"No. You saved yourself a lot of pain by coming to me to apologize. And you went to Maggie, too. No one made you do that."

Parnell's hand moved over about an inch. His gun's muzzle was pressed into his side.

"Not a muscle, Parnell, you aren't off the hook yet."

"You want him cuffed?" another boy offered.

"It's okay. He'll stay still. He might need to answer a call."

One of the other gang members returned and slipped into Brooks' seat. He picked up the rifle and stepped out of the car again. Parnell could hear the struggles and groans of his partner.

"I can't just sit here and let this happen!"

"You don't have any choice. Don't worry, it's nothing serious. Nothing that'll keep him in hospital."

"This is going too far. Assaulting an officer—"

"But beating down a handcuffed gang banger isn't? How is that suddenly right and this is wrong? Do you want to know why the charges against you and Brooks were dropped, Parnell?

Would you like to know that? Not because of no apologies. Because I can't afford it. This is a lot cheaper than court-justice."

"Worth prison, Enrik?"

"Maybe it is, Parnell. And maybe it isn't. Why don't I tell you when this has all blown over?"

The other Wildcat standing guard reached into the car and popped the hood. He went around the front of the car and Parnell couldn't see what was going on.

"What's he doing?"

"Siphoning your radiator. You'll need some water before you leave here or you'll overheat your engine."

"Enrik—"

"Enough, all right? Enough talk. What's done is done."

Parnell sat there, tense and silent, trying to block out the sounds of the beating. "Enrik, please…"

"What is it?"

"Revenge isn't worth it—"

"On the streets, revenge is everything," Larry declared.

"This isn't the streets. We aren't talking a street-fight here. We aren't talking about getting even with someone who double-crossed you. We're talking about a law enforcer, someone who's trying to keep decent people safe!"

"That would be true if you guys hadn't broken the rules. I wouldn't lay a hand on either one of you for doing your job. But you broke the law. When you come over to our side, our rules count."

Parnell kept quiet. A few minutes later, Enrik glanced over his shoulder. "Slide over to your partner's seat. If you take your hands down, make it real slow."

Parnell did as he was told. Brooks was dragged back to the car and folded into the empty seat. Parnell looked at him and up to the others silently. The group slowly dissolved until only Enrik was left.

"You'll pay for this," Parnell said quietly. "I'll see that you go to prison for this."

"No, you won't. He will, but you know I only took what I deserved."

"I won't let you get away with this."

"He's not badly hurt. He'll be back on the job before I will."

Larry held out Parnell's gun to him. Parnell sat there staring at it, then at length he shook his head. "Leave it in the lane so I have an excuse for not having shot you."

"Maybe you don't feel it yet, but you're pretty badly shook up. You're white as a ghost and you been shakin' since we got here. They'll understand you not shooting me."

Parnell took the gun. "How do you know I *won't?*"

"Because. You're a half-decent guy under that uniform."

He started to turn away, and Parnell raised the shaking gun to point at him. "You're under arrest, Enrik."

"You'd better not take the safety off." Larry didn't turn around to answer. "You're shaking so hard you're likely to pull the trigger."

He kept walking. Parnell lowered the gun and reached for his radio.

Black-Jack was sleeping quietly, so Lynn crawled out of the tent to talk to the others. All the children were asleep in their tents. Anne and Ron sat by the campfire talking. Janet sat down and joined them.

"How is he?"

"Still delirious. I don't know if he'll last the night."

"Serves him right," Ron muttered, staring down at the mug of coffee between his hands.

"I'm sorry. I don't think anyone deserves to die like this," Anne said.

"He didn't do anything," Janet said. "He hasn't done anything wrong."

"He tried to drown Ron," Anne pointed out.

"Talk to the children! Good grief, talk to Darla! She's twelve, she knows what she saw! It wasn't Black-Jack."

"If it wasn't Black-Jack, then who was it?" Ron demanded.

"Carlos."

Ron looked startled, then angry. "Carlos is the only one of the lot that's half-ways decent!"

"He's being decent to you so that you won't suspect him, Ron."

"He's a lot more decent than Black-Jack."

"You don't know either one of them. You haven't even talked to Black-Jack."

"He's a good-for-nothing hood running from the police!"

"He's a construction worker and he's trying to stay away from his father, who's a policeman."

Anne poked at the fire. "You're both only listening to one side of the story. Ron is listening to Carlos and you're listening to Black-Jack. No one is going to find out the truth that way."

There was a movement and soft moan from the tent and they all glanced towards it. Janet started to get up, but Anne put a hand on her shoulder. "I'll check on him," she volunteered, recognizing how exhausted Janet was.

Black-Jack had somehow slid down from being propped up and his face was purple with the effort of trying to breathe. Sammy was trying to lift him back up. It took all of Anne's strength for the two of them to get him propped up again. She felt Black-Jack tremble as she moved him. He lay there struggling for breath, his hand clutched at the bandages across his torso. Anne avoided his eyes and avoided looking at Sammy.

Jaslow wheeled Nicholas into the quiet corner office and parked him there. "Are you sure you want to talk to Duke?"

"Yes."

"Okay. As long as you're sure that's what you want."

They waited for Thompson, who had gone to fetch Duke. They both recognized Duke's step and his low rumbling voice as he spoke with Thompson, approaching the office. Duke stopped and stared when he stepped into the office.

"Where'd you find him?" he demanded. "Or have you had him all this time?"

"No, we didn't have him," Jaslow answered. "Though we've known where he was for a couple of days now. You see his new equipment?"

Duke looked over the computer panel. "Yeah, where'd that come from?"

"Social Services got a communications specialist to evaluate him and get him hooked up."

Duke shrugged. "So?"

"Hello, Duke," the synthesized voice spoke.

Duke gaped. "One of you did that! How did you do that?"

"We didn't. Nicholas did. He wants to talk to you."

"Talk? He's never talked in his life!"

"Listen to me," Nicholas' voice split the air again. "I'm charging you with abuse."

There was silence in the room. Duke slowly took this in. "I've never laid a finger on you."

"That's negligence. I meant abuse of Jacob."

"You can't prove anything."

"I was there."

"Nobody's going to listen to this circus act," Duke shouted, his face turning purple.

"How about murder? Do you think you can get away with that one?"

"What are you talking about?"

Jaslow had already started across the room, anticipating where Nicholas was going.

"If Jacob—"

Jaslow pushed the tablet away, abruptly cutting off Nicholas' power of speech.

"I think you've heard what Nicholas has to say to you," Jaslow said.

Duke breathed heavily, looking at Nicholas. His teeth were clenched. "When is he coming back home?"

"He won't be going back. He qualifies as a competent adult and he's made his wishes known. He doesn't want to go back to you."

"You can't do that."

"Nicholas can. He's spoken to Social Services."

"Where else is he going to go? Who else is going to look after him?"

"He's disabled. The government will ensure he's taken care of."

Duke stared at Nicholas, then at Jaslow. "Fine. He's old enough. If he says he wants to leave, that's his business."

He hesitated for a moment longer and then turned and walked back out of the room. Jaslow turned back to Nicholas. He carefully pushed the screen back into position so that Nicholas would be able to speak again.

"I thought we had a deal."

"Sorry."

"Duke is going to know nothing of Jacob's condition until we can get him out of the campsite. And he will know nothing of Jacob's whereabouts until we can take him in ourselves."

Chapter Forty-Four

WEATHER'S GOOD, HOW ABOUT going for a spin?"
Jaslow and Thompson turned and looked at Toni-toni.
Jaslow's eyes narrowed.

"You mean we can fly to the camp?" Thompson asked.

"You got it."

"You're gassed up and ready to go?"

Toni-toni nodded. Thompson and Jaslow exchanged glances.

"Okay, let's get this pulled together," Jaslow agreed.

He started making phone calls, getting everything organized. As soon as they could get ready, they were up on the helipad on the roof, getting into the chopper.

The last one on the roof was Duke, demanding to know where Jacob was. Jaslow swore in frustration. It was impossible to keep Duke away from the operation and eventually they made room for him and allowed him to go along.

Thompson's cell rang. He spoke quietly for a few minutes and turned to Jaslow. "Officer Brooks was assaulted on duty last night. Wildcats. Enrik was one of them."

"Tell them to arrest all the Wildcats they can, with a special warrant on Enrik."

"They've already got BOLO's out."

Toni-toni glanced at them. "Not Deke."

Jaslow looked at Toni-toni sharply. "He could have been in on it just as easily as any of the others."

"Not likely. I arranged for him to be taken to the Ranger station yesterday so he could go in with them once the weather broke."

"Then you don't need to worry about him getting arrested."

Toni-toni looked irritated. "Don't try to pull anything over on me. The Rangers get those bulletins too and they can arrest him as easily as any other cop."

"He can take his chances like the others. He knew that when he joined the gang."

"There's nothing illegal about joining a gang!"

Thompson had been watching Toni-toni grow more and more distracted. "Settle down, Toni-toni. Watch what you're doing," he warned quietly.

The pilot took his eyes off of Jaslow and slowly turned his attention back to his flying.

Janet was dozing after a long night looking after Black. He'd had a feverish, restless night. A helicopter was close by. Janet could hear the propeller beat the wind. Suddenly, Janet sat bolt upright. A helicopter? Another one? If Sarin hadn't noticed this time or had heard it like she had, without really comprehending it, maybe she could signal it…

She crawled out of the tent, looking towards the sound.

"Careful," warned Sarin from close by. "Don't do anything stupid, all right?"

The helicopter came into sight and she stared at it longingly. It was flying low. She could almost see inside it. Janet's heart skipped a beat. Wasn't it the same helicopter that had flown over before? She looked at Sarin, who was a pace behind her, studying the chopper with unconcerned interest. He didn't notice. He didn't realize. It might only be a tours helicopter, one that went over regularly, but on the other hand, it might not. It might be there for a specific purpose. For the purpose of saving them.

It flew over the camp without pausing or hanging over them like it had before. Janet's heart fell. They didn't know anything. Not a thing.

After landing on the ground just above the trail, Toni-toni got out with the officers. Jaslow looked at him.

"This has nothing to do with you, Taurus. Stay in the chopper."

Toni-toni shook his head stubbornly. "If Deke is with the Rangers, I want to talk to him. If he's been arrested, I want to talk to the Rangers."

"Stay here."

"You can't order me around. I'll come if I like. I won't be in the way, if that's what you're worried about."

Jaslow sighed.

The Rangers met up with the officers a little farther down the trail and Deke was with them. Toni-toni went to him immediately and they spoke to each other quietly. They were silent and watched the officers maneuver. Toni-toni stuck close to Thompson, which took some of the weight off of Jaslow's mind and left him free to give orders. The sharpshooters disappeared into the thick bush to circle the camp. Jaslow got their reports one by one as they got into position. Finally, Thompson made sure the emergency medical team—who came in their own chopper—were present and ready to go. He nodded to Jaslow.

There was a movement in the foliage ahead. Toni-toni's sharp eyes picked it out and he pointed the figure out to Deke as Jaslow got a report from one of the snipers. Deke watched tensely.

"It's only Andrews," he said to Thompson. "Don't shoot!"

"There won't be any shooting if we can help it."

Andrews suddenly became aware that something was wrong and he turned to shout over his shoulder. An officer stepped up directly behind him, gun raised. "Not a sound."

Andrews put his hands up and allowed himself to be escorted away from the camp. When a couple other officers came to help put cuffs on him and frisk him, he complied, showing no resistance.

"About time you guys got here, man."

"What's your name?" Jaslow demanded.

"Michael Andrews—"

"What's the situation back there?"

His words came out in a rush. "It's bad, man, real bad. Black-Jack, he ain't doing so good. Everyone is sick to death of Sarin and Carlos—Sarin by himself ain't bad, or Carlos, but together… they're poison! We shoulda been out of here a long time ago!"

Jaslow recognized his sentiments as similar to the ones that Deke had expressed earlier. They rang true. He hustled Andrews out of the way, into the custody of another officer. Everyone got into position.

Janet was startled by shouting. Not just the adolescent voices of the gang, but mature men's voices too, hard and harsh. Noises of running and crashing through the brush. A few of the motorcycles roared into life, but she could hear that they didn't get very far. She looked at Black-Jack, barely making it from one breath to the next, and at Sammy, watching wide-eyed from his corner. She knew she couldn't leave them alone to see what was happening. She was where she had to be and someone else would have to take care of the rest.

"Go, go, go!"

There were running feet right through the center of their camp now, heavy booted feet. Some of the children were crying or shrieking.

"Don't make a sound," a harsh voice whispered.

Janet turned around, startled, and saw that Carlos had crept in through the unzipped flap of the tent. He pointed his gun at Janet's chest. His face was flushed and sweaty. Janet looked at the gun.

"What's going on out there?" she asked, keeping her voice as calm and steady as possible.

"Cops. Looks like we're busted."

"What are you doing in here? You're not going to get anywhere by holding hostages."

His eyes flicked from her, out the flap of the tent, and back again. "Always good to have a purty lady on my arm," he said, his eyes narrow.

"It's not a good idea," Janet repeated.

"I'll be the judge of that."

He reached for her and Janet tried to avoid his grasp. She was crouched in an awkward position and there was not enough room in the enclosed space for her to keep away from him. He grabbed her arm with a steel grip and pulled her off balance, making her fall on her butt. Before she could get herself up and defend herself against him, he had his arm around her throat, laughing.

"You think you're any match for me, sweetheart?"

Janet grasped his arm, pulling as hard as she could, trying to twist out of his grip, while he laughed and pulled her backward toward the flap of the tent.

There was a loud sliding sound and Janet and Carlos both froze, their eyes going first to Black-Jack, who hadn't moved, and then to Sammy.

At first Carlos laughed. Just one short, sharp syllable, like a bark. But it stuck in his throat. Janet looked with horror into Sammy's eyes. Gone was the wide-eyed look of fear that she was used to seeing on his face. The naivety and the helplessness. Instead, his eyes were cold and calculating as he stared down the barrel of Black-Jack's rifle, having just loaded a round. The stock of the rifle was snug against his shoulder. His hands were steady.

"Sammy, no," Janet said. "Put down the gun. Someone will get hurt."

"L-l-let her g-go," Sammy ordered, the rifle pointed directly at Carlos.

It was obvious from Sammy's position and attitude that he knew what he was doing and had more than a passing familiarity with guns.

Carlos tried to laugh again but just raised his top lip in a twisted sneer. "You shoot me, you're going to hurt her."

Sammy didn't twitch, staring down the barrel. Janet saw him take a breath, hold it, and start to squeeze the trigger. She didn't dare move a muscle. Suddenly Carlos threw her to the side and dove out the flap of the tent. There were running boots and shouts. As Janet got up, she caught a glimpse of a couple of black-clothed policemen pinning Carlos to the ground. She took a deep breath.

"Okay, Sammy. It's all over."

He looked at her for a minute in silence, then lowered the gun. She watched him break it open again and unload the cartridge.

"That's right. Thank you. You were very brave."

Sammy laid the gun back down and pulled the blanket around him again. Black-Jack's eyes sought out Janet's.

"It's over," Janet said. "They're here to help. They'll fix you right up." Her voice choked up. "You're going to be okay."

"My dad's here," he whispered.

"Your dad? No. He's not here. You're safe. I promise you, you're safe."

Black-Jack looked at Sammy, who took him by the hand. Sammy's hand was tiny compared to Black-Jack's hard, work-worn hands, but he held tight.

"For N-n-nicky," Sammy whispered.

Black-Jack closed his eyes, giving an infinitesimal nod.

The tent flap was opened. "Come on out," one of the cops told them. "It's fine, you're safe. We need everybody out now."

"No, I have to take care of him—"

The cop looked in and saw Black-Jack and spoke immediately into his radio. "I've got Jacob Donell. The campsite is secured. Send in the EMTs."

He got static for a reply. He motioned to Janet. "Come on out, ma'am. They'll be right here to take care of him. Bring the youngster out."

Janet reached her hand out toward Sammy. He refused to take her proffered hand. "Come on, Sammy. The doctors are going to take a look at him. It will be okay."

As the EMTs were sent in, Duke clued into the fact that Jacob had been hurt. And that he was in serious condition.

"What happened to him?" he roared. "What's going on here? What happened to my kid?"

One of the YMCA supervisors, who had been removed from the camp and was trying to count and organize all of the children, turned and looked at Duke with big, round eyes.

"You're his father. You're Duke."

Duke nodded. "Who are you? What happened to him?"

"I'm a nurse. I've been trying to keep him alive. But you…"

Jaslow inserted himself between them and tried to divert Janet, taking her by the arm. "Ma'am, if you could just—"

She shook Jaslow off, her attention still focused on Duke. "If that boy dies, it rests on your conscience!"

"I didn't hurt him. What are you talking about?"

"You didn't hurt him? You beat on that boy! You're a drunk. A monster. This is on your head! You're the one he was running away from. The reason he came out here." Jaslow grasped her by the arm and tried to pull her away. "He's dying because of you!"

"Ma'am, please…"

"No one is going to die!" Duke shot back. "Don't you dare talk like that about my boy!"

Jaslow managed to get a better grip on Janet's arm and pulled her away, struggling.

Deke watched the paramedics make their way through the bush toward the Medivac helicopter with the heavily-loaded stretcher. As they walked past the watching group, Black's eyes met Deke's. His pallor was gray and Deke worried that he wouldn't even be able to make it to the hospital in time for them to do anything for him.

Deke tapped Toni-toni on the arm. "I got to go with him, Toni-toni, if they'll let me."

"You sure, kid? You might not want to see this…"

"I got to. You mind?"

"No, okay by me. Long as the cops and doctors will let you go. Call me when you're free. I'll be at home. I'll come pick you up."

"Thanks."

Deke followed the stretcher as closely as he could. He spotted Sammy standing there, alone, looking lost and close to tears. Hardly even thinking about what he was doing, Deke grabbed Sammy's hand and towed him along, still following the stretcher. Sammy's eyes were startled and at first he pulled back, but then he trotted to keep up with Deke.

The paramedics loaded the stretcher into the helicopter. "Nobody else is allowed in there," one of them told Deke, shaking his head. "Just the patient and the medical staff."

"We're brothers," Deke insisted. "You gotta let us go along. We'll keep him quiet."

"I thought it was only his dad. *He's* too big to fit anywhere."

"Me and Sammy can squeeze in. We'll hardly take any room. We won't get in the way and we'll help to keep him calm."

The paramedic looked undecided. Then he shrugged. "Squeeze in if you can. We've got to get on our way."

"This your notebook, Thompson?" Thompson turned to look at Toni-toni, who was holding Thompson's notebook in his hand. He was pale and croaked the words out.

"Oh, yeah. Thanks. Hey… are you okay, Taurus?"

"Yeah, sure. Who's this?" Toni-toni pointed to the name Pal Libra.

"That's one of the kids we interviewed at the Sunset Home. It's a shelter for juveniles. Why?"

"Can you describe him?"

Thompson frowned and flipped back a few pages.

"Tall and lanky. Slouches. Dirty blond, blue eyes, fair complexion. About fifteen. Why, you know him?"

"What's the address of Sunset Home?"

"You didn't answer my question."

"Don't you get it? I told you I had a brother named Parley who ran away! Libra is the sign he was born under. It's kind of a joke, calling himself Libra instead of Taurus."

Thompson blinked. He looked down at the notepad. "Looks like it could match up, doesn't it Taurus?"

"That's my Pal. I know it is."

"You want one of us to come with you to the Sunset Home?"

"I couldn't care less, Thompson. I been trying since I got out of prison to track him down and haven't been able to. The rest of them were all easier to find, even Deke. But I never could find Pal's trail…"

Thompson frowned, shaking his head slightly. "You're really close to your family, aren't you?"

"Not something you'd expect from someone who'd committed matricide?" he asked sarcastically.

"No, it isn't."

"I told you it was for those two, Thompson. It was worth every minute of prison if it would save those kids… it nearly killed me when the social worker said Pal was missing." He shook his head. "I could kill the old man for letting Pal run away, never even caring enough to try to track him down."

Jaslow came up to them. "They'll clean up here. If we want to fly back to the city while there's still light, we'd better be going now."

They hiked back up to the chopper. On the way back, Thompson told Jaslow in a low voice about his conversation with their pilot.

Chapter Forty-Five

BLACK'S EYES WERE CLOSED and his face was gradually losing the blue coloring around his mouth. Deke listened to the murmurs of the EMTs back and forth discussing his condition.

"Gotta get his pressure up," the older one advised. He was graying around the temples and his uniform was stitched with the name 'Rob.'

"Loading fluids," Marlin, the younger medic, acknowledged, checking the IV needle. "He's got good veins, but he's pretty shockie. I keep losing access."

"Try the jugular."

As Marlin repositioned Black's head, Deke could see the knife cut that had been stitched up. Black started to move his head back and forth in distress as Marlin tried to get the needle in place.

"Shh, hold still," Marlin murmured, trying to keep Black's head still while inserting the needle.

"Heart rate increasing," Rob warned.

Deke leaned forward. "Can I help keep him still?"

"Sure," Marlin agreed. "Hold him here," he guided Deke's hands so that they would be out of the way of the needle insertion site.

Deke did his best to hold Black's head still. "It's okay, man," he said. "They're just trying to help you."

"Pressure still dropping," Rob snapped.

"Doing my best… I think it's in…"

"No change."

They all sat tensely, waiting for the IV to make a difference. "Come on, man," Deke encouraged. "I ran for, like, two days to get you help. Don't give up on me now."

The needle was taped in place and Deke let go of Black's head and chin. He reached for Black's hand, squeezing it encouragingly.

"You gotta fight, Black-Jack. Just like when you were initiated. I never saw such a fighter. Don't give up now."

Sammy stirred beside him. Deke glanced at him. Sammy put his hand tentatively on Black's arm. He glanced around the crowded interior of the chopper and back at Deke. Deke nodded at him encouragingly. Sammy leaned closer to Black's ear.

"N-nicholas," he whispered.

It took Deke a minute to remember who Nicholas was and then he nodded vigorously to Sammy. "That's right. Remember Nicholas. Nicholas is waiting for you. Do you know how he's going to feel if you never come back?" He gripped Black's hand tighter. "I know what that's like, Black. I know what it's like when your brother goes away and never comes back." His voice was rough and he was a little embarrassed to be so emotional in front of Sammy and the EMTs. But he pushed the awkwardness aside, focusing on Black. "My brother went to prison for murder and I never saw him again until a few days ago. I never thought I would see him again. And my kid brother who ran away… I don't guess I will ever see him again. It kills me, Black. It just tears my guts out that he's gone."

Sammy looked at Deke intently and then back at Black, still touching his arm, stroking it gently. "M-me t-too."

Deke didn't think that Sammy was just saying 'me too' because he didn't know what else to say. There was pain in his voice. Maybe he'd lost a sibling too. Had an older brother run away. Deke put his arm around Sammy's shoulders and gave him a squeeze. Sammy didn't pull away. He just patted Black's arm.

"N-nicky," he encouraged Black. "F-for Nicky."

Black's lips moved slightly. Deke didn't think that he was conscious, but maybe something was getting through.

"Fight for Nicholas," he encouraged.

"Pressure's rising," Rob said. His fingers were over Black's radial pulse, his eyes intent on the various monitors hooked up to the boy. "Heart rate is good. Stabilizing."

Marlin pulled a blanket over Black's lower torso.

Deke looked at the bloody bandages over Black's chest, wondering why they weren't doing anything about the injury. He looked at the EMTs. "He'll be okay, right?"

"People are always surprising you," Marlin said, "pulling through and surviving seemingly impossible medical traumas."

Deke was not encouraged by this response. He didn't ask for any more details. Sammy shifted but didn't pull out of Deke's comforting grip. Deke patted his shoulder. "He'll be okay," Deke reassured. "You got older brothers?"

"N-no, y-y-younger."

"Yeah… I bet you're a good big brother."

Sammy nodded, looking down.

"You're in a gang?" Deke asked, indicating the twisted green bandana Sammy always wore, currently tied around Sammy's neck. "You're wearing colors."

He half-expected Sammy to deny it, to admit he was just trying to look like a banger, to get a rep for being tough. Kids did things like that. Deke had done it himself before joining the Wildcats. Before he figured out how dangerous it actually was to wear the colors of a gang that you weren't in. Or to look like a banger when you didn't have the protection of a gang behind you.

But Sammy nodded, fingering his bandana. "S-sixth."

"Sixth Street gang?" Deke raised his eyebrows. "Some tough dudes in Sixth."

"Yeah."

"That's good." Deke let his eyes travel over Black's face. One of his own gang brothers. "When you don't have a big brother looking out for you, you gotta have a gang. Sixth Street are tough dudes. Those brothers will look out for you." He stared at Black's closed eyes. "You stand behind each other."

Sammy nodded. He tapped Black's arm. "You h-h-helped B-b-black."

"Yeah." Deke felt a pang of guilt. "I shoulda done something sooner… or… if I coulda got Sarin to let me go, take my bike… I shoulda got help faster."

"W-why… S-sarin…?"

"You think he should care about one of his boys getting hurt…?" Deke paused, not really waiting for a response from Sammy, just marshaling his thoughts. "If it was anyone else, he woulda. Sarin looks after the Kittens. But… him and Black-Jack, they're sort of… I dunno. Rivals. Black would never want to lead the Kittens, but they'd sure like him to. Sarin just ain't got what he used to anymore. He doesn't got what Black-Jack's got and he knows it."

At the hospital, they had to wait a long time. The day stretched into night. When Sammy looked out the windows, he could see all of the lights sparkling, an ocean of stars. For a while, he and Deke just kicked around, waiting. But Sammy grew bored as the hours drew on. He went over to where Deke was sitting, watching a TV that hung from the ceiling, the sound turned down too low for anyone to hear it. Sammy stood beside Deke's chair and admired his Wildcats motorcycle jacket, brushing the badges on the sleeves lightly with his fingers.

Deke looked at him and patted him on the back. "How's it going, Sammy? You okay?"

Sammy nodded. With Deke sitting and Sammy standing, they were almost eye level with each other.

"T-tell m-me…" Sammy struggled to keep the words clear, "…your b-brothers."

"About my gang brothers?" Deke asked, looking around the waiting room as if he thought that some of the boys from the Wildcats might be there waiting with him. But they weren't.

"N-no. Your b-brothers."

"Oh." Deke stared out the dark window. He motioned to the chair beside him, for Sammy to sit down. "Toni-toni came back," he said. "He's my older brother. Went to prison for murder. And I didn't think he'd ever get out, but I found him a couple of days ago. He was the helicopter pilot that pulled me out when I ran to get help for Black-Jack." His voice cracked a little and he laughed. "Never thought I'd see him again."

Sammy thought about his lost siblings. Bunny was gone. Others who hadn't survived or had been taken away. Now it was just Sammy and Capo. Capo had already proven himself a fighter, battling his way through his birth defect and surgeries. Hopefully, that was a sign that he would be strong enough to survive and to grow up, like Sammy had.

"I know where the older ones are..." said Deke. "But they don't care about family. And then there's Pal..."

Sammy nodded encouragingly.

"He was so young when he ran away. Your age, probably. I don't know what happened to him... kids that age don't make it long on the streets. If he's still alive... I don't suppose I'll ever see him again."

"Yeah."

"Family is important." Deke ran his fingers through Sammy's hair. "You gotta... you gotta take care of your family."

Jacob knew that he'd been asleep for a long time. It was like being in a long, dark tunnel. He'd been there before, after being kidnapped by the Stars. This time was harder in ways. What was there to go back to? But they kept reminding him about Nicholas. Saying that he had to go back to Nicholas. He couldn't just leave Nicky at Sunset Home for other people to look after. They were brothers. Jacob had a responsibility. How would Nicholas feel if Jacob never came back? The only person who ever loved and cared for him?

Jacob opened his eyes reluctantly. There was a heaviness in his chest. He knew he was back in hospital. And that meant he was in trouble. The police would charge him with the harassment of the

YMCA camp. Duke would find out about him. Duke would demand to know where Nicholas was. But no matter what happened, Jacob wouldn't tell. He would still protect Nicholas.

But he got a shock when he looked around the hospital room. Nicholas' wheelchair was parked close to his bed. Nicky's eyes were closed. The window was black, late at night. Jacob stared blearily at the unfamiliar equipment attached to Nicky's wheelchair.

"Nicholas?" he whispered.

Nicky's eyes flew open. He focused on Jacob and the corners of his eyes angled up.

"Hey," Jacob greeted. "Who brought you here?"

Nicky's eyes moved away from him to the equipment on his chair and he blinked. "Hello, Jacob."

Jacob was startled by the electronic voice. He looked quickly around the room, making sure there was no one else there. The voice had come from Nicky's direction. But Jacob couldn't quite comprehend what was going on.

"What? Who was that?"

"Nicholas got a new voice."

"Nicky? Are you doing that? How?"

Nicky's eyes turned to Jacob and they communed in the old way.

"Your eyes? You can control it with your eyes?"

Nicky's gaze remained steady. Jacob was finding it hard to catch his breath. He closed his mouth and breathed in through his nose, fed by an oxygen tube. Concern flickered in Nicky's eyes.

"I'm okay," Jacob whispered.

Nicky's eyes left him, turning back to the speech synthesizer. "Don't talk. Need rest."

Jacob nodded.

"Close eyes. Sleep."

"Okay."

"I'll be here."

Jacob opened his mouth.

"Shh. Sleep."

Jacob didn't close his eyes right away. He lay still, gazing at Nicholas. Whatever else happened, Nicholas would be okay.

He finally had a voice of his own.

A nurse touched Deke on the shoulder, waking him up. Deke sat up, stretching, forcing Sammy to relinquish the comfortable spot on Deke's arm and to sit up as well.

"Come with me," the young nurse said softly.

Deke opened his mouth to inquire. She put her finger to her lips, her eyes darting around. "Shh. Just come."

Deke and Sammy looked at each other and went with her. They were a couple of hallways away before the nurse would speak to them, still leading them briskly along.

"I know you're not Jacob's brothers," she said.

"Oh, come on, we're—"

"You're his friends. And you've waited here all afternoon and evening to see him. I'm going to take you in there, but you only have a few minutes. We're not supposed to allow anyone but family."

Deke gave her a brilliant smile. "Thank you."

She smiled back. They stopped and she looked around covertly to make sure that no one was paying any attention. She opened the door and motioned them in. "Ten minutes. Then you'll have to go. But I thought you at least deserved a chance to see him."

Sammy followed Deke into the room. The door closed behind them. The nurse didn't enter. Black lay in the bed, still and quiet, hooked up to various machines and tubes. Sammy didn't get a good look at him before seeing the boy in the wheelchair beside him. He knew immediately who it was.

"N-n-nicky!"

Nicholas didn't move. Deke and Sammy got closer to the bed and to Nicholas.

"I am Nicholas," a robotic voice announced. "I don't know you."

Deke looked over the computer equipment and looked closely at Nicky's face. "Cool! How do you do that?"

"Eye gaze computer," Nicholas explained.

"Black never said anything about that. That's awesome!"

"It's new. After Jacob left. You a Wildcat?"

Deke nodded. "Deke. I'd shake your hand, but…"

Sammy wasn't as enamored with the speech computer as Deke. He touched Black-Jack's motionless fingers, resting on top of the sheet. Black-Jack didn't flinch, didn't make any sign. His color was better, probably due to the bag of blood hung on the IV stand. He had oxygen tubes feeding into his nose. Now dressed in a proper hospital gown, there wasn't a speck of visible blood. Other tubes that Sammy couldn't or didn't want to identify snaked in and out.

"Who is the little one?"

Sammy glanced over at Nicholas, flushing. He could have done with his own speech synthesizer. As it was, he didn't know how to begin explaining who he was and why he cared what happened to Black-Jack. He looked down at his feet.

"Uh, this is Sammy," Deke introduced. "It's… sort of complicated… Black saved him from a bear, that's how Black got hurt. Actually… I guess it's really not that complicated…"

"Good to meet you both. Jacob's friends."

Sammy ran his hand down Black-Jack's muscly, hairy arm. "B-be ok-kay?"

He tried to hear the emotion that Nicky's voice synthesizer couldn't express. "Doctor said surgery went well. He woke up once. Needs more blood."

"But he'll be okay?" Deke asked.

There was a long pause before Nicholas answered. "Hope so. I still need him."

Chapter Forty-Six

PAL STARED MOODILY AT the package in front of him. He lay on the bed, propped up on his elbows, with it on his pillow. Texas White had been surprised at him buying so much this time. Usually, Pal couldn't afford much. But a dealer was more than happy to sell his goods for the right price.

It was quiet. Supper was over and his roommate was out of town. No one would bother him until morning, at breakfast time.

Pal fingered the package. He had bought too much to hide safely. But then, Pal never planned to hide it. Or to sell it, as Texas had suspected.

Pal's thoughts wandered and were disjointed.

This was it. Swallow some pills and that would be all. No more pain.

With his pocket knife, Pal slit the plastic and let the tablets trickle out into his hand.

After the doorbell rang, Cassy heard Teresa call for Pal to go downstairs. When she didn't hear Pal come out, she went to his door. She knocked briefly and went in. Pal didn't usually answer anyway. She saw him facedown on the bed and drew in her breath sharply. She shook him, hoping he was merely asleep, but knowing he wasn't.

"Stoned?" David asked from the doorway.

"Out cold. What's Teresa want him for?"

"Cops are here asking for him."

Cassy shook him again. "Come on, Pal! What should we do?"

"Nothin'. It's his own problem, bound to catch up with him sooner or later."

Cassy came down the stairs slowly, clearly anxious and she entered the front room to face them. She saw Jaslow and Thompson and darted a glance at Toni-toni, unfamiliar to her. "Pal can't come down… he's sleeping."

"Sleeping?" Toni-toni repeated.

Cassy eyed him.

"If he's asleep, wake him up and send him down!"

Cassy shook her head. "He's sick. He just needs to sleep now. If you come back later…"

Toni-toni muttered an oath and pushed past her. Jaslow reached out to stop him but was too slow. Toni-toni was already bounding up the stairs.

Toni-toni reached the top of the stairs and found his path blocked by David.

"Which room is Pal's?"

"Who are you?" David demanded belligerently.

Toni-toni pushed past him and into the room with its door open. Toni-toni bent over Pal and shook him hard.

"Pal, buddy, it's me! It's Toni-toni. Pal, wake up! No… no!" He felt for a pulse, and in turning Pal over, saw the thin plastic pouch there, one or two pills left in the bottom. "Thompson!" Toni-toni yelled. "Get an ambulance! Quick!" His shout echoed all the way through the house.

Jaslow was at Pal's door a few moments later. He looked grimly at the boy and at the bag in Toni-toni's hand. He radioed to the dispatcher to get an ambulance. He looked at Toni-toni's face, white with anguish.

"Do something," Toni-toni whispered. "Jaslow, you gotta do something for him."

There was nothing to do but to wait for the ambulance.

Thompson left the hospital with an uneasy feeling about Toni-toni's father, worried that Toni-toni might have plans to harm him for letting Pal run away, and not bothering to track him down and get him back. This was a man who had already helped to kill one of his parents and showed no remorse whatsoever for it.

Jaslow was tired and shook his head irritably. "We can look him up tomorrow. It's been a long day, and I'm going home."

"I think we should look into it tonight."

"We're already working overtime. I'm too beat to do anything else. Besides, Taurus won't leave his brother's side. He's not going anywhere tonight."

"What if Pal doesn't pull through?"

"He will. The doctors said his chances were good. We found him in time."

"I suppose…"

"We'll check up on it tomorrow, first thing."

Chapter Forty-Seven

TONI-TONI LOOKED AT the dark house out the window through his binoculars. He had originally planned to wait another week or two, just to make sure he had accounted for every possibility. But now there was no point waiting. He went over specifics in his mind as he watched. Now she was leaving for work. The old man would be in the living room reading the paper. The blinds would be drawn so that he couldn't see across the street.

Toni-toni's mind drifted, taking him back to prison, talking to the psychologist about the murder.

"Do you know the difference between right and wrong, Toni?"

"If you aren't going to call me by my surname, that's Toni-toni."

"Why the nickname?"

"Because that's what I'm called."

"Are you going to answer my question?" she pressed.

"Of course I know the difference." Toni-toni was irritated. "I'm not a sociopath."

"Then you know that what you did was wrong."

"Yes," he agreed.

"Then why did you do it? Doesn't that make you feel anything?"

"Yes. But it was the only thing to do."

"Why is that?"

Toni-toni sighed. He'd gone over it all before. Time and time again. With one professional after another. "She was ruining them. I couldn't let her hurt them like the others."

"Hurt who?"

"Deke and Pal."

"And who are 'the others'?"

"Charley and Jimmi."

"And you? Are you including yourself in that statement?"

"I don't know. Maybe."

"What did she do to Charley and Jimmi?"

"She didn't care about them… the only one she cared about was herself, and getting ahead. She whipped 'em and made 'em work instead of sending them to school… she broke their spirits so that they couldn't stand up for themselves!"

"You're pretty well educated and your spirit doesn't seem to be broken."

"I didn't let her. I didn't trust her. I was never close to her like the others."

"Or anyone else? Have you ever felt close to anyone in your life?"

"You can't trust anyone. Look at me. I knew that, but I still trusted that idiot Cooper to get everything right when I agreed to help him. Look where that got me."

"You don't feel any guilt for what you did?"

"Of course I do. I know it was wrong, but it was the only solution."

"Do you have any religious beliefs, Toni-toni?"

"I don't know… I don't believe in an afterlife, but I believe you're punished for doing what's wrong. In this life. I don't know if I believe in a God, exactly… I think mankind has the power to judge for himself…"

"Is that how you see yourself?" she asked, eyes narrowing. "As a judge?"

"No… no, I don't mean that. I mean… There's right and wrong independent of any law… and inside, everyone understands that and knows what they are."

At his trial, the doctor had said that Toni-toni was sound of mind and that he wouldn't be a further danger to society. Toni-toni hadn't thought about his father back then. He'd thought only of his mother. What she'd done to them. He thought that with her out of the way, everything would be all right. He hadn't thought about the old man being a problem on his own. Or marrying the same kind of woman all over again. He didn't realize his mistake until the day that the social worker came to see him at the prison.

"Taurus, Antony?"

"That's me."

"When was the last time you had visitors here, Taurus?"

Toni-toni raised his brows. "Never."

"You haven't had any visitors since you came here?"

"I haven't had any visitors since I was arrested, other than people like you."

"Then you haven't seen your brother."

"No. Which one?"

"Parley."

"Nope. Why?"

"He's run away, apparently."

Toni-toni grabbed the table in front of him tightly to keep his balance, nearly blacking out. He stared at her. "He what?"

"Ran away. We thought it was possible he might have come here to talk to you first and not been registered on the list because he's a minor. But if he hasn't…" She stood up, tidying away her papers, "Well, that's all we wanted to know."

"Why? Why did he run away?"

"We don't know for sure. He seems to have kept quite an erratic schedule lately, so he must have had something on his mind for some time. Your father had noticed some behavioral changes, but he couldn't say if it was something that had started when he got remarried or with the arrival of the new baby. Probably a build-up of reasons."

That was the first time Toni-toni heard anything about the old man remarrying. They wouldn't tell him anything else. Pal had been so young when he ran away. Where had he gone? Somehow he had survived. Somehow he had found somewhere he was safe.

That was all in the past and there was no one who could give him those answers now.

Toni-toni put the binoculars down and checked his watch. He had lots of time. He closed his eyes and kneaded the tight knots of muscles in his throbbing head.

The officers on the shift before Jaslow and Thompson were in high spirits. "Was there ever a lot of action on patrol last night. Wow!"

"Like what?" Jaslow asked, sitting on the edge of his desk and having a sip of his coffee.

"Homicide, for one. And we arrested Enrik on that assault charge. That took some doing, I'll tell you. He didn't go quietly. Oh, and before I forget, the hospital was trying to get a hold of the two of you."

Jaslow was unworried about the hospital for the moment. "What was the homicide?"

"Funny name, just a second…" he checked his notebook. "Taurus, Lawrence James."

Jaslow was startled.

"Taurus?" Thompson echoed in dismay.

Jaslow looked at him. "Antony Taurus' father."

Thompson's face was slack with the shock. "He did it… you said he wouldn't leave the hospital."

Jaslow picked up the phone and dialed the hospital. He got to the doctor who had been trying to contact them.

He looked at Thompson.

"Parley Taurus aka Pal Libra died last night just after we went off duty. He never woke up."

They arrived at the scene of the crime. Jaslow stood on the sidewalk in front of Leo Taurus' house for a moment, staring at the building across the street. Toni-toni's condo. The homicide squad was there and Jaslow went to Parkinson, the officer in command. He was in the living room with the body, which was still seated in an easy chair, staring with sightless eyes at the blank TV screen.

"There's a man involved here who probably had every opportunity, the means, and the motive to kill your victim. He's living just across the street in that condo complex."

"And who is this suspect?"

"His son."

The officer frowned. "I make it my policy not to arrest family of the deceased without pretty conclusive evidence."

"Yesterday he said he was considering killing his father and he just recently got out of prison for the murder of his mother, the victim's first wife."

"I see. Well, that changes things a little." The officer gave instructions to a few of his underlings, and they went off to check Toni-toni's apartment. "He left his gun here. It's unregistered. From what we can tell, he was just cleaning it when the little one came in to see what all the noise was about. The killer put it down and slugged the kid hard enough to knock him out, but was so panicked that he left the scene without picking the gun up again."

"He put the gun down to hit the kid?" Jaslow asked, frowning.

"That's what it looks like. Most burglars would have hit him with the gun. But he put it down first."

"I suppose it makes sense for a half-brother. Any bullets left in the gun?"

"The magazine is empty. We haven't been able to count the bullets in this guy yet."

"Who discovered the body?"

"One of the kids was on his way to the kitchen to get his breakfast. Saw his father still asleep in front of the TV. The door wasn't forced, by the way. It was left unlocked. The killer just walked in and shot Taurus before he had a chance to stand up."

"How old was the kid who found him?"

"He's six."

"And kept his cool enough to phone the police?"

"Had the lungs to scream long and loud enough to bring the neighbors."

"Did you get any kind of description of the killer from the boy who was knocked out?"

"No. The kid's too young and confused, he wasn't any help."

Toni-toni slept deeply. He didn't awake to the sound of the door being unlocked by the super, or to the door opening. He started to come around as the officer came into the bedroom and let out a shout to the others. He stayed in a semi-conscious state until the officer shook him hard enough to bring him around. Toni-toni stared blearily at the officer and blinked his eyes. He moved sluggishly and reached under his pillow for his gun. Another officer grabbed his arm and pulled it back, lifting the pillow with the other hand, but found nothing there. Toni-toni stared at the bed, knowing his gun should be there, but it wasn't. The first officer hauled him off the bed.

"What's going on—" Toni-toni started.

"Shut-up!" ordered the officer and kicked him behind the knees so that he fell heavily to the floor. Toni-toni shook his head dizzily, trying to clear his thoughts; to force comprehension. All he knew was that he had a massive hangover and his gun was missing. He just sat there, watching the officers search his room. There was glass all over the carpet on one side of the room. One of the officers stepped on it and yelped in pain. He looked at the broken glass in surprise and looked at his foot, cut clear through the sole of his shoe.

All at once, it rushed back to Toni-toni. Pal had died. Pal was not just lost, he was dead. Toni-toni knew, though he couldn't remember, that he must have killed his father. He had been planning it for weeks, what else would he have done? It all came to him so quickly and powerfully and was too much for his already nauseated stomach. He was violently sick. Cursing, the cop holding onto him hauled him to his feet when the first wave of sickness passed and took him into the bathroom. Toni-toni could hardly keep his feet, even with help. He was sick again and then sat back, unable to focus on the room, barely conscious of anything. The cop said something to him, but Toni-toni couldn't focus on what it was.

His gun was missing… he must have hidden it somewhere so that he wouldn't be found out. At least he'd had the presence of mind to get rid of the murder weapon. But they must know, somehow. They were at least suspicious of him.

As Toni-toni's thoughts became more coherent, he was able to focus his eyes better and take in the room around him. The first thing he saw, right in front of his knee, was an empty pill bottle.

Sleeping pills. That was why he was so groggy.

He stared at the bottle and nausea washed over him again. Pal was dead. Pal had overdosed. He was gone. What was the use of hiding? Pal was dead and their father was dead. Deke would be all right with his gang. His gang brothers would help him.

"I did it," Toni-toni whispered, and his voice was harsh in his own ears. He covered his face, trying to shut everything else out. "I did it. I killed him."

Officer Hoyles shut the bathroom door, blocking out the noises of the other officers and their activities.

"What did you say?" he asked.

Toni-toni flinched. "I killed him. Laurence Taurus. He's dead, isn't he?"

"What makes you think that?"

Toni-toni's eyes rolled upward and he was sick again. When he stopped heaving, Hoyles handed him a cold, wet cloth. Toni-toni wiped his pale face and neck, his stomach still heaving sporadically.

"I've been watching him," Toni-toni confessed. What kind of a person killed his own father? "I've been watching him and every day it's the same. The lady goes to work and he sits and reads in the front room. He shuts the blinds. Then he sits and watches TV and he sometimes leaves the door open, so you can see in. He never locks it. He always does the same thing, every day. He sits there in the chair in the front room. He can't move fast. All you have to do is walk in and take aim. That's all. Pull the trigger. And it's done."

"Slow down, take it easy," Hoyles urged. "Nice and slow. Wait a minute."

Hoyles stuck his head out the door and spoke in a low, urgent tone. "Get me a recorder. And call Parkinson. Forget the murder site, we need him right here."

"He's already on his way," Hawerchuk assured him. "Be here any minute." He spoke to the other officers. "Anyone got a recorder?"

"Yeah, I got one here," one of the detectives announced.

"Great. Thanks."

Hoyles took it and withdrew into the bathroom, closing the door quietly. "For the record," he switched the voice recorder on. "Repeat what you just told me. Who did you kill?"

Toni-toni gave an exasperated sigh. "My father. Laurence Taurus. Leo Taurus. I've been planning it for months—"

"What have you been planning?"

"I got this apartment. It's expensive, I didn't have the money for it. It wasn't for sale. I had to wait, had to keep trying. I knew I had to get this place to watch him. So I did. And I watched him for weeks. Watched him from here, watched him from the street, from the back. Even talked to the kids a couple times. It had to be just right."

"When did you do this?"

"Last night. It was late. Pal… it was after the hospital…"

The door opened and Parkinson motioned for Hoyles to come out. They left Hawerchuk standing just outside the doorway watching Toni-toni in case he tried anything.

"Have you asked the punk if he wants an attorney?"

"Uh, no—"

"You'd better do it before he starts spilling his guts, I don't want this guy off on a technicality."

"Uh…" Hoyles shifted uncomfortably. "He's already talking. Admitted to the murder…"

"And you didn't tell him to get a lawyer?"

"No… sorry. He was in there, sick, puking his guts out, and then he just started talking…"

Parkinson swore. "Did you question him about it?"

"Well… a little."

Parkinson swore again. "That could cost us the case! Get in there and tell him to shut up until he talks to a lawyer. That's all we need, a psychopath off on a technicality!"

Hoyles grunted his agreement and went back to face Toni-toni. "I'm informing you of your right to see an attorney before you say anything. Do you understand that?"

Toni-toni moaned, holding his face. "Yes. I know."

"I'm telling you that you should talk to a lawyer before you talk to me, whether or not you're guilty. Do you understand that?"

"I don't want one."

"And you should understand that we can get you a lawyer to consult with at no cost, should you require it. There is a hotline where you can reach a lawyer any time of the night or day. Do you understand that?"

"Don't you understand?" Toni-toni pleaded. "I don't want a lawyer. I'm guilty. I did it. I admit it. They can put me in prison the rest of my life. They can put me in the electric chair. I don't care. I did it. I don't need a lawyer. I did it."

Hoyles said nothing else. He opened the door again and Parkinson was still standing nearby. "He won't stop. Doesn't want a lawyer. He said he understood his rights."

"You got that on tape?"

"Yes."

"Good. Take him down to the station, we'll question him there."

Chapter Forty-Eight

AFTER QUESTIONING THE YOUNG man for some time, Hoyles withdrew went to find Parkinson.

"Well, how's it going?" Parkinson demanded.

"I'm… not so sure he did it," Hoyles admitted. He raised his eyebrows and rolled his eyes a little, knowing that Parkinson wasn't going to like it and he'd better have more than a feeling to back him up.

"What? Why else would he admit to it?"

"I think he's covering up for someone. I don't know who, but I don't think he did it."

"Why not?"

"He doesn't know the details. I've asked him a few times to tell me in detail what happened and he just keeps giving me the same story. He walked in through the front door and fired. He hasn't said anything about the kid. He doesn't seem to realize the gun was left at the site. I think he knows who did it. Maybe he was even in on the plan, but I don't think he pulled the trigger."

Parkinson swore. "Check out his file, his background. Also, talk to these two officers," he scribbled the names on a sticky note and handed it over. "They know him, maybe they can tell you who he'd be covering for. And don't spread this around."

"Yessir."

An unfamiliar officer approached the bullpen, wiping sweating palms on his uniform pants before shaking hands. "The name's Hoyles. I'm wondering if you can help me."

Jaslow shrugged.

"What can we do for you?" Thompson asked.

"It's about Taurus. I understand you know him, a little bit about his history and so on."

"That's right."

"Listen, this is on the QT, but it doesn't look like he's the one who killed his father. We think he's covering for someone."

Thompson was startled. He looked at Jaslow.

Jaslow considered it. "The brother in the Wildcats gang. Taurus is very protective of him. That's who it's got to be."

"I supposed it could be Deke," Thompson said reluctantly, "but it was Toni-toni who threatened to kill their father."

"We're almost sure Taurus didn't," Hoyles said. "Why would this brother want to do it?"

"Same reason Toni-toni would," Jaslow shrugged. "Because they resented him. Maybe he was abusive. Because his brother Parley just died and he was upset. Why wouldn't he feel the same way as Toni-toni?"

Thompson thought it through. "I don't picture Deke as the type. If it was Deke, what's happened to Toni-toni's gun?"

"He ditched it. Or the murder weapon was Taurus's. The kid picked it up while he was sleeping or passed out. He may have been at Taurus's last night. Taurus said he was going to call him."

Thompson shook his head. "I don't know. I don't think he did it."

"Where does he live?" Hoyles asked. "We'll pick him up."

"Your best bet is to find the Wildcats."

When Deke arrived at Toni-toni's condo, he found a couple of police officers there locking the door. "Hey, I'm looking for Toni-toni. Is he… around?"

"Who are you?"

"Deke. His brother."

The officers looked at each other. "He's at the police station. We're headed over there. You want a lift?"

Deke figured Toni-toni must be working on some photography for the police. "Yeah, sure."

Deke went with them and was led to a small, quiet room off to the side to wait. The officer left him alone there, and after a long period of waiting, another one came in. He had a clipboard in his hand and put a voice recorder on the table and turned it on.

"Have you been informed of your right to see an attorney?"

"What?" Deke said, surprised.

"Have you been told you should see a lawyer?"

"I think you've got the wrong room," Deke said with a laugh. "I'm just here to see my brother."

Hoyles looked up at him, then back down at his clipboard. "Richard Taurus?"

"Deke. That's me."

"You're a person of interest in a murder. Do you want to see a lawyer?"

"I just came to talk to Toni-toni! No one told me I was under arrest! What's going on here?"

The cop took a deep breath. "Look, kid, we can't go on until you tell me whether you're gonna want a lawyer or not."

"No, *you* look, I'm just here to see…"

"I can't say anything to you until you confirm that you understand your rights."

"All right. I want a lawyer."

"That's better. Do you have a lawyer?"

"No."

"Is there someone you want to consult with to get a lawyer, or do you want us to get you one?"

Deke shrugged. "I don't know anyone."

"You want us to supply you one?"

"Yeah, I guess."

"Wait here. I shouldn't be long."

He walked out and shut the door behind him. Deke sat waiting, but not patiently or calmly now. His breathing was shallow and he started sweating. Murder? What did they want him for? It didn't make sense. It was like waiting for the punchline of a sick joke, the kind he knew he wasn't going to like. After what seemed like a long time, another man came into the room and sat down.

"Richard? My name's Anderson. I've been asked to represent you."

"Deke. Great, thanks."

"Now, why don't you tell me what's happening here, how you're involved in this mess?"

Deke took a deep breath. "All I know, is that when I called my brother last night and this morning, he didn't answer his phone. When I went to see him today, there were a couple of cops there. They said he was here and offered me a ride."

"When was the last time you saw your brother?"

"Yesterday. Hey, will you level with me? What's going on?"

"Let's get Officer Hoyles back in here, and he can tell you what's up."

"Okay, sure." Deke nodded. A bead of sweat ran down his spine.

When the officer came in, he wasn't ready to give any explanations. He wanted to ask questions. "When did you last see your father?"

"My father?" Deke thought about it and swore. "I don't know. I don't go back there much. I just stay with the gang. What's this all about?"

"Where were you last night?"

"My client has a right to know what he's being questioned about," the lawyer said flatly.

The officer favored him with a glare. "He knows what this is about."

"No, he doesn't. He has the right to know exactly what he's suspected of."

Hoyles turned and looked at Deke closely. "You're a person of interest in the murder of Laurence Taurus."

Deke stared for a moment before it clicked. "What? My dad?" he looked at them in confusion. "The murder of my dad?" he repeated, with dawning realization. He couldn't seem to draw a full breath. "My dad's dead? Why didn't someone tell me? What happened? When?"

"Take it easy, son. I'll ask the questions here."

"No, you tell me what's going on! When? When did this happen?"

"Why don't you tell me?"

"I don't know! What kind of a person do you think I am? You think I killed my own dad? I don't know anything about this, this is the first I've heard… anything!"

"Is that your story?"

"Tell me what happened! I want to know what happened! And Toni-toni? Is he mixed up in this too?"

The cop's mouth was a thin, uninformative line. "I'm afraid I can't tell you anything about the charges against your brother."

"What are they? You can tell me what he's under arrest for, can't you?"

"I don't have to tell you anything. Why don't you tell me what happened last night? It will be much easier on you if you tell the truth."

"I'm telling you the truth when I say I don't know what happened! Believe me! I spent last night at the hospital with Black and then out with the gang. I didn't even think about Dad. I called Toni-toni a couple times and couldn't get him. I haven't talked to him since yesterday."

"Who were you with specifically?"

Deke considered for a moment. "Talet… mostly it was the older guys. I don't know'em very well. The other guys are mostly in the can after the camping trip."

"Talet is being held for attempted murder."

"No way, man. He was there last night, I know that."

"How do you know that?"

"I saw him, talked to him. I'm tellin' ya, he's out. He didn't say anything about bein' in prison for murder. What's that all about?"

"Who else was there? That you know?"

"Uh… Keith, I'm sure he was. They were talking about Black-Jack, see. Everyone was talking about him. Talet talkin' about Black getting beat up by his old man all the time—"

"Hold it," Hoyles said sharply.

"What?"

"Watch what you say about other officers. You forget that I know him."

"His old man?" Deke shook his head. "How do you think Black got his name? His old man beat him black and blue! Believe me, he was gettin' smacked around at home. I felt sorry for the guy. I don't get along with my old man, but he never laid a hand on me like my mom or step-mom."

"So we come back to your father."

Deke bit his lip when he realized what he had said. "I fought with him, sure. Everyone fights with their folks. I moved out. That's it. End of story. I stayed with the gang and I went back to say hey now and then and there weren't any hard feelings. There wasn't really any bad blood between us."

"What about your other brothers?"

Deke frowned, thinking back to the older brothers who had abandoned him to his fate. "I don't associate with Charley and Jimmi. And until a few days ago, I didn't even know about Toni-toni bein' out. As for Dad's other kids, I don't really know 'em."

"You've missed one."

"Pal?" Deke shook his head. "It's years since I seen him. He was really just a little tyke when he ran away. He'd be… maybe fifteen now… if he's even still alive." Deke ran his fingers through his hair. "Couldn't'a' been more than ten when he ran away."

"So you don't know about Pal."

Deke's heart skipped a beat. "What do you mean… know about Pal?"

"Toni-toni found him."

"What?" Deke yelled. "Where? Why didn't he tell me about it? He should have told me!"

"He just found him yesterday. At the shelter where Jacob Donell had been staying."

Deke couldn't suppress a huge grin over this news. "Well, don't that take the cake! That's some kind of coincidence, huh? Right there, maybe even talkin' to Black-Jack the same day as I did! Hey, I gotta see him! What's he like?"

Hoyles hesitated a moment. "He died at the General last night."

Deke clutched the arms of his chair for support, a wave of vertigo washing over him. He swallowed. "Man, you got some nerve, you know that?" His voice rough and his mouth dry. "Questioning me like this, tellin' me someone killed my dad and then that someone killed the brother I ain't seen in years just like it was the most natural thing in the world! What kind of a person do you think I am? I don't believe you."

"It's the truth," the cop said, putting up his hands defensively. "Where were you last night when you managed to contact Toni-toni?"

"I said I never talked to Toni-toni last night," Deke shot back. "What happened to Pal? I want to know what happened."

"You talked to Toni-toni. You know what happened."

"I don't know!"

Hoyles took a long, slow drink of his coffee and then stood up. "I think you and your lawyer need to discuss your strategy here. Consider a plea." He walked out of the room.

Deke looked at Anderson. "A big help you are! Why don't you make them tell me what's going on?"

"I'll do what I can. But I can't promise you anything."

"What about Toni-toni? Can you find out what exactly happened?"

"Stay here, I'll see what I can find out."

Deke was left by himself again.

Anderson watched Toni-toni and Hoyles through the observation window for a while and then got permission to go in.

"I understand you aren't being represented."

Toni-toni looked at him for a moment. "I don't need a lawyer," he said slowly, "especially not an ambulance chaser."

"I'm representing your brother. I thought it might make things easier if we all got together."

Toni-toni stared at him for a few minutes, blankly, unable to gather his wits to reason this through. Then understanding and anger grew in his eyes. "Deke? They're not charging Deke with this…!"

"Now that's interesting," Hoyles spoke up, "I understood that you have several brothers. What makes you think it was Deke who we were charging?"

"He's the only one around… none of the others are even in town."

"I see."

"How can you be charging Deke? He was… he was…"

"What's the matter? Can't think of an alibi?"

"I don't know what he was doin' last night. It's not like I could call him. But I know he wasn't the one to shoot my old man because I did it. I did!"

"I came here to see you because your brother asked me to," Anderson interrupted, trying to get back into the conversation. "He's worried about what's going on. Seeing as you don't have any representation, I wanted to offer my services…?"

"I keep saying I don't want a lawyer, doesn't anyone here understand English? I'm guilty, I don't need a lawyer!"

It was the end of a long day. Deke had been expecting to be transported to juvie on the end-of-day bus, but last call came and went, and he was still sitting at the police station. Finally, Anderson came to see him for the last time. He was looking tired. There were lines across his forehead and around his eyes, and a five o'clock shadow smudging his jaw.

"Well, good news, Deke. They are releasing you. You're free to go."

"Does that mean it's over? For good? Or are they gonna come after me again?"

Anderson shook his head. "Right now, there's no evidence against you. Not even a clear motive. They were just fishing."

"And Toni-toni? What about him?"

"He *did* confess to the murder," Anderson reminded him.

"Yeah. So I guess there's not much you can do to get him off."

"Hoyles doesn't believe that he did it. There are just too many holes in his story. It doesn't match up. And he hadn't been advised of his rights when he confessed, which is a procedural problem."

Deke shook his head. "Does that mean they're letting him go?"

"It looks like it. They won't give me many details, since I'm not representing him, but I suspect that they will let him go, at least until they can gather more evidence against him."

"Good."

Anderson raised an eyebrow. "He did it, though. That's pretty obvious."

"He's already served time. Why not just let him live his life now?"

"Because you can't just go around killing people when you don't like their choices or lifestyle."

"No…" Deke agreed. "But you don't know what he was like. The old man. Some people… they just can't be allowed to keep messing up kids' lives."

Anderson studied him in silence for a long moment. "Was it you?" he asked finally.

Deke blinked. "I was out with the guys. I've got an alibi."

Chapter Forty-Nine

DEKE SAT ON THE front steps, smoking and waiting. He wasn't sure how long it would take Toni-toni to get home. Maybe Anderson was wrong and they weren't ready to release him yet. The sky was darkening and Deke was considering going to find the gang when he saw Toni-toni making his way down the street. His head was bowed and he slouched over, looking tired and defeated. He was almost up to the door when he finally noticed Deke sitting on the steps. He stopped and gave Deke a forced smile, lines of fatigue around his eyes. He couldn't hold the expression for long.

Deke stood up and held out his arm to Toni-toni. They gave each other an awkward half-hug, clapping each other on the back, then they walked side-by-side up the steps into Toni-toni's building. When they got to his apartment door, Deke looked up into Toni-toni's face.

"You okay?"

Toni-toni stood with his hand on the doorknob, not putting his key in the lock. Finally, he nodded. "I'll be fine."

"Pal—" Deke started, then he choked up, unable to get any words out or to think of what he wanted to say.

Toni-toni put his key in the lock and opened the door, putting his hand on Deke's back to walk him in. His expression was bleak. "You're my only family now." He went directly to the kitchen and looked through cupboards, eventually pulling out a bottle. Deke saw him eye the bottle for a minute before pulling out glasses, pouring them each a half-tumblerful and then deliberately putting the bottle back away.

Deke took his glass from Toni-toni and they each took a sip. Neither of them gulped it down.

"You didn't have to confess, Toni-toni," Deke said.

Toni-toni met his eye.

"They've got nothing on me," Deke said. "Nothing on either of us. Just your confession. You shouldn't have done that."

Toni-toni took another sip. "Maybe not."

"It's just you and me now. We gotta stick together. You can't—don't do anything stupid."

"Like what?"

Deke just met his eyes and held his gaze. Toni-toni shrugged and looked away.

"Don't go away again," Deke pleaded. "Don't… don't run away from me."

Toni-toni nodded. "Okay, little bro." He stared out the apartment window, toward the crime scene. "Okay."

Sammy sighed, standing outside of the house in the slightly-too-big shoes that the hospital had managed to find for him before sending him on his way. At least they weren't too small. Sammy hoped that they didn't come from some dead kid, but he tried not to think about that.

"Hey, our boy is back."

Sammy turned around to see Zed strolling down the street, heading down toward the gang's house. Sammy smiled slightly at the greeting.

"You eat lots of marshmallows at camp? Come on down after you've had a chance to see your mama," Zed told him. "I'm gonna have some jobs for you."

Sammy nodded.

Zed continued on his way. Sammy dragged his feet up the walk to the house and climbed the stairs to the room. He opened the door and went into the room, mixed emotions rolling around in his stomach. On one hand, he was glad to be home, to have the drama of all that had happened at the camp over, to be in a familiar place, where he belonged and could see his mom and Capo. But at the same time, he wished he didn't have to go home. Back to the anxiety and abuse. Living hand-to-mouth. Worrying about his baby brother.

Marisol was sitting on the bed, bent over a glass pipe, holding the flame of her lighter under the bowl. She looked up, startled, at Sammy's entrance.

"Shut the door," she ordered around the pipe.

Sammy obeyed and went over to the window to open it. Marisol pulled the foul-smelling smoke into her lungs. "Are you back early? What day is it?"

"Th-thursday."

While she was preoccupied with the pipe, Sammy went to get Capo out of his makeshift crib. The normally wiry baby felt soft and doughy and didn't respond to Sammy's touch as he unwrapped the blankets. There was a sick lump in Sammy's stomach. Capo was warm and he stirred as Sammy picked him up. Sammy looked at his face. There was a long split in the skin above the top of the baby's nose, and his eyes looked sunken and bruised. Sammy stroked his cheek.

"Capo… C-capo…"

After a few more calls and some poking and shaking his arm, the baby roused a little, opening his eyes and looking glassily at Sammy. He didn't smile or cling to Sammy like usual.

Sammy looked at his mother, sitting on the bed with the pipe, paying him no attention. He got up to make a bottle to see if he could get Capo to drink. There was a bottle of water, but no can of formula powder on top of the dresser. Sammy looked inside the top drawer and then beside the dresser where there had previously been a whole case of formula that Marisol had bought with the money Sammy got from Zed. But there was nothing. Sammy looked around for it. There was no way they had used all of those cans yet. But the box was gone. All sold for drug money?

Sammy looked at his mother again. She hadn't moved. Cradling Capo in his arm, he walked out of the room, down the stairs and out of the house. Once outside, he wasn't sure what to do. He sat down on the front steps and looked down at the baby.

He couldn't stop thinking about Black-Jack's fevered ramblings back in Janet's tent. About Nicholas, how helpless he was. Black still had to take care of him just like a baby, carrying him, feeding him, changing him. Because when he was little he got a head injury and had never been the same since. Sammy touched the split above Capo's nose, trying to see if he could feel any fracture line beneath it. Black had lived with abuse for years, all so that he could take care of Nicholas. And even though Black-Jack was so big—bigger than anyone Sammy knew—his dad still hurt him.

Sammy had always told himself that it would stop. Once he was bigger. Once the babies were bigger. But now... now he knew it wouldn't. It would never stop.

Sammy sniffled and wiped his nose with the back of his hand. Capo's eyes were closing again. He lay limp in Sammy's arms. Sammy stood back up and walked out to the sidewalk. He looked up and down the street, his stomach like a lump of lead.

He was lost. He didn't know what to do. Taking a glance down toward the gang's crib, he decided to walk the other way. He didn't want to go see Zed and find out what errands the banger wanted him to run. He didn't want to see any of them. He thought of the way that Sarin and Carlos had treated Black-Jack. When he got hurt, they hadn't cared that Black-Jack was part of their gang. They showed him no loyalty. Sammy wondered how Zed and Marcos and the others would react if Sammy were badly hurt or killed. Would they care about Sammy any more than Sarin had cared about Black-Jack?

Deke had told Sammy that gang brothers mattered. But Sammy saw by his actions how much more his real brothers meant to him. The gang brotherhood was important to Deke. Black-Jack was part of that brotherhood and Deke had tried to help him. But it wasn't the same as having made contact with Toni-toni. It wasn't the same way as he felt about his missing little brother, Pal. Sammy heard the pain in Deke's voice when he talked about missing Pal, and Sammy felt it too.

A car pulled up beside Sammy. He scrubbed his eyes with one fist and looked over. It was a police car. He stopped and looked through the window, expecting it to be Smith. But it wasn't, it was one of the other neighborhood beat cops. Sammy faced him. He took a step toward the squad car and stopped. The window went down.

"Everything okay, son?"

Sammy looked at the cop, trying to speak. The officer waited, looking at him. Sammy took another halting step toward the car.

"What is it?" the cop asked.

"S-s-smith?" Sammy whispered, barely able to get any sound out.

The cop looked at him for a minute, as if trying to decode a puzzle. He reached over and shifted the car into park. He opened his door. Sammy looked over his shoulder, his heart speeding up, trying to decide whether to run. The officer made a downward motion with his hands.

"It's okay. Come here and sit down." He opened the door to the back seat for Sammy. Sammy sat down, not swinging his feet inside, just sitting with them hanging outside the car, cuddling Capo close to him. The officer leaned down to eye level. "You want me to get Officer Smith? Is that what you want?"

Sammy nodded.

"Okay, sit tight. I'll get him."

Sammy sat and waited, rubbing Capo's tangled locks. The minutes ticked by. The hot lump in Sammy's throat wouldn't go away. He heard the other car pull up but didn't turn to look at it.

Smith came over, leaning down to speak to him. "Sammy? Hey, is everything okay?"

Sammy shook his head. Looking down at Capo, he held the baby out hesitantly. Smith pulled back the blanket.

"Oh, no… what happened?" Smith looked over his shoulder at the other cop. "Call an ambulance."

Sammy gulped. "She h-hits him," he said around the painful lump.

"Your mom?"

Sammy sniffled, nodding.

"Okay. You did right telling me. We'll take care of it, okay?"

"Ok-k-kay."

Smith pulled open one of Capo's eyes and then shook his shoulder a few times. Capo roused a little.

"H-h-hector t-too."

"Your mom's boyfriend?"

"Uh-huh."

Smith patted him on the shoulder. Sammy didn't pull away. He needed that encouraging touch. Another human who cared. "We're going to protect him. They won't hurt him anymore. Or you, Sammy."

They waited, watching Capo breathe, eyes closed, very still in Sammy's arms. Finally, Sammy heard the approaching whine of a siren. The ambulance pulled into the street. The EMTs got out and came over. One listened to Capo's chest with a stethoscope and shone lights in his eyes, nose, and ears. They gently removed him from Sammy's arms, putting him onto a backboard on a gurney.

"Was he dropped? Do you know? Did anyone see what happened?"

Sammy shook his head. They continued to work over Capo, putting something around his head and taping it tightly in place. They pulled straps across his body. Capo didn't stir or make any protest. Tears started to run down Sammy's cheeks. He thought of Nicholas, locked inside his body forever, unable to move or smile.

Sammy glanced over at Smith. The officer's face was flushed.

"Sammy, you wait here, okay? I'm going to go up and see your mom now. Stay here with Officer Pierson."

Sammy watched Smith go into the house. His stomach felt sick. He might throw up. Smith was going to arrest Marisol. Sammy couldn't back out now. He looked away from the house once Smith was in the door and looked back at Capo. They had him all stretched out and pinned down, and he looked so tiny on the stretcher. Sammy wiped at the tears on his cheeks as the EMT's loaded the gurney into the ambulance.

They were still there when Smith brought Marisol out of the building. Her hands were cuffed behind her back. She wasn't fighting him and she didn't see Sammy in the police car and start screaming at him. Her expression was vague. She didn't even look at the ambulance. Smith steered her into his squad car.

Smith came back over to Sammy, shaking his head. "There will be a social worker coming to get you," he explained. "She'll get you settled somewhere safe, so don't be scared, okay?"

Sammy nodded. He watched the ambulance pull out, taking Capo away. "B-be ok-kay?"

"They'll take good care of him. Sammy, I need to know where Hector works so we can pick him up before he hears about this and runs."

Sammy nodded, staring down at his hands.

The social worker was a long time in coming. She took Sammy in her car to an office where he had to sit and wait again for most of the afternoon. People walked back and forth past him, not saying anything. The social worker had given him crayons and paper, but Sammy didn't color.

Finally, the social worker returned. She looked at Sammy's blank sheets of paper and raised her eyebrows. "All right, Samuel," she said. "Everything is set. You ready to get out of here?"

Sammy nodded. He stood up. "H-how's C-capo?" he asked.

She looked at him. "Capo?"

"M-my b-b-brother."

"I thought his name was Hector."

"Uh-huh."

She put her hand on Sammy's head. "I talked to the hospital and they think he'll make a full recovery, given time. It's a good thing that you got him help when you did."

Sammy swallowed.

She transferred her hand to his shoulder. "Come along, then."

She took him back out of the building to her old blue car. She made sure that Sammy got buckled in properly, which he didn't actually need her help with. Then he watched the scenery pass by outside the window. The familiar streets quickly fell away and it was like he was in a different country. Almost as much of a wilderness for him as the forest where they had camped. Eventually, she stopped in front of a brick house. Sammy trailed the social worker up to the front door, feeling scared and alone.

An old woman with a tanned face opened the door. She gave Sammy a smile. "And this is the new boy. Sammy, is it?"

Sammy nodded.

"Come in, come in."

The social worker waited for Sammy to go by her first, then followed him in. Sammy took a couple of steps into the room.

There were two young children playing with wooden train tracks on the floor. They looked up at Sammy.

One was a three-year-old girl, with fine blond hair and a round, pink face. She looked at Sammy and their eyes met.

Her mouth formed a small 'o'.

Sammy's heart throbbed so hard and fast he thought he would burst.

The little girl jumped to her feet. "Sammy? My Sammy!" she shrieked.

Sammy caught Bunny as she flung herself at him. He lifted her up and swung her around in an exuberant circle. "B-b-bunny!"

She reached out and gave him a big hug, strangling him with her tight grip. "Sammy, Sammy, Sammy!" she trilled.

He pulled her away from his throat and she put her hands on his cheeks, holding his face in front of hers. He drank in her sweet, glowing face.

He'd thought he would never see her again. He'd thought she might be dead.

But she looked good. Her thin face had rounded out. Her eyes sparkled with life and mischief.

"Why don't you come sit down?" the social worker invited.

Sammy walked over and sat down on the couch beside her, cuddling Bunny to him and kissing her on the smooth skin of her neck.

"You won't mind staying here with your sister?" the social worker teased.

Sammy shook his head. "No."

"Mrs. Hinkel will take in Hector—Capo—when he's out of hospital, too."

Sammy looked at the foster mother, ducking his head shyly. She nodded confirmation. He gave her a smile of appreciation. Sammy buried his face in Bunny's hair and inhaled the sweet strawberry-infused scent.

Black-Jack and Deke… they were right about family.

Family took care of each other. Protected each other.

Family mattered.

Lynn pressed the button for the lift, lowering Nicholas in his wheelchair from the van's floor level to the ground. Jacob hovered close by and once it came to a stop, moved in to release the brakes on the wheels and pull the chair off of the lift.

"Be careful," Lynn warned. "Maybe I should do that…"

Jacob shook his head. "I can do it."

"The doctor said that you're not to exert yourself. You have to let yourself heal."

"He's not heavy."

"Just be careful. You can't do everything that you're used to being able to yet."

Jacob backed the wheelchair out of the lift and bent over to look at Nicky's face. "She thinks the wheelchair is too heavy for me to push."

"He picked me up right after he got out of hospital before," Nicholas said. "And after getting shot."

Lynn shook her head, putting her hands on her hips. "That doesn't mean that it's wise! You nearly died. The YMCA nurse never thought you'd get out of there alive. Same with the

Medivac. You are going to need time to heal completely." She gave him a warning look. "You'd better not be picking Nicholas up today. I've been looking after him while you were in hospital. I can move him."

Jacob eyed her. Nicholas was less than a hundred pounds. If Lynn could lift him, Jacob certainly could...

"I mean it," Lynn warned. "If you don't listen to me, I'll kick you out."

Jacob sighed and rolled his eyes. "Fine. I have to go over to Pat's anyway. See if I can start work again."

She opened her mouth to object, her eyes widening. Then she stopped. She looked at Jacob's face, and then at Nicky's, eyes narrowed. "You're getting to be quite the tease now, since you've come out of your shell."

"He always was," Nicholas said. "Just not with strangers."

Jacob ducked his head, blushing. "Never had anyone who could rat on me before."

"Evil laughter," Nicky's flat, robotic voice intoned.

Jacob snorted. Lynn giggled, shaking her head. "You guys are going to be a lot of fun to have around. I'm glad everything worked out."

Jacob looked into Nicky's smiling eyes and nodded. There was an unexpected lump in his throat. He tried to swallow it. A few short weeks ago, Jacob had never imagined that he would end up in a place where he and Nicky could both be safe and welcome. That they could let down their guard and not have to worry that Duke, now awaiting a court hearing on abuse charges, would hurt one of them. Jacob had never imagined that he would ever be able to hear Nicky's words.

They were home.

Once brothers, always brothers.

Did you enjoy this book? Reviews and recommendations
are vital to making a book successful. Please leave a review
at your favorite book store or review site and share it with
your friends.

Don't miss the following bonus material:
Sign up for mailing list to get a free ebook
Other books by P.D. Workman
Read a sneak preview chapter
Learn more about the author

Also by this Author

Mystery/Suspense:

Looking Over Your Shoulder
Lion Within
Pursued by the Past

Young Adult Fiction:

Breaking the Pattern:
Deviation
Diversion
By-Pass

Between the Cracks:
Ruby
June and Justin
Michelle (Coming Soon)

Stand Alone

Tattooed Teardrops

Don't Forget Steven

Those Who Believe

Cynthia has a Secret

Questing for a Dream

Once Brothers

Sneak Preview

Michelle was in her room with a book when her daddy got home from a long haul with Marcie. She listened to June greet Justin and Marcie. Kenny, sitting on the bed staring at his schoolbooks, got up and went out to the front room.

"Kenny, get out of here and back to your homework," June told him.

Kenny said nothing. He rarely had anything to say.

"Kenny…" she raised her voice warningly.

"Leave him alone, June," Justin told her.

"I told him no TV before his homework is done."

"Well then, I guess his homework is done."

There was silence for a couple of minutes, while they probably glared at each other, trying to decide whether to have an out-and-out argument over it.

"Where's Michelle?"

"In the bedroom with her nose in a book, like always."

A moment later Justin was in the doorway. "Hi, pumpkin."

"Hi, Daddy."

He walked in and sat down on the edge of the bed. "How are you doing, Michelle?" When she moved, he saw her black eye. "Oh, sweetie. What happened?"

Michelle shrugged and didn't answer. She didn't need to. He knew what had happened. "I wish I was Marcie and could go with you all the time."

"Well, you need to go to school. Marcie doesn't."

Michelle nodded. "I wish I was like her."

Justin touched Michelle's bruised face. "You don't wish you had CP."

June walked in. "What are you doing?" she demanded sharply.

"I'm talking to Michelle."

"Get your hands off her!"

Justin withdrew his hand and frowned at June. "What's the matter, June?"

"You think I don't know what's going on? Get out of here and leave her alone."

Justin stood up, his brow creased in consternation. "Do you think I'm hurting her? I would never do that. We were just talking."

"She doesn't need you in here, putting ideas in her head and touching her."

Justin walked out of the room. June also left. Michelle went back to reading her book. A while later, June yelled at her to come for dinner.

"I'm not hungry."

"You have to eat."

"I don't want anything."

"Leave her alone," Justin told June.

"Fine, it's less money spent on groceries if she doesn't eat," June grumbled.

"June, have a drink and relax. You're usually happy to see me when I've been away on a long haul."

June said nothing. Michelle listened to the clinking dishes and glasses.

Michelle was asleep when Kenny came in. She woke up and watched him slowly undress for bed. Justin had put Marcie to bed with Michelle earlier and she was fast asleep with Michelle's arms encircling her. Kenny stayed up watching TV late as usual, waiting until long after dark when everyone had gone to sleep and the apartment was totally silent. June and Justin had gone to bed together an hour or two earlier. Michelle didn't know how they could fight and argue all night and then go off to bed together as if nothing was wrong.

"Goodnight Kenny," Michelle said softly.

He flapped a hand in her direction and climbed into bed.

Two days later, Justin was off to work again and Kenny and Michelle were left alone with June. June was quiet and easier to get along with for a couple of days, as she always was after Justin had been home. But it didn't last. It never lasted.

Kenny was in trouble at school again. Not for fighting this time, but because he was failing, and failing in everything. Usually, they advanced him a grade anyway, but they called home to try to motivate him to work harder.

"You are so stupid," June berated him. "How come you can't pay attention in class and make the teachers think you got something between your ears besides rocks? You're so dumb!"

"Leave him alone," Michelle protested.

June turned on Michelle. "You stay out of it, missy! This has got nothing to do with you."

"Kenny is good at school, he doesn't bother anyone. He's quiet…"

"And he's thick as a post! If I want to hear from little Miss A Plus, I'll tell you."

Michelle opened her mouth to argue and June raised her hand. Michelle ducked back and went to her room, shutting the door. She turned her radio on loud to drown out the sound of June's voice as she continued to castigate Kenny.

He came into the room later, avoiding her eyes as he went over to his bed and lay down.

"Are you okay?" Michelle questioned, and went over to him, sitting down beside him. Kenny covered his face. Michelle looked at him.

"I hate her," she muttered. She opened the door and looked around covertly for June. She couldn't see or hear June. Michelle went to the bathroom and was back a moment later with cotton and peroxide.

"Okay, let's see now." She held Kenny's hand away from his face and dabbed at the cuts. "Hold still. We gotta get you fixed up."

He let her clean the cuts and grazes without protest. When she was done, they just sat in silence looking at each other.

"Do you have any homework?" Michelle asked finally.

"Uh-huh."

Michelle looked around for his books. "Where is your bag?"

He looked away. "I forgot it at school."

"Oh. What were you supposed to do?"

"Dunno."

"You gotta bring your bag home. I can help you with your homework, but you gotta bring it home."

"Yeah."

"I'll help you," Michelle repeated.

He nodded. Michelle went back over to her bed and picked up her latest book. Kenny lay staring up at the ceiling in silence.

Kenny was ten and Michelle was eight. It was pretty young to be on their own, but Michelle was considering it. Justin was rarely ever home and June wasn't getting any less abusive. Things weren't going to get any better.

Michelle honestly hadn't realized how bizarre June's behavior was getting. Justin got home after a long haul one day and June refused to let him get close to Michelle.

"You just leave her alone. Stay away from her. You understand?"

Justin didn't get angry. He just looked at June. "You don't even know why you're doing this, do you?"

"Doing what?"

"I didn't figure it out last time either." June was looking at him like he was crazy. "How old is Michelle?"

"You know as well as I do she's eight."

"And what happened when you were eight?"

June stared at him, understanding flooding her features.

Michelle looked at them. "What happened when Mama was eight, Daddy?"

"Go to your room and let your mom and me talk."

Justin wasn't usually strict with Michelle so she pressed further. "What happened?"

"You heard me." His voice was firm and he raised one eyebrow.

Michelle went to her room, wondering what was going on.

June's place at the dinner table was empty. June was in her room with the door shut. The children all looked at each other.

"What's wrong with Mama, Daddy?" Michelle asked.

"Mama's got some things to think about. You just stay out of her way for a while." Justin was preparing to feed Marcie and didn't look at Michelle when he spoke.

"Daddy… can't we come with you when you leave this time?"

"Honey, you know I can't go dragging three kids around the country with me. I have a hard enough time with some of my bosses over taking Marcie with me."

"Why don't you ever take me or Kenny with you instead?"

"I have to take Marcie because June can't take care of her. There's nowhere else for Marcie to go." Justin inserted a spoonful of pureed peas into Marcie's mouth.

"What if Mama can't take care of us either?" Michelle persisted.

"You guys can take care of yourselves. Marcie can't."

Michelle looked pointedly at Kenny. He could take care of himself? "You don't know what it's like."

Justin finally looked at her, his face sad. "Sweetie, if I could be here all the time, I would. But somebody has to pay the bills."

"You don't know what it's like," Michelle repeated desperately.

He studied her. "You're a smart girl," he said. "Smarter than anyone I've ever met. You tell me what you think I should do."

"Is mama going to be better after this?"

"You know she's not going to get any better."

"Then I don't want to stay here anymore."

Justin was silent for a while. "You want to go to foster care?"

"Yes."

"I'll call Social Services," he said finally, after another long silence, during which he fed Marcie.

"They have to keep us together," Michelle said.

Justin nodded. "If we can," he said quietly, "but you gotta know, they could separate you. And even if they don't, there's no guarantee you'll like it any better than here."

"I know."

Justin looked at Kenny. "What do you think, Kenny?"

Kenny didn't look up from his plate. He shrugged.

"You want to come with me if I go away, right?" Michelle prompted.

Kenny nodded. Michelle and Justin sat looking at him.

"Do you understand what that means?" Justin asked.

Kenny didn't answer.

Justin went back to feeding Marcie, silent.

"I'd like to talk to the children separately," the social worker told Justin.

"Marcie can't talk. Besides, she'll be staying with me. Kenny won't talk to you. But you are welcome to talk to Michelle."

Marsden looked at Marcie in her wheelchair and discounted her. She looked at Kenny and Michelle. "I'll talk to the boy first," she challenged.

She took him by the arm and led him into the conference room. She sat him down in a chair across from her. "So how are you, Kenny?"

He shrugged and didn't say anything.

"Why don't you tell me why you don't want to live with your mom anymore," Marsden suggested.

He didn't make any response.

"Do you want to go with Michelle?"

He nodded.

"Why do you want to go with Michelle? Is that what your daddy told you to say?"

She expected him to shake his head, but he didn't do anything. He just sat there looking at his feet.

"Does your mom hit you, Kenny?"

Again there was no response. His head sunk lower. His eyes didn't leave his feet.

Marsden tried approaching it from several angles, but got no response. She abandoned the topic and tried to engage him in a casual conversation about himself or his interests. But Kenny just sat there as still as a statue, not looking at her. Eventually, Marsden gave up. She took Kenny back out to his father and motioned to Michelle.

"Come with me, honey."

Michelle followed her. She sat down in the chair, shifting uncomfortably.

"So maybe you can tell me why you don't want to stay at home anymore."

Michelle looked around. "I'd like it if Daddy was there. Mama's okay when he is. But he's not home very much. He's a trucker."

"Yes, he is. Why don't you want to stay with just your mom?"

Michelle looked down at her hands and scratched at the arm of the chair. "Mama can't take good care of us," she said cautiously.

"Why not?"

"She gets mad… and then she gets mean to Kenny."

"What does she do to Kenny?"

Michelle bit her lip. "Sometimes when he gets in trouble at school she hits him."

"Is that what your dad told you to say?"

"No. She doesn't do it when he's home."

"Does she spank him or hit him hard?"

Michelle shrugged. "Hard."

"Does she 'get mean' to you too?"

Marsden held her gaze and Michelle looked away from her. "Uh-huh."

"What does she get mad at you for?"

"Sometimes… I forget to help with dinner… or I try to stop her from getting mean to Kenny."

Marsden nodded. "Okay, Michelle."

"I get into trouble at school too, sometimes," Michelle added, "because I talk too much. The teachers say I'm disruptive."

"Okay. Let's go back out and see your dad."

~ ~ ~

Michelle, Book 3 of **Between the Cracks** by P.D. Workman is coming soon!

About the Author

FOR AS LONG AS P.D. Workman can remember, the blank page has held an incredible allure. After a number of false starts, she finally wrote her first complete novel at the age of twelve. It was full of fantastic ideas. It was the spring board for many stories over the next few years. Then, forty-some novels later, P.D. Workman finally decided to start publishing. Lots more are on the way!

P.D. Workman is a devout wife and a mother of one, born and raised in Alberta, Canada. She is a homeschooler and an Executive Assistant. She has a passion for art and nature, creative cooking for special diets, and running. She loves to read, to listen to audio books, and to share books out loud with her family. She is a technology geek with a love for all kinds of gadgets and tools to make her writing and work easier and more fun. In person, she is far less well-spoken than on the written page and tends to be shy and reserved with all but those closest to her.

~ ~ ~

Please visit P.D. Workman at pdworkman.com to see what else she is working on, to join her mailing list, and to link to her social networks.

~ ~ ~

If you enjoyed this book, please take the time to recommend it to other purchasers with a review or star rating and share it with your friends!